Praise for
The Lamia

"**Buckle up. Drop anchor. Trim your nails. Get a flu shot. Twice. And make sure a nurse, security guard or a psychologist is in attendance while reading.** If only someone had a new book about a world-wide pandemic caused by a bat. Oh, wait.

"In acclaimed author Steven G. Jackson's latest work, *The Lamia*, a bat infects a young girl in the Costa Rican jungle and threatens to start a global pandemic. And while this book is so 2020 it is far scarier, and so terrifying (you will wish you had installed special locks on every door and window).

"Jackson is a master craftsman of thrillers, with a clear understanding of story structure and character-first storytelling, and this is his finest work yet. Be prepared for psychological terror as characters face decisions so horrific that your insides will scream and you will ponder 'what would I do in this impossible situation?'

"*The Lamia* is too thrilling to put down, and you'll want to finish it in one shot. But it's also so psychologically horrifying you may need an occasional break to brace yourself for what happens next. My advice, beyond buying this book, is to buy a dependable night light (and perhaps a bottle of Scotch). You'll need both, at the least. And consider booking a rubber room after finishing, as this book is so skillfully written it will chill your soul.

"Again, Jackson is a magnificent writer and creator of thrills and suspense, and *The Lamia* is without a doubt a dark hole of terror that will birth horrifying nightmares and sleepless nights. Enjoy."

—Lorenzo Porricelli, CEO & President, Gun Hill Road Productions Co.;
President, Southern California Writers Association;
Co-Founder, Orange County Screenwriters Association;
Hollywood Film Historian

"Psychological terror at its finest.

"A father questions everything, including his own sanity, when he battles to save his daughter from a seemingly all powerful evil capable of attacking its enemies from the outside—and more terrifyingly—from within. Steven G. Jackson delivers another tightly woven plot that will keep you turning pages and wondering what's going to happen next."

—Maddie Margarita, writer and host of "Lit Up! OC" and "Character Floss the Podcast"

"Here's a thriller that never stops.

"A hideous presence grips young girls in a Costa Rican jungle, looms over the wintry community of Salem, Oregon, and threatens to infect and possess the world. When a prominent psychiatrist's daughter is afflicted, he reaches out for help from law, religion, medicine, witchery, and a tribal shaman—with chilling results. A year after reading an early draft, the horrifying images continue to haunt me."

—Sandra Homicz, California Writers Circle

THE
LAMIA

EVIL IS COMING

STEVEN G. JACKSON

King Family Press
Shanghai
San Francisco

Book Cover and Interior Design by Monkey C Media
Edited by Sandra Homicz
Author Photo by Ryan C. Jackson

First Edition
Printed in the United States of America

ISBN: 978-1-7355528-0-4 (Trade Paperback)
ISBN: 978-1-7355528-1-1 (Ebook)

Library of Congress Control Number: 2020916562

This is dedicated to my Mom, who made me believe in my creative side, and my Dad, who continues to teach me how to be a good man.

CHAPTER 1

Playa Pelada, Costa Rica, the Wednesday before Thanksgiving

R ed paint bled on the sign's rotting wood, and even though the message looked old, dried, and worn, a thick goo stuck to Dr. Richard Morgan's fingertips when the compulsion to touch it overcame him.

Aviso. No entre.

He shuddered. Sticky sea air permeated his nose and throat. The taste and smell conspired to burn his insides. "Looks like a warning." He dug his toes into the smooth sand on the isolated, empty cove and scanned the encircling jungle beyond their rental home. Bright green leaves the size of prehistoric fronds masked what might be lurking in there. Morgan thought he saw eyes staring at them through tiny black gaps. "I wonder who put it here?"

Morgan peered past the warning sign to the isle twenty yards offshore. It featured a level plateau five feet above the waterline, and a rock outcropping resembling a volcano, with a lone, full-bodied tree perched high at its apex. The flat mesa acted as both a foundation for the towering mound and a footpath. "We better stay on shore and forget about exploring that island."

He turned to his companions and his apprehension dissolved into the absurdity of farce, a tragic comedy come to life. His girlfriend Azra to his left, his ex-wife Michelle to his right, both glaring daggers at him. Between them stood Taylor, his daughter, ambivalent to his vexation. *Who goes on vacation with his sweetheart, ex, and teen daughter? And I'm a psychiatrist.*

Azra's black hair rippled in the island breeze. "I agree with Richard." Even after a year of dating, her Pakistani accent still sent chills up Morgan's spine. "With all the wild animals in this jungle, who knows what we'd find on that islet?"

Michelle and Taylor—*can Taylor really be fifteen?*—stood their ground. All three women wore shorts and tops in combinations of beige and white, shirt tails tied around their waists. *Are they doing that just to mess with me, gaslighting me?* In addition, Taylor's tee had an arrow and the words 'I'm with Stupid.' When he and Michelle were at Taylor's side, Morgan sought to arrange for the pointer to be directed at her mother, but Michelle consistently outmaneuvered him. *Exactly like our short-lived marriage.*

Taylor, her golden skin a blend of Morgan's Caucasian paste and Michelle's African-American heritage, skipped down the beach past Morgan. "Come on, Dad," she said in her sweet, lyrical voice. "When did *you* grow into a worry-wart?"

Morgan caught her arm before she entered the surf. An unfamiliar apprehension gnawed at his gut. He recalled a recent psychiatry lecture at the University of Vienna. *Ignoring the voices that implore us to stop compels us toward disaster.* "Hang on. What's *aviso* mean?"

"It says to be careful." Taylor rolled her eyes. "Which you always are. Dad, please. If you're this cautious at forty, what are you going to be like at fifty? You promised we could wade out to the island. It's not that far. Don't crush my holiday."

Ruin your vacation? Ouch.

Crossing looked simple enough. Low tide. Calm seas. Large stones for easy passage. And steps carved into the side of the island going from sea level to the elevated plain. At the far point of the island, the ocean splashed and giggled. *Imagine sitting on the edge, my tired dogs dangling over the waves, soaking in the day's final rays and getting a perfect view of the sunset. It* will *be spectacular. Nothing comes close to this in Salem.* But something tormented him.

Azra distanced herself from the ocean. "Are we leaving?"

Taylor's eyes begged him to go across the stepstones and explore. *No way I'm disappointing Taylor. We go.* But Azra's orbs flashed a stern warning.

"I'm thinking," Morgan stammered.

"*Now* you're exercising judgment? Seriously? Where was your reasoning when you coerced me to join your dysfunctional family-fest to this remote tropical forest instead of a peaceful Thanksgiving holiday at home?" Azra glared at Michelle. "And with your ex, no less. For a shrink, you can be clueless."

What gave me away?

"Nobody made you come," Michelle said. In contrast to Azra, Michelle was New York City personified. Her amped-up tone challenged Azra. "You think *I* like this? My daughter insists on bringing her dad, and he brings *you*? You're lucky I don't clock you."

Morgan's face turned crimson. "Hey, knock it off. This trip is for Taylor. This is her only week off from school until Christmas, and you both nixed *that* idea. You agreed you could handle traveling together."

"Is it true they don't have any turkey?" Azra asked. "We're having *chicken* for Thanksgiving dinner?"

"Freshly slaughtered and dropped on our doorstep." Morgan gave her a stern expression. "I'm sure you'll like it."

Azra scowled, but held her tongue.

"Come on, let's go!" Taylor pleaded. "Before the sun sets."

Morgan stared into his daughter's brown eyes. *After my myriad of screwups, how many more chances will I get with you?*

As if she'd read his mind, she said, "It's okay, Dad."

He didn't know if she referred to the island, or his child-rearing skills. He bolstered his self-esteem and chose parenting.

Which still left the open question. *Is it safe?*

Jason Mraz's lyrics from *Living in the Moment* reenforced his swagger. *Don't worry about things that will never happen.* "Thanks, sweetie. You're right. The sea is tranquil, and the tide is low. Follow me."

Morgan reached for Taylor's hand, but Michelle took it first. She started with Taylor for the island.

Morgan next tried Azra's, but she withdrew it.

"I refuse to be a consolation prize," Azra said. She stormed toward the crossing.

"Azra, please. Be patient." He sought to catch up to her. "I'm doing my best here."

Michelle grinned back at him from her spot at the head of the group.

You're enjoying this, aren't you? Morgan gave Michelle a sarcastic smile. He fell in behind the ladies. They crossed the shallow water to the islet without incident, stepping from one stone to another. Once on the island, they marched along a narrow path of solid rock, worn to a glossy finish by the surf.

Morgan's reflection in puddles on the shiny stone foundation made him appear shorter and wider than his six-one, one hundred eighty pounds. His hazel eyes floated behind bookish glasses. *Taylor's right. I look like a nerd.*

"Azra, wait up," Morgan said.

This time, she allowed him to catch her. She slumped into him. "I'm not mad. It's been a long day. You know I'm not armed with your eternal optimism. Or your sarcastic wit. This place creeps me out."

Morgan reassured her with a kiss. "I'm sorry. Sometimes I can be a pain in the you-know-what."

"Sometimes?"

Relief washed over him. *I just might survive this trip with my relationship intact.* He picked up the pace to keep up with Taylor and Michelle.

The farther they distanced themselves from the serenity of the beach, the more the weather changed. A calm day turned ominous. The Pacific Ocean churned, and the wind stiffened. A single cloud with wicked intentions formed over the isolated tree at the top of the isle. The usually pleasant smells of coconut and salt air shifted to something malignant. *What'd they do, build a sewer under here?*

Morgan pointed skyward. "Gang, check out that cloud. Weird, huh? Like the island has its own weather system."

A stinging wind blew seawater in his face and raised the filament on his arms. *Maybe we should turn back.*

"Richard," Azra said, her voice an octave lower than normal, "are you sure this is safe? We're pretty exposed out here. It'll be dark soon."

"We're close to the end of the trail, Dad." Taylor looked at Morgan with her patented blend of hope and warning. "You promised."

Michelle gave Morgan a defiant stance. "You *did* promise."

Still double-teaming me. The Siren voices of the coaxing temptresses. "Okay. Let's keep moving."

Michelle bestowed Taylor a wink, and Taylor's eyes celebrated.

But Azra's peepers narrowed.

Morgan looked aside, pretending to focus on the island. *Azra nailed it. I am clueless. If my patients only knew. I hope she'll forgive me for this.* "Once we reach the end, we'll turn around. Before we lose the twilight."

"This reminds me of the three of us in Bermuda," Michelle said, smirking at Azra. "Remember?"

Morgan's skin tingled. "Best trip ever." He blushed, then cast a guilty squint at Azra, whose mood didn't appear to be improving. "I mean, yeah, fun."

Taylor and Michelle charged ahead, leaving Morgan and Azra alone.

Violent surf crashed behind them. *The weather's still changing. Stay alert.* Morgan checked his footing and found small holes in the otherwise-polished rock. *What are those?*

He dropped to one knee and lowered his head near one of the rock's orifices. A calm he didn't understand settled over him. Then, a sudden sucking pressure grabbed his knee joint. *Like being pulled into the opening.* "You feel this?"

"The oppressive heat and humidity?" Azra said.

"No. I swear I'm being sucked in." He gave her a quizzical look. "Do you think we're in some spooky zone where the laws of physics don't apply, like the Bermuda Triangle or something?"

"Stop trying to scare me," Azra said. "Gravity doesn't act differently in Costa Rica. They're called *laws* for a reason."

Morgan recalled a disastrous trip to Hawaii. *Some principles don't believe in physics.* "Maybe."

He tried to stand, but the pulling sensation increased, holding him in place. *These sucking holes—they're like the curious hollows in Algernon Blackwood's story, "The Willows" where the mark found on a dead body matched a shape encountered all over the island.*

Unable to swallow, he panicked. *We've got to get away from here.*

Being sure to avoid more holes, Morgan pushed to a standing position. He grabbed Azra and pulled her until they'd caught Taylor and Michelle.

Queasiness assaulted him. *Like the morning after a robust bender.* As if on cue, his stomach growled loud enough to wake the late Blackwood himself. He spit out a load of pukish-green bile.

"Jesus, Richard," Azra said. "You okay?"

"Gross," Taylor said, holding her nose.

Run now! a voice in his head screamed with startling clarity. "We need to get off this island."

But Taylor skipped away. "We're almost there."

Before Morgan could stop Taylor, Michelle doubled over, grasping her stomach.

Distracted, he let Taylor escape and went to Michelle. "You okay?"

"A little lightheaded." Michelle straightened.

Morgan tried to take her hand. "Let's bail."

She pulled it away, keeping his shutout intact. "Hell, no. It's just the humidity. And I thought summer in New York was ungodly. Go with Taylor."

"I'll wait until you feel better."

"Don't you dare."

It is *more humid than earlier. Like the sun's rays have weight to them, pressing down on us. Is it getting harder to breathe?* "Stay hydrated. Doctor's orders."

Michelle flipped him off.

"Look out!" Azra pointed to the sea.

The ocean had morphed into a raging beast. White caps, whipped by an invisible gale, pranced atop the crests.

Taylor rejoined them.

"Dad?" Her body shook.

A threatening swell raced toward them, just as an attack of vertigo struck Morgan. He couldn't tell up from down. Nausea assaulted him.

"Hang on!" He grabbed who he could reach—Taylor and Azra. The wave caught Morgan in the chest, sending the three of them careening to the ground.

Morgan choked on ocean water. He struggled to his knees, and spit out what he'd inhaled, burning his nose. He labored to rise, still dizzy, and helped Azra and Taylor stand. "Run! Before the next wave!"

Taylor dug her nails into his arm, drawing blood. "Where's Mom?"

Morgan turned, wide-eyed, and didn't spot her on the plateau.

His pulse double-timed, but an adrenaline surge counteracted the vertigo. He took a deep breath and his light-headedness retreated. He plodded to the rocky edge and checked the sea five feet below. "Michelle! Where are you?" *Stay calm. Find her.*

"Dad! Watch out!"

Another colossal wave knocked Morgan into Azra and Taylor. They tumbled to the base of the volcano-like mound.

The cloud piled on with pelting, oppressive rain.

Morgan scrambled to his feet, and, not seeing Michelle, prepared to dive into the ocean to search for her. But Taylor screamed. He followed her horrified stare to the far end of the island where he'd dreamt of watching the sunset an eternity ago.

An undulating wave of living creatures pulsed towards them along the path. He gasped. *What the hell?*

Crabs. Hundreds. *No. Thousands.* Oversized black crustaceans with anterior legs resembling Popeye's arms and giant razor claws. Ten yards away. The throng charged sideways straight at them with malicious intent. Morgan couldn't help but wonder, with a sudden but brief spark of insanity, if these mutants might not speak to him, as King's lobstrocities spoke to Roland Deschain on the beach bordering the Western Sea in Mid-World. "Run!"

"What about Mom?" Taylor screamed.

The tide had risen, their stone crossing to shore now covered in angry surf. The water level surged to the height of the plateau.

Aviso. No entre. The sign taunted him.

"I'll find her. You and Azra go back."

But another blur, bigger than the crabs, came splashing for them from the other direction.

Oh, Christ. What now? Morgan weighed the hazards. *Better risk the unknown.* "Hurry!"

Azra dragged Taylor toward the steps they'd used to climb onto the trail, and the safety of the shore.

The advancing shadow from the beach came into focus—a big black dog. *Man's best friend. Not so horrifying.*

Temporary relief dissolved into fear. The hound barked and growled, then charged, fangs exposed, white drool falling onto its gigantic, splashing paws.

"Richard." Michelle's voice, faint and desperate.

Morgan's heart skipped a beat. "Michelle! Where are you?"

"Ocean."

The crabs advanced, pinchers clapping above their heads like a Calypso dancer. *Only sixty seconds until they overrun me.* He staggered to the path's edge and spotted Michelle holding onto rocks at the root of the island. "Hang on. I'm coming."

"Taylor?" Panic in Michelle's voice.

Peril surrounded his daughter. The surf raged and, as Taylor clung to Azra, the giant black Lab closed in on them.

"She's fine." *No, she's not.* "Almost to shore."

"You're still a lousy liar. I've got a good grip here. Make sure Taylor's safe."

Forty-five seconds. Morgan stepped onto the first layer of unstable rocks on the crag, teetering in the wind.

"Don't you think about climbing down here," Michelle shouted. "Too dangerous. I'll scramble along the foundation to shore. Save Taylor."

"Taylor's protected by Azra." *But who will defend Azra?* "I can't leave you in the water."

"Go, goddamnit!" Michelle screamed. She fought against the rushing water.

Thirty seconds. Morgan studied the rocky embankment between the path and Michelle. *I'll never get to her without cracking my head open. But I have to try.* "I'm coming in." Morgan picked out another steppingstone. He chanced a step and nearly crashed as the edge of the ridge tipped sideways.

"Richard, I'm fine! Your only job right now is Taylor!"

Morgan returned to the stability of the path and checked on the crabs. *Shit. Fifteen seconds.* "Okay, you win. I'll get Taylor to shore and then swim around to meet you."

"Take care of Taylor. Promise me."

"I swear. Stay where you are. I'll be right back."

Morgan sprinted after Taylor and Azra on the slick path. The crabs chased after him.

He worried he was making the wrong choice and wondered if Michelle could hold on through repeated volleys of rough surf.

CHAPTER 2

Morgan stumbled racing down the path, but kept his balance. The crabs' pinchers clicked at his heels and their claws scraped as they closed in on him. A grinding sound, like nails on a chalkboard, spiked through Morgan's brain. The crabs' smell matched something that had died and returned from the grave. Bile climbed up his throat.

Morgan caught up with Taylor and Azra. *Another twenty feet to the steps. Then I can go after Michelle.*

The mutant crustaceans, mere seconds behind him, laughed aloud, bringing Morgan to the verge of insanity.

The charging dog barked. White drool gave a rabid vibe. The hound, fangs exposed, leapt. Morgan braced himself, shielding Taylor and Azra.

But, instead of landing on Morgan, the canine blocked the crabs from reaching him. The black Lab picked one up in his mouth, killed it with a shake of his head, and tossed the besieger aside.

The assaulters reacted as a single organism and fled the way they'd come. *Like birds changing course.* The dog pounced on the strays, opening them up for a bite of crab meat, his tail wagging.

Morgan heaved a sigh. He hugged Taylor. "You okay?"

"What about Mom?"

"She's secure. I'm going after her now."

A bright light cracked the sky open and thunder screamed at them. The island shook. A dense limb from the tree at the apex split off in a crescendo of sparks and fell toward them. Morgan protected Taylor's skull with his arms. The branch flew past him and hit Azra on the leg. Her blood dripped onto the plateau and vanished into the holes with a horrifying gurgle.

"Richard!" Azra screamed. "Help me!"

He yanked her away from the bloody hole. "Both of you hold on." *I have to get them to shore. Michelle will have to wait.* "I'm taking you to safety." *Hurry.*

"Did you *see* that?" Azra asked, checking her wound. "It's like the ground was drinking my blood."

"Can you walk?" Morgan asked Azra.

Taylor tugged on him. "Forget her. Save Mom! We can make it back."

Before Morgan could respond, a brown bat with the wingspan of a hawk swooped past them. Its membranous wings made an abnormal swooshing sound. It circled Taylor's head. Azra and Taylor screamed.

"Run!" Morgan yelled.

They sprinted toward the steps leading to the path and the shore.

Morgan swatted at the bat, but it plunged onto Taylor's scalp.

Taylor shrieked. She reached for her head and came back with bloody globs. "Holy shit! It bit me." She turned to Morgan. "Am I going to get a coronavirus?"

The bat flitted into the air, hovered, then soared to the tree remains.

Morgan checked Taylor's head. Two punctures. Streaks of blood mixed with the rainwater covered her face. *Jesus. What else can go wrong?* "Azra has a first-aid kit. You'll be fine." *Now hurry. Help Michelle.*

"Can't *you* treat it?" Taylor protested. "She just does dead people."

Azra flinched. "I'm an internist. I ran a department at the CDC before switching to forensic pathology. Just because I run the Medical Examiner's Office instead of a plush private practice doesn't mean I'm not a great doctor."

"Not now!" Morgan said. "You two head for the beach. I've got to find Michelle and make sure she's safe."

"Richard, don't go," Azra said. "The tide's up and the surf is rough. I don't know if I can get Taylor across."

Morgan glared at her. "Michelle's hanging onto a rock in that storm. All you need to do is cross to the beach. Can you do that for me?"

Azra nodded. She took Taylor's hand, re-gripped it when Taylor feinted a wish to pull away, then led Taylor to the submerged steps, now five feet deep.

Morgan veered to the open sea and dove into a raging swell.

Rain pounded Morgan in the churning surf. The current drove him against the rocks. He crashed into a jagged edge, his ribcage taking the brunt of the blow. Air exploded out of his lungs. He doubled over in pain. Fractured rib kind of pain.

He grabbed hold of a rock and checked on Taylor and Azra. They'd reached shore and had collapsed on the sand. *They're safe. Thank God.*

The wooden sign blew over and skimmed along the beach toward Morgan. *It's taunting me. Aviso. No entre.*

The last remnant of sunlight vanished. A lightning flash illuminated Michelle, twenty feet away, moving hand-over-hand along the rocks. Morgan kicked, using his left arm to swim, but the current kept forcing him toward the islet.

"I'm almost there," he yelled, and, to Morgan's relief, the downpour ended.

The clouds over the island shifted, blending into gray waves of their own, providing a hint of light from the partial moon, and a glimpse of his ex.

A large wave pummeled her, and Michelle disappeared below the surface.

"No!" Morgan descended to the sea bottom, searching for her above the fine-grained sand. The warm water gave him an advantage—no seaweed. Ribbons of blood danced in the ocean, the byproduct of his collision with the rocks.

I bet they have sharks in Costa Rica. Big mothers. He shook that thought aside. Not as far as he'd hoped, but enough to continue. *Where is she?*

Morgan returned to the surface and gulped a bottomless breath. The crabs watched him along the island's rocky ledge. *They think I'm dinner.*

A shadow in the water caught his attention. *There!*

Ribs aching, lungs on fire, he swam to Michelle, pulling her head above the roiling waves. "Breathe, Michelle, breathe!" He pulled her toward shore, but she didn't respond.

When he could touch the bottom, he called for help. "Azra. Taylor. Help me!"

Arms grabbed him, pulling him and Michelle to land. They turned Michelle onto her side. Azra leaned over, checked Michelle's pulse, and started chest compressions. "She's not breathing."

"Dad, *do* something."

"Azra, let me do that. It's Michelle."

"No," Azra said as she pumped. "I'm more experienced. And detached."

Morgan's eyes flooded. *Come on, Michelle. Breathe.*

A motion caught his peripheral vision. The sign was standing upright again. *What the hell?*

Taylor fell to her knees at Michelle's side. "Push faster. Harder. You're not trying hard enough."

"Rushing only hurts. Her best chance is if I stay calm and follow the process." Azra glanced at Morgan. "Richard, you're bleeding."

Morgan touched his side, a painful, sticky mess. "Don't worry about me. Focus on Michelle."

Azra alternated pumping Michelle's chest and checking for a pulse. "She's not responding."

Morgan choked on his own spit. Time stopped. *This can't be happening.* He looked to his daughter. Taylor's complexion whitened, defying her ancestry. *She looks like a ghost.* Tears streamed down her cheeks, mixing with dried blood. She chomped on her nails, leaving chipped fragments in the sand.

A lightning bolt struck the warning sign, obliterating it. The force knocked Morgan onto his back. *Holy shit.* He labored to his feet.

Taylor and Azra were oblivious to the sign's destruction.

Azra stopped pumping and looked up at Morgan. "I'm sorry. She's gone."

Taylor shoved Azra out of the way and tried giving her mother mouth-to-mouth.

Morgan fell to his knees next to Taylor. *Not again.* He slammed a fist into the sand. "Michelle?" He wiped away tears. "I'm so sorry. For everything. You deserved better."

Taylor stopped CPR and scowled at her father. "This is all your fault. You let her die." She jumped to her feet. "I hate you."

Morgan's spirit collapsed under the weight of Taylor's words.

Taylor shrieked to the heavens and raced away along the coastline.

CHAPTER 3

A jolt of wind pounded Morgan. The moon ducked behind ominous clouds. The surf mocked him with thunderous explosions as it burst upon the shoreline.

Morgan called after Taylor. "Wait!"

But Taylor charged ahead, disappearing in the gloom.

Morgan addressed Azra. "Can you watch Michelle while I find Taylor?"

"You think it's a good idea to be out here alone?" She glanced at the jungle, twenty yards away. "Who knows what's lurking in there? Maybe something bigger than that bat, which was way too big to begin with."

She's right. But I have to locate Taylor. "Sorry. Wasn't thinking. Come with me." *And hope no animal comes for Michelle's body.*

The two of them chased after Taylor's footprints in the wet sand. They passed the path that led to their rental. Taylor had stayed along the coastline.

"Taylor," Morgan called. "Please stop."

They found her around a bend where the beach jutted left. Taylor stood frozen, her tears glimmering in the reflection of torches from a nearby farm, a streak of blood falling along her left ear. Morgan reached her first and grabbed her. "Taylor. Thank heavens."

She tried to push him aside. "Leave me alone." But her eyes registered fear.

Morgan followed her gaze. The black Lab, its shiny wet coat a reminder of their ordeal, growled at Taylor in the flickering light. Behind the hound, a short man in jeans and a white t-shirt held a bloody cleaver. A pig rotated over an open flame. Burning animal flesh assaulted Morgan's nostrils in the thick air.

Morgan put his arm around his daughter and acknowledged the stranger. "Excuse the intrusion." He pointed inland. "We're renting the house behind your farm. There's been a horrible accident."

The man, surrounded by four tall, flaming torches stuck in the sand, directed the tip of the cleaver at them. "I know who you are. I am delivering your Thanksgiving chicken in the morning." His frown thickened. "Go home. The jungle is no place for you at night."

The canine continued to growl.

"Can you call off your dog?" Azra said. "He's scaring the girl."

The farmer cocked his head. "Cocoa. Down." Cocoa, focused on Taylor, dropped to his stomach. "Aren't there four of you? Another woman?"

Morgan swallowed hard. His voice shook. "She drowned."

"She is dead?" The man narrowed his eyes, then jammed his cleaver into a butcher block stained in slaughtered animal blood. "Was she near the island?"

"Yeah," Morgan said. "I need to report it."

The hound snarled at Taylor again. Morgan stepped in front of her and Azra. "Your dog doesn't seem friendly. Can you put him on a leash or something?"

"He will not hurt you unless I tell him to. I am Juan. I will call the police."

Unless he orders it? A warning shot across the bow? Morgan attempted to get on the farmer's good side. "Cocoa was a big help to us on the island. Chased a bunch of aggressive crabs away. You sure grow them big in the tropics."

Juan gasped. "You went *onto* the island?"

"Yeah, we did. And then a storm came out of nowhere and swept my ex-wife out to sea. I couldn't save her."

Juan considered the dog growling at Taylor. "My dog never growls. Did anything happen to your daughter while you were out there?"

"A bat attacked her. Minor cut to her head. No big deal."

Juan grimaced. "You should not have gone out there. It is a bastion of evil."

Azra cleared her throat. "What do you mean?"

"He means, you should have obeyed the warning." A woman, no bigger than Juan emerged from the jungle. "I am Margarita. Juan's wife."

"Richard Morgan. Sorry to be in a hurry, but my ex is out there, unprotected. You'll send someone?"

Margarita and Juan exchanged glances. Only Juan showed remorse.

"I will inform the proper authorities," Margarita said. She pulled a walkie-talkie from her rumpled shirt pocket and hurried toward the farmhouse. But not before Morgan overheard. "*Margarita to campamento base. Tengo un ataque confirmado. Enviar equipo de contención.*"

Morgan addressed Juan. "Is she calling the police?"

Juan didn't meet his gaze. "Why did you go near the demons?"

Azra rolled her eyes at Morgan. "Jesus, Richard," she whispered. "What century is he in?"

Cocoa jumped up and showed his fangs. He snarled at Taylor.

Juan furrowed his brow. "I fear it infected your daughter. Cocoa senses the evil."

Taylor sagged into him. "Dad? What's he talking about? Is it COVID-19? Or another pandemic-causing virus?"

Morgan swallowed back bile. His ribs made deep breathing a nasty chore. "It's nothing to worry about, Sweetie. We've all been vaccinated. Come on, let's go back to your mother."

Juan snapped his fingers, and Cocoa whined. A second snap got the dog moving into the farm. "The police will reach the doctor. Maybe he will arrive before the armed branch of the task force." Juan's eyes teared.

Morgan shivered. *Armed?*

"You have a medical examiner here?" Azra said.

Juan glanced at Taylor, then back at Morgan. "No. The doctor will take care of the body, as well as inspect your daughter for the plague."

"You have plague?" Azra said. "Bubonic?"

"Worse," Juan said.

Taylor blanched. "I *knew* it. They have their own pandemic brewing, don't they? Something new."

"Taylor, calm down. Whatever it is, we'll handle it." Morgan looked to Azra. *Worse than Bubonic?*

"Your father's right." Azra reached for her, but Taylor flinched and pulled away. "There are no reports of plague, nor a new pandemic, in this region. Richard, I'll take Taylor to the house. She shouldn't have to see her mother like that."

"*Like that?*" Taylor yelled. "You mean dead. Because Dad saved you instead."

Morgan sagged. "Taylor, I tried."

"Yeah? Well, Mom's gone, and your girlfriend's alive." Taylor broke free of Azra and raced toward their rental house.

Azra chased after Taylor. "I'll get her. You handle Michelle."

Juan pulled out a cell phone and dialed. "Dominguez. Juan. A drowning at the island. *Tourista*. We require the doctor to check a girl before *La Contención de la Plaga* takes over." He eyed Morgan's shirt. "Lots of blood." He hung up. "The physician will come."

"What we need is a coroner to take care of Michelle."

Juan picked up the cleaver. "Our doctor is for your daughter. *La Contención de la Plaga*, the plague containment task force, will not let you leave the country until they are convinced she is free of infection."

19

An iciness flowed throughout Morgan's backbone. "You can't hold us here against our will."

"The task force can impose a quarantine."

"I understand the concern after the COVID-19 pandemic." Morgan eyed the butcher's knife. "But we'll handle it. Is this task force your version of our CDC?"

"It is a long story."

Morgan squirmed. "I'd like to hear it, but I need to get to my ex."

Juan raised the cleaver to his shoulder.

"You planning to butcher something?" Morgan said.

Juan gazed at the knife, then planted it back into the block. "*Chancho*. Pig. But not now. I will join you."

Morgan didn't feel like talking on the hike to Michelle, but broke the awkward silence after a solitary minute. "Your family been here long?"

"Five years. We come here from Bribri village to get our daughter away from the demons attacking our tribe."

Jesus. More with the demons.

"But we were too late. We did not know the demon had already infected our daughter. When we brought her with us, we spread the disease." Juan choked back a cry. "Our daughter died. But not before infecting other girls."

"Only girls?"

"The nature of the beast. I know you are grieving now for your ex-wife, *señor*, but losing a daughter is something different. And, knowing we allowed the plague to spread is horrifying."

Juan checked over his shoulder. "Margarita has dedicated the rest of her life to see this plague contained. She joined *La Contención de la Plaga*, and they monitor the entire country. *La Contención* is not sanctioned. The government will probably arrest Margarita someday. But she does not care."

Juan looked into Morgan's eyes. "*La Contención de la Plaga* is ruthless, *señor*. We need our doctor to examine your daughter before they arrive. To clear her. The task force will not let her leave if there is any doubt."

They passed the bend. The clouds parted, and the moon shone on Michelle.

Shadows pranced around the corpse in the moonlight. "Hey, get away from her!" Morgan sprinted to Michelle, sending a howler monkey and a genetic hybrid between a lizard and an armadillo scrambling back into the jungle. *Thank God. No mutilation.*

When Juan reached them, he bowed and mouthed what Morgan assumed was a prayer.

Seems like an okay guy.

The sewer smell returned, causing Morgan's stomach to turn. On the island, wind whistled through the heavy branches, inducing the tree at the top to sway back and forth. *Like it's alive.*

"When I pass this island, I have same feeling as when in Bribri village. I think *Bé* is here."

"*Bé?*"

"The race of demons. Trying to destroy all humans."

Morgan didn't know what to say. "And you believe in these demons?"

Juan wiped his eyes. "They killed my daughter."

Morgan changed the subject. "I hiked up in the Bribri area once. In the mountains by Panama. One of the last indigenous tribes."

"*Sí.* Did you hear about the plagues?"

"No. Some local guy tried to run me off. Figured he didn't want any white dudes around."

"It is bad there, *señor.* The plague destroyed almost all the young girls. So many lives wasted. And we will soon be out of Bribri women to reproduce, to continue our civilization."

Morgan looked down on Michelle. A heavy shroud of remorse descended on him as he pondered her death, and then he thought of another loss. "I once lost someone else I cherished to a legend of an ancient culture."

21

"We experience these legends firsthand," Juan said, "and we believe. No matter what logic tells us."

Morgan didn't want to go down that rabbit hole. "I appreciate your help. But my daughter has a routine bat bite. Even if this bat's spreading COVID-19, Taylor's been vaccinated. We have treatments now."

"You have no medicine for this plague. But I hope she is okay. I do not want to see another innocent girl destroyed."

Blood drained from Morgan's face. "Destroyed?"

"Margarita will do anything to keep the plague from spreading." He stared at Morgan. "Anything."

"Are you telling me to run?"

Juan gazed to the sky. "It is for *Sibú* to decide now."

"Sibú?"

"He controls the top tiers of the Bribri universe."

Morgan scratched his head. "Sorry. I don't understand."

"Our universe has many layers. On top is *Sibú's* realm. Then the sky and forest, then the earth, then the underworld, where we bury the deceased. The abode of the dead is *Kudo's* kingdom."

If Azra were here, she'd go nuts.

"*Kudo*," Juan continued, "also watches over the plants and animals. If someone is killing either without the proper respect, he orders the jungle's natural inhabitants to attack the people. That is why the bat attacked your daughter."

"My girl hasn't killed anything. She adores nature."

"Her behavior will not deter *Kudo*. Look at our rain forest. She is a victim of other people's actions."

Morgan rubbed his chin. "And you and your tribe still believe this?"

"Some of it is hard to accept. The legend says *Sibú* sent a vampire bat to cut his sister, Tapir, and her blood formed the earth. Our version of creation. But I have seen enough to know the plague is real."

"My daughter will be fine." But his voice wavered. *When it comes to bat bites, everything has changed. It could be something new.*

Juan grunted. "We've lost many an *Awá* fighting the demons, for the souls of our girls."

"*Awá?*"

"Our tribe's shaman. Our holy men. Only they can exorcise the demon. And then, only rarely. Often, the beast wins and the *Awá* dies."

Morgan chose silence over a debate.

"The doctor will check your daughter for a white ring around the bite. If she does not have it, she is not infected, and I can help you escape before the task force arrives."

"I inspected the wound. No white ring."

"I hope it has not appeared since you checked her. But, I must be honest. Cocoa can tell. You should prepare yourself."

CHAPTER 4

Surrounded by exotic jungle cries, Morgan kneeled into the soft sand and touched Michelle's icy cheek.

"You brought your ex-wife and current girlfriend," Juan said. "A puzzling choice."

Morgan stared at the horizon. "Yeah. I only get one trip a year with Taylor, and last time she bailed when I refused to include her mother. So what could I do? I convinced Azra to come with me. In hindsight, that probably wasn't my smartest decision."

"You are a brave man, *señor*. Foolish, but brave. Like me, you have tension with your loved one. Perhaps we are kindred spirits."

"I hope you're better at dealing with women than I am. I'm the poster child for failed relationships." After a short lag, he continued. "I drank when I couldn't face my responsibilities. My wife left me. Not my best moment."

"Most unfortunate."

"My relationship with my daughter is already strained. Now this."

"Family can overcome anything."

Morgan winced. *He sounds like me with my patients. But I'm proof that's not true.* He changed the conversation's direction before the hammering in his head got any louder. "Maybe you can answer a question for me."

"I will try."

"On the island, there were these holes. You know what I mean?"

"*Sí.* One of many *sobrenatural* things out there."

"They sucked blood from a cut on Azra's knee. They pulled on me, too."

"Like I told you. It is an evil place."

Morgan's peripheral view sighted an image. A paunchy Hispanic man dressed in white, with short black hair and a gold badge on his left breast pocket, approached with a tiny chap carrying a medical bag. They reminded Morgan of Laurel and Hardy. He rose and brushed the sand off his shorts and legs.

The officer reached Morgan first but didn't bother with any pleasantries. He kicked at the dead body.

"Hey." Morgan pushed him from Michelle.

The policeman moved his hand to his holster. "Shove me again, and I *will* arrest you."

"Touch *her* again," Morgan said, "and I'll kick your ass."

They stared each other down until the constable laughed. "American *touristas.* Always playing the cowboy." His words dragged as if too exhausted to finish his sentences. "And with a dead ex-wife on my beach. Lucky me."

The doctor examined Michelle's body. "Where is the daughter?"

"Back at our rental."

The physician addressed the police officer. "It's urgent I examine her."

The stout gent nodded. "My name is Dominguez. You are the girl's father?"

"Yes, and ex-husband to the deceased."

"Can you bring her? The doctor needs to check her for infection."

"When we're done with this."

The M.D. stood. "Could be a drowning. I must examine her to be sure. Take me to the girl."

"Hang on." Dominguez pulled out a small notepad.

"Can't that wait?" the doctor said. "You understand what's at stake."

"I won't be long." Dominguez narrowed his eyes at Morgan. "What happened?"

Morgan swallowed and pointed to the island. "We went hiking out there. It started out calm. But a storm blew in, and a wave knocked her into the ocean. By the time I reached her, she'd drowned."

"You dove in after her?"

"After I got my daughter and girlfriend off the island."

"So, not right away."

"No."

Dominguez scribbled in his notebook. "You trained in ocean rescues?"

"No," Morgan said. "I did a tour in the army, but I didn't do much water stuff."

Dominguez closed the pad. "Consider yourself lucky. We lose many *touristas* here."

Morgan's chest tightened. "I see nothing fortunate about any of this."

Taylor appeared on the path to their rental, followed by Azra, who struggled to stay even. Taylor ran to her mother, not making eye contact with Morgan.

"This is the girl?" The doctor said.

Azra caught up to the group. "So you're the medical examiner?"

"I am what there is. *Me llama* Pietro. I need to check the girl's wound."

Morgan stepped between them. "My girlfriend and I are both doctors. We'll handle it."

"Señor, please." Juan said. "I beg you. The task force will be here soon."

"No."

Before Morgan could interfere, Dominguez grabbed his wrists and pinned his arms behind him. The shooting pain in his ribs caused his eyes to water.

"Hey, let go of me!"

"It is for your own good," Dominguez said.

Morgan fought, but Dominguez held him. Taylor came to his defense, but Pietro intercepted her and flashed a light at Taylor's scalp. Juan shielded Azra from Taylor.

The constant whir of noise from the jungle stopped, as if a conductor had signaled for a pause in the performance.

"She is infected," Pietro said, a deep sadness in his voice.

And the jungle came back to life.

A spear of fright struck Morgan in the chest.

"Are you sure?" Dominguez asked.

"Positive," Pietro said. "We must wait for the task force."

Morgan couldn't pull apart from Dominguez's powerful grip. "What are you talking about?"

"What if we take her to the Bribri before they arrive?" Juan said.

"An infected girl?" Petro said. "They will never let her into the tribe."

"You are right," Dominguez said. He released Morgan and shoved him toward Azra and Taylor. He pulled out his pistol. "Step away from the girl."

Morgan put his arms around Taylor and Azra. "No."

"Dad?" Taylor said. "Don't let them take me."

"I've got you. You're not going anywhere with them."

"Are you people all insane?" Azra spun on Pietro. "What are you, some kind of witch doctor? We haven't even diagnosed her yet. You can't know what she has. *If* anything."

Pietro handed her his penlight. "See for yourself."

Azra hesitated, then took the light. She pointed it at the bite.

Morgan stepped closer. "What is it?"

"I treated the area around the bite," Azra said. "But, the wound is behaving in a way I'm not comfortable with."

"It doesn't mean she's infected with anything," Morgan said, his irritation clear.

"Look."

Morgan squinted. A red scratch along the top of Taylor's head was surrounded by a silvery ring. "What's the white stuff around the laceration? It looks like it's growing."

"Not growing. Throbbing." Azra shut off the light and gave Morgan a look that scared him. "I've never seen anything like it. Have you?"

"No." Anxiety rushed through Morgan.

Taylor collapsed into Morgan. "Dad? Am I going to die?"

Morgan kissed her forehead. "No. But we're getting you back to Salem." He turned to Juan. "Listen, I understand you're spooked about the bats. Lots of tribal stories about plagues. But we have modern pharmaceuticals at our disposal. We can treat whatever this is."

Pietro huffed. "You think our medicine does not compare to yours? You consider us uncivilized? Let me tell you something. No medical science will help her."

"Azra," Morgan said, "tell him you can fix her."

Azra sighed. "Richard, you know we can't be certain until we understand what we're dealing with. There are many diseases in remote areas that don't have known cures. We all know what happened with COVID-19."

Taylor crowded in tighter. "Dad, I'm scared."

Morgan held her. "Officer, we're United States' citizens. I demand to speak to someone at the US Embassy."

A woman's voice spoke from behind them. "Everybody freeze!"

Morgan turned and faced Margarita, flanked by two men with automatic rifles pointed in their direction.

CHAPTER 5

The stench magnified as if the island was reacting to the confrontation on the beach. Howler monkeys preached. Salt water vapor drifted into Morgan's throat, and he gagged. He stepped in front of Taylor. "Nobody comes near my daughter."

Dominguez pointed his pistol at Margarita. "Tell your soldiers to lower their weapons. I have the situation under control."

"Like with my daughter?" Margarita said.

"An unfortunate development."

Margarita stared at Juan, then at Dominguez. "Unfortunate? It was tragic. We all understood what she had become. We all knew she had to be destroyed." She poked herself in the chest. "I offered to do it. To kill my own daughter. But you stopped me, saying you and the doctor wanted more time. To study her. To find a cure. And what happened?"

Dominguez and Pietro shared an expression of remorse.

"She escaped and infected more girls," Margarita said. "Whom I had to destroy. I *knew* those families. You might as well have killed those girls yourself."

Dominguez shook his head. "This is different. The bite is new. She is not yet a threat."

Margarita scoffed. "Not for you to decide. I am taking the girl by authority of *La Contención de la Plaga*."

"You and your task force have no power here," Dominguez said. "I will not allow you to be a vigilante on my beach."

Margarita let out a grave breath. "I see. Then you leave me no choice." She pulled a pistol and shot Dominguez in the forehead.

Taylor and Azra screamed.

For Morgan, something inside exploded, as if Margarita had dropped a lit match in a pool of gasoline at his feet. Every sense went into hyperdrive. Every muscle prepared for battle.

He backed up into Taylor and Azra, trying to act as a shield. *She was willing to kill her own daughter over this perceived disease. Assassinated the local sheriff. She'll kill us all.*

Dominguez dropped to his knees, then face-planted into the sand. The policeman's weapon fell five feet from Morgan.

Pietro staggered to Dominguez's body and checked his pulse. He bowed his head in obvious sorrow.

Juan stepped back. "Margarita. What have you done?"

"Dominguez did this to himself," Margarita said. "You know we cannot let the plague spread."

Taylor and Azra each stood wide-eyed behind Morgan. He wanted to reassure them, but didn't know how.

Instead, Morgan focused on his surroundings. *I've got to get Dominguez's weapon.*

"What are you going to do with them?" Juan asked Margarita, pointing at Morgan and Azra. "They are not infected and have done nothing wrong."

"They will never accept what must be done." Margarita pointed her pistol at Morgan. "I derive no pleasure from this. You cannot understand."

Morgan called up his army training, skills he never expected to need again. He judged the distance to Dominguez's weapon as three long leaps. *Not good odds. Even if my next move is a surprise her two guards will gun me down.*

He tensed for an assault anyway, knowing doing nothing meant certain death for them. *Remember, aim for the midsection. Best chance to hit something.*

"Wait," Juan said. "He and his family deserve a proper burial."

Margarita hesitated.

Morgan pounced on her hesitation. "Yes. We're Catholic. Are you?"

Azra pushed away. "*We're* Catholic? I don't even believe in God. And if I did, I'd find no solace in having a meaningless ceremony before being murdered." She pointed at Margarita. "And murder is what this is. Superstitious hysteria."

Margarita wagged her weapon at Morgan. "On your knees."

"Margarita," Juan said, "please do not do this. We will find another way."

She turned her head toward her husband, and both guards flanking her followed her gaze.

Morgan took advantage. He dropped to the sand and retrieved Dominguez's weapon. Before Margarita and her team could react Morgan winged both guards. They grabbed their legs and their weapons fell.

Morgan's side raged from his ordeal in the ocean. He guzzled air and aimed at Margarita's heart. "Drop your weapon."

Margarita narrowed her eyes, her weapon pointed at the sand. "Juan, you distracted me on purpose."

Juan stood his ground. "We must give the doctors a chance."

"A waste of time," Margarita said. "And you know it."

"Drop the weapon," Morgan said. "I won't ask again."

Margarita looked at Morgan with a hatred he recognized from his practice.

She's lost it. A clear risk to others. Don't hesitate to take her out.

Juan begged Morgan. "Please do not hurt her. She is my wife."

"She needs to give up her pistol," Morgan insisted.

Margarita ran her tongue along her lips. "Our task force is everywhere, *señor*. You will never escape Costa Rica alive."

"I'll take my chances," Morgan said.

"And," Margarita said, "even if you do, we will hunt you like dogs, wherever you try to hide. We will find the girl, and we will destroy her." She spit in Taylor's direction. "Before she destroys all of us."

Morgan's teeth chattered. *She'll never stop. You have to end this. For Taylor.*

"Dad," Taylor said, "can we please go? She's scaring me."

Morgan's finger tensed on the trigger. "Last chance. Lose the weapon."

"Richard," Azra said, "what do you plan to do?"

"Protect Taylor. And you."

"There has to be an alternative," Azra said. "We're not killers."

No, we're not. "I'll do whatever I have to."

Margarita slumped and released her pistol. "Fine. I will leave you to the task force." She turned to Juan. "Why did you help them?"

Juan came up and squeezed her. "I cannot let what happened to our princess crush my soul."

Morgan took Margarita's weapon and turned to Pietro, "Throw the goon's rifles in the ocean." He pointed Margarita's automatic rifle at him. "And don't even think about aiming one in our direction."

Pietro walked to the shore and tossed the guards' automatic weapons into the sea.

Morgan turned his attention to Azra and Taylor. "We need to go."

"I'm not leaving without Mom," Taylor said.

"We can't take her, honey. Leaving the country will be hard enough as it is."

"No," Taylor said. "Just because you guys don't care doesn't mean I don't."

Morgan felt a pain in his chest. *Don't care? If you only knew.* "Juan, can we borrow the truck? I didn't rent a vehicle, and we need to get to the airport in Liberia. I can pay."

"You will never make it to Liberia. Margarita is right. The task force will already have a national alert out for your daughter. They will watch the airports."

"The police?"

"Perhaps not. Cooperation between the task force and the authorities is sometimes, how you say it, resisted."

"Then we'll leave the country by car. Which way?"

"South on the main highway, to Panama." He tossed his keys to Morgan.

"Juan," Margarita exclaimed, "what are you doing? You cannot help them escape."

Juan held her. "I am sorry, my love. But the girl deserves a chance."

"A chance at what? She's *infected*. You *know* what that means. And the police captain is dead, with two of my guards shot. The doctor must treat them at the hospital. He will talk. How will you explain that?"

"I don't know. But it is in our best interest not to admit what happened here. The police would lock you up for murder." Juan looked at Morgan. "Go. Before I change my mind."

"I can't thank you enough." Morgan handed Juan a wad of cash. "It's all I've got on me, but there's more in the safe at the house. It's all yours. And I'll leave the truck for you at the main airport in Panama. I assume you have border guards?"

"*Sí.*" Juan hesitated, then pocketed the money. "But, because they work for the government, they are unlikely to communicate with the task force."

Morgan motioned toward the vehicle. "No time to waste. Taylor, Azra will arrange with their M.E. to ship your Mom home."

Taylor broke free from Azra and pounded Morgan on his arms. "We can't leave Mom."

He held her. "Sorry, sweetie. It's the only way." She fought him, but he forced her toward the truck.

They passed the wailing guards and Morgan approached Pietro. "Save these two, but let me save my daughter. I'm begging you, one doctor to another. Let me take her home. She's no threat to your people."

Pietro stared at Margarita. "I will not be party to Margarita's arrest. We need her." He glowered at Morgan. "Get the hell out of here."

Morgan and Azra loaded a protesting Taylor between them on the front bench seat.

"Remember the Bribri." Juan crossed himself. "The *Awá* may be your only hope."

Morgan shifted into drive and sped toward the border.

CHAPTER 6

On a bumpy and narrow thoroughfare, in pitch darkness, Juan's truck jerked and coughed, but plowed ahead. Morgan's head bounced into the ceiling and a dull pain permeated his skull.

"The military monitors this highway," Morgan said. "It's the link between Mexico and Columbia for drug traffic. Let's pray we don't run into a random checkpoint."

After a long delay, Azra replied. "You know praying is a waste." After letting that sink in, she continued, "How are you holding up? You did things."

"I'm okay. Did what I had to do."

"Who knew such superstitious crap still existed? I don't understand."

Morgan glanced at Taylor. Even wedged in, she'd fallen asleep. "How's her wound?"

"Once we stop I'll apply another antibiotic. It'll have to do until we get home and her doctor can give her a full workup. Rabies shots, blood tests, anti-virals." Azra pointed to Morgan's side. "I need to check you."

"I'm fine. Bleeding's stopped. How's your knee?"

"Not bad. Already treated it."

They reached the Panama border without being stopped. The jungle, with its mysterious squawks and rancid smells, surrounded them. The wind shifted layers of green vegetation. One car stood between them and escape.

"Passports?" Morgan said.

"Got 'em," Azra said. "What about the blood on your shirt?"

"If I lean into the door, they won't see it." *I hope.*

Taylor shifted. "Where are we?"

"At the border. Once across, we'll catch the next flight home."

"You left Mom."

Morgan gnawed on his lip. "There wasn't any other way."

"You didn't even *try* to save her."

"Don't speak to your father like that." Azra said. "He saved our lives in an impossible situation."

"Not *Mom's.*"

Morgan squeezed Taylor's hand. "Something I'll always regret. But we have to get you out of Costa Rica."

The auto in front crossed into Panama and Morgan pulled up to the gate. He rolled the manual window down, leaning into the door. "Evening."

"Passports," the heavy guard said.

Morgan handed them over. The thin guard flashed a light inside the car, then shifted to the truck bed.

"You flew into Liberia," the heavy guard said. "Coming back?"

"Yes, sir," Morgan said. "Going to see the canal. Returning in a few days."

The guard stamped the passports and returned them. "Proceed."

Morgan's entire body relaxed. *Yes!* "Thanks. Have a good night."

The thin guard moved to the far side of the cab and focused his light on Taylor's head. "Wait. Is that blood?"

Oh, shit. "A hiking mishap," Morgan said, trying to keep his voice level. "We're doctors. Nothing to worry about."

"Looks like a bite."

"Lost my footing and took a header," Taylor said. "What can I say? I'm a klutz."

"You two," the thin guard said to Morgan. "Step out, please."

Morgan clenched his teeth. *This is bad. They'll notice the blood on my shirt.* Lacking another choice, Morgan opened his door and stepped out. "Is this necessary?"

"You're bleeding."

"Like I said, we fell."

Three cars pulled up behind the truck, their headlights illuminating Morgan.

"Forget it," the heavy guard said. "Let's keep the line moving."

The thin guard stood his ground. "You know about those mountain stories. Vampire bats. Plagues and shit."

Morgan tensed. *Not these guys, too.*

The heavy guard hesitated. "You don't believe in that Bribri crap, do you?"

"My friend works for *La Contención de la Plaga*," the thin guard said. "I should call. Make sure there's no alert out."

No, no, no. Let us pass. "Guys," Morgan said, his voice cracking. "It's nothing."

The small guard backed away, his face blanching. "The wound on her head is moving."

"Moving?" The big guard stepped back.

"Yeah. Like it's alive, or something."

Morgan checked the gate. *If I floor it, can I ram through it?*

They'll alert the Panamanian police. We'll never get away.

"It's an illusion," Azra said. "The light plays tricks on our vision at night. Trust me. She's fine."

"She doesn't look fine," the thin guard said. He waved for Taylor to exit the car. "Let's go inside while I make a call."

"She's not going anywhere," Morgan said.

"Calm down, *señor*," the thin guard said, his hand on his holster, looking like a Central American version of Clint Eastwood. "You can go with her."

"I'll take her," the heavy guard said. "Open the gate for these other cars."

Morgan and Taylor joined the guard inside the station, a tiny room with two chairs, a counter, and a combination phone and fax machine. The guard pointed to the seats. "Sit."

"Listen," Morgan said, "if it's money you want I can get some."

A scratching noise on the front window interrupted him. Morgan squinted to find the source.

His heart raced as a brown blur came into focus. *Bats. Dozens writhing against the glass.* "What the hell?" Jagged lines formed on the glass. "Will that glass hold?"

The window shattered, and the room filled with bats. Taylor screamed. A brown hurricane swirled around them. Morgan covered Taylor the best he could.

The bats pounced on the guard, who shrieked. He reached for his pistol, but they ripped his eyes from their sockets, and he fell to the floor.

"What's going on in there?" the thin guard yelled. He scrambled into the station, his weapon drawn. But the bat's onslaught overwhelmed the pistol. They picked his eyes clean and carried them off as trophies. He screamed until he passed out.

Morgan huddled with Taylor in the corner, his heart jammed against his chest. *Did that just happen?*

The heavyset guard moaned. Even though he was unable to see, he looked in Taylor's direction. "You did this."

Morgan shielded Taylor's face from the carnage. "You hurt?"

"No."

"Me, neither. Almost like they were targeting the guards."

Azra ran in, then slid to a stop. "What happened? I heard glass breaking. Screaming." She saw the guards on the floor. "You attacked the guards?"

"Bats," Morgan said.

She held her stomach. "Jesus. Why would they do that? What kind of country is this?"

The guard mumbled before passing out. "*La Plaga.*"

Azra checked his pulse. "He needs an ambulance." She shifted to the bigger guard and felt under his jaw. "This one needs a coroner." She stood. "We have to call somebody."

"We can't afford to wait for help to arrive." Morgan lifted Taylor in his arms and stepped over the eyeless bodies. "We'll call from Panama."

Azra let out a deep breath. "I agree. Get us out of here. Before anything else happens."

They jumped back into the car and crossed the border.

CHAPTER 7

Salem, Oregon - the day after Thanksgiving

After their ordeal in the steaming tropics, Morgan celebrated seeing the frigid, drizzly city he called his own. He, Taylor, and Azra picked up his yellow Lab, Bear, and arrived at Morgan's home after sunset to a chilly and dark interior. Even his modest two-bedroom house with its decaying wood trim brightened his spirits after three flights, including airline and terminal changes.

Taylor stormed to the room she'd grown up in before she and Michelle had moved out after the divorce, followed by the wagging dog. "Leave me alone."

"Azra has to change the dressing on your wound," Morgan called to her. He motioned for Azra to follow. "Not optional."

Morgan proceeded to the master bathroom and pulled his shirt over his head. An ugly cut on his ribcage stared back at him. A reminder of Michelle's drowning. He fought back tears as Azra joined him.

"How's Taylor?" Morgan asked.

"I gave her a sedative. She'll sleep for a while. Her gash looks normal. Maybe the weather down there caused it to pulse. Anyway, her pediatrician can do a full workup."

"I'd rather you did it."

Azra pulled out a sterile pack containing a needle and surgical thread from her medical bag. "Okay."

"Thanks."

"Sit still." Azra ran the tip through the flab above Morgan's hip. He winced. "Ouch."

"Don't be a wimp," Azra said. She looked up and squinted. "You look awful. Your complexion is ghost-like, even for you. And your hair. It's like a coagulum of sticky goo."

Morgan grunted. "A warm shower will fix everything." Somewhere behind his eyeballs, a riveter made the music of migraines.

Azra finished patching up his side. "That'll hold until you see your physician."

She doesn't look much better than I do. Guess I shouldn't share that. "Sorry about Thanksgiving, and, well, everything."

"You should rest. I'll come back and check on Taylor and you tomorrow."

"You're leaving?"

"I need to go home and unpack, get into my own hot shower, and Taylor will need time to settle into her old bedroom. Easier if I'm not here."

"My shower's plenty big enough for both of us."

"Not tonight, Richard."

Morgan took her hand. "Can I do this?"

"Do what?"

"Raise Taylor. I don't know the first thing about raising a teenage girl."

"You'll figure it out," Azra said.

"I'm used to counseling adults, not teenagers. What if I mess up?"

"You sound like her therapist. She's not a patient. She's your daughter. Parenting is hard. There's no manual. You do your best, and you live with the results."

Morgan pressed her hand. "No offense, but you don't exactly have much experience on the subject. You said you're afraid to have kids."

41

Azra's eyes flashed anger, and she pulled away. "I never said I was *afraid*. My career is my passion. I won't compromise it."

"And if Taylor is living with me? What will that do to *us*?"

"You're all she has now. I must take a back seat." Azra's expression gave away nothing.

Is she expecting me to argue with her? Is this a test?

When Morgan didn't respond, Azra narrowed her eyes. "What about your parents? You've never talked about them. Can they help?"

A glaciation descended on Morgan. "Dead."

"I'm sorry. And about *us*, every time I bring that up you change the subject. What is it you want, Richard?"

"You know I care about you."

Azra retreated. "*Care* won't cut it. If that's all this is, I shouldn't keep hanging around, hoping you decide on a committed relationship."

"You should never say *committed* to a shrink." His try at humor failed. "Come on. I'm getting there."

Azra poked him in the thorax. "I still haven't seen a ring. Or been asked."

Morgan groaned. "I'm working on it. Baby steps."

"I'd prefer adult steps."

Morgan tried to kiss her on the lips, but she angled her head so he only smeared the side of her face. "Are we good?"

"We both have a lot to consider." She kissed him on the cheek. "Get some sleep."

"Is Taylor going to be okay? Those people in Costa Rica said some scary shit."

"She'll be fine. There's no fever. The slash will heal."

"You don't think they'll come after her?"

"Here? Hell, no. Without work visas Homeland Security would flag them. They'd need money, passports, a weapon. Even if they could figure out where you live, they'd never pull it off."

"I suppose."

"That Margarita woman got to you, didn't she?"

Morgan exhaled. "Hard not to think about her."

"And those poor border guards. Whatever possessed the bats to swoop in?"

"No clue. Could the locals have a scent that triggered them?"

Azra looked puzzled. "Damn peculiar."

Morgan followed her to the front door. She pecked him on the cheek again and vanished into the rain.

Twice on the chops? Not good.

His mind returned to Margarita's last words. *We will chase you down wherever you try to hide. We will find the girl, and we will destroy her.*

Anxiety rushed through Morgan, pushing him to check on Taylor. Bear, her yellow lab, lay at the edge of her bed. He wagged his tail at the sight of Morgan.

Taylor sat up, clutching a stuffed dog he recognized from long ago - brown with a white stomach and oversized, floppy, white ears.

Azra said she sedated her. "Taylor? You okay?"

Taylor eased her head around until she faced him. Her neck swiveled and creaked. "I heard you with Azra. You wish I'd never been born."

Morgan rushed to her, but she vaulted under her blanket and hid.

"Go away. You let Mom die. I know you did. Now I'm the only thing standing between you and your girlfriend."

Pain pierced Morgan's chest. "Taylor, no."

"Go away!"

Morgan stood his ground for a moment, then slumped and retreated. *She hates me. Blamed me even though it was Michelle who bailed from our marriage.*

He dragged himself to his own room and collapsed onto the bed. He closed his eyes and fell asleep to nightmares of bats, guns, and the deceased love of his life.

CHAPTER 8

Morgan awoke Saturday drenched in perspiration, his throat caked in crud. The room spun, approximating a merry-go-round on steroids. He coughed up a chunk of bile, then forced his way to the bathroom sink to flush it out.

A dash of light peeked in through his bedroom window. He wanted to go on an early morning run—*nothing like a Salem jog in November, unless it's in December, January, or February*—but knew his ribs couldn't handle it and instead dialed Father Javier Garcia.

Garcia answered. "Pennywise? That you?"

"Yeah." Morgan rubbed his aching head. *Still with the Pennywise. High school was a long time ago, dude.* But the attribution comforted him. He recalled Garcia pinning him with it at their Senior Prom. *Class jester. Biggest wiseass. Never picking up the check. Pennywise.* He'd accepted the moniker, a Steven King reference, over the threatened alternative—BTC, or Bozo the Clown.

"You're back early, man. Everything okay?"

"Javi, Michelle's dead. Drowned in a storm. I pulled her to shore but couldn't resuscitate her."

"Oh, no. Taylor? Azra?"

Morgan sagged onto the bed. "Taylor's here. But the three of us barely busted out of Costa Rica alive."

"What? Why?"

"Taylor got bit by a bat and the locals freaked. Claimed she had the plague. They planned to execute us all. I had to leave Michelle behind."

"That's loco, man. You had Taylor checked out, right?"

"Azra treated her. She's fine. But I had to shoot two Costa Ricans to escape. Didn't kill them, but, still."

After a lengthy delay, Garcia responded in a subdued voice. "You did what?"

"I had no choice."

Another pause. "I believe you. But, man, that's intense."

Morgan grabbed his head. "I'm in trouble, Javi. I can talk to you, and it stays privileged, right? As my priest?"

"As your priest, yes." After a short delay, he continued. "I am still your priest, right?"

"Of course."

"Well, it *has* been almost over a year since we've seen you in church. Since the divorce."

Morgan grunted. "Can we not do this now?"

"Sorry. What can I do?"

"I'm worried Taylor will never forgive me for not saving her mom."

"If you couldn't save Michelle, she couldn't be saved. Taylor will come around."

"I'm not so sure about either."

"Why's that?"

Morgan debated sharing his most private secret. "To give you the complete picture, I need to explain what happened with my former fiancée, Ginger, twenty years ago. Two years before Michelle. You remember her?"

"Sure. You two were quite the couple." Garcia hesitated. "Until her tragic death."

"That's what I need to tell you about. Can you come by? I can't leave Taylor."

"Should I bring the confessional cabinet? It's pretty heavy."

"Shut up, smart-ass. Just get over here."

* * *

Father Garcia arrived in street clothes carrying his worn, leather-bound Bible. He gave Morgan a bearhug. "Good to see you, man."

"You want coffee?"

"No time. Just spill what you have to tell me."

They sat on the living room sofa in front of the TV. "Hold on to the Good Book you've got there," Morgan said. "You might need it. You're about to learn the truth about your best friend."

* * *

Ohe'o Gulch, Maui, Hawaii - Twenty years earlier

Morgan and Ginger arrived at the Haleakala National Park beyond Hana at three in the afternoon, two hours before sunset. A hike to the 400 foot-high Waimoku Falls would take an hour each way.

A severe storm had drenched the mountain, raising the water to flash flood levels. Dark clouds hovered.

"My parents referred to this as the 'Seven Deadly Pools' instead of 'Seven Sacred Pools.'" Morgan said. *Back before my Dad destroyed everything.*

"That's the first time you've mentioned your family," Ginger said. "I wondered if you have some dark secret. When will I get to meet them?"

Morgan blanched. *Idiot. Why'd you bring that up?* "A conversation for another day."

"We *are* getting married, you know. Shouldn't you tell me a little?"

Morgan marched on for fifteen minutes. They reached the first of the seven waterfalls, Makahiku Falls and its 200 foot drop. The sun now hid behind the mountains and clammy spray thickened the air. The sky darkened as if lowered by a dimmer switch.

They hiked into the bamboo forest where giant stalks blocked out any remaining light. Man-made wood slats covered the underbrush here and there, allowing them to walk between the stalks, a welcome break from the mud and slippery rocks. Their boots created a comical squishing sound. The wind scraped against them. The reeds applauded.

"It's like they're trying to tell us something," he said. *Something urgent.*

By the time they reached Waimoku Falls, their clothes were water-logged by the thick mist from the gushing cascade.

"We should head back," Morgan said. "It'll be pitch dark soon."

"Hang on. I want a souvenir." She picked up a stray lava rock and placed it in her backpack.

"You're not supposed to take anything out. Especially lava. Hawaiian religion says it's bad juju. Pisses off Pele."

"It's the twenty-first century," Ginger laughed. "Besides, I make my own luck."

She didn't wait for a reply. She made a u-turn and reentered the forest. Morgan raced to stay even.

The wind gusted, and the hollow stems clapped violently, dancing as if alive. Rain pounded them. Shoots darted to the beat, grinding like a knives and forks slashing across each other.

The trail vanished under gushing mud.

Morgan gripped Ginger's hand. "Keep moving."

He led them along the raised wood-slatted pathway. The last glimmer of daylight disappeared. The bamboo continued their ritualistic performance.

Anxious sweat poured from Morgan's temples. *Don't let Ginger see how concerned I am. Need to keep her calm.*

The cascading water sped up, racing under the wood slats. They plowed forward, their feet splashing.

A bamboo shoot snapped, missing them by inches. Morgan's head twisted skyward. Faces in the clouds, illuminated in the black-hearted sky, laughed and taunted.

A heavy stalk crashed into his arm, sending it numb, and he involuntarily released Ginger. She screamed as a torrent of flood water lifted her, and she careened into the river, vanishing over Makahiku Falls.

* * *

Salem, Oregon

"I let her take the lava," Morgan told Garcia. Deep lines carved crevices in the priests's face. *They get deeper every year. Must be hell to hear about the parishioner's sins. Like mine.* "I didn't protect her."

"The rock didn't sweep her away. A flash flood did."

"I'm responsible." Morgan's stomach lurched. "You're in the business of accepting what you can't prove. How can you be sure taking the lava didn't factor into her death?"

"The Holy Catholic Church isn't based on superstition. If you've been beating yourself up all these years, it's time to stop."

Morgan squirmed. "It gets worse. Ginger's parents had me arrested for murder."

"What?"

"After his own investigation, the DA dropped the charges." Morgan looked his friend in the eye. "The two women I loved end up dead." *Three if you count my mother.* "What if I'm bad news for the women in my life?"

"That's nonsense." Garcia put his free hand on Morgan's shoulder. "Be strong, man. For Taylor's sake, and yours."

"Is that code for stay off the booze?"

"We both know drinking is no solution. Besides, a sober Pennywise is a fun guy. A happy fellow. The drunk version, not so much."

Morgan focused on a scratch in the hardwood floor. "I don't have a clue how to raise Taylor."

"You're her father. You'll figure it out."

"*Absentee* dad. And a lame one at that." Morgan pawed at the scrape with his tennis shoe. "I can't believe Michelle is gone. I need to call her parents."

"They don't know about Michelle?"

"Not yet."

"It seems they would have been your initial call." Garcia's calm voice hinted of accusation. He rose. "Keep me informed on how Taylor's doing. Her youth group misses her." He let himself out.

Morgan stayed riveted to the sofa, head in hands. *He's right. I can't put this off any longer.* He stared at his cell phone. *I should make breakfast first. Taylor will wake up any sec.*

Cracking eggs into a pan calmed him. He added sharp cheddar and bacon, then scrambled them to create a Taylor's favorite. As if on cue, Taylor appeared in her pajamas. Her complexion lacked its typical warmth, but otherwise she looked healthy. *But that scowl. Not like her at all.* "How you feeling?"

"Mom's dead. How do you think I'm feeling?"

"I know. It's rough, but we can try to get through this together. I made breakfast."

"I'm not hungry. Can I go to the mall?"

"Azra's taking your blood today. Once the results come back, you can go if you feel up to it."

"I want to be with friends. Get my mind off everything."

Taylor disappeared into her room and closed the door.

The eggs on the stove grew cold, untouched, while Morgan wondered how to handle Taylor without Michelle and how to tell Michelle's parents their daughter was gone. *So much for delaying the inevitable.*

But before he could dial, his cell rang. The caller ID said Isaiah Carter. *Shit.* He answered. "Isaiah. I was about to call you."

"You son of a bitch. You killed my little girl."

Morgan choked a denial. *Who told you?*

"I know what you did," Carter continued. "The American Embassy in Costa Rica called. Did you think I wouldn't find out you killed her? Then left her body on pagan soil. No proper burial at our church."

"She drowned. An accident. I tried to rescue her."

"Save your breath. We're flying to Salem. I'll see you get the needle for killing my daughter. I'm taking our granddaughter away from you before you can harm *her* too."

CHAPTER 9

Morgan hung up on Carter. His heart pounded. *Still the same bully.* Michelle's last words invaded his thoughts. *Take care of Taylor. Promise me.* A charge ran through his body. *Like hell you're taking my daughter.*

He knocked on Taylor's door.

"Leave me alone."

"May I come in?"

She answered after a protracted delay. "It's your house."

Morgan stepped in. Taylor sat on her bed in pj's. Near-arctic air from her open window filled the room.

"Jeez, kiddo. It's freezing in here."

"I was hot."

He checked her forehead. "No fever. Azra will be here soon to do a thorough exam and draw some blood."

"Yay," Taylor said, with irony thick as cold porridge. "Then she can verify I've got some new disease. At least I'll be famous. Patient Zero."

"Bat bites happen all the time and nothing bad happens. A rabies shot and you'll be good as new."

He gazed down on her. *Still the same angelic face. She's the little girl I brought into this world. With Michelle.* He reached out and touched her cheek. She allowed it, but eyed him with suspicion.

"Taylor," he said, "I let you down. I'm determined to change. I want you here with me. Please say you want to be here."

Taylor scowled. "What about Azra? I heard you guys."

"Chalk it up to exhaustion and stress from the trip." He sat next to her. "Taylor, I never wanted our family to break up. I never stopped loving your mother. I want to be a family again."

"Azra will be pissed."

"If she can't deal with it, then she's not right for me. For us."

Taylor showed no emotion. She curled up with her stuffed dog and closed her eyes.

* * *

Azra arrived at noon and examined Taylor. After drawing blood, and assuring Taylor she checked out normal, Azra joined Morgan in his living room.

"She's okay?" Morgan said.

"Stop worrying." Azra took Morgan's hand. "I'll need the blood test results to be certain, but she seems fine. I'll have them tonight."

Morgan squirmed. "I have something important to talk to you about."

Azra's eyes sparkled. "Is this the question I've been waiting for?"

Shit. She thinks I'm proposing. "You know I adore you. But I need to focus on Taylor right now."

Azra's spark faded, and she withdrew. "I'm sure that's best."

Morgan ground his teeth. "I realize it's not what you want to hear."

"I understand."

"If I don't give Taylor everything I have, I'll regret it, and it will impact us."

"Will there be an us?"

He pulled her in tight and held her. She let him hold her. "I hope so."

Azra didn't respond.

* * *

After Azra's car pulled away from Morgan's home, a new set of headlights approached under a sky of menacing clouds. Morgan felt an involuntary shiver.

A short, stocky man with a round face and a two-day growth got out of the car. His black raincoat, overly long for him, scraped along the wet asphalt. He wore a cap with "Grandpa" stitched on the front and dangled an unlit cigar from his mouth. Morgan noticed the "Montecristo Habana" band wrapped around the thin smoke.

"Dr. Morgan?"

"Who's asking?"

The man stepped under the porch's overhang and pulled his coat back, revealing a shield.

"Lieutenant Gerald Smokey, Head of Criminal Investigations for the Salem Police." His voice sounded as if it was coming through a coffee grinder. "May I come in?"

"Smokey? Is that like the bear, or the cop chasing the bandit?"

Smokey didn't look amused. "Gee, Doc. Think of that all by yourself? Now, can I come in?"

Morgan waved him in. "What can I do for you?"

"I received an interesting call from the police department in Nosara, Costa Rica."

Morgan flinched. *How'd they find us so fast? And, if they did, then Margarita can.* "My ex-wife, Michelle, drowned down there day before yesterday. Swept out to sea in a storm."

Smokey jotted something down in his notepad. "That's not how they tell it. They found evidence of foul play. Looks to them like you killed her."

Morgan gasped. "That's ridiculous."

"They also say you refused to cooperate with their investigation, and you killed a police officer and shot two locals. Then fled the country, attacking two border guards. Claim you ripped their eyes out. The border guys might not make it."

"I didn't touch those guards." Morgan flopped onto the couch. *They're trying to frame me.*

Smokey scribbled more notes. "They filed an extradition request."

Morgan blanched.

"They want your daughter back, too. Claim she's an accomplice."

Morgan sank deeper into the couch. "You can't extradite us. They tried to kill us. That's why we ran."

"Who tried to kill you?"

"They have this task force. Sort of a secret police. They want to finish the job."

Smokey slapped the notepad shut. "A secret police."

"I appreciate how that sounds. Nuts, right? But that's what happened."

Smokey cleared his throat. "Did you know I met Michelle? And your daughter?"

"No."

"At Saint Edward's. Been a regular for thirty years. Met Michelle kneeling in a pew a few months ago. My granddaughter is in the middle-school youth group your daughter leads."

"Small world."

Smokey angled closer. "Indeed, Dr. Morgan. You know what I can't stomach? People in my town being murdered. I really can't stand that."

"Nobody murdered Michelle. It was an accident."

Smokey grunted. "Humph. You'll excuse me if I don't take your word on that."

"You can't ship us to Costa Rica. They'll execute us both."

"Michelle is my case, so you're not going anywhere until I'm done investigating her death. Once I'm done, well, the Costa Ricans will want justice for their citizens."

Morgan's heart pounded. *He intends to send me back there. And maybe Taylor. I can't let that happen.* "Any chance you can have

Michelle's body shipped here? That would mean so much to us. And her parents."

"I asked them," Smokey said. "Said they'll trade her corpse for you and the girl. They seemed more interested in your daughter. What did she do?"

"Nothing. I told you, they're corrupt. And deranged."

"Humph. Well, they're faxing over their official report now. I need you to come downtown for a chat."

Morgan's head spun. "You're arresting me?"

"I didn't say that."

"Do I need an attorney?"

Smokey's stared at Morgan. "I don't know. *Do you?*"

"You make it sound like I'm a suspect."

"You are."

"Then I need an attorney."

Smokey shrugged. "Up to you, Doc."

Morgan thought about leaving Taylor alone. "It'll be short, right?"

Smokey opened the door. "I hope so. I've got lunch with my granddaughter this afternoon."

Morgan's hands shook. *I need a drink*. He shuddered, arguing with himself. *No! One year sober.*

* * *

The Salem Police Department resided in the same building as the Salem Community Development Department and Municipal Court, with a large fountain separating it from the Public Library. Morgan met his attorney, Dorothy Prescott, inside. Dorothy stood half his height and weight and had fiery red hair, which matched her reputation as the toughest lawyer in Salem. An officer escorted them to a gloomy interview room.

Outside, the wind whipped a fir tree around like a rag doll, battering against the room's lone window, a two-by-two square of opaque, bulletproof, shatterproof glass. Raindrops the size of marbles pelted it.

The door swung open and Lieutenant Smokey shuffled in with a handful of papers. He dumped them on the table and sat across from Morgan and Dorothy.

"Doc," Smokey said, "the report's in. We've got evidence you need to explain." He rifled through the stack. "The Costa Rican police found your fingerprints on Michelle's neck and bruising consistent with strangulation."

Morgan looked at Dorothy, who didn't react. "Not possible."

"Further, your fingerprints were on the gun used to kill their policeman and shoot two citizens. And in the border station where someone mutilated two guards."

"I didn't kill anybody. The crazy lady from that task force killed the policeman. I maimed two armed guards on the beach in self-defense. Bats attacked the border guards."

"Bats."

I know it sounds bizarre, but, "Yeah."

Smokey twirled the cigar in his mouth. "Why would the police lie about the evidence?"

"The task force convinced the police Taylor was a threat to them because of a bat bite."

"Ah, yes. Your secret police. Or is it the shadow government?"

"I'm serious. They said they'd track us down."

Smokey and Dorothy exchanged glances.

"I know how it sounds," Morgan said. "Batshit crazy. You think I'm doctor Looney-tunes. If you don't believe *me*, ask Azra. She'll tell you."

"I spoke with Dr. Khan," Smokey said. "As the CME, she's held in high regard. Now, she's your girl, so there's that. But she backed you up." He pointed his cigar at Morgan. "I also got a call from Michelle's father today. He's convinced you did it. Says you've been threatening Michelle for years."

Morgan shifted in his seat. "He never liked me. He's a bigwig in his local church and didn't approve of our Catholic wedding." *Or perhaps he just thinks I'm a jerk.*

"Humph. Well, he and his wife are flying in to provide, what he calls, significant evidence to show you've been planning this for years. He hired a big-shot lawyer to petition for custody of your daughter."

"I knew I should have bought all the broomsticks in Utah."

"What?" Smokey tipped his head to the side. "Oh, I get it. You're a funny guy, Doc."

"Most people don't think so. But Carter's got nothing."

"Maybe." Smokey slouched back. "Guess what I did."

"I'm in no mood for guessing games."

"I searched for dirt on you. Found a homicide file from twenty years ago. Remember that?"

Morgan sagged. "Of course I remember. They exonerated me."

"Yes. But it's peculiar, don't you agree? Being investigated for two deaths. Both in water. Both your women."

Dorothy got in the game. "The past isn't relevant, and you know it."

Smokey raised his eyebrows. "Perhaps it is. Perhaps it isn't. Don't go wandering off, Doc. I'll be investigating."

Morgan knew he and Taylor wouldn't last long in Costa Rica. "How long do you figure it'll take to clear me?"

Smokey grunted. "If I had Michelle's body, and my forensic team, I'd get to the truth in no time. Without it, humph, I'm not sure. Maybe your in-laws will shed light on my investigation."

Morgan shivered. "So, I have that long to convince you not to send me to Costa Rica."

"Don't get your hopes up, Doc. Even if we determine Michelle drowned, you have other crimes to answer for. Policemen are passionate about cop killers. Professional courtesy extends a long way."

"But I didn't do it."

Smokey stood. "That sounds like something you'll have to prove in their court, not ours."

Morgan shivered. *If extradited, I'll never see a courtroom.* "Dorothy, you've got to keep us here. Our lives depend on it."

CHAPTER 10

Sunday

The clock chimed midnight. Sitting alone in his tiny closet of a bedroom on the rectory's top floor, Garcia studied his daily prayer requests. *Too many. And rarely an answer.* He kicked at the leg of the table. *Is it because I'm not worthy to do God's work?*

Despite the frigid temperature outside, his room steamed in the isolated space. From the washstand a faucet's constant drip pecked at his mind.

His phone broke the bitter silence. *Morgan.*

"Pennywise," he answered. "How's Taylor?"

"Good. Blood work came back clean. No rabies. No COVID-19. Nothing unusual."

Garcia glanced at the prayer list. *One I can mark off.* "And you?"

"I got called into the police station today," Morgan said, his voice lower. "The authorities in Costa Rica claim I killed Michelle."

"That's loco, man. Why would they say that?"

"They're trying to get Taylor and me extradited by manufacturing evidence. But Detective Smokey plans to investigate Michelle's death before agreeing to that. You know him from church, right?"

Garcia scanned the invocation list. Nothing from Smokey. "He's been a parishioner for years. Great guy."

Morgan laughed. "Your so-called great guy is trying to have your best friend arrested for murder."

"He's fair, and good at his job. He'll sort it out and exonerate you."

"I hope you're right. He says he met Michelle at your church, and his granddaughter is in Taylor's youth group."

"True." Garcia looked at the large wooden cross above his bed. It hung askew. *Like my faith.* "Speaking of Taylor's youth group, when do you figure she can come back and run it? They meet again Tuesday. If that's too soon, I can get a sub."

"She might go to school Monday. And the church group the next day if she feels up to it. She's been through hell."

Garcia swallowed. *Hades. We each have our own view of what that might be.* He thought about two teenage girls from his early days in the Church, Reggie and Patti. A sharp pain struck deep within his chest. *Maybe it's reserved for priests who've failed.*

"Will I see you two at church today?"

"I think Taylor needs another day of total rest."

"And when she's better, will I see you at services."

"Can we not do this right now?"

Garcia looked at his prayer list. Morgan was at the top. "Up to you, Pennywise. But don't wait until it's too late."

"What's that mean?"

"We're all on the clock. We just don't know what time it is. Only God knows."

CHAPTER 11

Monday

*Y*ou *let Mom die.*
Morgan awoke in a mattress soaked in perspiration, his heart trying to thrum its way through his chest. The wind rattled windows and bored through cracks in the house's armor, rendering the home's antiquated heating system impotent. Simultaneously warm and icy, he quivered and checked the time.

Three o'clock in the morning. An hour since the last horrid dream had awakened him.

He heard a noise down the hall.

Taylor. Another nightmare. He put on a pair of pink bunny slippers, a Father's Day gift from Taylor. Their last Father's Day as a family. His breath came in short, white spurts. He shuffled to her room, then listened through the closed door.

The bed box spring squeaked, followed by a whine from Bear.

Morgan tapped on her door and whispered. "Taylor? You awake?"

"Go away."

Morgan pressed ahead. "Can I get you anything?"

The door flew open. Taylor blocked the doorway. She shivered in bare feet, black shorts, and a black tank top, her skin rising in goosebumps. Bear whined and paced behind her.

He took a step inside. "Jeez, Taylor, you're freezing."

She held her ground. "I said, go away." She tried to slam the door, but he blocked it with his arm and pushed it open.

"Hey, I'm trying to help."

She glared at him and retreated to her antique sleigh bed, stripped to the pink sheet and matching pillowcase. "I don't need your help. And I'm not cold. It's sweltering in here."

Biting wind and bursts of snow rushed in through an open window. White shirts, pants, skirts, and dresses littered the floor. He stepped across and closed her window, then lowered the shade. *Snow's come early this year. It's going to be a hell of a winter.* "You'll catch pneumonia like this."

She sat on the bed, erect. "I told you, I'm hot."

He sat next to her and tested her forehead. Warm, but not feverish. "Did you have a bad dream?"

She mocked him with her laugh. "Are there any other kind?"

"It *will* get better."

She flopped onto the bed. "Whatever. I want to sleep now." She reached under her pillow and retrieved her stuffed dog, the one Garcia gave Taylor when he baptized her, pulling double duty as priest and godfather.

"I see you found Mr. Snuggles," he said.

"I didn't *find* him. He wasn't lost."

"Right. How does Bear feel about him?"

"He's a dog. How would he know anything?"

Morgan stroked his chin. "You love Bear."

"Whatever. At least Mr. Snuggles won't die."

Morgan held her. "Nobody else will die."

Her eyes flashed and her voice dropped an octave. "You don't know anything."

Morgan flinched. *That voice. Eerie.* "I promise everything is okay now."

Taylor smirked.

"What's with the clothes on the floor?" Morgan said.

"I don't want them anymore."

"I notice it's all your white stuff. Did white become a fashion no-no?"

Taylor picked at a spot on the sheet. "Isn't that what you do when you're in mourning? Wear black?"

"Some do. But you don't have to throw everything else out."

"Are we going to have a funeral for Mom?"

"We'll have a service. I'm hoping to get her back soon. I think we should wait. Don't you?"

"I guess."

Morgan placed a blanket on her, which she kicked off. "Try to sleep."

"Are *you* able to sleep?"

"Not much."

"Do you miss her?"

Morgan swallowed. "I do." Tears descended. "I should never have given her a reason to kick me out."

Taylor closed her eyes.

After a minute of silence, he sensed she might have dozed off. "Good night, Taylor. I love you."

He hung around, hoping for a response, then sank his head and plodded to his own room.

* * *

Taylor, dressed in black, her backpack slung over her shoulder, burst into the kitchen while Morgan made breakfast. "Holiday's over. Can you take me to school?"

Morgan checked on the weather through his kitchen window. The snow had stopped, leaving a thin blanket on the ground. But the sky gave every indication of a freezing, slushy, miserable day. "You sure? It's okay to wait. They'll understand."

"If I sit around here, all I'll do is think about Mom. I *need* this. To heal."

Morgan admired her lovely face. *Maybe she's right.* "Okay. But call me if you don't feel well. I can pick you up any time. Deal?"

"Deal."

* * *

Morgan dropped Taylor off at her high school, then drove to his office at the Oregon State Hospital, famous as the filming location for *One Flew Over the Cuckoo's Nest.* Appropriate, he reasoned. The tall spire atop the stone building gave off a pinkish hue in a sliver of dawn sun trying to force its way through the dark clouds.

A film crew met him out front. *Not this again.*

"Dr. Morgan, Jill Moncrief from ABC News." The woman wore a blue jacket with an ABC logo. "Any comment on recent patient escapes? Given two-thirds of the patients here are criminally insane?"

Morgan waved her off and ducked inside. He found his office as he left it—locked, organized and neat. A wood desk, one wall-to-wall bookcase, a leather desk chair, a table flanked by two armchairs, and a couch. And a locked cabinet housing prescription drugs.

He set his briefcase on the desk and turned on his office computer. *Paperwork catch-up day.*

That plan lasted thirty seconds. Someone knocked on the door, and he looked up to find Bob Allister, a patient from the marriage counseling segment of his practice.

"Dr. Morgan. Sorry to bother you without an appointment."

Morgan motioned for Allister to join him. "Bob. How are you?"

Allister stepped inside. "Better, thanks to you."

Morgan rose, and they shook hands across the desk. "Take a seat. What have you been up to?"

Allister sat at the edge of the chair. "Back from a recruiting trip for my Ducks. Hoping Coach can get us over the top."

Morgan recalled Allister owned a business jet and made it available to the University of Oregon football staff during recruiting season. "I guess that's one perk of retiring as the CEO of a major corporation. Your own jet and the chance to help your alma mater."

"It's a sweet deal, no doubt. But it meant nothing when I thought my marriage was going down the tubes."

"How is Marcia?"

"She's great. We're great. Looking forward to a second chance." Allister bent forward. "I heard what happened to you, losing Michelle in Costa Rica. Must've been awful."

Morgan's face turned red. *How does he know? Boy. Never underestimate the drumbeats of a small town.* "Thanks. Yeah, it was brutal."

"Is there anything I can do for you? Anything at all? You saved my life."

"Thanks, Bob. Michelle's gone, and I have to deal with it. But I appreciate the offer."

Allister looked disappointed. "Okay. But the offer stands. Any time."

Morgan wanted the conversation to be over. "Thanks, Bob. It means a lot."

"No sweat. I'll leave you to your work. You have a good day."

After Allister left, Morgan put his head in his hands. A grunt broke him out of his spell, and he glanced at the doorway.

Lieutenant Smokey filled the passage, an unlit cigar dangling in its usual spot.

Morgan sagged. "Detective. What now?"

Smokey slogged in. "Still more questions than answers." He stopped at the far side of the desk and removed the cigar.

Morgan decided to go on the offensive and poke the bear. "Aren't Cuban cigars illegal in this country?"

Smokey admired his smoke. "They were when I got this. But anyone here can have them now, as long as you don't resell them."

"So you *did* get it when it was illegal. Kind of ironic, don't you think?"

"What can I say. Being the a detective has its perks." Smokey smiled, and Morgan noticed two gold crowns deep inside his mouth.

"And aren't they expensive?" Morgan asked, his voice needling. "Too much for a detective's salary?"

"Chief of detectives." Smokey pointed at Morgan. "I'm not the one under investigation."

Morgan closed his eyes and took a deep breath. "Do I need my attorney here?"

"Nah. I came by to see where you hang your shingle."

"Any progress with the police in Costa Rica?"

"They're pissed I haven't shipped you back. Still holding Michelle's body as leverage."

Morgan opened his eyes. "I didn't do it."

"Humph. We'll see." Smokey nodded to Morgan and disappeared.

Javi better be right about Smokey. Taylor's life depends on him.

Morgan's cell buzzed. A call from Taylor's school. "This is Morgan."

"Doctor Morgan, this is Principal Franks. You need to get down here. Taylor punched a classmate."

CHAPTER 12

Morgan picked up Taylor from the principal's office, apologized to the headmaster, and rushed her to the car. The weather had morphed to an electrical storm, and his arm hair stood at attention. Once he got Taylor settled out of the tempest, he fired up the auto and sped away.

"You hit a student?"

Taylor yawned. "He had it coming."

"He?"

"Yeah. It's no big deal."

Morgan squirmed. "It's a huge deal. Since when do we use violence to resolve our differences?"

"Starting today, I guess."

"That's unacceptable behavior, and you know better."

"Mom wouldn't care. She understood men are lame."

Morgan clenched his teeth and took a moment to calm himself. "Tell me what happened."

"Nothing."

"Did he provoke you?"

Taylor grinned. "He didn't do anything. I snuck up on him and clocked him. He never saw it coming." She laughed. "You should have seen the shock on his face."

She's enjoying this. "Come on. He must have done *something*."

"He's a boy. I hate boys."

Morgan swallowed. "You hate boys. Just out of nowhere?"

"That's right. Your good Catholic daughter can't stand boys. From now on, I'm into girls. How do you like that?"

The clinical side of Morgan kicked in. *What is this? Questioning her own sexuality? Has the shock caused this, or has it been festering? Is she in a healthy emotional or mental condition to come to this conclusion?* "We'll talk more about this later. After I decide on an appropriate punishment."

He winced at the blast of a police siren. Red and blue lights flashed in his rear-view mirror. *Shit.*

He pulled over and lowered his driver-side window. Through his side mirror he watched a heavyset officer amble toward him. *Hey. I know that guy. I counseled he and his wife. I think they reconciled.*

The officer reached the window and smiled. "Doctor Morgan." He put his ticket pad away. "It's good to see you."

"Nice to see you, Officer Phillips. How's Emily?"

"We're great. Thanks to you."

"You two did the heavy lifting. So, what'd I do?"

"You ran a red light back there." He glanced at Taylor. "You okay?"

"I'm good. Distracted, I guess. I don't know if you heard, but my ex drowned."

The officer nodded. "I did. I'm so sorry. You okay to drive home? I can escort you."

"Thanks. Not necessary." Morgan gave the officer a sheepish grin. "You going to write me up?"

"Hell, no. After what you did for me and Emily. I'm forever in your debt. You have a good day." The officer tipped his cap and returned to his vehicle.

Morgan drove the rest of the way in uneasy silence. Taylor hummed a dirge of "I am Woman" and "Another One Bites the Dust."

* * *

68

Morgan and Azra sat at his kitchen table in front of three bowls of canned clam chowder. "She's not herself. Wears only black. Never smiles. Then, she punches a kid. Her justification? All boys suck. Is she having a sexuality crisis?"

"Her mother drowned in a foreign land. She got attacked by a bat. Targeted by crazy vigilantes who wanted to kill her. Then watched you shoot two armed men. And the bats with those guards. It's a miracle any of us are coping."

Taylor entered in a black tee and matching shorts, her face grim and her skin tone subdued. "Is *that* what's for dinner?"

Morgan reacted with a puzzled expression. "You love chowder."

Taylor spun on him. "Mom made it from scratch. You don't know shit. Stop pretending you do."

Azra clanked her spoon on the bowl. Her cheeks turned bright red.

"Taylor," Morgan said, "you don't have to eat it, but there's no reason to swear at me. I'm doing my best here."

Taylor's cackling mimicked the Wicked Witch of the West. "Your best sucks." She shivered. "I think you got to Mom in time to save her, then let her drown." She spun on Azra. "You and your slut."

Morgan's heart twitched. He jumped to his feet. "That's enough. Go to your room."

A look of regret formed, but before speaking, Taylor returned to her irate state, and stormed away. She slammed her bedroom door.

Morgan turned to Azra, who sat hunched over her food. "Sorry. She had no right."

Azra looked up, her chin quivering.

Morgan slid his chair next to hers. "I don't know what to do. One moment, she's a hurting girl needing my love. Then, bam, she hates me."

"You must see similar behavior at your office."

"It's different when it's your own kid. Hard to stay detached. I want to prescribe something. She's not sleeping. Claims to feel great and has lots of energy, but, even when she's acting normally, there's an underlying sadness. She consistently regresses."

"Sounds like my manic-depressive cousin."

Morgan winced. "It's too early to diagnose that. But I need to send her to another therapist. Get an independent opinion."

Azra rose. "I should go."

"Please stay."

She put her hand on his shoulder. "You should focus on her. I'm in the way."

"You've been different since we got back."

"Let's take things a day at a time. Help Taylor. Give her all your attention."

Morgan stood. "I don't want to lose you over this." His vertigo returned, and he steadied himself by grabbing the table. *And I don't know if I can do this alone.*

Azra's eyes teared. "I'll call you in a few days. See how you two are doing."

Without another word or a kiss, she left. Morgan watched her car speed away. *She didn't sign up for this.*

His head stabilized. He walked back to Taylor's room and knocked. When she didn't respond he cracked the door open. "Taylor? You should eat something."

Morgan's frosty breath floated into the blackness. Concerned, he stepped inside and turned the light on.

Taylor lay on top of her bed, in just the tee shirt and shorts, no covers, asleep. The room was freezing due to the open window. Her breath turned to frost and lingered. Bear sat in the corner trembling, his attention riveted on Taylor.

Morgan shook his head. *How can she sleep in this?* He latched the window closed, then covered her with a blanket. After watching her for a full ten minutes, he withdrew to his room.

He dozed off fully clothed, including sneakers. Morgan passed between a blurred, semi-alert state to a land of nightmares, crossing and uncrossing the boundary between consciousness and unconsciousness, sanity and insanity.

* * *

Tuesday

When Morgan awoke at sunrise, he trudged to the bathroom. He stared into the mirror, horrified by his blanched complexion. His clothes clung to his body drenched in perspiration.

He'd been dreaming of Michelle. *Oh, sweetie, how did it ever come to this?* He splashed cold water on his face. *How will I survive losing you and having Taylor go through this?* His bloodshot red eyes stared back. *No more whining. Taylor needs help. Time to find her another therapist.*

First, breakfast. He started for the kitchen, but froze halfway there.

A single trail of muddy footprints tracked across the wood floor from Taylor's room to his bedroom. *Bare feet. Taylor-sized, not Bear's. Did Taylor go outside during the night?*

Or did someone else come in?

He surged into her bedroom. She snored, safely tucked under a sheet. The freezing air from her open window jolted him. *Jesus, the window again?*

At least she's okay. Now confirm no one's here.

Morgan rushed around checking the rooms and behind doors. Other than the mud between his room and hers he found nothing. Back at her door, he stared at the trail, confounded. He knew his feet were too large to have made the prints, but he checked for sludge. Nothing.

It came from outside. But no trail from the front door. How'd she get out? And why?

Morgan examined her room and found stains under her window. He gulped and checked her feet.

He almost collapsed under the weight of his discovery. *Mud. Oh, Christ, she climbed out her window?*

Taylor grunted and kicked off her sheet.

Morgan stabilized himself. "Taylor, you awake?"

"I'm tired. Leave me alone."

He sat on the edge of the bed. *No. I have to know.* "Taylor, you have dirt on your feet. And you left a trail from your window. Did you climb outside last night?"

She laughed, her eyes still closed. "What are you talking about? Why would I go through there?"

"But the tracks only come from the window."

Taylor shot up at her waist, seated and erect. Her bloodshot eyes flew open and bored into him. "I said I didn't do it."

Morgan tensed at her hostility, but stayed true to his quest for answers. "Then who did? Somebody with feet about your size was in here."

"I have no idea. You sure it isn't just Bear making a mess?"

"The prints look too big for Bear."

Taylor lay back and closed her eyes.

"You skipped dinner. You must be starving."

"Not hungry." Her voice had lost its edge.

"You need to eat. Can I trust you to go to school?"

Taylor opened her eyes and smiled. "I'm sorry about yesterday. I'll be good."

"You're lucky they didn't suspend you. Or worse. I convinced them to waive the zero tolerance punishment due to the extenuating circumstances surrounding your mother. But you won't get another chance."

"I appreciate you going to bat for me. It won't happen again."

Morgan studied her face. *Maybe Azra's right. She's been through hell. Might need my support and some slack more than anything.* "I'll throw a few protein bars in your backpack."

"Thanks." She sat up. "Dad?"

Jeez, she sounds almost normal. No hatred. Morgan teared up. "I'm right here."

72

"I'm also sorry about last night. I owe you and Azra an apology."

"Apology accepted. We know you've been through a lot."

"Can I go to my church group after school? Brianna had to lead it all by herself while I was gone. She needs me. And she's eighteen, so it's like having an adult with me. It'll help me stop thinking about Mom."

Morgan licked his lips. "Taking care of other kids might be too much right now."

"Dad, it's a dozen middle-school girls. Between Brianna and me, it's easy-peasy. And Father Javier is always watching."

Morgan closed his eyes. *Can I let her out of my sight? Leave her in charge of children? And what about getting her in to see a psychotherapist?*

"Please, Dad. Nothing bad will happen."

Maybe this is what she needs. Back in her routine, in a safe place. The shrink can wait a day.

"Okay."

CHAPTER 13

Morgan swabbed wet towels along the wood floors, cleaning the dried mud. *She must have walked in her sleep. People do all kinds of crazy shit while sleepwalking. That's why she can't remember.*

The electrical storm had blown through, leaving a crispness seldom experienced in Salem. Fresh pine fragrances leaked through the crevices in the walls and added to his own cleaning effort, giving Morgan's home that just-cleaned scent.

Once the floors were clean, Morgan paced through his living room, Bear following. *At least no word from the school today.* But he couldn't shake the feeling that something wicked loomed.

Morning rolled into afternoon. *School's over, and Taylor's with Javi by now. I should check in with him. Just to make sure.* But he shook away his paranoia. *Treating her like nothing's wrong will help her get acclimated and heal.*

As the clock donged four, Morgan's ringing cell saved him the trouble of a call to Garcia. "Everything okay?"

"Richard, we have a crisis."

Richard? You haven't called me that in twenty-five years. Morgan wilted. *Oh, shit.*

"I can't believe this is happening," Garcia continued.

What was I thinking? "What happened?"

"Katy Wilson is missing."

Relief washed over Morgan. Then he chided himself. "Where?"

"We took the youth group to Keizer Rapids Park. Brianna, Taylor, and I. You remember the loop there?"

"Yeah."

"Brianna took half the kids one way, and Taylor and I took the rest on the other trail, so we'd meet in the middle. It's a short hike - thirty minutes tops."

"And when you met them Katy was gone?"

"*Sí*. Neither Brianna nor the other kids saw her separate from the group. I called the police, and the parents, but I can use help here. It'll be dark soon."

"Taylor's okay, right? Not freaked out?"

"Actually, she's the calmest one here."

Morgan let out a breath. *I guess that's good.*

"I'll be there in fifteen minutes." Morgan shivered. "The Willamette River is down the cliff. You don't think she hiked down there?"

"I don't know what to believe."

* * *

Morgan pulled into the park under dark clouds and a setting sun. A brisk, roaring wind foretold a chilling evening. Any child unprotected in the elements overnight would be in serious trouble.

Blue and red lights flashed atop police cars in the parking lot. Morgan counted a dozen middle-school girls standing together, with Garcia, Brianna, and Taylor surrounding them. Officers grabbed high-powered flashlights and charged into the recreation area.

Morgan ran toward Taylor, but stopped at the sound of a familiar voice.

"Doc." He turned to find Smokey rushing in the same direction. "What are you doing out here?"

"Father Garcia asked me to help look for the girl. Your granddaughter? She's here?"

"Yes." Smokey veered off. "Daylight's fading fast. We need to hustle."

Smokey ran off and Morgan reached Taylor. She stood out as the only one not wearing a jacket. She'd changed into a white dress. *White? That's new. Does she keep a change of clothes at the church?* "Taylor. You okay?"

Taylor showed no emotion. "Richard. Why are you here?"

Richard? Where'd that come from? "Javi called me. Aren't you cold? I have a blanket in the car."

"I'm fine."

Garcia appeared, clutched his Bible. His knuckles were white. "*Gracias* for coming."

"What can I do?" Morgan said.

"Help watch the girls? I need to show the police where Katy was last seen."

Two officers ran by with netting used to dredge a river. Morgan's heart sank. "Go."

Garcia raced off with a handful of policemen.

Morgan focused on Taylor. "Javi tells me he was with you when you met up with Brianna's group. Is that when you discovered Katy was missing?"

"She's exactly where she belongs."

Morgan tensed. "What do you mean? You know where she is?"

Taylor looked past Morgan. "She's sleeping."

Before Morgan could react, Smokey stepped next to him with a young girl. "Your daughter okay?" Smokey asked.

"She's fine. Your granddaughter?"

Smokey held her close. "Seems okay. Not saying much. None of the girls are."

Morgan noticed Smokey's perusal of the children. *Smokey's right. The girls are staring at Taylor. Like they're frozen in place.*

"Maybe they're frightened," Smokey said.

"Maybe." Morgan looked back at Taylor. Her dress floated about in the icy wind. "Excuse me, Lieutenant. I need to get Taylor in something warmer. I promised the Father I'd look after the kids. Can you cover for me? I'll be right back."

"Sure, Doc."

"I'm glad your granddaughter is safe."

"Thanks, Doc. Glad your daughter is fine, too. We better locate Katy Wilson."

"The entire community is looking. We'll find her." Morgan placed his arms around Taylor's shoulders. "Let's get you warm." He took her back to his car where she continued to stare into the woods. He put a blanket around her shoulders.

"Taylor, why did you say Katy's sleeping? Do you know something?"

She laughed. "I know *everything*."

Morgan swallowed hard. "About Katy?"

She gave him an unnerving look that sent shivers down his spinal column.

Shouts from the park interrupted them. Excited voices. Lights flashing.

"They found her," Taylor said. She turned to Morgan and her eyes bored into him.

He flinched. He recognized the expression from his practice. *A glimpse into insanity.* He shivered. *Something is wrong. I can feel it.*

"Can we go now?" Taylor said.

The voices from the park got louder. The lights moved closer. Paramedics rolled Katy on a gurney into the parking lot, her parents at her side. An ambulance whisked her away.

"Thank God," Morgan said.

"I told you," Taylor said. "She's doing great."

"Doc," Smokey called from the crowd. "I need you two back at Saint Edwards. I have questions."

Of course you do.
So do I.

* * *

On the drive over, the wind picked up and howled with an eerie pitch. Morgan's head pounded.

Once back, Smokey spun his unlit cigar with his tongue. Morgan, Taylor, and Brianna sat next to each other on the worn couch in the youth group center facing Smokey and Garcia. Two police officers stood in the background.

"Tell me what happened," Smokey said to Brianna.

"I wish I knew. We went for a walk in the park, and somehow she got separated from us. We realized it when the other group met us."

"When's the last time you remember seeing her?" Smokey said.

"I guess right before Father Garcia checked in."

Smokey looked at Garcia. "And when was that?"

"I ducked into a restroom at the halfway point," Garcia said. "I called then."

Smokey bit into his cigar.

"I asked Taylor to wait outside," Garcia said. "Then we met Brianna and her group right where we said we would."

Smokey sat silently for a few minutes. Morgan eventually ran out of patience. "How's Katy?"

"She's awake, and doesn't seem worse for wear," Smokey said. "No cuts or bruises. They took her to the ER, to be safe."

"I'm sorry, Father," Brianna said. "I'm so confused."

"It's okay."

Smokey pulled his notepad from his back pants pocket. Turning to a page in the middle, he scanned it, then looked at Taylor. "Before Katy left for the hospital, she gave me a statement. Says she was with the group, and a beautiful girl in a white dress appeared in a fog, beckoning her from the forest. Couldn't make out who it was. That's the last thing she remembered before we woke her up."

Taylor glimpsed at Morgan, then back at Smokey. "So?"

"Your dress matches Katy's description."

Morgan shot out of his seat. "You son of a bitch."

Taylor settled deeper into the couch. "Father Javier told you I was with him."

Smokey didn't flinch. "I follow the evidence, Doc. She matches the depiction of the girl, and she's part of the group here. I wouldn't be doing my job if I didn't ask."

Garcia stepped between them and reached for Morgan. "Richard, you need to calm down."

Morgan pulled his arm away. "He's making it personal."

Smokey extricated the cigar from his mouth and pointed it at Morgan. "Know what, Doc? I take missing kids very personally. And murder."

"Are we done here?" Morgan said.

"Not quite," Smokey said. "Padre, how long a walk do you suppose it is from that restroom to where we found Katy? If you cut through the woods instead of taking the trail?"

Garcia pinched his nose as if trying to fight off a sneeze. "Not far. Two minutes tops. But the forest is dense. You'd have a rough time getting through there."

Smokey jotted something into his notebook. "And how long were you in the restroom?"

Garcia blushed. "Long enough to take a leak, man."

"You have any communication with Taylor while in there?" Smokey said.

"No."

Smokey made another note. "Humph."

"What are you implying?" Morgan said.

"Not implying anything, Doc. Trying to determine the facts."

Morgan turned to Garcia. "Javi, do you think it's possible to go through that brush without getting cut?"

"I don't see how. The brush out there is full of sharp branches, thorns. Plus mud." He looked at Taylor's pristine, white dress. "You'd have stains."

Morgan pointed at Taylor. "Lieutenant, do you see any sign Taylor could have gotten through the brush?"

"I sure don't, Doc."

"Good. Now, can we go?" Morgan stood.

"After I ask Taylor a few more questions."

Before Morgan responded, Azra rushed in, breathless. "Richard, are you two okay?"

"We're all right. What are you doing here?"

"Father Garcia called me."

Taylor started to hum. Softy at first, a pleasant, joyful sound, which converted to a growling cadence. Her eyes rolled in their sockets, and she shook.

Azra rushed to Taylor, but the shaking grew more rapid and the growling louder.

"Call 9-1-1," she ordered. "She's convulsing. Richard, there's a cloth in my bag. Get it. We need to suppress her tongue."

Taylor's pupils lowered until they stared into Azra's. With a wide grin, she stuck out her tongue and bit down violently. Blood sprayed into Azra's face.

Taylor cackled like a witch in a Brothers Grimm fairy tale. Azra jumped backward, almost tipping over.

Morgan's knees buckled. Only Smokey's quick catch saved him from crashing. *What is happening to my daughter?*

CHAPTER 14

Two male nurses held Morgan as he strained toward Taylor in the antiseptic emergency room. Strapped in a gurney at Salem Hospital with an IV in her arm, Taylor writhed and screamed. Two other nurses held her steady while a doctor took her vitals.

"What's wrong with her?" Morgan shouted. "They sedated her at the church."

"They need to up the dose because she isn't responding," Azra said.

A sharp pain ripped through Morgan's clenched hands. He forced himself to relax, then opened and closed both fists to relieve the stress.

Garcia's eyes were closed, lips mouthing a prayer. Smokey bowed his head and prayed.

Morgan kneeled on the floor and closed his eyes. *She needs help. More than I can provide.* "God, I need Taylor to be okay. Please forgive me for my role in the divorce. I'll come back to church. I'll do anything."

Taylor stopped screaming.

Morgan looked up, finding Azra staring at him with a bewildered expression. Garcia looked as puzzled as she did.

Morgan rose and approached the bed. Blood gurgled from Taylor's mouth. She appeared to be asleep, the convulsions gone. "Is she okay?"

Azra regarded him with curiosity while the doctors took Taylor's vitals.

"The convulsions stopped," the doctor replied. "We don't understand what caused them. I've scheduled a battery of tests."

"How long before you identify what's wrong?" Morgan said.

"Impossible to say," the doctor said. "As soon as I have any information, you'll have it."

Azra stepped towards Morgan. "The tests will take several hours. You should eat. They'll call if there's any change."

Morgan watched Taylor. "I should stay."

Azra took his arm. "She'll be out for hours. Let's get dinner. It might be a long night."

"Okay." Morgan turned to Garcia. "Care to join us?"

"*Sí.*"

They walked out.

Smokey called to Morgan. "I hope she's okay, Doc. I'll be praying for her."

"Thanks. I appreciate that."

* * *

Garcia set his greasy cheeseburger next to his fries and chocolate shake to answer his cell phone. He responded to the caller, then hung up. "Katy checked out fine."

"Thank God," Morgan said, picking at his food.

Azra stopped in mid-bite and set her half-eaten burger back on the plate. "Thank God? Richard, what's with all this praying, and thanking God?"

Garcia shifted, keeping his head lowered.

Morgan took a bite, chewed, then swallowed. "Just an expression."

"Really?" Azra said. "I've never seen you pray before."

"So?"

"So," Azra said, "you don't believe in God."

Garcia turned to Morgan, unable to contain his grin.

"You know I'm Catholic," Morgan said. "Michelle and I used to attend Javi's services and continued after Taylor was old enough."

"I thought you were past that phase," Azra said.

"Can we not do this now?" Morgan tilted his head toward Garcia. "You're making Javi uncomfortable."

Azra's eyes widened. "Oh, Father, I'm so sorry. I didn't mean to offend you."

Garcia chuckled. "Oh, please don't stop on my account. Truth is, I've got more questions than answers these days. Besides, I like it when you give Pennywise a hard time. It keeps his know-it-all ego in check."

Morgan poked him. "Smart ass." Then, to Azra, "Thank you for apologizing."

"I didn't apologize to you," she said. "He has no choice. You do."

Morgan glared at her. "What can I say? I prayed for Taylor. Seemed like the right thing to do. And maybe it helped. Taylor stopped convulsing."

Azra stared at him. "She stopped convulsing for medical reasons. Surely, you comprehend that."

Morgan pitched toward her. "Like me, you learned about the power of prayer in med school."

Azra didn't respond.

"All I know is the doctors gave her medicine," Morgan continued, "Javi and I prayed, and she got better. If prayer had something to do with it, then I'm thankful our prayers were heard."

Azra swerved back. Her face turned a shade darker.

Morgan held her hand. She didn't resist, but she didn't squeeze back. "I'm grateful you were there to help her. Don't make a big deal out of this. Let's finish our meal and get back to the hospital."

Garcia popped the last fry on his plate into his mouth and grinned. "Amen, man."

Azra did not look amused.

* * *

In Taylor's hospital room, an antiseptic mix of linoleum, white paint, and shiny stainless steel accessories, Morgan stood by Taylor. Smokey sat in the back, and Garcia and Azra flanked Morgan.

"Can she hear me?" Morgan said.

"She's sedated," Azra said. "But it's possible."

"Taylor," Morgan said. "You'll be fine. I won't let anything happen to you."

"Be careful," Azra said.

"About what?" Morgan said.

Azra lowered her voice. "Med school 101. Remember? They told you not to make promises. Some outcomes are beyond our control."

"Similar to a lecture in seminary," Garcia said. "Although the purpose was different. We shouldn't promise things only God can deliver."

Azra rolled her eyes. "So now we're comparing medical school to seminary?"

Smokey cleared his throat. "What if Taylor can hear you?" He stood. "Going to check on Katy. She's right down the hall." He shuffled out.

"Smokey's right," Garcia said.

Azra crossed her arms across her chest. An awkward silence followed.

Smokey ambled back in, focused on a cell phone. Instead of taking his seat, he leaned against the wall.

"Whatcha got there?" Garcia asked.

Smokey raised his head, eyes locked in on Morgan. "A development in the Katy situation. Her parents found a photo on her phone." He turned the phone for them.

As the photo came into focus, Morgan recognized Taylor in her white dress, with green bushes in the background.

Smokey shifted the phone's screen back to himself. "Seems Katy took a picture of Taylor at the park."

"Why's that important?" Morgan said.

"Taylor's the only photo she took. Katy claims Taylor appeared to her when she was on the hike with Brianna and wanted to capture her beauty. She also says it's the last thing she remembers before she woke up."

"She must be confused," Morgan said. "Must have taken it before they split up."

Smokey tapped on the screen. "Humph. Time stamp says otherwise. Lines up with when the Padre was on the phone with Brianna."

Garcia stared at Morgan, puzzled. Fear in his eyes. "He's right."

A shiver ran along Morgan's vertebrae. "But Taylor was with Father Garcia. She couldn't have made it to Brianna's group and back in time, without a trace of dirt on her."

"So how do you explain the photo?" Smokey asked.

"Why does it need explaining?" Azra said. "Even if Taylor was there, who cares? Katy wasn't hurt. So what if she wandered off and fell asleep?"

Smokey stepped up to the foot of the bed, watching Taylor. "I'm stuck on a few things. Why would Taylor lie about seeing Katy? Why doesn't Katy remember what happened? And why didn't one of the other girls see anything? My own granddaughter didn't see Taylor there." He addressed Morgan. "I don't believe in coincidences, Doc. And I don't like unexplained circumstances. We need to know what happened."

Morgan's experience in Costa Rica flashed by. *The plague. Margarita. Young girls. Could this be related?*

Stop it! Stay in reality.

"Any chance the time stamp is off?" Morgan said.

"The phone's clock is right," Smokey said.

"I'll say it again," Azra said, her voice elevated. "Why does it matter? Nothing happened. No crime here. A little girl got separated. Happens all the time. There's no boogey-man. No pedophile. No harm, no foul."

"Humph. But it could have gone *very* badly. The river. An abduction. Katy's parents don't buy she fell asleep. They want answers."

"We all want answers," Garcia said. "I'm responsible for those children, man. Brianna has always been reliable. I trust her." He looked at Morgan. "I trust Taylor, too. But I need to make sure nothing like this happens again."

"You can't legislate everything," Azra said. "Accidents happen. They were only out of your sight for fifteen minutes. You escorted the group with the youngest leader. You checked in regularly with the other group. Sounds like you did your job."

"I don't think the parents will agree." Garcia said. "Am I right, detective?"

Smokey pulled out a fresh cigar. "Nobody's blaming you, Padre. But, speaking as a grandparent, I don't like it."

"Nothing happened!" Azra cried out.

Morgan shushed them. "Enough. If you insist on arguing, take it outside. Taylor's the one person who's not okay. I'm spending my energy on her."

Garcia and Azra looked sheepishly at each other. Smokey plopped his cigar in his mouth.

A shadow at the doorway caught Morgan's attention. A young girl in a pale-blue gown stood there, staring at the bed. White as a bleached ghost.

The fibers on Morgan's arm came to attention. "Can I help you?"

Smokey approached her. "Katy. Where are your parents?"

Morgan shivered. *Look at her eyes. Wide open. But like they don't see anything.*

Smokey took her arm. "Come on, sweetie. Let's go find your parents."

"The doctor told them it was okay to get dinner," Katy said, her voice without emotion.

"Okay," Smokey said. "You need to get back in bed. Come with me."

"I want to stay with Taylor."

Morgan gulped. *This is creepy. Maybe Taylor's not the only one who needs psychiatric care.*

Smokey escorted Katy out. Morgan followed them to the door, watching them ease past the nurses' station.

A figure at the end of the hall drew Morgan's circumspection. Female. Shortish. Head shrouded in secrecy. Dark skin.

Panic set in. *No. It can't be.* He shook his head. *Margarita. She found us.* He wanted to charge her, but lightheadedness kept him from moving. *She's come to kill Taylor.* "Smokey. Stop that woman!"

Smokey had reached Katy's room, where he turned Katy over to a nurse. He gave Morgan a puzzled expression. "What?"

Morgan fought off his dizziness and broke for the lady. "The end of the hall. She's the one who threatened to kill Taylor."

Morgan passed Smokey, who followed. The woman didn't move, her back to Morgan. Morgan closed in and he recalled Margarita's warning. *We will chase you down wherever you try to hide. We will find the girl, and we will destroy her.*

Twenty feet. Ten feet. The figure didn't turn.

I've got you, bitch.

He reached her and twirled her around.

The elderly woman screamed. *Not Margarita.* Morgan collapsed to his knees.

Smokey reached Morgan. "What the hell, Doc."

The woman pointed at Morgan. "This man groped me."

"I'm sorry." Morgan said. "I mistook you for somebody else."

"And that makes it okay?" the woman huffed.

"No. It's not okay. I apologize."

The woman contemplated this, then narrowed her eyes at Smokey. "He's not one of those perverts, is he?"

Smokey led Morgan away. "He's not, ma'am. Just a misunderstanding. You have a nice night."

"I don't trust him," the woman yelled after them.

"What was that, Doc?" Smokey said, back in Taylor's hospital room.

Morgan looked to Azra for support. He got none. "I thought it was Margarita. She said she'd come looking for us."

"Why would she do that?" Smokey said. "They know I plan to ship you down there once I'm through with you."

Because she's invested in killing Taylor. She'll never stop.

CHAPTER 15

Wednesday

The sunrise peeked through the blinds in Taylor's hospital room, displaying clouds etched in pink borders and white, fluffy insides. The space smelled of disinfectant, masked by air freshener, then engulfed with bug spray. Morgan looked on, eyes watering and taste buds vandalized, Azra at his side, while Taylor's ER doctor flipped through his charts.

"Every test came back normal. Normal EEG. No brain lesions. No dangerous sign of pooling fluids. Nothing to explain the seizures. Follow up with Neuro, but I see no reason she can't go home."

Morgan wanted to feel good about the news, but his mind didn't cooperate. *She's not normal. At least not mentally.*

Taylor pouted. "I want to leave. Hospitals give me the creeps."

"Then that's what we'll do," Morgan said.

Azra tugged on Morgan's arm and pulled him aside. "What if it happens again?" she murmured. "What if we're not there?"

"You heard him," Morgan whispered back. "She's fine." He glanced at Taylor, checking to see if she was listening. "She'll recover better at home." *And maybe I can keep a lid on her seizures. No need to turn her life into a spectacle.*

* * *

The neurologist's office was clean and cushy. Morgan and Azra watched as Taylor went through a battery of tests throughout the morning.

"She was okay last night?" Azra asked for the second time.

"I told you. All good."

The Neurologist finished up with Taylor and the four of them retired to his office. Plush chairs and couches surrounded a mahogany desk. Taylor took a chair by herself. Morgan sat next to Azra on a couch.

"I've completed a cursory exam," the neurologist began. "X-rays and tests of Taylor's brain activity found no abnormalities. Electrical stimulation is normal. Red and white blood cells, normal. Spinal tap, nothing. Your daughter appears to be in peak physical condition."

Morgan shifted. "No indication of what caused her seizure?"

"No symptoms."

Taylor stared straight ahead as if the conversation had nothing to do with her.

"What about stress?" Azra asked. "She's been through a horrible ordeal. At one point she was convicted she was carrying a new virus that could start a pandemic."

"Dr. Morgan's the finest psychiatrist in the area, so I'm certain he has a handle on Taylor's mental care," the neurologist said. "But, I can understand the clinical complication of treating your own daughter." He jotted a note on a pad. "Dr. Elliott is the best neuropsychiatrist in town." He smiled at Morgan. "You probably know him."

"I do," Morgan said. "His professional reputation is top-shelf."

"Are you sure Taylor should be home?" Azra asked.

"I'm fine," Taylor barked. "I'd be even better if you'd leave me and my Dad alone."

Azra blushed.

Morgan gripped Azra's hand, which was cool to the touch. "Taylor, don't speak to Azra like that. She's trying to help."

"Like she helped mom?" Taylor stood and stormed out.

Morgan rushed after her, leaving Azra to sit and stew.

* * *

Morning sun dissolved into Salem gray. Azra didn't say a word as Morgan drove the three of them back to his place. Once there, Taylor vanished into her room. Morgan didn't bring up her attack on Azra, instead hoping rest would do her good.

"You could have done more to defend me," Azra said. Her scowl made it clear he was wading in treacherous waters.

Morgan chose levity to defuse the situation. "If you think about it, she was really attacking me. I should sign up for a self-defense class."

Azra balked. "You know, Richard, humor isn't the solution to everything. And sarcasm isn't even wit. It's a trait of a lazy mind. I deserve better." She bolted out the door and sped away in her car.

Morgan thought about calling her cell phone and asking why she was with him if she couldn't stand his personality, but was afraid of the answer, and dropped the idea.

He sat and studied the clinical experience of Dr. Elliott for over an hour. But Azra's voice haunted him. *Are you sure Taylor should be home?*

His own voice countered. *Taylor hasn't shown any more symptoms. I did the right thing.*

Azra's voice again. *I deserve better.*

Yeah, maybe you do.

Taylor screamed, breaking his trance. Morgan tried to stand, but his legs were jelly. He stumbled into her bedroom, finding her sitting up in her nightshirt, soaked with sweat. Bear paced and whined.

Morgan sat beside her. Tried to make eye contact. "Taylor. It's okay. You're safe."

Taylor looked around the room, wild-eyed, before focusing her attention on Morgan. Recognition settled in and she grasped him. "Dad, why am I having these horrible dreams?"

Morgan stroked her hair. *Because you've been through hell. And I've been inept at helping you.* He took her by the shoulders and eased her back. "About your Mom?"

"Some. But there are others. Something worse."

Than your mother dying in front of you? "Like what?"

She shivered. "I don't want to think about it."

Morgan tapped her on the nose. "Okay. You have your first session with Dr. Elliott after school. He'll give you some tools to deal with whatever your subconscious is bringing to the surface."

Taylor looked apprehensive. "Why can't you treat me? It's what you do, isn't it?"

"It's called emotional detachment. I might make health decisions based on love, and that's not best for you. You also need an environment where anything you say is confidential."

"But I trust *you*, Dad."

Morgan fought back his tears. "I'm so glad, honey. Dr. Elliott will take great care of you. You'll like him. And you can tell him to share what he finds with me. Then I'll know what to do when you're with me."

He hugged her and glanced over at Bear, pacing near the room's nook. "Need to go out, Bear?"

Bear whined and fell on his stomach. His brown eyes stared at Taylor.

"That's weird," Morgan said. "He always goes out the doggie door when he needs to."

"He's been acting strange," Taylor said. "I don't think he likes me."

Morgan squeezed her harder. "Don't be silly. Bear loves you."

Bear stood and peed.

CHAPTER 16

Thursday

Taylor sat across from Dr. Elliott is his oversized office. He smelled of stale cigarettes, his furniture appeared slept in, and he cocked his head continuously, reminding her of an exotic bird. Her father waited in the outer room with the receptionist.

Halfway through an hour session, Taylor recounted the previous night's nightmare.

"I'm in Nosara, I'm hiking on this huge boulder. It's like a small island. It's sunset. The sky gets dark fast. Dad's there, then he's gone. I don't know where. Bear is at my side."

She swallowed. "There's music. No, not a song. More like a humming. I want to find the source so I hike to the far end of the island. The surf is pounding. Crabs lurk there and I'm afraid they might attack at any moment. They hear the thrumming too. They're being told to leave me alone, at least for now."

Taylor gulped the stale air in Dr. Elliott's office.

"I try to block out the sound. I look at the top of the rock. It's a thick jungle. Then I notice something. A pair of red eyes."

Taylor shuddered. Elliott stayed silent.

"I'm being called. Someone wants me up there. I glance at Bear, but he's whining and backing away. So I climb the rock myself. It's super steep. The rocks have sharp edges, and I'm getting cut all over. Blood is pouring down my legs as I ascend. And the more I bleed, the louder the humming gets. Like it gets off on it."

She wiped away a flow of tears.

"I'm almost to the top. It's freezing cold, which is weird, right, since I'm in the tropics. I'm shaking, and it slows my ability to climb. That's when I notice Bear's head is severed—just a red stump. I bawl and retreat to comfort him.

"Which pisses off whoever is calling me. It wants me up there, and now."

Taylor paused, shivering. She pulled her legs up and wrapped her arms around them, trying to create a bundle of heat.

"The sun's gone down, and there's no light, other than the crimson eyes staring at me, commanding me to climb to the top. I don't like the look of those eyes and scale down. But those crabs are scrambling up the rock now. Threatening me."

Taylor closed her eyes, another tear forming. Still, Elliott kept quiet.

"I panic and scramble to the top. The fiery eyes are waiting for me. I scream, trying to wake myself. And then a voice comes from the bushes.

"It says, call me *Bé*."

* * *

Morgan and Elliott faced each other after the session. Taylor went downstairs for ice cream with Elliott's administrative assistant.

"Richard," Elliott began, "she articulated, in great detail, her dream from last night."

"That's good," Morgan said.

"Yes. I think your instincts are correct. Her experience in Costa Rica affected her severely, and it's manifesting itself mentally and

94

physically. She didn't mention her mother once. Her mother's drowning may be the cause of the dreams, but she's not in them."

"Odd. What's next?"

"She's probably repressing feelings about her mother. I'd like to try hypnosis at our next session. See if we can break down that barrier."

"Okay. When?"

"Saturday?"

"Sure."

"Perfect. My calendar is clear—it's my golf day, but my foursome bailed on me." He lowered his voice. "Which they hate to do, because I always end up owing them money."

Morgan stiffened. "Are you saying my daughter's well-being hinges on your golf schedule? Do I have to remind you whose recommendation got you into this hospital?"

Elliott put up his hands. "No. I didn't mean it like that. I assure you, Taylor is my top priority."

"Good. Same time, then?"

"Yes."

Morgan started to leave, then turned back. "Since you didn't mention it, I can assume she's not a danger to herself? Or others?"

Elliott shook his head. "I see no reason to worry. Once we bring her repressed memories to the surface, she'll be her old self again."

CHAPTER 17

Friday

Morgan listened for the familiar creak in his home's walls. The sound of raccoons scampering on his roof. He inhaled the aroma of the nearby forest. Sounds and smells that comforted him.

Home. Once the happy residence for the three of us. Then, after the divorce, my lonely retreat. Now, a distressed daughter. An angry girlfriend. A detective after me. What happened? And that crazy bitch in Costa Rica. Who knows if she'll ever stop.

Morgan and Taylor sat at the kitchen dinette, sharing breakfast burritos stuffed with eggs, sausage, bacon, sharp cheddar and jalapeño jack cheeses, red and yellow peppers, and a spoonful of cilantro. They washed it down with fresh-squeezed orange juice.

"The Petersons asked if I can babysit Jennifer from six to eight tonight," Taylor said.

Morgan shoveled more burrito into his mouth.

"So, can I?" Taylor's tone dripped with honey.

"I don't know, sweetie. You still need lots of rest."

"It's two hours. I've babysat her like a jillion times. She's easy-peasy. I read to her, play games, watch TV. Nothing to it."

"It's only been three days since your episode."

Taylor scowled, and her voice changed to a lower, darker octave. "C'mon. You haven't allowed me to do *anything*. How much trouble can I get into with a ten-year-old?"

"We're making sure you're okay."

"The doctors all said I'm fine, and not contagious. It's been, like, forever."

Morgan weighed how much to debate her. *I don't want her to worry.* "How about this? There's a diner near their house. I'll eat dinner while you watch Jennifer. We can talk by phone every fifteen minutes. You may get tired quicker than you realize."

Taylor started to protest, then agreed.

"Maybe I can even convince Azra to have dinner with me," Morgan said.

"Are you two still fighting?"

"It's not much of a fight if nobody's speaking. But, yeah, she's not taking my calls."

"It's about me, isn't it?"

Morgan stood and kissed her on the forehead. "No. You're perfect. It's silly adult stuff. We'll work it out."

"You didn't figure it out with Mom." Taylor's anger radiated throughout the room.

He picked up his plate. "Something I regret every day. Your Mom was great. I screwed up."

Taylor glared at him, which puzzled Morgan.

"You okay?" he asked her.

"I wish you'd saved her," she said.

Morgan couldn't mask the pain. "Me, too. I tried. I really tried." He exhaled. "I'll tell Mrs. Peterson you can watch Jennifer. Now go brush your teeth and get ready for school. Don't forget to feed Bear."

* * *

Morgan dropped Taylor off at the Peterson's home at six. Jennifer clapped at her arrival and the two girls sat on the rug to play a game of Chutes and Ladders. Morgan exchanged brief pleasantries with the Petersons, then forced himself to leave.

"Remember, Taylor. Every fifteen minutes."

"Got it."

He found Azra waiting in a booth at Denny's. She refused to smile, but he counted her presence as a small victory.

"Hey, I'm so glad to see you. Thanks for coming." Morgan sat across from her.

"It's not every day a girl gets invited to a night out like this," she said, waving at the meager ambiance.

Morgan paused, a warmth of embarrassment spreading through his face. *She's still pissed. Maybe this isn't a good idea.*

Azra broke into a big grin. "Richard, lighten up. It's a joke." She looked around the room. "You have to admit, as make-up dinners go, this is pretty lame." She reached across the table and took his palms in hers. "But I'm delighted you called, and I'm elated we're here. The last week has been awful for me."

"Me, too. I'm sorry I upset you. It's not any more complicated than me wanting Taylor to get better."

"It's a little more complex, but nothing we can't work through. You know my feelings about religion, and the cases I see when children are denied proper medical attention by their parents, due to religious beliefs. They end up on my table. It drives me insane."

"I understand. It would drive me crazy, too. Don't worry. I'm not going over the deep end and denying Taylor the care she needs. There's no reason I can't believe in both, is there?"

The waitress showed up and took their order—a BLT and lemonade for Morgan, a tuna melt and coffee for Azra—and scurried away.

"You really startled me," Azra said. "You told me you swore off the Catholic Church, and all it represents. Lack of religion is an area of common ground for us. An important one."

"Yeah, I understand. And I was sincere when I told you my views about the Church. But seeing Javi and Lieutenant Smokey praying over her, I realized I dropped the Church out of anger over my own failures, not because I stopped believing in God. I hope you can live with that. I don't want to lose you over this."

Azra squirmed in her chair. "It's disconcerting. You didn't believe in prayer a week ago. Now, you're praying. You don't have any other surprising beliefs, do you?"

"No." Morgan crossed his heart. "I promise."

"I hope not."

The food arrived, and they ate in silence. Halfway through his fish and chips Morgan called Taylor's cell phone. After five rings it went to voicemail. "Taylor was supposed to call. She's not answering."

"She might have turned the ringer off by mistake. Happens all the time."

Maybe. "I have a bad feeling."

"Welcome to life with a teenage girl. Not the most reliable."

Morgan thought back to the incident at Keizer Rapids Park. His insides bunched up. "I have to go check on her."

"Before we finish?"

"I'm sorry. Something's not right."

Azra slid out after him. "Okay, but you owe me the rest of a tuna melt."

They hustled to the Peterson's. Sweat turned to ice along Morgan's hairline, and his heart beat faster than it should. *Please, God. Let Taylor be okay.*

Morgan rang the doorbell, then stepped to the side to peek in a window.

Taylor and Jennifer sat in their same spots in front of the board game, staring at each other.

Neither reacted to the doorbell.

Jennifer's expression reminded Morgan of Katy's at the hospital. *Distant. Lost.*

"Are they there?" Azra said.

"Yeah. But something's wrong. It's like they're in a trance or something."

Morgan found the door locked. He pounded on the door with his fist, rattling the surrounding walls. "Taylor! Open the door. It's Dad."

After a moment of silence, he knocked again. "Taylor!"

The door creaked open. Taylor stood there, a puzzled expression on her face. "What are you doing?" she said, annoyed.

Morgan exhaled. "We agreed you'd call. You didn't answer your phone."

Taylor shook her head. "You two need to chill. We're playing." She returned to her spot on the floor across from Jennifer, who hadn't budged. Morgan and Azra stepped inside. The game pieces still sat on their opening squares.

Azra circled around and approached Jennifer from behind. "Young lady, how you doing?"

Jennifer didn't react until Taylor cleared her throat and spoke to her. "She asked how you are."

Jennifer turned to Azra. "I'm well, thank you. How are you?"

Azra and Morgan exchanged glances. Azra performed a cursory exam. "The girl has a slight fever. We should watch her until her parents return."

Morgan tried to gauge Taylor's temperature.

She veered back to avoid his touch. "What are you doing?" Taylor said, her voice an octave higher, and her pace of speech a tick faster, than normal.

"Making sure you aren't coming down with something." Morgan tested her forehead. "I think Taylor's okay."

"I'm fine," Taylor said, a subtle anger in her statement. "Can't you leave us to our game?"

"I'll get water." Azra left for the kitchen.

"The pieces are still on the opening square," Morgan said.

Taylor rolled her eyes. "Jeez, Dad. We're about to start a new game."

Is that what's happening here? He cleared his throat. "Who won the last one?"

Taylor scowled. "I did. Can we have a little privacy now?"

100

Morgan sat on the couch. "Not with Jennifer having a fever. We'll hang out until the Peterson's get back. Shouldn't be long."

Taylor returned her attention to Jennifer. "Okay, Jennifer, you go first."

The children played.

But a tingle ran along Morgan's arms and legs. *This sure doesn't feel right.*

CHAPTER 18

Saturday

Morgan watched Taylor doze off as Dr. Elliott concluded his hypnosis countdown. *I sure hope this works. I don't like making Taylor relive her Costa Rican tragedy.*

"Taylor, this is Dr. Elliott. I'll ask you some questions. Just relax."

"Okay," she replied.

"Good," Elliott said. "Let's go back to your dream about the island. Is your mother there?"

"She's far away. With Dad."

Morgan narrowed his eyes. *She still sees us together. Might be significant.*

"Anything else?" Elliott asked.

"Mom can't help me. Neither of them can stop the torture."

Morgan and Elliott exchanged glances.

"You have pain?" Elliott asked.

"In my chest. And in my mouth. Some of my teeth ache."

"Do you recognize these discomforts?" Elliott said.

"No."

"Focus on your ribcage," the therapist said. "Describe what it feels like."

"Like someone is in there," Taylor said. "Pressing on everything. Making room."

Morgan gulped. *Making room? Oh Taylor. You must be terrified. I know what would help me through this. A drink.*

Shut up!

"Do you think this causes the seizures?" Elliott said.

"Yes."

The wind picked up, and a branch scratched the window. Morgan's heart leapt to his throat.

"The doctors don't know what to look for," Taylor continued.

"Who told you that?" Elliott said.

Taylor paused before answering. "Nobody."

Morgan swayed forward, breaking his silence. "Sweetie, this is Dad. What do *you* think you have?"

Taylor tensed. "I know. But I can't say."

"Sweetie, you can tell us anything. Nobody can hurt you."

Taylor shook, slowly at first, then more rapidly.

Morgan rose. "She's convulsing again." He gripped her by the shoulders. "Taylor, it's okay."

The convulsions grew wilder.

Morgan turned to Elliott. "Wake her up!"

Elliott stood, eyeing the scene with confusion. "Whatever's bothering her can resist the hypnotic state. Very unusual."

"Hurry!"

"Right. Taylor, I'm going to count to three. At the sound of three, you'll wake up, feeling refreshed and unafraid."

Taylor squirmed, almost breaking loose from Morgan's hold.

"One."

Taylor's eyes flew open, glaring at Morgan. Her irises turned darker.

What the hell? Irises can't change color.

"Two."

Taylor stopped convulsing, then sneered at Morgan. "This won't help her," she said in a deep, mocking voice.

Morgan's knees wobbled.

"Three."

Taylor spasmed, then wrapped her arms around herself. She grimaced in terror. "What happened? Why are you staring at me?"

Morgan swallowed. Her eyes looked normal again. *I must have imagined her eyes turning darker.* He brushed the locks from her damp forehead. "It's okay, sweetie. It's all going to be okay."

"Did I say anything helpful?"

Morgan looked at Elliott, then returned his attention to Taylor.

"Yes," Morgan said, trying to sound convincing and upbeat. "How do you feel?"

Taylor shrugged. "Fine, I guess."

"Any pressure in your chest?" Morgan said.

She gave him a queer squint. "No." Her expression turned serious. "You think I have heart trouble?"

"No, sweetie. Your heart's fine. How about your teeth? Any pain there?"

Taylor's brow wrinkled. "Who told you about my teeth?"

"You mentioned it while hypnotized. They're bothering you?"

"Kinda sore."

Morgan tipped forward. "How long?"

"A day, I guess. It's no big deal. Right?"

You're my daughter. Any abnormal condition is a huge deal. "I'm sure it's nothing."

"Can we go home now? I'm tired."

Morgan helped her up off the couch and glanced at Elliott. "Yeah."

Taylor extended her hand. Elliott hesitated, then took it in his. "Rest up, Taylor. I'll see you on Tuesday. And don't worry. We'll sort this out and have you feeling great soon."

"Okay. Thanks."

"Can you wait outside for a sec?" Morgan asked her. "I need to speak with Dr. Elliott. Won't take long."

When they were alone Morgan asked Elliott, "Did you see her eyes? Her irises changed color."

Elliott frowned. "You certain? I've never heard of such a thing."

"I'm sure." *Aren't I?* "And referring to herself in third person. Strange under hypnosis."

"I hate to suggest it, but that's often the sign of a true multiple personality. I don't have to tell you how rare those are."

Morgan took a massive breath. "Almost unheard of."

He replayed her words in his mind. *Like someone is in there. Pressing on everything. Making room.*

This won't help her. In that deep voice.

Oh, Taylor. What's going on?

CHAPTER 19

Taylor felt a pinch as Azra hooked her up to a portable EKG machine. "Will this tell you what's happening?"

Morgan stood next to Azra. Bear sat in the corner, his head on his paws. "It will show us your heart activity. In case that pressure you're feeling is heart-related."

A voice within Taylor laughed.

"What's wrong with me, Dad?"

"We will find out, sweetie. Trust me."

The voice howled louder.

"What happens if my heart pumps too fast?"

"Then we send you to a heart specialist. They have medications to control that. So, even if we find something, it's nothing to worry about."

Taylor tried to look cheerful. But the voice worried her.

"You also mentioned your teeth are sore," Azra said. "May I?"

Taylor opened wide, and Azra used a penlight to inspect. "Your gums are a little inflamed in a few spots. Have you been brushing and flossing regularly?"

"Twice a day."

"I'll give you something to ease the inflammation. It's no big deal. Happens all the time."

Azra finished attaching the sensors and turned on her EKG. Taylor's heart rate displayed on the screen. "Okay. Your heart rate is regular."

Taylor curled into a ball. "I'm exhausted. Can I sleep now?"

Morgan kissed her forehead. "Goodnight, angel. Try to do what Dr. Elliott suggested. Think happy thoughts as you fall asleep."

* * *

Her dreams came at once.

The rock island. Crabs. Bats. Her mother slipping into the sea.

Her father, standing on the Costa Rican shore, in the distance.

She ran toward him, but the gap between them stayed constant. He didn't respond when she screamed.

She stopped running and realized she didn't recognize her surroundings. The beach morphed into a jungle, deep in the mountains. Colorful spiders hung from the branches.

Then the wind came up, calmly at first, but speeding into a gale. The dense vegetation dove in threatening jabs. She called out again, begging for someone to save her.

And the eyes. Blood red. On fire. Hiding in the trees directly in front of her. She tried to see more, but the leaves thrashed around, camouflaging the eyes just enough to hide their source.

"Are you here to help me?" she said, though she knew the answer.

The red, glowing eyes darted toward her.

* * *

Taylor jerked up to a sitting position, perspiration matted her cheeks. Morgan and Azra sat next to her, and Morgan held her. Bear whined.

"It's okay, sweetie. Bad dream?"

"Yeah. Did you find anything?"

Azra shook her head. "Everything's normal."

"You said something in your sleep," Morgan said.

Taylor crinkled her brow. "What?"

"You said, 'you're wasting your time.' Do you remember that?"

Her lips pouted. "I was back in Costa Rica. You and Mom were there, and red eyes in the jungle."

"An animal?"

"I don't know. I think it wanted to eat me."

Morgan embraced her. "Nobody will hurt you on my watch."

Taylor forced an unconvincing smile, then lay back. The voice was silent now, but the push in her chest intensified. And her teeth ached more.

I'm scared.

Don't be, the voice of the red eyes replied. *I will protect you.*

CHAPTER 20

Azra departed once Taylor fell asleep for the night. Morgan watched her car drive off, then gazed out the kitchen window toward the forest. Shadows danced in the moonlight. The scent of burning logs crackling in his fireplace soothed him.

A woman with dark hair stepped into the light at the edge of the woods, dressed in a drab winter coat and bright red tennis shoes.

That's funny. Then Morgan tensed. *Margarita?*

Before he could react, she vanished.

You're overreacting. Taylor's safe.

He poured himself a cup of coffee. He stared into the black abyss, trying to make sense of how best to care for Taylor.

A grating noise came from the front yard. He dismissed it as the wind. But the sound repeated, louder this time.

Did the woman come back?

Bear ran to the door, made his well-trained single bark to alert Morgan, then sniffed. He backed away, his tail between his legs. He whined.

"Bear? What's wrong?"

Bear scurried to Morgan's bedroom, leaving a trickle of piss along the floor. "Seriously, Bear. What's up with you?"

The scratching repeated.

Morgan held his breath. *Did Margarita find us?* He grabbed a kitchen knife and stepped over to the window and peeked outside.

Jennifer Peterson and Katy Wilson stood on his porch in their pajamas, their quick breaths white clouds pounding against the door.

What the hell?

Morgan threw the door open and checked for their parents. *Not here.* He pulled them inside and closed the door. "It's freezing out there. Where are your parents?"

Jennifer slowly craned her neck to face Morgan. "We came to see Taylor."

Goosebumps rose on their exposed arms. Morgan grabbed two blankets from the linen closet, wrapping each of them up. "Taylor's asleep. We need to call your parents."

"No," Katy said in a monotone voice. "Taylor wants to see us."

Morgan's gut cramped. *Why would you think that?*

Jennifer and Katy started toward Taylor's bedroom.

Morgan cut them off. "You can't go back there. Tell me your parents' numbers."

Neither one answered.

Feeling as if he had no choice, Morgan dialed 9-1-1.

An operator answered. "Nine-one-one. What is the nature of your emergency?"

Morgan looked at the two rigid children.

"This is Dr. Morgan. Remember the Wilson girl, from the park?"

"What about her?"

"She's here, along with a kid from a few blocks down. I don't have the phone numbers for the parents, so I called you guys."

After a long pause, the operator answered. "Are they hurt?"

"Just cold. In their pj's. Can you send someone over here to take them home?"

"I'll inform Lieutenant Smokey."

Morgan's shoulders slumped. "Great." He grimaced. *Another opportunity for Smokey to pile on.*

* * *

Smokey arrived first. He walked straight to the two girls. "Hey, kids. Everyone okay?"

Neither child made eye contact with the detective.

"I'm from the police department. Your parents are on their way. Wanna tell me what you're doing here?"

No response.

"They've been like this since I found them outside," Morgan said. *Eerie.*

Smokey pressed on. "If you're scared, you have nothing to worry about. I'm here to make sure you're okay."

More silence. *We've officially transitioned from eerie to frightening. This silence is so loud my bones are vibrating.*

Smokey turned back to Morgan. "Damn peculiar. They showed up like this?"

"I think peculiar left the station a long time ago," Morgan said.

"Is Taylor awake?"

"Nope."

Smokey exhaled and looked at his watch. "The parents should be here soon. They're freaking out, as you can imagine."

"Am I in trouble here? I didn't touch them."

Smokey looked at Morgan and shook his head. "Not yet." He paused. "Look, Doc, I know you think I'm after you. But I've got nothing personal against you." He lowered his voice. "Fact is, I'm rooting for you. The Padre says you're a good guy."

Brisk pounding on the front door interrupted them. Morgan swung it open, and the Petersons and Wilsons both charged in. They ran to their respective girls, wrapped them in ski parkas, and shielded them from Morgan.

Mr. Peterson spoke first. "Can somebody tell me how my daughter ended up three blocks away like this?" He glared at Morgan. "Did you touch her?"

Smokey stepped between them. "Everybody stay calm. Best we can figure, the kids came here on their own looking for Taylor."

"Why would they do that?" Peterson said.

"We don't know," Smokey said. "She babysits for Jennifer, and Katy's part of the church youth group she supervises. Any other connection you can think of?"

Mr. Wilson shook his head. "No. But Katy went missing in the park. We found Taylor's picture on her phone. Now this. Something's going on, and Taylor's the one constant. I want her investigated."

"For what?" Smokey said.

A floorboard creaked in the hallway, and they all turned to see Taylor, in a black nightgown, standing stiff and erect. Her normal chocolate complexion had turned pale. Her bloodshot eyes showed little white left.

Morgan squirmed. *Like a ghost.* He grit his teeth. *Stop it.*

Jennifer and Katy came alive at her appearance and tried to free themselves from their parents' arms, their eyes riveted on Taylor.

Mrs. Peterson stepped between Jennifer and Taylor, cutting off her line of sight, and ricked her daughter gently. "Jennifer. What's wrong? Did she do something to you?"

Jennifer ignored her, trying to get to Taylor.

Taylor watched the commotion, then spoke in a calm voice, but one deeper than normal. "Jennifer. Katy. Go home. You don't belong here now."

The children immediately stopped struggling.

Morgan, used to looking for subtle word choices in his practice, gulped. *Now? And what's with your voice?*

Mr. Peterson picked Jennifer up, and she put her arms around his neck. He turned to Morgan. "I don't know what your game is, but you keep your family away from mine. Understand?"

Mr. Wilson clutched Katy and followed them out, turning at the door. "I'll be insisting Father Garcia remove Taylor from the church group."

They left the door ajar. Smokey closed it, staying inside.

Taylor turned to Morgan. "What were they doing here?"

"We were hoping you could tell us," Morgan said.

"Strange," Taylor said. "I never told them where I live."

"So no idea why they'd come here?" Smokey said.

"No," she replied. "Do you think I'll be allowed to lead the youth group?"

"Father Garcia knows you," Morgan said. "I understand why Katy's father's upset, but he's not in charge. Get some sleep. Okay?"

Taylor walked back to her room. Bear peered around the hallway corner. Taylor called out for him.

"Bear. C'mon, boy. Come back to your bed." But Bear retreated into Morgan's room. She tried one more time, with desperation and pleading. "Bear? Please come back."

After a moment she gave up waiting, slouched her shoulders and returned to her room.

Morgan's heart tugged. *What's bugging Bear?*

"Doc," Smokey said, "if you think of anything, let me know."

"I will. And I appreciate what you said."

Smokey twirled his unlit cigar in his mouth. "Remember, Doc, I follow the evidence."

"Are you any closer to resolving Michelle's case?"

"Your in-laws arrived today. Gave me a file. Haven't gotten through it all."

"I'm guessing I don't come off well."

Smokey laughed. "You could say that."

"Carter's a liar, you know."

"Humph. So you've said."

"And you still plan to extradite me to Costa Rica when you're done?"

"Nothing's changed, Doc."

Morgan angled in. "If you must send me, fine. But don't doom Taylor. They'll kill her."

Smokey bit into his cigar, without comment.

* * *

Before turning in, Morgan checked in on Taylor. *Asleep. Good.*

But her stuffed dog, a treasure her entire life, lay strewn across the bed, its head removed, stuffing spread across the blanket.

Taylor opened her eyes. Dead black irises stared back at him.

Morgan fell to his knees.. "No, no, no." He bowed his head. *God, I don't understand. Please help me.*

CHAPTER 21

Monday

After a quiet Sunday at home, Morgan dropped Taylor at school, then pulled in to Saint Edwards to meet with Garcia on what his friend termed "an urgent matter." Morgan surmised from his tone it involved Taylor and wasn't good news.

Why should his message be any different?

Garcia stood inside the church's main entrance, Bible held securely, and motioned for Morgan to join him in the last row of pews. A single beam of light refracted off the stained glass image of the Virgin Mary, creating a rainbow collage around the priest. Melting candle wax gave off a hint of lavender. Someone was practicing on the organ. He or she needed the repetition.

Should I divulge about her stuffed animal? He gave it to her. If I tell him, he'll have more reason to take her group away. He shook the thought aside and joined Garcia. "What's up, Javi?"

"Richard."

Richard again. Not good.

"I need to pull Taylor from the youth group. If I don't, the program will collapse. It may, anyway. The entire congregation is in an uproar."

"Because of the park?"

Garcia wiped moisture from his brows even though the church air was nippy. "Katy's parents emailed every other church family. Described Katy wandering to your home late last night and claimed Taylor was responsible for Katy's disappearance in the park. They said Taylor is evil."

"Evil? Seriously?"

"Afraid so."

"No one will listen to that nonsense."

Garcia's shoulders drooped. "They are, man. The other parents may not buy she's evil, but they're not interested in having their children anywhere near her right now. I have to remove her. Even changing leaders might not be enough."

Morgan stomped his foot on the marble floor. "You know what she's going through. She's a good kid. That youth group is one of the few joys in her life these days."

"I know. And I'm sorry. But my first responsibility is to the church."

Morgan rose and stood over Garcia. "What do *you* believe?"

Garcia eased up to face Morgan, his eyes showing concern. "I think Taylor isn't well. I'll pray for her. And you."

Morgan recalled the stuffed dog, strewn over Taylor's bed. *Can I blame Javi?* "You're her Godfather. You're making things worse."

"I'm sorry. I can't risk losing my parish."

Morgan fought the urge to lash out, instead turning and dragging himself out of the church.

* * *

Still reeling from his confrontation with Garcia, Morgan lingered in Dr. Elliott's waiting room after school. Taylor emerged from her private session an hour later, tears streaming down her face, her eyes bloodshot where they'd otherwise be white. Elliott looked like a trapped animal. Morgan approached Taylor to comfort her.

She shot him a nasty expression. "I'll be at the car."

"Hang on." But she stormed out. Morgan turned to Elliott. "What happened?"

"Richard, she's deteriorating. I think we need to find her a new doctor."

"What are you talking about?" Morgan said.

"My style of therapy isn't helping. I'm sorry."

Morgan grabbed his arm. "What happened in there?"

Elliott shivered. "I've never dealt with anything resembling this. She's showing signs of another personality." He looked at the floor and whispered, "A violent, evil persona. Even named it *Bé*. It seems to be the source of her nightmares." He raised his eyebrows. "More than losing her mother."

Morgan let go of Elliott's arm. "You're going with multiple personality disorder again?"

"That's what I see. And it requires special treatment, therapy I'm not qualified to give." Elliott shook his head. "I wish I was more help." He hesitated, then started to walk back into his office.

"Wait. There's something else, isn't there?"

Elliott turned back, his face an ashen gray.

"You look petrified," Morgan said.

Elliott chose his words carefully. "Her expression changed when the other personality took control. I think her other personality is dangerous. To herself, and to those around her. She could hurt someone."

"So you're dropping her."

"She needs an expert. I'm sorry."

But Morgan recognized Elliott wasn't sorry. *He's relieved.*

* * *

Back in the car, Morgan told Taylor about taking a break from her church group. Much to his surprise, the crooks of her mouth turned up, and she stared out her window in silence.

* * *

Richard, take care of Taylor. Please. Promise me. No matter what.

After Taylor disappeared into her room Morgan gazed at his empty glass, wondering if scotch would help. Bear scratched the front door.

Trying to escape? "Et tu, Brute?" Morgan sank his head. *What am I going to do?*

He ran through the list of issues dogging him. *She's not responding to traditional treatment. Smokey might arrest me for killing Michelle. The more he sees Taylor, the more he suspects her of something. And, even if he doesn't arrest us, he'll ship us back to Costa Rica. Where they'll kill us both.*

Speaking of which where is Dorothy on fighting the extradition?

He shivered. He held out his arms to Bear, who stood with some hesitation, then stepped over to him. Morgan let Bear lick his face.

And what happens if they extradite me, but leave Taylor here? Who will care for her?

The Carters will always take her. Not ideal, but at least she'll be safe.

Bear nudged Morgan's head with his own. Morgan rubbed him behind the ears, and Bear fell to the floor, legs up, waiting for a belly-rub, which Morgan gave him.

If by some miracle I keep us out of Costa Rica, Margarita is probably lurking, waiting to finish the job herself. And, don't forget, my best friend, and her Godfather, abandoned us. And it seems inevitable Azra will split up with me.

He stared at the glass. *Helping Taylor is up to me. And, the best way to keep her safe, is to hunker down here. No school. Or church. No visitors. And no Smokey. Don't give him any more ammunition.*

He called Azra.

* * *

Morgan and Azra finished an impromptu dinner.

"Everybody is bailing on her," Morgan said, keeping his voice low so Taylor, in her room with the door closed, wouldn't hear. "Father Garcia, Dr. Elliott, her friends. Bear. How is she supposed to get better?"

Azra put down her fork. "Not everyone, darling. You haven't. I haven't."

"You notice her eyes? Constantly bloodshot now."

"I did. Likely lack of sleep."

"Maybe." Morgan inhaled and exhaled deeply. "I'm responsible to Taylor and Michelle to protect her."

Azra smoldered. "Michelle's gone. You only owe it to Taylor."

"I made a promise." A sharp pain rattled around in Morgan's temple. "I've made a decision."

"What's that?"

"I'm going to homeschool Taylor. Give her a safe environment here."

Azra blinked. "Wow. What about your practice?"

"I'll take a leave."

"You can afford to stop working?"

"For a while."

Azra gripped him. "What can I do to help?"

"You're being an angel. I worry I'm asking too much."

"There's no such thing."

Morgan forced a swallow. *I can't do this alone. She can help me save Taylor. Save myself.* "Azra?"

"Yeah?"

"Before we went on vacation, you asked me where I thought this relationship was going. Now I'm sure. Will you marry me?"

Azra released him. She narrowed her eyes. "Don't joke about something like this."

Morgan clenched his teeth. "I realize the timing sucks, but I'm serious."

"And Taylor? She just lost her mother. Who you still think a lot about."

"We don't have to tell Taylor," Morgan said. Azra slumped. "Yet. Or anyone. It can be our secret. Until things settle down and you feel comfortable telling everyone."

Azra stared at him. "You're so excited about marrying me you don't want anyone to know."

Morgan grabbed her hand. "That's not what I meant. You said you were worried about Taylor."

"Aren't you?"

"Of course I am. She's in a fragile state right now."

Azra put her free palm up. "Stop. I'm messing with you. You know I love you. Yes, I'll marry you."

Morgan caressed her. He wanted to describe his joy at their engagement, but he didn't like to lie. "This calls for a celebration. Since neither of us drinks, we'll have to settle for some serious sex."

She laughed, but pulled away. "Not with Taylor in the next room. I shouldn't stay here until she knows."

Morgan gave her his best sad face. "I can be quiet."

"Since when? We can wait. She comes first. Right?"

"Right." *Sometimes, doing the right thing sucks.*

* * *

After Azra left, Morgan logged onto the internet. He found a local gun store and picked out a firearm online.

In case Margarita shows up.

But, in the dark recesses of his mind, there was more to it.

CHAPTER 22

After he ordered a pistol online, Morgan's doorbell rang. He bitched to himself about the late interruption and checked through the front window. Nothing but darkness. *Damn light must be burned out.* He swung the door open.

A huge shadow stood in the dark, with a backdrop of falling snow. Morgan froze, his apprehension mounting. A man's outline stepped forward and a smaller figure appeared behind it.

"Richard," the man boomed. "Mind if we come in. It's pretty uncomfortable out here."

Morgan recognized the voice, and then the silhouettes. His heart hiccuped. *Oh, shit. Isaiah and Laila Carter. What are Michelle's parents doing here?* "Isaiah. Laila. Come in."

They stepped inside, each dusting snow off their shoulders. Isaiah towered over Morgan, and his pack fell on Laila, who did double duty clearing it from her rail-thin frame. Isaiah didn't notice.

"Been a long time," Morgan said, not sure how to proceed.

"Cut the crap, Richard. We know you killed our daughter. You've got our granddaughter. We came to take her home with us. Before you can hurt her."

Morgan's face turned crimson. "How dare you?" He stepped between them and the hallway to Taylor's room and sucked in his gut. "I did everything I could to save Michelle. And Taylor stays with me."

Carter glared at Morgan. "We can do this the easy way, or the hard way."

Morgan bristled. "Your threats have no currency here. Get out."

Carter glanced at his wife, still beauty-pageant bewitching, although Morgan sensed something unhealthy going on there, and huffed. "I told you he'd be this way." He confronted Morgan. "Our attorney is ready to file papers. You won't win. Let's be reasonable. We both want what's best for Taylor, and what's best is to be with us."

Morgan got up into Carter's chest. "I'll never give her up."

Carter laughed. "Son, as you know, I'm a religious man." He motioned toward Laila. "We're a spiritual family. Elders at our church. We don't fight about our problems, we pray on them. And the Lord has made it clear. We need to watch over Taylor and see she's raised proper. Not like you, who moved Michelle to this bastion of evil, and are the prime suspect in her murder."

"Bastion of evil?" Morgan said. "What are you talking about?"

"Some places are wicked," Carter said. "The name Salem is synonymous with evil. The Massachusetts version had witches. Lord knows what denizens of hell you've got wandering around here."

Morgan stared at him. "You're insane."

Carter tried to walk past him. "And you're a pitiful little man with no moral compass."

"I'll show you a moral compass." Morgan may have made up with God, but he wasn't above throwing a punch at Carter. His roundhouse right landed square on Carter's chin, knocking him back. "There's your moral compass, asshole."

Carter grabbed his face, his eyes watering. "Now why'd you do that?" He turned to Laila. "Looks like we'll have to file those court papers. And an assault and battery charge with the police."

"How long will it take before we can get her back?" Laila said.

"Our attorney says he can get a hearing right quick, given the circumstances," Carter said. "No judge will rule in favor of this guy. Not with what's happened to Michelle and his likely role in it."

"I didn't kill Michelle," Morgan said. His knuckles throbbed, and he shook them. He hated himself for doing that in front of Carter.

"Save it for the judge," Carter said. "Michelle was my daughter, and I can't bring her back. But I can make sure Taylor grows up safe. Now, we'd like to see her."

"Hell, no," Morgan said. "She's asleep and I won't have her disturbed." He pointed to the front door. "You're not welcome here. Leave, or I'll call the police."

Laila shivered, then grabbed Carter's arm. "We should go."

Carter pondered this, then backed them both outside. "We'll be seeing you in court."

* * *

Tuesday

The next morning, Morgan sat with Taylor. She picked at her breakfast.

"Not hungry?" Morgan asked.

"Not really."

"Teeth sore?"

"A little."

Morgan swallowed. "Listen, I need to talk to you about something. I think it's best if I homeschool you for the rest of the year. I know you'll miss your friends, and the social aspect of school." He held his breath, expecting a fight.

"Okay," Taylor said. "I have other ways to meet girls."

Morgan grimaced. *What does that mean? A sexuality revelation? Remember what they said in Costa Rica?*

He rattled his head. *Stop it.*

* * *

After lunch, Morgan answered the house phone on the second ring. "Hello?"

"I need you at the station," Smokey said. "Bring your attorney. I called Azra."

"Is this about punching Carter?"

"Wait. You punched Carter?"

"He came by last night, trying to take Taylor. I didn't let him."

"Humph. I hope he doesn't press charges. I've got enough paperwork."

"Taylor's here."

"The officers outside will watch her. Get down here. And don't hit anybody." Smokey hung up.

* * *

Morgan stepped into the interrogation room, first seeing Azra in a dark pantsuit with her arms folded, and then Dorothy, dressed in muted red, matching her hair. He crossed and sat next to Azra. "Hey, beautiful. Do you know why we're here?"

Azra ignored the compliment. She shook her head.

"I'm sure it's nothing," he said. "Right, Dorothy?"

Before Dorothy commented, Smokey entered, followed by a tall man in a dark blue suit, dark hair, and power tie.

"This is District Attorney Crawford," Smokey said.

They sat across from Morgan, Dorothy, and Azra.

"Okay, detective," Morgan said. "What's up?"

Smokey chewed on his cigar. "The investigation into Michelle's death has taken a new turn. Do you have anything you'd like to confess, Dr. Morgan?"

"Don't answer that," Dorothy said.

Morgan waved her off. "I already told you. Michelle drowned. I tried to save her."

"Well," Smokey said, "I have a witness who heard you threaten your ex-wife. Claims you boasted of having a foolproof way to kill her on the trip, using the drug ketamine to weaken her, and then take her swimming. In powder form, it'd be easy to pack. Ring a bell?"

"That's absurd," Morgan said. "Who is this clown? Some bozo you dredged up at Witnesses-R-Us?"

"Do either of you have access to ketamine?" Smokey said.

"I use it for certain types of depression," Morgan said. "But it's locked up in my office, and the hospital keeps records of any time it's checked out or used."

"What about you" Smokey asked Azra.

Azra shot up. "What are you accusing me of?"

"Sit down," Smokey said. "You didn't answer my question."

Azra looked at Morgan for help, and when she didn't receive any, plunged back into her seat and crossed her arms and legs. "An anesthetic? An anti-depressive? My patients are already dead. They've kinda moved past the need."

"But you can get it, right?" Smokey said.

"Any doctor can procure it," Azra said.

Smokey bit down on his smoke. "We asked Costa Rica for a tox screen on Michelle last night. Results should be in any minute."

"That won't be admissible," Dorothy said. "Not without the body to substantiate it."

Crawford broke his silence. "It's enough to get a warrant to search for evidence. If we use the tox screen at trial, you'll get your chance to verify the findings."

"Michelle's been dead for over a week," Morgan said. "Can they still test for ketamine in her system?"

"They can," Azra said. "It's too late to find it in her urine, but they can detect it in the blood for up to two weeks. Even if blood viability has passed, it'll stay in a corpse's hair follicles for three months."

"Worried, Doc?" Smokey said.

"Your witness is a liar.," Morgan said. "I never said those things. They won't find any drugs in Michelle's system."

"Humph."

Morgan gestured to Dorothy. "It's Isaiah Carter. He's after Taylor. That's why a third party comes forward now and makes this up."

Dorothy considered this, then addressed Crawford. "Bill, the timing *is* suspicious. Who's this witness?"

Smokey twirled his cigar. "Turns out Michelle had a boyfriend. Claims the Doc wanted Michelle dead. Maybe jealousy has reared its ugly head."

"Michelle didn't have a boyfriend," Morgan said. "I'd have known."

"Maybe you *did* know," Smokey said. "And you didn't like it."

"Why would this witness wait until now to come forward?" Dorothy said. "It makes no sense."

"I can't ignore it, Dorothy," Crawford said.

"This is all bogus." Morgan turned to Smokey. "You'll see. A tox screen will rule out drugs."

An officer knocked and entered, then handed Smokey a piece of paper.

Smokey studied it for a full minute, then cleared his throat. "Costa Rican authorities found ketamine in Michelle's hair follicles. Matches the witness' story."

Morgan fell back into his chair, his head spinning like the tea cups at Disneyland. "Impossible." He fought off the urge to throw up.

"Humph. I have the report right here."

"They're lying. Hoping to convince you to send me to them. Hoping to get Taylor back, too."

Smokey gravitated toward Morgan. "That's an awful lot of people you say are perverting the truth. Isn't it more likely you're the one lying?"

Morgan looked at Azra, pleading for support. She looked stunned.

"I'm issuing search warrants for both of you," Smokey said. "Homes and offices. Officers will escort you both to your home and do a search. Another team will be at your work."

"But no charges are being filed?" Dorothy said.

"The DA wants a direct link to you giving her the drugs, and to vet this witness more," Smokey said. "So, you're both free to go. But don't leave town."

As Azra stood to leave, Smokey continued. "There's more. Dr. Khan, you're being suspended from your Coroner's duties. Until this gets cleared up."

"You must be joking," Azra said.

Smokey shook his head. "There's nothing funny about any of this."

Azra shot a glare at Morgan that pained him.

"I'm sorry." Morgan moved to take her in his arms, but she repelled his advance. "Where are you going?"

"My livelihood's at risk. I need my own attorney." She bolted.

So, how's the engagement going? Morgan faced Dorothy. "Where do we stand on fighting the extradition?"

Dorothy looked up at him. "I have a filing ready. But extradition may be the least of your worries."

CHAPTER 23

A police officer escorted Morgan inside his home. He found Taylor on the couch, folded into herself.

"You cool?" Morgan asked her.

"Why are the police here?"

Morgan hugged her. "No biggie. A routine search."

"In my room?"

"The whole house."

"Bear's in my bedroom. He's not right."

"You have a dog?" the officer said. "I need you to tie him up outside."

"He's friendly," Morgan said. "I'll take him out. Bear, come."

After a moment, without an appearance by Bear, Morgan checked Taylor's bedroom. The blinds were closed, resulting in a pitch dark aura. A guttural growl emanated from the corner.

Morgan's vision adjusted. Bear's eyes glowed in the dark. Morgan's breath halted. *What the hell?* The room smelled of excrement and urine. "Bear, it's me."

Bear growled again, then rose to his full height.

"Come here, boy."

As Bear turned his head, the radiance in his eyes vanished. Morgan glanced at the light in the hallway behind him and exhaled. *Ah. Just a reflection.*

"What's wrong with him?" Taylor said.

"Maybe the policeman spooks him."

The stench reached Taylor. "Jesus, what did he do in there?"

Morgan stepped toward Bear. "Come on, buddy."

Bear took a step, then stopped and whimpered.

Morgan dropped to his knees and put his arms out. Bear lowered his head, whined, then ran to his master. Morgan choked back his own bile at the stench under his nose. His palms slid across Bear's moist back.

Taylor turned on the lights and gasped. Bear, covered in excrement, growled at her.

"Bear," Morgan said, "it's Taylor."

Bear fought hard to escape, his paws flying across the floorboards like a cartoon character.

A tear fell down Taylor's cheek. "See. He doesn't like me anymore."

Morgan picked up the struggling Bear and carried him to the bathroom. "Don't say that, Sweetie. Probably something he ate. You know Labs."

"No, you won't," Taylor said, in a deep, scratchy voice Morgan hardly recognized.

Morgan set Bear in the tub. "Taylor? You okay?"

"She's better than ever," Taylor said. Her irises turned darker.

The room spun. *The second personality? But that doesn't explain her eyes.* "She? Who is this?"

Before Taylor answered, Bear jumped from the tub and challenged Taylor with fierce barking and snarling. Taylor stepped back and hissed at the dog.

Morgan grabbed Bear by the collar. "Hey, buddy, it's Taylor. Calm down." Bear strained to go after Taylor. Morgan held tight. "Hey! Down!"

Bear sank to the floor and whined.

Taylor shook violently, then sat with a thud. In her normal voice, she said, "See, Dad. Bear hates me."

Morgan stared at her, then the canine. *Her eyes are brown again. This would be clinically fascinating if it weren't my daughter being afflicted.*

"Taylor, do you remember talking in a different voice?"

"Get a grip, Dad. I think you're losing it."

Morgan put a calmer Bear back in the bath and ran the water. "You said Bear wouldn't get better, and then you referred to yourself in the third person."

"Why would I say that?"

A river of sweat poured down Morgan's face. *Why, indeed.*

CHAPTER 24

Wednesday

Dorothy's call woke Morgan the next morning. His head pounded, and his night of nervous listening for any sign of movement in Taylor's room left him spent and irritable. He noted the time. *Seven? This can't be good.*

"This is Morgan."

"Richard, there's been a development. Lieutenant Smokey and I need to see you right away."

"You're with Smokey?"

"He called me as a courtesy. I won't lie to you. It's bad."

"He's arresting me?"

"That's up to him. He knows Taylor is at the house. He's agreed to meet you there. We'll be there in ten." She hung up.

Morgan's stomach roiled. *Stay calm. Maybe it's not so awful. She said it* was *bad.*

He shook off the thought and got dressed in jeans and a long-sleeve cardigan. *At least I'll look sharp for my mug shot.*

He checked on Taylor, still sound asleep. *Good. Better make her breakfast.*

Hands shaking, Morgan burned the eggs and toast, then knocked over the orange juice, spilling the sticky liquid across the kitchen floor.

Jesus Christ. Get a grip. He stared at the mess. *Is this a metaphor for my life?*

Morgan tossed the food and mopped the floor, deciding cold cereal might prove more his speed. He jumped at the sound of the doorbell. "It's open."

Lieutenant Smokey stepped in wearing his "Grandpa" hat, but without a cigar in his mouth. "Doc. Thanks for agreeing to see me at this hour." He left the door ajar.

"I wasn't aware I had a choice."

Smokey shrugged. "Your attorney on the way?"

"Yeah. What's this about?"

Smokey observed the residue on the hardwood. "What happened there?"

"Sorry to disappoint you, but it's not blood. Just OJ. Did you know eggs are harder to cook when you're being falsely accused?"

Smokey didn't respond. He peered past Morgan into the home. "I heard you took Taylor out of school. Is she okay?"

"How'd you hear?"

"I'm well connected around here."

"I bet you are. It's nothing. I've decided to homeschool her."

Smokey scratched his head through the top of his cap. "Sounds like a big move, Doc."

"You worried we're making a break for it?"

"Humph. You wouldn't get far." He gave Morgan a knowing expression. "Is Taylor up?"

"Not yet."

"She's doing well?"

"She's fine."

Smokey grunted. "I see." After a moment, he continued. "I'm worried about her."

"I appreciate the whole concerned grandfather act, but can we get down to business?"

Smokey pulled a cigar out and plopped it into his mouth. "They completed the inventory of your office. Guess what they can't locate?"

"Surprise me."

"Your prescription log."

Morgan frowned. "It's in my five-drawer, right where I told you."

"They didn't find it. Makes this witness seem more credible now, doesn't it?"

"I'm telling you, the Carters are behind this," Morgan said. *Oh, God. They might get away with this. They might take Taylor away from me. And have me shipped to Costa Rica.*

Smokey ran his tongue in front of his lower teeth. "I can't help wonder if it incriminates you. It shows you checked out the ketamine before your trip."

Dorothy rapped on the door as she entered. "You're not interrogating my client without his attorney present, are you detective?"

"Just having a friendly conversation. I told him about the prescription log."

"And, without it," Dorothy said, "you've got no evidence my client did anything unlawful."

"I've got a witness. That's enough." Smokey took out his handcuffs. "Turn around, Doc. You're under arrest for the murder of Michelle Morgan."

Morgan looked to Dorothy for help. She offered none.

Smokey's phone interrupted him. He frowned, suspended cuffing Morgan, and answered. "Smokey. What?" He eyed Morgan. "Get every available unit on this. Top priority."

Smokey hung up and put his handcuffs back. "That's mighty convenient for you, Doc. My witness bugged out through a back window from the safe house. You have anything to do with that?"

"Don't be absurd." A crushing weight fell from Morgan's shoulders. "So, no arrest?" He tried not to sound giddy, but failed.

"Don't get too excited, Doc. I'll find him."

Morgan let out an enormous breath. "Taylor would know about a boyfriend, too. No way that witness is genuine."

"Well, he's legit about a few things," Smokey said. "We checked the bar where he said you two met. The security video places you there. And then we have the Ketamine being available in your office, and a missing log for it."

"I'll say it again. It's the Carters."

Smokey rubbed his nose. "Would her parents know about a boyfriend?"

"Not sure," Morgan said. "Trust me, I want him found as much as you do."

"Humph. I'm not in the trust business, Doc. But, like I said, I'll find him. I always do."

Taylor stepped into the room. "What's going on?"

"Nothing important," Morgan said.

Smokey scowled.

Dorothy stepped forward. "Hi, Taylor. It's nice to meet you. I've heard so many nice things about you. I'm Dorothy Prescott. Your family's attorney."

Taylor's expression grew darker, and her voice dropped an octave. "I'm in hell. Can you do something about that? Or are you as worthless as everybody says."

Dorothy blanched.

Morgan stepped between them. "Taylor! Why would you say such a thing? Ms. Prescott is a great attorney. And you're surrounded by love. You're not in hell."

"You don't understand hell," Taylor laughed. "But you will."

Morgan's mouth went dry. He wanted to respond, but no words came out.

Taylor yawned, then started down the hallway. "You have no idea."

"About what?" Morgan said, apprehensive of the answer.

Taylor gave him a provocative glance usually reserved for older, flirtatious girls before she disappeared into her room. "You'll find out soon enough."

Morgan wanted to rush after her and chew her out, but held off with Dorothy and Smokey standing there. He turned to Dorothy instead. She looked shaken. "I'm sorry. She's been through a lot. Has these episodes, almost like a different person."

"She's getting appropriate professional help?"

"Yes."

Dorothy sat on the couch, keeping an eye on the hallway. "I have more bad news, Richard. The judge has granted a hearing on Taylor's custody. In two weeks."

"How can he do that?" Morgan said. "They've got no witness."

"I need to be honest with you. Their case is strong."

Morgan sat across from her. "But it's all circumstantial, right?"

"It's true there's no smoking gun, but even indirect evidence can become overwhelming. The drugs in Michelle's system. Your fingerprints on her neck. The witness claims. The missing log sheet. I think the only reason you're not in jail is because Costa Rica refuses to return Michelle's body."

Morgan's stomach lurched. His head throbbed.

"Then there are the other murder charges waiting for you in Costa Rica," Dorothy continued. "The chance of winning the fight against extradition is small. And I won't be able to help you down there."

An even sharper pain dug into Morgan's gut. "I'll never see the inside of a courtroom down there. I'm screwed, aren't I?"

"There's also this incident with Katy and Jennifer. The town is talking, Richard. Can you recover from all this in Salem?"

Morgan's frustration overwhelmed him, and he raised his voice. "You're advising me, if we get through this without being jailed or extradited, we should move?"

"I'm saying you should prepare yourself for contingencies. If you get arrested, what's your plan for Taylor?"

He waved her off and glared at Smokey. "I didn't do anything. Neither has she."

Smokey cleared his throat. "I hate to pile on, Doc, but I must ask Taylor about the incident in the park. And with those girls here."

"Why?" Morgan said. "Nothing happened."

"I beg to differ, Doc. *Something* happened. I aim to find out what. I figured you'd rather I do it here. Or, we can all go downtown."

Morgan looked at Dorothy. "Can he do this?"

Dorothy stood. "He can, but Taylor has rights. We'll both go with him."

"Shouldn't you be spending your time finding Michelle's alleged boyfriend?" Morgan said to Smokey.

"We're following all leads. Sent his picture all over the state. We'll find him. Where's Taylor?"

"In her room," Morgan said. "Want me to get her?"

"Let me speak with her first," Dorothy said. She turned to Smokey. "Agreed?"

"Of course," Smokey said. "I don't want to make this difficult on her."

Morgan led Dorothy to Taylor's room and knocked on the door. "Taylor, Ms. Prescott needs to speak with you."

"Go away," came a booming voice, barely recognizable as Taylor's.

Morgan flinched. "Taylor, that's no way to talk to me." He opened the door.

Taylor stood on top of her bed, naked, writhing to a heavy metal band blasting through her earphones. She grinned at the sight of Dorothy and called to her in a throaty voice. "Hey, girlfriend. Come to party?"

Her eyes. The irises are black, not brown.

Morgan's legs buckled, and he dropped to one knee in the fight to stay conscious. After composing himself, he crossed to the bed and grabbed a blanket, throwing it around Taylor. "Taylor! What's the matter with you?"

Taylor fought him for a moment, then sagged against him, suddenly calm.

Smokey stepped into Taylor's room. "What happened?"

Morgan shook his head. "Teenage stuff."

Taylor perked up at this and turned her head, smiling fiendishly at him. Her irises were black rather than brown. "Teenage stuff? You *are* clueless."

Morgan looked into Taylor's eyes. *What the hell can cause her irises to change color?* "Who are you?"

Taylor squeezed her eyes shut. "I'll tell you when I'm ready."

Dorothy backed up, bumping into the wall. Her face lost its pigment, and her legs wobbled.

Morgan shook Taylor gently as if trying to stir a child in a deep sleep. "Taylor! Look at me!"

Taylor opened her eyes and looked like her old self again. "Dad? What's going on?" She peered at herself in the blanket. "Where are my clothes?"

Morgan exhaled and stroked her hair. "You had a spell, sweetie. It's over, now."

"A convulsion again?"

"Sort of. Do you remember any of it?"

Taylor shook her head, looking at the concerned looks on everyone's face. "No. It must have been bad. You all look spooked."

Morgan checked on Smokey and Dorothy.

Dorothy reclined against the wall. "I think I should be going."

"No. You should be here when Smokey talks to her." Morgan said.

Dorothy looked at Taylor, at Smokey, then back at Morgan. "I don't think legal answers are what you need."

"What do you mean?"

"Don't you see what we all see?" Dorothy said. "She's not well. She needs psychiatric help. What do you expect me to do for her?"

Morgan stiffened. "Your job. You're her attorney."

Dorothy shook her head. "Richard, I can't continue as your family attorney. Find someone else to represent you."

Smokey stepped into the hall.

Morgan's heart hurt. "You don't mean that."

Dorothy gave Taylor a sideways glance and shivered. "I'm afraid I do."

Morgan recognized that shiver from his practice. "You're scared, aren't you?"

She looked at the floor.

"You can't quit," Morgan said. "If I want to drop a patient, I have to find them another doctor. I'm responsible for their care until they do."

"This is different," Dorothy said. "You haven't paid me a retainer, so I'm not technically obligated."

"Obligated? You've been my family attorney for years."

"I'm sorry. And, before you ask, I won't refer your case to a colleague. I wouldn't feel right involving anyone I know."

"She's a little girl," Morgan said. "Why are you afraid?"

Dorothy looked up at him, tears forming around her eyes. "The real question is, why aren't *you*?" She raced out of the house, never looking back.

Taylor dressed herself in private. After she gave them the all-clear Morgan and Smokey reentered her bedroom. Smokey retrieved a small notebook from his jacket pocket and opened it to a blank page. Pencil in hand, he waited for Taylor and Morgan to sit on the edge of the bed. "Taylor, this won't take long. I'm here on official police business, to ask you about the day Katy went missing from the youth group."

"I wasn't with her group," Taylor said. "She was with Brianna."

"So you said. But there's a picture of you on Katy's phone. The time stamp is consistent with the timeframe she vanished."

"But Father Javier and Brianna told you I wasn't there," Taylor said.

Smokey rubbed his forehead while Morgan looked on, ready to pounce if Smokey said anything accusatory. "Humph. So you say."

Taylor's eyes narrowed, and she sat up straighter. "What's the BFD? Katy's fine. She's home, and nothing happened to her."

Morgan reached toward her. "Taylor, answer his questions."

Taylor swirled around and glowered at Morgan. "Maybe he should ask you. You had Katy here at the house without her parents' consent. Maybe you've got the hots for young girls, and *you're* the one who needs help."

Morgan's face flushed. He took a step back, trying to contain his rage "Taylor! How can you suggest such a vile thing?"

She started to speak, then shivered and sagged. She reached across and embraced Morgan. "I'm sorry, Dad. I don't know what's wrong with me."

Morgan didn't know whether to feel confusion or relief. He hugged her back.

Smokey chewed on his cigar. "That's enough for now, Doc. We'll continue this later."

CHAPTER 25

That night, Katy Wilson woke up to the sound of scratching on her second-floor window. The moon lurked near the horizon aside a shadow with two red spheres.

And a voice. Sweet. Singing. The sonnet of angels.

Katy beamed. *I am beautiful. Content. Safe.*

The figure beckoned her. "Invite me in."

Katy rose.

CHAPTER 26

Smokey sat across from Garcia in a red-vinyl booth under flickering lights. The smell of burning oil permeated the deserted late-night diner. The lone waitress whistled while reading a magazine at the counter.

Smokey's instincts told him the next shoe would drop soon on the series of bizarre incidents. He took another hit of his black coffee. "I don't know. You say she's a great girl, a warm-hearted *Catholic* girl, but everywhere I turn, she's in the middle of trouble."

Garcia sipped his lemonade. "I know it's driving you nuts, but I've known them a long time, and they're top-shelf people."

Smokey rubbed the back of his neck. "I want to believe you, Padre. I really do. But the picture of her in the white dress. And her behavior. There's something wrong there."

"Sometimes earthly signs don't tell the whole story. Don't you agree?"

"Playing the God card, Padre? Well, devout as I am, my job is to follow the evidence."

"In my heart, I know neither Pennywise nor Taylor are guilty of anything."

"Pennywise?" Smokey said.

"Sorry. Nickname for Richard."

"The evil clown in *It*? Kind of on the nose, don't you think?"

Garcia smirked. "A freaky coincidence. No matter what you call him, Richard's one of the good guys."

Smokey took one last hit on his coffee, long since cooled off, and rose. "I hope you're right, Padre. I must admit I kinda like them. Seems like they've been through hell. I hope the evidence turns in a new direction."

His phone rang. "Smokey." He slammed his fist onto the table. "I'll be there in five." He hung up, his bewilderment obvious. "It's Katy Wilson. Some kind of animal attacked her."

"What? Where?"

"In her bedroom. I'm off to check it out."

"I'm coming with you," Garcia said.

"This is police business. Best if you return to your parish."

"She's my parishioner, and I'm going. The family may need comfort."

Smokey considered this. "Okay. But you need to brace yourself. She's in bad shape."

* * *

Smokey pulled up to the Wilson residence in his Impala, followed by Garcia in the parish's late-model Honda. They rushed to the gurney outside a parked ambulance in the street. Tubes probed Katy's arms, and a compress lay on her forehead. Her eyes were open but spacey. Her skin had been shredded from her neck to both shoulders.

Wilson confronted Smokey. "It's the Morgan girl. She's responsible for all of this. Why haven't you done anything?"

Smokey put his palm up to halt the advancing parent. "Tell me what happened."

"Something attacked my daughter while she slept. *In her room.* There are teeth marks on her. *Bites*, for Christ's sake."

Garcia bent over her. "Katy, it's Father Garcia. Can you hear me?"

Katy looked at him vaguely, then hissed.

Garcia jumped back.

"I'm telling you, it's Taylor Morgan," Wilson growled.

"If it is," Smokey said, "we'll handle it." He stepped aside to speak to a paramedic. "What's her condition?"

"Multiple bite marks around the neck, extending out to her shoulders. Looks like something was gnawing on her. Broke the skin in a few spots, but she's not in imminent danger. They'll treat her at the hospital."

"Ever seen these kinds of bite marks before? Could they be human?"

"More like an animal."

Smokey turned to Wilson. "The house was locked?"

"Sealed tight."

"Open windows?" Smokey said.

"Just Katy's." Wilson pointed at her window. "But her bedroom's upstairs."

A police officer stepped in. "No sign of forced entry. No evidence of a ladder or footprints under Katy's window. Originally, I suspected a raccoon climbed in from the roof. But we found a ripped piece of white fabric, sir. Stuck to the blood on her neck. Kinda frilly."

Smokey motioned to see it, and the officer brought him the clear evidence bag. It contained a one inch patch.

Same pattern as Taylor's dress from the debacle at the park.

Garcia rejoined Smokey. "What's that?"

"If I'm not mistaken, a solid lead." Smokey turned to the policeman. "Get me a DNA swab off the victim's wounds. And a second kit for a suspect. If I'm right, we'll finally have proof."

He studied Garcia. "You should come with me, Padre. The Doc may need your kind of support tonight."

* * *

Morgan gave up on reading, instead staring across the living room at the clock striking ten. Exhaustion invaded every ounce of his being, but he didn't feel like sleep. *Bad things happen when I hit the sack.*

A rapping sound came from the front entry. *Now what?*

He opened the door and found Smokey and Garcia on the porch. Morgan gave them a double-take, not surprised to find Smokey there, but never expecting Garcia to be with him.

"Again?" Morgan said.

"Can we come in?" Smokey said. "It's important."

Morgan waved them through. "Of course it is. Let me guess. I'm now the prime suspect in stealing the offering from the church."

Garcia looked sullen. "This is serious."

Morgan recognized that tone of voice—*what else can go wrong*—and dropped onto the couch. Smokey and Garcia remained standing.

"The Wilson girl was attacked in her bedroom tonight," Smokey said. "Bitten."

"Bitten?" Morgan said. "In the house? Is she okay?"

"At the hospital," Smokey said. "She'll recover. Unfortunately, she has no recollection of the attack. According to the parents all the doors and windows downstairs were locked, but her second-floor window was open."

"That poor girl," Morgan said.

"Humph." Smokey retrieved the evidence pouch from his coat pocket. "We found this at the scene. It looks like it matches the dress wore the night Katie went missing."

"Seriously?" Morgan said. "You think Taylor's the only girl in town with a white dress?"

Smokey pulled a piece of paper out of his other pocket. "I have a court order here for Taylor's DNA, and to collect the dress. I brought the DNA collection kit with me, so she doesn't have to come down to the station."

"Why do you need her DNA?" Morgan said.

"The bite might be human," Smokey said.

"You think Taylor *bit* her?" Morgan said. "After scaling the side of the house?"

"I don't know what to think. But the wound gives us a chance to catch the perp."

"And clear Taylor," Garcia said, though not convincingly.

"Is she here?" Smokey said.

"She's sleeping," Morgan said.

Garcia stepped up to Morgan. "Has she been here all night?"

"Yeah. Went to bed around ten."

"Could she have slipped out?" Garcia said. "How often did you check on her?"

Morgan stood to face Garcia. "I didn't *need* to check her. She couldn't get past me."

"Humph. Unless she used her window."

Morgan's cheeks turned red. *The mud tracks the other night. It's possible.* He regrouped and glared at them both. "Seriously? Javi, you've known her for her entire life. You're her Godfather, for crying out loud. Biting people? You know better."

Garcia stared at the floor.

"The DNA test, Doc. Here, or at the station?"

Morgan exhaled. "Fine. We'll do it here. Get this nonsense resolved." He turned on Garcia. "I won't forget this."

"Pennywise, I'm sorry. But this will clear her."

Morgan motioned for silence. "Save it. Let's get this charade over with."

They trudged to her room and Morgan knocked lightly. When no one answered, he opened the door slowly, allowing the hallway light to creep in. He froze at the sight of her empty bed. The open window let in a frigid wind. *Taylor? Don't tell me you climbed out again.*

Smokey nudged in, followed by Garcia. "Couldn't get past you, huh?" Smokey said.

Morgan's insides churned. "I don't understand."

"Understand what?" Taylor spoke from behind him, a toothbrush in her mouth.

Morgan spun around to find her coming out of the second bathroom in a black nightgown. His heart nearly burst from his chest. "Taylor, you're here."

"Where else would I be," she mumbled through toothpaste residue. "Father Javier!" She charged in and embraced him, almost jostling his Bible free from his hand. "What are you doing here? It's the middle of the night." Then she noticed Smokey. "What's going on?"

Morgan gripped her hand. "Katy Wilson was attacked tonight. The detective wants to take your DNA. It's standard to use it to eliminate people as suspects."

Taylor looked confused. She licked her lips clean. "Isn't it also used to find who's guilty?"

"It can," Morgan said, "but you've been in your bedroom all night."

Smokey cleared his throat. "Is that true?"

"Yeah." She looked at Garcia. "You believe me, right?"

Garcia nodded vigorously. "*Sí.*"

"She always leave her window open, Doc?" Smokey asked Morgan. "Seems awfully drafty."

"She gets warm sometimes." Morgan stepped over to slide it shut.

Smokey followed him over and checked the window frame and the floor. "No evidence she climbed in or out."

"She told you," Morgan said. "She's been in her room all evening. Take your sample and get out."

Smokey pulled out the DNA kit. "Open wide, Taylor. This won't hurt a bit." He unscrewed the plastic bottle, removed a Q-Tip, and sat on the bed next to her. He dabbed the inside her mouth. "All done." He sealed the sample and rose.

"So this will clear me?" Taylor said.

"It will," Morgan said.

"One more thing," Smokey said. "I need to take her dress."

Taylor looked to Morgan for help. "They need to take my clothes? Can they do that?"

"They have a warrant," Morgan said. "It's nothing to worry about."

Smokey crossed to the closet and opened it. After a moment of rifling through hangers, he pulled a white dress out and raised it up.

A piece, matching the size of the fabric in evidence, was missing from the right sleeve.

Smokey held the cloth up to the dress, and all four of them stared at the damning confirmation before them.

"What's that mean, Dad?"

Shit. This is bad. "Don't say anything else, Taylor," Morgan said.

Garcia approached the bed. "Taylor, I'd like to say a prayer."

"I'd like that, Father Javier."

Smokey took the clue and left the bedroom. Morgan followed him to the living room, leaving Garcia and Taylor alone.

"Doc," Smokey whispered, "find another attorney. She can stay here for now, but this doesn't look good."

Morgan stood frozen. "I don't believe it. She wouldn't, couldn't."

Garcia joined them. He took hold of his friend's arm. "It looks like she was there."

Morgan pulled away. "No. There's another explanation. The dress could have been ripped another time. Maybe somebody's framing her. Like that witness tried to do to me."

"I'd like to believe that," Garcia said. "But it's not so easy right now."

Morgan made a fist. "You think your goddaughter is a predator?"

"No. But you have to admit she's not herself."

"You sound like you're condemning her already," Morgan said. "Without even waiting for the DNA results."

"I care for both girls," Garcia said. "Katy deserves my pastoral love as much as Taylor does. The community needs answers. If there's a predator out there, we need to know."

"Don't leave the house, Doc. You or the girl."

"How long to run the test?" Morgan said.

"We have a new Rapid DNA Testing machine," Smokey said. "I can have results tomorrow."

CHAPTER 27

After Smokey left and Taylor finally asleep, Morgan retired to the sofa to watch a University of Oregon basketball game in Hawaii, hoping to take his mind off the impending DNA test. He kept the sound low, not so much for Taylor's sake, but to hear anything going on in her room. Or outside her window.

The game ended, and he watched sports highlights.. Despite his best efforts to stay awake he dozed off.

Dreams came quickly. Costa Rica. Taylor overrun by crabs. Taylor pleading for him to save Michelle.

He awoke and wiped his soaked forehead. Damp matted hair stuck to his temples.

A sliding clatter broke from Taylor's room.

Shit. She opened the window.

A scraping hiss followed.

She's climbing out. Morgan ran outside. He listed into a stiff, dank norwester gale and checked along the side of the house.

Nobody there. Get a grip. She's probably hot.

He fought the wind when shutting the door. *Going to be a miserable night.*

He tried returning to the sports highlights but an uncomfortable feeling surged through him.

How can anyone be roasting in this weather? Could she have slipped out too fast for me to see her? No way. Nobody's that agile. But the thought gnawed at him. *I'll go knock to say goodnight. Then I can relax.*

Satisfied with this scheme, he walked to her room and rapped on the door. "Taylor. I'm turning in. Need anything?"

He waited for five seconds, which seemed more like minutes, each second of silence built on the other, adding to his anxiety.

"Taylor?" Morgan reached for the doorknob, pausing before turning it. "I'm coming in."

He pushed the door ajar, revealing an empty bedroom and an open window. He gasped, struggling for breath. *Dammit!*

More pissed than panicked, he charged into the freezing rain. *Great. She'll catch pneumonia in this.*

"Bear, come."

Bear stood his ground inside the entryway.

Morgan raised his voice. "Bear. Where's Taylor?"

Bear whined, stepped outside, then sniffed the sod beneath her bedroom. The soulful Lab peered at the window, whimpered again, and turned back to Morgan.

"Find Taylor," he ordered again.

Finally, Bear lowered his nose and sniffed. After scarcely a moment's hesitation, he lunged forward, toward the rear of their home which backed up against Bush's Pasture Park and the maze of trees that led to the John Lewis Field and McCulloch Stadium. Bear raced past the tree-line, dodging branches and bushes, pushing into the park's interior. Morgan fought to stay even.

The rain turned to sleet as Morgan ducked limbs. Succeeding only half the time in avoiding the pointed boughs, his face bled. Still, he charged ahead, attempting to keep pace with Bear.

They popped out of the trees and into a pasture of knee-high grass, short of Pringle Creek which separated the woods from the park. Mist, resembling a layer of snow, clung to the ground. Sleet turned to hail. Bear slowed and sniffed the sodden earth.

"Bear. Find Taylor. Hurry, buddy."

Bear dropped to his stomach and whined. Morgan looked up to follow Bear's gaze. An indistinguishable shadow moved toward them.

"Taylor? Is that you?"

Before Morgan could step closer, a pack of rats ran across the meadow, from the silhouette to the creek. Then a wolfish howl echoed through the woods. Morgan froze, his breath coming in halted quakes. "Taylor?"

The figure, Taylor's height and dressed in black, stepped further into view, approaching slowly, but didn't respond. Morgan strained to see but the combination of darkness, hail, and fog made it impossible. He shivered, his skin covered in moisture from the elements.

Who else would be out here in this mess? Hell, why is Taylor out here?

A golf-ball-sized hailstone struck his head, knocking him to his knees. Stunned but conscious, he ran his right hand along his noggin. Blood smeared across his palm.

I've got to get to Taylor.

The hail fell faster and harder, and Morgan scampered toward the trees, where he might get a reprieve. Instead, he slipped and slammed face-first into the hard, slick soil. Pellets of ice bruised his back though his shirt.

Bear's bark turned into a hysterical crescendo.

Taylor, swathed in a gauzy black nightgown, emerged from the brush a dozen yards ahead. Her feet appeared to glide through the ground fog. Her dry and angelic skin showed no ill effects from the hailstorm.

Morgan tried to swallow, but found no saliva to work with. His head ached. Sticky blood fell down his cheeks. *She looks like something out of a Stephen King novel.*

Bear let out a howl and spun on Morgan. His eyes looked like a wolf on the prowl. Bear's guttural growl made it clear he considered Morgan a threat.

To Taylor? Why?

Morgan gave his full attention to Bear. "Bear. It's okay, boy. It's me."

Taylor closed in. Bear heeled, snarling at Morgan.

"Taylor, thank God you're okay."

"You shouldn't have come," Taylor said, no hint of emotion in her voice.

Morgan leaned forward, examining her eyes. The sclera burned bright red rather than the expected white. He flinched backwards. *Jesus. They look identical to Bear's. But that's way beyond bloodshot. And medically impossible. Must be my imagination. Maybe I hit my head harder than I thought.*

Another sharp pellet of hail struck Morgan. He winced. "It's too dangerous for you out here. I'm bleeding."

"I know. It smells delicious."

Morgan stiffened. "What did you say?"

"Bear can smell it, too."

This can not *be happening.* His heart raced. *Keep it together. I'm a psychiatrist, for Christ's sake. There has to be a rational explanation.*

"Help me up," he said. "We need to go back to the house."

Bear snarled and took a few hostile steps toward him.

"What's wrong with him?" Morgan said. "Storm must have him spooked."

Taylor grinned, with sparkling red eyes. She replied a full octave higher. "Yeth. It must be the tempest."

That's not her normal voice or smile. The grin's like a clown's with painted, exaggerated lips. And her irises have converted to red now, with the sclera white again. What is going on with my daughter?

Another figure appeared surrounded by a misty fog behind Taylor, filling Morgan with a combination of horror and despair.

The cloud of vapor divided, forming a path directly to Taylor, like the parting of the Red Sea. Jennifer Peterson strolled up to Taylor in bare feet, wearing only pajamas. She stared up at Taylor with devotion, even as the hail bruised and cut her face.

What the hell? Bile ran up Morgan's throat. He forced it back. "Jennifer!" Morgan yelled. "What are you doing out here?"

Morgan struggled to his feet, but hesitated when Bear growled and barked, showing his fangs.

"Bear, it's me. Down!"

Bear hesitated, then stopped barking and fell onto his belly.

"Stay!" Morgan commanded, and Bear put his head on his front paws, staring at Morgan. "Good boy."

Morgan turned to Taylor and Jennifer. His temporary relief dissolved as Taylor placed her face against Jennifer's neck.

"Taylor, what are you doing?" Morgan yelled, confused. *It's like The Twilight Zone.* He chased away a sick thought. *Or a porn scene.*

Taylor made eye contact with Morgan. She opened her mouth and let it sit over Jennifer.

Morgan's head spun. "No!" He screamed and raced toward them. "Taylor, stop!"

Taylor chomped, and a river of blood ran down Jennifer's neck, combining with the rainwater. She lapped at the red gold.

Morgan's adrenaline kicked in. He closed the gap between them in seconds, ignoring the hail and the new stinging cuts on his face. He grabbed Taylor by the shoulders and pulled her away from Jennifer.

Oh, Christ, Taylor's DNA will match the bites on Katy. And the dress.

He checked Jennifer. Blood trickled into her pajama top from her ripped neck. Her expression blank, her eyes vacant.

"I'm so sorry, Jennifer. I don't know what got into Taylor." Morgan turned on Taylor. "What the hell's wrong with you?"

Taylor's lips were crimson with Jennifer's blood. She expanded her mouth wide to give Morgan an unobstructed view. Her incisors were abnormally long, like fangs. And razor sharp.

Morgan gasped. Revulsion ran through his gut. *What medical condition causes that?*

Taylor tried to escape from Morgan's grasp and feast on Jennifer's throat. Morgan held her off, finding her unusually powerful but not strong enough to break free. He managed to pull her aside.

"Jesus, Taylor, stop for God's sake!"

When Taylor continued her fierce fight to reach her prey, Morgan slapped her.

Stunned, she shook her head and looked at Morgan, disoriented. "Dad? What are we doing out here?"

Morgan froze, amazed at the return of Taylor's innocent voice. Her teeth no longer appeared as long or as sharp. Her irises were brown. *Was it just my imagination? My mind and eyes playing tricks on me in the hailstorm?* He shelved that debate for another time. Overwhelmed with relief at having his daughter back he squeezed her. Then he checked on Jennifer, who stood statue-like in the dwindling hail, her blood congealing on her neck.

"Jennifer, you okay?"

She didn't react.

Morgan assessed the wound, found it shallow, and carried Jennifer toward the house. "Follow me."

Before he took a step a silhouette deeper in the forest appeared in his peripheral vision.

"Is someone there?"

A horrified face peered through the trees. He recognized it and his vertigo returned. *The same lady was out here last week. Could she be part of Margarita's task force?*

"Hey," he called, "I know you're out there. What do you want?"

The face retreated into the brush.

"Are you with Margarita?" He held his breath, waiting for a response.

Again, no reply.

Taylor rested against him. "Dad? Is it the crazy Costa Rican lady?" Between the vertigo, Jennifer's dead weight, and Taylor's inclining into him he almost toppled into the mud.

"No," he said, surprised at how convincing he sounded. "She'll never find you. Let's go home."

He led the way, Taylor's arm looped around his, and Bear obediently prancing behind. *I better not let Smokey find out about this. After the DNA test confirms his suspicions, he'll already have enough evidence to ship us both to Costa Rica.*

CHAPTER 28

Once inside the house, Bear retreated to Morgan's bedroom, keeping as far away as possible when he passed Taylor's room.

Morgan, still shivering from the fright with Taylor as much as from the hail, wiped blood from his forehead. He settled Jennifer in a chair. Her pulse checked out, but her vacant expression terrified him. "Jennifer? Can you hear me?"

When she didn't respond, he wrapped a blanket around her and waited, hoping to see her recover.

"What happened, Dad?"

Morgan debated what to tell Taylor. He settled for, "She got scratched."

He pulled the blinds and checked outside the house. *No sign of the woman. Must have been a coincidence.* But deep inside he wondered, and he shivered.

Then he called Jennifer's father. "Mr. Peterson? It's Dr. Morgan, Taylor's father."

"What do you want?"

"I don't mean to upset you, but I found Jennifer in Bush's Pasture Park. In her pajamas in the hailstorm. She's got a few cuts, but I think she's okay."

"What are you talking about? Jennifer's upstairs, asleep."

"I'm afraid not. You better get over here."

Muffled voices rose on the other end of the line. "I'll be right there. Don't you or your girl lay a hand on her." He hung up.

What kind of monster does he think I am? He studied the damage to Jennifer's neck and his gut cramped.

"What do you recall, Taylor?" he said, wiping off the last streak of blood from Jennifer's neck. He rubbed antibiotic cream into the small wound, the size of two jagged incisors.

Taylor shook her head. "I don't remember anything after going to bed. What were we doing out there?"

Morgan applied a bandage to Jennifer's neck. "I went to say goodnight, and you were gone. So Bear and I searched for you. We found Jennifer out there with you." He patted Jennifer on the cheek. She could have passed for a stone statue. Even her facial muscles felt hard to the touch. "Jennifer. Snap out of it."

Jennifer snapped to attention. Her forehead creased in consternation. "Dr. Morgan? What are you doing here?" She glanced over at Taylor. "Taylor? Are you babysitting me tonight?"

She doesn't know where she is. "Jennifer, you're at our house. How do you feel?"

"I'm good. Why?"

"You don't feel weak? Cold? Thirsty?"

"No. Should I?"

"We found you in the woods. Any idea why you were out there?"

"I don't know."

At least it wasn't to see Taylor.

"Your Dad's on his way. Can I get you anything? Hot chocolate?"

"No, thanks," Jennifer said.

"Okay." He focused on Taylor. Blood dripped around her mouth. *Jesus. Peterson can't see that.*

He wiped Taylor's face with a wet cloth. "What about you, Taylor?"

"I'm not thirsty."

I'll bet you're not.

A car skid to a stop in the driveway. Seconds later Peterson pounded on the door. "Morgan. Open up!"

Morgan let him in. Peterson ran past him to his daughter. "Are you okay, Jenny?"

"I'm fine, Papa."

Peterson opened the bandage and checked the marks, then glared at Taylor. "Did Taylor do this?"

Morgan tensed.

"No, Papa."

Morgan exhaled. *She doesn't remember. What a break.* He mustered his training and spoke calmly. "I saw the cut on her neck, maybe from the branches, and so I applied antibiotic ointment and bandaged it."

Peterson turned on Morgan, anger etched on his face. "This is what happened to Katy Wilson." He pointed at Taylor. "This is *her* doing. I called the police."

Shit. Just what we need.

An approaching siren confirmed Peterson's story. Followed by more tires screeching on the driveway. Moments later, Smokey stood on the landing in a heavy coat and fur-lined boots, shivering. Morgan waved him in. "I'm glad you're here, detective. I was going to call you myself."

Smokey stepped in from the cold. "Humph. Why's that?"

"I saw Jennifer outside in the storm," Morgan said. "I immediately called her father."

Smokey ran his tongue inside his cheek. "Was Taylor out there with her?"

Morgan glanced at Jennifer, and then Taylor. Either might expose his story. He drew a breath, his stomach in knots. *Here goes nothing.* "No. Taylor hasn't left the house."

"Bullshit," Peterson said. "Jennifer wouldn't go wandering off on her own. Taylor must have convinced Jennifer to follow her back here."

Smokey approached Jennifer. "Hi, Jennifer. Can you tell me what happened?"

"All I remember is Dr. Morgan taking care of me."

"You don't remember leaving your house?" Smokey asked.

"No."

"Or seeing Taylor?"

Jennifer glanced at Taylor, then rumpled her brow. "It happened like Dr. Morgan said."

Taylor grinned.

Morgan tried not to give away his surprise. *My lucky day. But why?*

"Humph. Seems we've got quite a puzzle here."

Peterson grumbled. "There's no mystery. She's a predator. She did something to Katy in the park, then attacked her in her own home. And now this. Why aren't you arresting her?"

"The lab finished the DNA test on Katy's bite marks," Smokey said, looking at Taylor. "Not a match for Taylor."

Morgan blushed at the good news. "No match?"

"Not to Taylor. She didn't attack Katy."

Morgan looked at Taylor, beaming. Taylor sat emotionless, watching them both.

Smokey turned to Peterson. "Can I see the wound?"

Peterson peeled the bandage back, revealing two tiny marks.

Smokey studied them, then looked at Peterson. "They're not like the bites on Katy. Those were tears, maybe from an animal without sharp teeth. These are precise and made from something pointed. Like a branch."

Peterson bristled, pointing at Morgan. "They're responsible for this."

Morgan continued his offensive. "Hey, enough with your accusations. I understand you're upset, but the responsibility here is all yours. Keep your kid at home, where she belongs, will you?"

Peterson made a move toward Morgan.

Smokey stepped between them. "Enough. Jim, unless you've got other evidence for me, I've got no reason to suspect the Doc of anything. Or his daughter. I know it seems like a huge coincidence, but she tested clean on the Wilson girl, and these marks don't match those, anyway. And the Doc has a point. How's Jennifer getting out of the house? At this hour? In this weather?"

Peterson glared at Smokey, gave Morgan a hateful glance, and picked Jennifer up in his arms.

"Stay away from her," he said to Morgan. "You and that sick girl of yours. Understand?"

"You keep your daughter away from here, and we'll all be fine."

Peterson stormed out with Jennifer.

Morgan turned to Taylor. "You okay?"

She skipped toward her room. "Perfect. Time to sleep."

She knows she got away with something. A piercing pain rippled through his chest. He looked at Smokey. "Anything else?"

Smokey opened the front door and examined the area. "Convenient the weather erased any sign of footprints," he said matter-of-factly. "Makes it impossible to see how many of you were out there."

"I told you—just me, detective."

"That's what you said, all right. Well, we still have a lot to figure out. The dress matched the fabric found on the victim, so possibly we're looking at two perps."

Morgan's enthusiasm sagged. "Seriously? There's no evidence to suggest two, is there?"

"Not yet."

"Taylor says she tore the dress on a bush. Perhaps somebody really is trying to frame her."

"Maybe."

"So are we free to leave the house now?"

"Yep. But don't leave town. You're both still persons of interest." Smokey started to leave, then turned. "Keen interest."

Morgan watched Smokey drive away, then knocked on Taylor's door.

"Go away."

"We need to talk. I'm coming in." He waited five seconds, then opened her door.

Taylor was in bed in her nightgown with the covers on the floor, her window opened wide. "You can't come in here without permission."

"I'm your father. I can do whatever is necessary to keep you safe." He crossed her room and closed the window, latching it shut. "It's freezing in here."

Taylor glowered. "I want that open."

Morgan licked his parched lips. "Too bad. You know the black dress with the piece missing?"

"Yeah."

"Any idea how the torn piece from your dress could have gotten on Katy?"

Taylor eyed the closet. She smiled in a way that made Morgan uncomfortable. "Maybe she bumped into it the night she came here."

Morgan approached her. "Open your mouth."

Taylor complied. Her teeth appeared normal. *Maybe it* was *my imagination.*

"I saw you bite Jennifer. Why would you do that?"

Taylor stared defiantly. "Can you leave now? I'd like to sleep."

"I need an answer. We can't cure you if I don't know what I'm dealing with."

"I don't need to be *cured*. I've never felt better. The seizures have stopped. My heart checks out. Can't you let me sleep?"

Morgan backed away. "Fine. I'll let you sleep. But you can't go anywhere until I get some answers about your behavior." *Medical or psychological.*

"So now I'm in prison?"

"It's for your own safety." *And the security of others.*

* * *

Morgan sat at his dinette table, holding a glass of water he would have traded for scotch, staring at a web search, trying to match her symptoms with known conditions. He'd turned up bupkis.

She attacked Jennifer.

Did she attack Katy, too?

No. The DNA test cleared her.

But what are the odds of a second perpetrator with the same M.O.?

He closed his eyes and focused through his exhaustion.

Okay, let's address this logically. There are two possible scientific explanations. She has a medical condition. One that's previously undiscovered, at least not one that's recognized. Causes her irises to change color. Causes her teeth to change shape. In which case I have to get the medical specialists involved.

He sipped from the glass and stared in despair at the ceiling.

Or it's her psyche, and I can treat her. A multiple personality disorder or schizophrenic paranoia.

Either way, I have to trust science to solve this.

His mind wandered to his fiancee. *So, do I tell Azra about tonight's attack? Have her look for a medical explanation?*

No! They'll lock her up. Take her away from me. Or, send us to Costa Rica, to be killed. No one else can know. Not until I rule out the psychological possibilities.

A third choice barged into his head. *What if it's me? What if my own observations are compromised? Can my sleep-deprivation be causing delirium?* He swallowed. *Maybe I'm the one that's losing it.*

He glanced at the clock. Almost midnight.

All I know for sure is I will protect her. No matter what.

And Azra? She'll be pissed if I shut her out. I could lose her.

Morgan finished his water. The kitchen light created a prism in the glass, and Morgan stared at it, mesmerized.

Taylor comes first.

He looked up at the sound of footsteps. Taylor approached, lines across her forehead.

"In case you get any ideas," she said in a deep voice, "I won't let you torment her."

Who? Jennifer? "I would never hurt anyone."

Taylor grunted and returned to her room. Morgan lowered his head and succumbed to his exhaustion.

CHAPTER 29

Thursday

Morgan gave up trying to sleep at sunrise after a night of checking on Taylor every fifteen minutes. He kept her door ajar and each time he checked the window was open. He shut it, only to find it agape again during the next check.

The sun broke through the clouds and bright sunshine poured into Taylor's room. Taylor bolted upright as a sliver of sunlight crossed her legs.

"Close those fucking blinds!" she roared.

"Hey," Morgan said. "Language." He shut the shades, putting the bedroom in darkness. "Listen, I have to go into the office to contact my patients about my leave of absence. I'll see if Azra can come over."

"Why do we need Azra? I always stay home alone."

"I'm thinking about the seizures." *Among other things.* "Humor me, okay?"

She turned her back to him and huddled into a fetal position. "Whatever."

He called Azra, who answered on the first ring. "Richard, I have good news. They lifted my suspension this morning."

"That's great. You never deserved any suspicion."

"I know. The ME office is swamped. This deal with Katy getting attacked has the mayor going nuts."

"I bet. Nothing stirs up a community like children being assailed."

Azra paused before continuing, her voice lower. "I heard about the Peterson incident at your house. And the DNA results. At least that's a relief."

"Can I ask for a favor? I need to go to the office for an hour. Any chance you can watch Taylor while I clear my calendar at the hospital?"

"Can we do it now? So I can get to work by nine?"

"Deal. Thanks."

"That's what fiancees do, right? Be there for our man."

* * *

Morgan's second floor office, never a bastion of decor and ambiance, struck him as particularly morose, despite a rare day of December sunshine trying to peek in through the closed blinds. He considered opening them, exposing the southern view.

That will only remind me of Taylor's outburst. No thanks.

The room smelled stale, so he turned on the air. He scanned his appointments for the next month. He needed to call several colleagues and arrange for referrals for each of his patients, then inform them of the transition.

Professional ethics be damned. I've got a daughter to save.

Besides, the doctor is definitely not in. He recalled Lucy in "Peanuts." *Five cents. What my advice is worth right now. They'll be better off with someone else.* He pulled out his desk drawer.

A paper fell at his feet. An invoice from the hospital's drug repository.

I refiled these after the police returned them. Did I drop one?

He lifted it off the floor and eyed it. The date on the page floored him. *The day before our trip to Costa Rica.*

What the hell? I didn't order any prescriptions. He began to perspire. *It says I checked out a vial of Ketamine that day from the hospital. This might explain the discrepancy.*

Morgan stared at the itemization, frozen.

That's not possible.

He looked at his desk drawer. A tiny pocket hid between the side of the desk and the compartment.

The invoice must have lodged in there. Somehow the police didn't find it.

Did I hide it? Why don't I remember?

He rose and walked to the locked repository that contained his prescription medications. He kept two logs—one inside the cabinet, and another on his computer. He fumbled the keys twice before navigating the lock. Finally, he pulled out the inventory and returned to his desktop. He compared the files.

They match. Thank God!

He took the list back to the cabinet and checked the stock on his shelves, examining each entry against the ID number on the vial.

Everything checked out until he got to the last record.

The Ketamine. It's not here.

He stumbled back and bumped into his desk. Dizziness flooded him.

I took Ketamine, like the witness said. I don't remember, but that's my signature. The hospital signed and dated it.

He returned his gaze to the invoice.

The vial's not here. Did I really kill Michelle and then block the memory? Am I following my father's legacy?

Morgan inhaled to steady himself. He dropped the paper. His eyes focused on a different vial. *Sodium thiopental.* He picked up the barbiturate and pocketed it for reasons his conscious mind didn't understand.

A knock on the door startled him. "Yes?"

A middle-aged Hispanic woman, professionally dressed in a navy blazer and skirt, stood at the entrance. Dark rings hung under her eyes. Her face showed the leathery crinkling of too much sun, and excessive stress.

"Can I help you?" Morgan said.

The woman let herself in and sat. "Actually, I'm here to help you."

Morgan squinted. "How's that?"

"I know what's wrong with your daughter."

Morgan eased into his chair. *I know this lady from somewhere.* "Excuse me?"

"My daughter was infected the same way." Her accent hinted of South America.

"What makes you think there's something wrong with my daughter?"

The woman handed Morgan a business card. "My name is Linda Copeland. I was a professor of ancient civilizations at the university in Lima."

Morgan inspected the introduction. "Dr. Copeland."

"Please call me Linda. Everybody does."

"I'm sorry, I don't understand why you're here. My daughter's fine."

"Your teenage girl is *not* fine. And she will get worse. And then she'll kill."

Morgan leapt to his feet. "Now, see here. You have no right to talk about my daughter like that."

Linda shot out of her seat. "I have every right. I lost my daughter to this *evil*. She died because of the demon behind it all."

Morgan's face paled. *She lost her daughter? I can't even imagine.*

She sat back down. "Sorry. I'm here only to help you. And to get justice."

"I'm sorry about your daughter, Professor."

"As I said, it's Linda. I gave up my professorship to track down this monster."

Do I know her from somewhere? "I'm sorry, Linda. But your tragedy has nothing to do with me. Or my daughter. If someone killed your daughter, perhaps you should talk with the police. If you're here for grief counseling, I'm afraid I'm not taking new patients right now."

"I tracked you from Costa Rica. You'll want to hear what I have to say."

Oh, shit. Margarita's task force. And I left Taylor at home with Azra.

"You leave my daughter alone!" Panicked, he dialed Taylor's cell phone from his land line. No one picked up. *Am I too late?*

"I'm not here to harm your daughter. I only want you to listen."

Morgan called Azra's number and got no answer. He slammed his phone down. *Why aren't they answering?*

"I was in the forest when your daughter attacked that girl."

The park. Those red shoes. "I remember you. You've been watching my house. You're part of that crazy task force."

"They're not crazy. But, no, I'm not with them. I work alone."

If she's been watching the house, she could have gone after Taylor many times. But didn't. "It sounds like you're a stalker. Why, I don't know, but I'll have the police on your ass if you don't stop."

"And have me tell them what I saw?" Linda raised her eyebrows. "I don't think so."

Morgan sagged into the chair. "What do you want? Money? Drugs?"

"Don't be absurd. I came hoping we'll help each other."

"I told you, I don't need any help."

Linda teetered back. "I'll make you a deal. You give me ten minutes to tell you my story, and, if you still want me to leave, I'll leave you and your daughter alone."

Morgan considered her offer. *She didn't turn Taylor in when she could have.* "Okay. Ten minutes."

"You're a smart man, Dr. Morgan."

"Tick, tock."

"I was on sabbatical, traveling with my daughter. My husband, an American stationed at the university, passed away from a heart attack, and I wanted my daughter to get away. I took her to the

Bribri village in Costa Rica, near the Panama border. My goal was to do a deep dive into their culture, to start a class on one of the last unchanged indigenous tribes left on the planet." She brushed away a tear. "Little did I know, my daughter wouldn't survive the trip."

The counselor in Morgan kicked in. "What happened to her?"

"A vampire bat attacked her in the jungle. I thought it was no big deal. A minor scratch." This time she broke down.

Morgan's training was to not interrupt a patient baring their soul, but he offered a tissue, anyway. *Jesus. Another bat.*

"I'm sorry, Dr. Morgan. It's still an open wound."

Yes. The kind that never really heals. "It's good to let it out."

Linda cleared her throat. "I treated the bite but my daughter changed. We were a long way from civilization and the disease progressed rapidly. The people in the village took me to their *Awá*. He did incantations, then proclaimed my daughter infected by a plague. Said if I'd brought her sooner he might have been able to help." She wiped away a tear. "I was too late."

Eerily similar to our experience in Costa Rica. "Did they try to hold her there? Hurt her?"

"They planned to kill her. So I sneaked my daughter into the jungle. We hiked into Panama. Then a boat home to Peru."

"Fortunate you escaped."

Linda stared at the floor. "No, it wasn't."

Morgan checked the time. Five minutes. "Why's that?"

"Because she wasn't my daughter any longer."

"I don't understand."

Linda's head popped up. "She changed into a vampire, Dr. Morgan. Like your daughter will."

A vampire? That's the best you've got? She's lost touch with reality. "Look, I feel bad about your loss, but I don't have time for ghost stories."

"Tell me about your daughter's eyes."

"Her eyes?"

"That's the first sign. Her eyes are bloodshot all the time, aren't they?"

How does she know?

"I can see from your face they are," Linda continued. "Here's what's happening, unbelievable as it may sound. The bat transferred a demon to her. The demon will stay in the shadows at first, but show itself more over time. When the demon wants to show itself, your daughter will speak in a deep voice. Her irises will turn dead black, and her skin will look puke-green."

Morgan sat up straighter. *Holy shit.* As worried as he felt for Taylor, his medical instincts also kicked in. *If Linda's daughter had this same thing, maybe she's the key to finding a medical solution for Taylor? I wonder if we can dig up her daughter's body to run tests?* He decided to skip that part of his thoughts and go with denial for now. "I assure you, I've seen none of that."

"Good. Maybe there's still time to stop *it*."

"Stop it from what?"

"Turning your daughter into a vampire that preys on girls."

"That's ridiculous. There's no such thing."

Linda marched ahead with her story. "The symptoms will start subtly. The most obvious change will be her incisors. They'll grow. Her skin color will fade. Her irises will change to bright red. Then her voice will squeak and, as *it* matures, she'll develop a lisp."

Morgan's heart stopped long enough to cause a rush of dizziness. *Red eyes. Lisp. It is the same condition.* "Red. I thought you said they'd turn black."

"When the demon shows itself, they go black. You'll be able to tell who's in control of her body and mind by the signs. Red irises means the vampire. Black, the demon."

How do I get her to agree to exhume her daughter's body? This could be a break for Taylor and a medical breakthrough for the ages. An unknown pathogen from deep in the Costa Rican jungle, just waiting for its chance to evolve and spread.

Linda continued. "The more the vampire takes control, the more prominent her symptoms and the obvious signs will be. Eventually, she won't be recognizable. Your daughter will be gone, replaced by a monster. A lamia."

What's a lamia?

"I chained my daughter to a stake in the ground, like a wild animal, to keep her from attacking the girls in our community."

"You chained your own daughter?"

"Just as will you, Dr. Morgan. When you can no longer control her. When she is a murderer. And worse."

Morgan drummed his fingers on his desk. The sound echoed throughout the office. *I need to get back to Taylor and time to think about having her daughter's body examined.* "Linda, I've heard enough. I'm truly sorry for your tragedy, but I can't help you."

"After a while, the Costa Rican task force found us. To finish its job."

"Finish?"

"They killed her."

This poor woman. She's been through unimaginable horror.

"You want to know the horrible truth? The truth you will someday face?"

Morgan waited on the edge of his chair.

"The truth is, I was relieved when they killed her."

Morgan's skin flushed, and a burning sensation ran down his arms. "You *wanted* them to kill your daughter?"

Linda pounded her fist on the desk. "I could not save her! It was the only way!" She wept.

Morgan didn't know whether to call the police or admit her to a psychiatric ward. "That's a tragic story, Linda. Like I said, I'm sorry for your loss." He handed her another tissue. "May I ask if the medical examiner did an autopsy?"

"He did. But all the symptoms vanished when the task force beheaded her."

"They *beheaded* her?" The image barged into his mind. Only this time, it was Taylor, not Linda's daughter that he saw. He chased the horrid vision away, but he could feel his sweat in every pore.

"Both the *Awá* and the task force said it's the only way to kill the lamia." Linda shook her head. "And it could have been worse. I secured my daughter before she could wound any more girls. The task force said the disease spreads quickly if the lamia attacks more girls. Imagine if that happened. It could spread exponentially."

Wooziness assaulted Morgan, and he barely stayed conscious. "Were the killers arrested?"

"Some were. Most escaped."

Morgan shook his head. *That could have been us.* "I can't tell you how sorry I am. No one should be put through that."

"I left the university. To identify and track the demon. To educate people. I've traced it to the beginning of time."

"You believe the demon story? You're an educated person. You must know better."

Linda pointed at Morgan. "I do believe. And you will, too. If you don't already."

A thought rose from within Morgan's psyche. *What if she's right?* He forced it back into the darkness. "You say you want to find the demon?"

"I will destroy it."

"How?"

Linda looked down. "I think I have a way to capture it. Once I have it contained, I can keep it from possessing anyone else. But the only success in exorcising the demon through the centuries has been by the Bribri *Awá*."

Morgan stood. "You came here to get my daughter? To take her back to Costa Rica?"

"I'm hoping you'll see it as your daughter's only chance. You have a responsibility to see it doesn't spread."

Her words stunned Morgan, followed by anger. He pointed to the door. "Time's up, Professor."

She rose and gave him a sad expression. "I'm afraid your daughter's time is up. Come with me to see the *Awá*. He's her only chance."

"Goodbye, Professor."

Linda hung her head and retreated.

CHAPTER 30

A Greyhound bus pulled into the Salem station. A single passenger in a floppy hat and sunglasses disembarked.

She plucked the address, one provided by a surprising ally, from her gym bag. The fellow conspirator thought she would see Dr. Morgan brought to justice. By the time the moron realized her true target, it would be too late.

Step one—buy a machete. Then find the girl.

Margarita pulled out a photo of her true target.

Taylor Morgan. I'm coming for you. And your offspring.

CHAPTER 31

The wind picked up and rocked his car on the drive home. Morgan called Garcia from his hands-free phone. "Javi, it's Pennywise."

An unfriendly voice answered. "I'm busy. What do you need?"

"I know I said some things. Forgive me? I don't know who else to turn to."

"Well, I *am* a priest. What choice do I have?" Garcia grunted. "What's wrong?"

"I may have committed a mortal sin. I'm worried I killed Michelle."

"What?" Garcia whispered. "Why would you say that?"

"I discovered new evidence. A trail pointing at me."

"What evidence?"

Morgan spoke in a monotone. "I checked out Ketamine the day before we left for Costa Rica. That's the drug they found in Michelle's system. And I hid the receipt. The vial isn't here. I'm so confused."

"Slow down. You took Ketamine to Costa Rica, and they found that prescription in Michelle?"

"Yeah."

"And there's a discrepancy between the official drug log you keep?"

Hearing the question out loud made Morgan flinch. "I guess there is."

"And you don't remember anything?"

"No."

"There must be a logical explanation. You'd never hurt Michelle. And if you treated her you'd remember, right?"

"My mind might have blocked it. Happens sometimes with extreme guilt." He squirmed. "Do you think I'm capable? With my family history?"

"What motive would you have? You never stopped loving Michelle."

Morgan recalled his father's violations. His stomach churned. "Even love has its flaws."

Garcia didn't immediately respond. Morgan waited, tense and scared.

Finally, the priest replied. "This is very confusing, Pennywise. Did you tell Smokey?"

"Not yet. Figured I'd confess to you first. Maybe score a few points upstairs before I'm damned to Hell."

"I'm not in the damnation business. And this isn't a proper confession. Did you tell Taylor?"

"What am I going to tell her? That she was right about me wanting her mother dead?" Morgan stared at the floor.

"You must get to the truth. What about confiding in Azra? She was there. She might remember something."

Morgan flinched. "That's not a good idea." *I'm already keeping things from her. Go, team fiancee.*

"Why not?"

"It's complicated." *How's that for the lamest excuse ever? I sound like one of my patients.*

"You asked for help. I'm trying to offer some."

"I know. Sometimes I'm not the easiest guy to befriend."

"My advice? Tell Azra and Smokey. You might learn something that helps you remember. Not for absolution. For yourself."

Morgan squirmed.

"I'm glad you called. I'm always here for you. Even when you're a pain in the ass."

"I appreciate that, Javi. But I may need more help than you can provide."

"Truth first. Forgiveness later."

Morgan sagged. *If I killed Michelle, I don't deserve forgiveness.* "There's more."

"Hit me."

"A professor came to my office just now. Claims her daughter died of the same malady Taylor's got."

"Died? How?"

"Claims the unique plague that Margarita woman warned me about is real." His skin crawled.

"You believe her?"

"Some of it's too far-fetched. But Taylor is showing hard to explain symptoms. Her irises change color. Her teeth are growing. And a second personality." *Should I tell him about Taylor attacking Jennifer in the park? Better not go down that path with anyone else. That will link Taylor to Katy's assault.*

"You think she's got multiple personality disorder?"

"It's more likely she's exhibiting schizophrenic paranoia. She's approaching the age it manifests itself. But her symptoms aren't classic for it. And the professor's daughter showed the same peculiarities."

"So that plague might be a more plausible explanation."

"Except they haven't found anything in Taylor's tests to substantiate any disease. It's a mystery." *Should I even mention Linda's talk of a demon? No. Even a Catholic priest will laugh at me.* "The professor's girl underwent an autopsy, but if we could get the body back here to Azra, she might find something important. Not just for Taylor, but for mankind."

"Will the professor go for that?"

"She believes in a supernatural cause. I doubt she'd be open to it."

"What can I do?"

"For now, thanks for listening. I'm pulling in. I'll call you later."

CHAPTER 32

Morgan met Azra at the front door. Bear stood next to her, wagging his tail.

Azra pecked Morgan on his cheek. "Gotta run. Did everything at the office go okay?"

No. "Yeah. Any sign of Taylor?"

"Not a peep. I looked in on her a few times, but she's still asleep."

"Cool. Thanks for helping." Morgan reached for her, but she passed him and he turned to watch her race away.

Footsteps came up behind him. He turned and found Taylor in white shorts and a lime green halter top. *Hey. No black clothes.* Temporary relief dissolved as Bear whimpered to his bedroom, and Taylor stared in his direction.

Her eyes. Morgan froze. *Black again. What do I do now?*

"She's hungry," Taylor said in a low, masculine voice.

"She?"

"The sow."

Morgan swallowed. "The sow?"

Taylor laughed. "Your daughter, you dimwit."

A second personality? "Can I speak with Taylor?"

"No."

"What does she want?"

"You can't give her what she wants."

"Try me."

"Soon, she will only drink."

"Why's that?" Morgan said, trying to follow his professional training and remain calm. But, inside, his guts were churning.

Taylor grinned, then shook her head. "It is for me to know, and you to discover."

"I see. I'd like to talk to Taylor."

The Taylor-creature spat at him. A spray of red and yellow pus landed on his cheek. "I decide who will orate."

Morgan gagged. *Who talks like that? You sound like you're from ancient Rome.* He wiped the stench off his face with his sleeve. "Well, I'm done talking until I can speak with Taylor."

"Another thing. No more sun. No more going out during the day. Only at night." She shuddered and gave Morgan a puzzled expression. Her irises switched to brown, and she spoke in her normal voice. "I'm so tired. Time for a nap."

Morgan stepped toward her. "Taylor?"

"Who else would it be?" She shook her head as if mystified at his words and went to her room. Morgan followed her, but she slammed the door in his face. He considered forcing his way in but decided against it.

Was that a second, independent self? Or, is Linda's demon real? Should I get Javi involved?

Steady, cowboy. Stay with science. Psychological rationale will get us both through this.

* * *

Taylor slept all afternoon. Morgan checked her several times. Finding the windows and blinds closed and her room dim, he opened the shades each time, only to find them closed when he returned. The room reeked like roadkill on a hot August afternoon.

Once the sun retired for the day, rustling sounds occurred. Morgan eased down the hall and tapped on the door. "Taylor? You up?"

Something slammed against the door, causing Morgan to step back. "Taylor?"

"Go away!" came the response, with that deeper than normal voice.

Morgan steeled himself. "I'm coming in."

He tried to open the door but something interfered. He pushed it open a crack and found the dresser against it. *What's this doing over here?* He put his shoulder into it and forced the cabinet away far enough to squeeze inside.

The bedroom looked like a hurricane swept through. The bed and night stands sat askew several feet. Clothes were scattered across the room. The mirror over the dresser was shattered, and shards of slivered glass littered the floor.

Taylor sat on the bed in a torn t-shirt with one shoulder bared and jean shorts ripped up the side seams, exposing her thighs and hips. Her ghoulishly pale face glowed, lighting up the room. Blood trickled down her chin from bleeding lips. She held tufts of her own black locks in her claws.

"Taylor? What's wrong?"

Taylor's bloodshot eyes glared at him, and her sneer mocked him. She shrieked in a hideous high-pitched wail.

For the first time, Morgan was afraid of his daughter. Not just *for* his daughter. *Of* her. *The black irises. The long teeth. Her fingernails. Her face. Taylor, what is happening to you?* He approached her cautiously. "Taylor? It's Dad."

"Leave me alone!" came the guttural response.

"You're bleeding."

A howl of laughter. "Taylor loves blood." Her mouth opened, exposing pointed incisors, which chomped on her lips and started a new flow. She lapped at the crimson liquid, like a dog at a water bowl. "Mmm. Tasty."

Morgan, blinded by a rush of tears, stumbled toward the bed and sat next to her. He placed his hands on her shoulders. "Taylor, stop."

Taylor bared her fangs in a snarl toward him.

Jesus Christ. Her teeth. Longer. Sharper. Morgan sprang backward to the edge of the bed, his heart pounding against his chest.

A growl. "Taylor is gone."

Morgan wiped at his tears. "Who am I speaking with?"

"I've had other names, but the Bribri call me *Bé*."

Finally. A name for the second personality. Maybe that's progress. "Where's Taylor?"

Taylor laughed, more animal than human. "Gone."

Morgan gulped. "I want to speak with Taylor."

"She is never coming back. I live here now."

Morgan shook her shoulders gently, hoping to bring Taylor back in control.

Taylor opened her mouth wide to show off incredible fangs. "Does this look like Taylor?"

Morgan gasped. *If she bit someone, she could kill them.*

"I can see your fear," the Taylor-thing said. "Smell it. Shall I taste it?"

"You don't scare me. I demand to speak with my daughter! Now!"

Taylor cackled. "You will never see her again. Her transmutation is almost complete."

Transmutation? What's she talking about? "You're not welcome here. I command you to leave my daughter."

"Do you miss her?" she said.

"Taylor, you're right in front of me."

Taylor's face turned red. "You are a fool."

"Why's that?"

"You refuse to believe anything that doesn't match your belief system. Another foolish human."

"You mean science? Medicine? Psychiatry?"

"All beliefs from your world. You're in *my* domain now."

"What world is that?"

"The Bribri call it the realm of *Sibú*. Satan uses other names."

"And who's *Sibú*? A make-believe god?"

Taylor hawked phlegm onto his cheek.

Morgan closed his eyes. His left arm ached. *A heart attack? No. Just stress. Stay calm and get her to talk.* He brushed the ugly glop away with his sleeve. "My calling *Sibú* a false god makes you angry?"

"All humans make me furious."

"I can help you get rid of that anger. It's what I do."

Taylor laughed the laugh of a thousand jackals. "I am not the one who needs help. I am in control. You are not."

"I want to talk with Taylor."

"She's dead."

Morgan shook his head. "She's not dead."

Taylor narrowed her eyes. "*Try* to find her."

"I will. I'm going to rid her of you, forever."

"Oh, I will depart soon. But what I leave behind, you won't recognize."

Morgan gagged a swallow. His heart rate convinced him to stop their conversation. *Keep it together. Try not to think of her as your daughter. She's a patient. Be clinical. It's her best chance.* He mocked himself. *Like I can be detached. It* is *Taylor.* "Wait here. I have a gift for you."

Morgan entered his bedroom and found Bear cowering in the far corner, giving him an accusing and confused glare. He grabbed a wet washcloth and a syringe full of sodium thiopental. When he returned to Taylor's room, she stood on top of her bed, arms out to her sides, perpendicular to her body in a crucifixion pose. Morgan's chest tightened at the sight. "You say you're leaving. Before you do, tell me what you call this condition."

"Lamia."

That's the term Linda used. "Is there a treatment for it?"

Taylor laughed again. "There is nothing you can do for her. Or the children she's spawned. You are an inconsequential human."

Morgan's vertigo returned. He held onto the bed for support. *Spawned. What a horrifying term.* "If it's contagious, how come I'm not infected?"

"We want only young girls."

A numbness ran along Morgan's spine. *Like Margarita and Linda said.* He pointed at Taylor. "I think you're full of it. You don't belong here, and it's time you left."

"I don't think so." Taylor spit a glob of green muck at him, hitting him on the chin. "I like it in here."

Morgan wiped the goop away with his wrist. "It's time for you to leave. It's time for Taylor to talk."

"She's gone. It's me and the lamia now."

The lamia? "I thought lamia was the name of the disease."

Taylor pounded her chest. "They call me *Bé*. She is lamia."

"So what's this disorder called?"

When Taylor refused to answer, Morgan pulled the syringe out.

Taylor shrieked at the sight. "No! The lamia must complete her mission."

Morgan stepped forward and raised the syringe. "Get the hell away from my daughter!"

Taylor hissed and grabbed his arm, stopping the advance of the needle in midair.

Morgan's arm muscles cramped. *Damn. She's strong.*

Taylor twisted his arm until his shoulder socket screamed. The needle tilted, now aimed at his own torso.

"No, you don't." He grabbed her around the waist with his other arm and freed his wrist while keeping the syringe steady. He called on all his strength and jabbed the needle into her thigh.

As he plunged the thiopental into her, Taylor screamed like nothing Morgan had ever heard before. Goosebumps formed over his entire body. Her hold on his arm weakened. She drooped onto the bed. "You're an arrogant loser. And you're wasting your time.

Soon, even this won't slow me down." She closed her eyes, and she collapsed.

Morgan caught her and laid her on the bed. Once his adrenalin slowed, the room spun, and he plopped onto the floor.

What's going on here?

Another familiar voice from deep inside him rose. *I need a drink.*

He slapped himself, hard. *No!* He got to his knees, then to his feet.

Morgan cleaned Taylor's face with the washcloth, then drew a blanket over her. He pulled out her lip, staring at her enlarged incisors. *A split personality doesn't cause that.* He shook his head, releasing her lip. He lifted her eyelids and gasped. Her irises had changed from black to bright red.

Exactly what Linda described. If anyone finds out about these teeth, those eyes..... Until I figure this out, I can't let anyone else see her.

He beheld her ashen face—once so incandescent—while she slept under the influence of the sedative.

My poor angel. Hang on, Sweetie. I will fix this.

* * *

Morgan fell into the dinette chair in front of his laptop. *Let's see if there's any reference to Lamia, Bé, or Sibú.*

Lamia turned up several hits. "A mythical monster, with the body of a woman or with the head and breasts of a woman and the torso of a snake. Sucks the blood of children. References going back to Greek mythology. In literature and movies, a race of vampires. Or demons."

A search for *Bé* and *Sibú* resulted in several links to the Bribri culture in Costa Rica. "Bé is a race of demons who seek to destroy humankind. Sibú watches over the dead." The words shaman and Awá kept surfacing. Morgan dug deeper. "Aha. They refer to a medicine man."

All consistent with what Margarita and Linda described. Is a supernatural cause even possible? He teared. *My God, Taylor. What's happening?*

Morgan shut his eyes and slumped. *Wait. What if Taylor read this? Could her subconscious be driving a delusion and she's along for the ride? If so, I can treat her.*

He grabbed two textbooks from his bookshelf. He searched for Taylor's symptoms, but came up empty.

Overcome with exhaustion, he slumped at his desk and succumbed to the nightmares ahead.

CHAPTER 33

Friday

Morgan awoke at sunrise with his face resting on his warm laptop keyboard, the fan humming in his ear. *Shit. Didn't mean to fall asleep. Is Taylor here?* Recalling terrifying nightmares, he crawled out of his chair and rushed to check on Taylor.

She lay on the bare mattress, her bedding on the floor. Her window was wide open, and a freezing wind assaulted the room. Morgan closed the window, noticing a patch of blue sky amidst the clouds, and covered Taylor with a blanket.

The phone rang. *Azra.* "Hey, honey," he said, fatigued. "How you doing?"

"Richard, there's been a development."

"What now?"

"I'm helping the crime lab out. Someone attacked the Aldridge's daughter, Haley, last night."

Morgan's face blanched, and his knees weakened. *Not another one.* "Where?"

"In her bedroom on the second floor. All the doors and windows locked. Just like Katy Wilson."

"Is she okay?"

"She isn't hurt too bad. More gnawing than biting. Again, like Katy. You know the family?"

"Not well. I met the father a few times at soccer when Taylor was playing. Nice guy." *And now, a tortured guy.* Morgan's heart tugged at him.

"Taylor?"

"What about her?" Morgan asked.

"Does *she* know Haley?"

"Classmates, that sort of thing. But they don't hang out." Morgan recognized the doubt in his own answer, and the hurried response. *Keep it together. I sedated her.*

"You should ask her. The police will."

"She was here with me all night."

After an awkward silence, Azra replied. "I've got to get back. I'll come over as soon as we process the scene. Let's hope the DNA tests aren't a match for Taylor." She hung up.

Moments later, a loud pounding hammered the front door. He swung it open.

Smokey pulled a cigar from his mouth and pocketed it, his demeanor all business. "Morning, Doc. I need to speak to Taylor."

"About what?"

"May I come in?"

Morgan's defiance blew in with a layer of fog. "You have a warrant?"

Smokey stiffened. "I don't need a warrant to question someone."

"That sounds like an interrogation. Is it?"

"I'm trying to avoid bringing her downtown." Smokey, still on the porch, eyed Morgan. "You hear about Haley Aldridge?"

"Azra just called to tell me. That's awful."

"They're classmates, right? Used to play on the same soccer team."

"That was years ago. I'm sorry, but I don't think Taylor can help you solve this tragedy."

"Humph. Her wounds were like Katy Wilson's."

Morgan kept his mouth shut. *He's fishing. Still suspicious of Taylor. Don't give him anything.*

Smokey pressed on. "We did a rapid DNA test on Haley's wounds."

Morgan tensed. *Please don't be Taylor.*

"It came back with Jennifer Peterson's DNA. Why do you think that is, Doc?"

The weight of the world fell off Morgan's shoulders "Really?" *The Peterson girl?*

"Yeah. The lab places her at the scene. The adults don't know each other, and Jennifer's never been to Katy's home. But her DNA is in the bite marks, and her fingerprints are in the room. I'll have them recheck the results on Katy. Maybe she attacked her, too."

Morgan shook his head, trying to wrap his mind around that news. His skin crawled. *Are Jennifer and Taylor linked to this? Taylor said this infection would cause her to attack other girls, and it would spread. Linda and Margarita said the same thing. What am I dealing with?* "If you know it's Jennifer's DNA, why question Taylor?"

Smokey remained motionless. "Because my gut tells me to. But it's probably best if I gather more evidence before I do. Don't go anywhere, Doc. I'm not through with you. Or your daughter."

* * *

Moments after Smokey left, the doorbell rang. "Forget something?"

"Pennywise," Garcia's voice came through the front. "It's me. Are you and Taylor okay?"

Morgan opened the door. "We're fine. Why?"

I wonder if that lie is enough to send me straight to Hell.

"There's been another attack. Another parish child."

Morgan's shoulders sagged. "I heard. In fact, Smokey just left."

"Rounding up the usual suspects?"

Morgan winced. "Not really the time for me to channel my inner Casablanca."

"Sorry. Sometimes the lines just flow out. You and Taylor were home all night, right?"

"Yeah." *Though the window was open.* "They found Jennifer Peterson's DNA at the scene. Maybe you should go over there."

"No way!"

"Afraid so."

Garcia paced. "Haley's parents found an upstairs window open. It's all so strange, man. Someone climbed up to the second floor, and then someone else opened the window from the inside. At least that's what the father told me. He called, asking if the church could do anything."

"The church?"

"*Sí.* He's hoping I have some special prayer or ritual to keep evil spirits out of his home."

"Really?"

Garcia cleared his throat. "He says Haley was in a trance this morning. And he knows about the other kids who've been attacked. The entire community is freaking out."

"But the church? Sounds like a job for the police. Smokey's all over it."

Garcia coughed. "Is Taylor any better?"

"No. Still searching for the right treatment. I'm sure her issues are triggered by her mother's death." Morgan glanced at the ceiling, half expecting a lightning strike from an angry God. *Forgive me, Javi, but I can't tell you.*

"You talking therapy?"

"That's all there is, right? I mean, short of an exorcism."

Garcia stared at him blankly.

"I'm kidding," Morgan said. "You know, a little Catholic humor."

"There is nothing funny about an exorcism."

Morgan watched his friend closely. "You guys don't do those anymore, do you?"

"They are a necessary rite in a world with demons." Garcia wiped his brow with a sleeve.

"You really believe in demons?"

Garcia faced his friend. "Demons are part of the spiritual world. May as well ask me if I believe in Christ."

"You okay, Javi? You look shook up."

Garcia re-clutched his Bible. "Exorcisms and demons are a disturbing subject."

Morgan whistled. "You act like *you've* done an exorcism."

Garcia squirmed. "Even if I took part in one, I'm not at liberty to discuss it."

"Holy crap. You *did* do one. Why didn't you tell me?"

"It has the same rights to privacy as a confession. And, well, the church doesn't like to advertise them. As the world loses its collective faith, people like to mock some of our traditions. We keep a low profile on rituals like this."

"Did they try therapy? Medical treatment?"

"The church requires all medical and psychological efforts be made first. Exorcisms are only done as a last resort."

"Do they work?"

Garcia wiped away a tear. "Sometimes." He drew a deep breath. "Mine almost killed me." He shivered. "I mean, they can be devastating to the priests involved."

Morgan looked at his friend with a renewed sense of interest. "You should be a star in those beer commercials. You're the most interesting priest in the world."

"If the qualification is performing an exorcism, I'll pass. Demons are menacing, not only to those they possess but also to those who try to intervene. They can move from one host to another. They will reach into your mind and find your greatest fears and use them against you. Alter your sense of reality. They are as evil as evil can be."

Taylor's deep voice boomed from her bedroom. "Father Chancho! We meet again."

Garcia staggered into Morgan, who strained to keep him from collapsing. He bent over and grabbed his knees.

Morgan held him up. "You okay?"

"I recognize that voice."

"Where?"

Garcia stood and backed to the front door, his face ashen. "I'm sorry, but I have to go. You should be careful, Pennywise. I sense an evil you aren't equipped to handle."

CHAPTER 34

Garcia knelt at his bedside, shaking. The brilliant morning sun poured in, but he felt neither warmth nor joy at the majesty of a rare sunny day. Instead, he resisted saying the prayer he intended, haunted by the mocking voice at Morgan's home, and the failed exorcism a decade earlier that shook his confidence and faith.

That voice. Can it be the same demon?

His stomach cramped. *I did everything right at that exorcism. But the demon wouldn't leave.*

He recalled the horrified look on Patti's face during her exorcism. Her body contorted in inhuman ways. His despair when he, then a young priest assisting a seasoned exorcist, sagged to the floor in defeat and exhaustion. The victory in the demon's eyes.

A flood of thoughts he'd kept hidden deep inside gushed from their containment. *Why didn't it leave? If the power of Christ can't rid a young girl of a demon, what can it do? Is my calling a waste of time? Was I not worthy? Did she die because I didn't believe?*

Garcia rose and stared at his favorite possession, his Bible. His stomach churned and his throat burned after swallowing. He threw his Bible into the wall and wept.

My Godchild is afflicted with something evil. Maybe possessed by a demon. Perhaps the same evil spirit, mocking me. He bit his lip, drawing blood. *I need to grow a pair and warn Pennywise.*

Hold on. Two demonic possessions challenging me? Unlikely. Don't get Pennywise riled up for no reason.

Besides, even if it's a case of demonic possession, am I up to facing an exorcism again?

He looked up at the ceiling. "Is it you, Satan, who mocks me? Torments me? Tortures me? Or is it you, God? What did I do to cause you to forsake me?"

Though he had duties to attend to in the sanctuary, he collapsed and slept, without uttering a prayer.

CHAPTER 35

Morgan watched Taylor sleeping on her back, her mouth wide open. Her breath filled the room with a foul stench. Her complexion was transitioning from the earth tones to a shallow green. *She hasn't budged all morning. Since the sun came over the horizon.*

Azra announced herself at the front door.

"In Taylor's room." *Should I close her mouth? No. Might as well get to it.*

Azra entered wearing her white work smock with her name stenciled on the left breast.

"Thanks for coming during your lunch hour," Morgan said.

She came up and kissed him. "Always happy to have an excuse to come by."

"You need to see something." Morgan stepped aside, exposing Taylor's mouth and incisors.

Azra froze. "What happened to her teeth?"

"I'm hoping you can tell me. One thing's clear. Her condition isn't only mental."

Azra moved in cautiously. "How long?"

"Looks like a half inch."

Azra glared at him. "This is serious, Richard!"

Guilt ran along Morgan's backbone. "Sorry." *Even shrink's have to cope.* "A few days."

"And you didn't *call?*"

"They weren't this pronounced until today."

Azra slipped on a pair of latex gloves. "Her skin is almost pale green. She asleep?"

"Sedated."

Azra felt around Taylor's gum line, then examined the teeth. Morgan tensed, half expecting Taylor to chomp and cut off Azra's fingers. He kept that fear to himself, which brought on a new layer of guilt.

"What can cause this?" Morgan said.

"Not a clue. Tooth enamel shouldn't grow this fast. Any other symptoms?"

"She hates sunlight."

Azra continued her examination. "Not uncommon. Anything else?"

"The second personality is dominant now. Claims to be taking over."

"Are you ready to admit her to a psych ward?"

Morgan gently pulled Azra to the side. "I don't know what to believe. Remember Margarita? What she said would happen?"

"That lunatic? Surely, you're not falling for her nonsense?"

"Look at her, Azra. She attacked Jennifer, tried to bite her. She tells me she'll infect others. And now we know Jennifer assaulted another girl."

Azra stared back at Morgan.

"Say something," Morgan said.

"I think you're under a lot of stress. Whatever is going on here, it's a medical condition, perhaps both mental and physical. We're doctors. We'll find a solution."

"No, you won't," came a voice from the hallway.

Morgan spun and found Linda Copeland standing at the bedroom door in lime shorts and a yellow tank top, with her red shoes. *Shorts in Salem? In November? She looks like a fruitcake.*

"Hey," Morgan said. "You can't barge into my house."

Linda stepped into the room. "You're lucky I did. You're almost out of time."

Morgan flinched. "Out of time?"

"Based on my experience and research," Linda said, "your daughter has less than a week before she's lost forever."

His chest tightened again. *Lost forever?* "A week?"

"My best estimate," Linda said. "It might be less. I might be too late."

Morgan's knees buckled before he righted himself. *Too late?* He swallowed hard. *It can't be!*

"Who is this?" Azra said.

"My name's Linda Copeland. Professor of Indigenous Cultures, including the Bribri. I barged in at Dr. Morgan's office. I came to warn him."

"About what?" Azra said.

"About the monster his daughter has become."

Azra gave Morgan an exasperated glance. "Seriously, Richard?"

Morgan drew a breath. "I didn't take her seriously." He stared at Taylor. "Not then, anyway."

"*Not then?*" Azra exclaimed.

Linda stood over Taylor. "My daughter looked like this, before she died." Tears fell down Linda's cheeks. "So innocent. So deadly." She broke down and sobbed.

Azra lowered her voice. "You lost your daughter to something similar?"

"Not *similar. Exactly* this."

"Did her doctors ever diagnose what was wrong with her?" Azra said.

Linda shook her head and wiped tears away. "This girl is possessed by a demon. Being converted into a lamia. The Bribri *Awá* has some success with curing the victims. If it's not too late." She turned to Morgan. "If it *is* too late, she needs to be destroyed."

Destroyed. Morgan turned white.

Azra forced her way between Linda and Taylor. "Possessed? A demon? Destroyed? What's the matter with you? And what the hell is a lamia?"

Linda didn't back down. "It's a vampire who turns young girls into other lamias." She faced Morgan. "Has her language degraded yet?"

"What do you mean?" Morgan asked.

"Like I told you in your office, the lamia speaks in incomplete sentences. She'll have a lisp, a high voice, and bad grammar. Unlike the demon who is *very* clever, the lamia is not too intelligent."

"You're out of your mind," Azra said. "And don't you dare talk that nonsense around Taylor. You'll scare her."

Linda took another step closer. "You know I'm right."

Azra pushed Linda away from her fiancée. "Richard, aren't you going to do something?"

Morgan studied Taylor. *Her teeth. Her ghoulish complexion. And her thirst for blood. Her aversion to sunlight. Her irises. It's everything Linda and Margarita warned me about. I know it now. Why can't Azra see too?* He shifted his eyes to Azra, to Taylor, and back to Azra.

"Well?" Azra said.

Morgan felt pressured. He grabbed Linda's arm and escorted her into the hallway. "You need to go." When Linda refused to budge, Morgan whispered, "I need you to leave. I believe you, but I can't have you here while I persuade Azra."

Linda's mouth widened. She nodded her head in agreement and left.

Azra stepped into the hallway with Morgan. "What did you say to her?"

"I asked her to leave."

198

Azra studied Morgan's face, which blushed. "Can you believe the audacity? The insanity. That lady should be in *your* hospital."

Morgan followed Azra into the living room. *I'm convinced Linda's right. I wish I wasn't, but I am. And Taylor's life is at stake.*

If I'm too late, what will I do? Kill my daughter? Is that what's required to end her suffering?

"Richard, are you listening?"

Morgan shook himself. "I'm right here."

"You should report that woman."

"To who?"

"To someone. She's delusional."

Morgan sat with Azra on the sofa. "We should cut her some slack. She did lose her daughter."

"And I'm sorry for her loss. But to barge in here and say Taylor is some kind of monster?"

Morgan looked past Azra, toward Taylor's room. *A monster. Oh, Michelle. I could sure use your help.*

"Richard! What is it with you? It's like you're not even here."

"I'm here, Michelle."

Azra bolted to her feet. "Michelle? Seriously?"

"What?"

"You called me Michelle."

Morgan grimaced. "Oh, sorry."

"Sorry? That's it?"

Morgan stood up straight. An internal anger boiled over. "You need to stop criticizing me. My daughter's dying in there."

Azra hesitated at the force in Morgan's accusation. "She's not dying. We'll figure it out."

"I think Professor Copeland is telling the truth."

Azra backed away. "*What?*"

"Something unique infected Taylor in Costa Rica. The symptoms don't match any known pathogen, and it hasn't responded to traditional medicine."

Azra's eyes widened. "And we'll isolate it. Treat it. It's called *medicine*, for Christ's sake."

A painful spike pierced Morgan's mind. *Over and over again, the same shit. There must be a shortcut we can take through this repeated scene.* "How can you be sure? Wasn't it you who said there can be undiscovered diseases in the jungles?"

"I did. And, if that's the case here, we'll identify it and cure it."

"And if there's no medical treatment? What then?"

"It's way too early to jump to that kind of conclusion."

"There's no harm in listening to the professor," Morgan said. "We can follow both paths simultaneously."

Azra stiffened. "No, *we* can't."

"So, it's your way, or the highway?"

"I'm not willing to compromise everything I believe because we have a crisis. We need to stick to our training. And, have you considered your professional reputation? Your career is finished if word gets out you're promoting some kind of voodoo solution to an obvious psychological problem."

Morgan sagged. *She will never compromise. About Taylor's treatment or our relationship.* He held his head. "I can't let her infect anyone else."

"There's zero sign of contagion in the test results. None. Nada. Zilch."

"And yet, Jennifer looks to be infected. By Taylor."

"You don't know that."

Morgan stood up and gave Azra a stern look. "Yeah. I do. Taylor attacked Jennifer."

Azra's face flushed. "She what?"

"Taylor bit Jennifer. Jennifer welcomed it. Now these girls act like Taylor has some sort of spell over them."

Azra opened her mouth, but no sound emerged.

"Her incisors are turning into fangs," Morgan said, his voice rising until he approached yelling at her. "Why can't you see it?

She's barely recognizable. I'll tell you one thing. This charade you can cure her is over. It's time we faced the truth. And dealt with it."

"I see." Azra's lips pursed. "I'm a charade."

"That's not what I meant."

"It's exactly what you meant." She bit down on her lip. "To think I was going to build a life with you."

"Azra, don't do this."

"No!" She scrambled to the door. "You're right. It's time we dealt with it. Goodbye, Richard. Enjoy fantasizing about your ex."

"I'm not dreaming about Michelle. It's just her death and the impact on Taylor bumping around in my head."

"Enough! We're through. Do me one favor, will you? Get Taylor the help she needs. Not this crazy shit you're spouting off. Find her a *real* psychiatrist." She slammed the door on her way out.

Morgan took one step after her, but froze. *Let her go*. He went back to Taylor's room, put a sheet over her, and rushed to his bedroom, where Bear put his head on Morgan's knee.

"Looks like it's just us, buddy."

Morgan fell onto his bed, eyes closed, and broke down. Confused and exhausted, he wept. Bear whined, then licked his face, wiping his tears away.

"You're a good boy." Morgan rubbed Bear's head.

Bear wagged his tail.

"Can I tell you a secret? I know I should feel bad about Azra. I'm supposed to fight for her. But I can't."

Bear put his front paws on the bed.

"As soon as I realized Azra wasn't going to be able to help Taylor, I didn't care if she stayed. Maybe I'm the monster."

Bear jumped onto the mattress.

Morgan rubbed the Lab's stomach. "Appreciate the unconditional love. But we still have a problem. What are we going to do about Taylor?"

CHAPTER 36

After an unsatisfying dinner of canned soup, Morgan checked on Taylor. She continued to sleep, but someone had opened her window. Again? *What the hell? She's out cold. Isn't she?*

A wisp of snow blew inside. Morgan slid the window closed and latched it. His head ached, and he suffered from a tinge of remorse about his encounter with Azra. He considered calling Linda, his new ally, and a rush of adrenaline hit him, replacing the regret. *Who knew breaking off an engagement would be so cathartic?*

He set aside the concern Linda might want to destroy Taylor. *Surely she knows something that can lead us to a cure. I refuse to accept it's too late.*

Another notion gave him hope. *Maybe Javi can fix her. Perhaps an exorcism is the answer.*

His doorbell rang. *Is that Azra, wanting to make up? What do I tell her?*

He opened the front door without looking to see who had rung. Instead of Azra, he found an erect, tall man in spectacles and a pressed dark blue suit. Flicks of fresh snow like dandruff covered his black bowler. Morgan smelled lilac.

"Can I help you?" Morgan said.

The man first regarded Morgan's slippers, his brow furrowing.

"Yeah, they're bunnies," Morgan said. "And I don't give a shit if you like them or not. What do you want?"

The man returned his attention to Morgan's face, his own showing no emotion. He handed Morgan a business card and spoke in a strong British accent. "Allow me to introduce myself. Nathanial Quinn. Demon Specialist."

Morgan didn't know whether to laugh or cry. "Demon specialist?"

"Correct," Quinn said. "May I come in?"

"No, you may not." Morgan handed the card back. "Whatever you're selling, I'm not interested."

Morgan tried to close the door, but Quinn lodged his foot in.

"Dr. Morgan, I'm your one chance to save your daughter."

Morgan narrowed his eyes. "Who told you she needs saving?"

"Let me in, and I'll reveal everything."

"Did Professor Copeland send you?"

"No. I dare say, you don't have time to waste. Hear me out."

"You'll explain it from out there, or not at all."

Quinn reached inside his jacket and retrieved a piece of paper. "Jolly good. Have a look at this."

Morgan took the page. It contained a long list of names. "What's this?"

"References. People I've saved. Look into them. Their stories are all a matter of public record. When you realize I'm your best chance, call me."

"You still haven't explained how you know about my daughter."

"It's my job to follow all demon afflictions," Quinn said.

"You with a church?"

"Oh, no. My technique isn't based on religious doctrine. It's more of a medical procedure."

Morgan ran his tongue around his gums. Despite trying to suppress his excitement, his heart raced. *Medical? And believes she's possessed? Is this guy the best of both worlds?*

Careful. He sounds too good to be true. "Medical? Sorry, bud. We're full up with doctors trying to solve this." *In fact, I chased one away. And she had sex with me.*

"Are you going to allow me in? It's bloody bitter out here."

It can't hurt to listen. Morgan swung the door open. "Five minutes. Take a seat."

Quinn followed directions. "I am sorry. Bad luck to run into this demon. Nasty bugger. Calls itself *Bé*, right?"

Morgan sat across from him, stunned. "You're familiar with *Bé*?"

"I am. One of Satan's original demons. Came to America with the Spaniards. Embedded itself in the Bribri tribe and took their culture's moniker."

"What do you do, exactly?"

"Purge victims like your daughter of the demon inside. For good. Guaranteed."

Morgan scoffed. "Yeah, right."

"I'm dead serious, Dr. Morgan. I can save your daughter. If we act quickly."

Morgan's skin crawled at the implied urgency. *This guy can't be for real, can he?* "If you were to treat my daughter, what would it entail?"

"I'm sorry. That's proprietary."

Morgan laughed. "You want me to turn my daughter's life over to you, and you won't tell me what you plan to do?"

"I intend to cure her. This demon has a specific fear. I can make it leave. And isn't chasing it away your only aim?"

Absolutely. And he collaborates Linda's story. Plus, we wouldn't have to go to Costa Rica to save her. But I can't put her through anything I don't understand.

"Uh huh. Well, your five minutes are up, Mr. Quinn. Have a nice life."

Quinn rose and retreated in his perfect posture. "Check my references, Dr. Morgan. Call me. But please hurry. The point of no return is imminent."

"I'm not calling you."

Quinn did his best Cheshire Cat impression. "Oh, you'll call." He walked away from the house.

Morgan grabbed his cell and dialed Garcia. "Javi, I need your help."

Garcia's answered in a subdued voice. "Pennywise. What time is it?"

"Six in the evening. Did I wake you?"

"I must have dozed off. Good thing you called. I have the after-school groups arriving soon."

"Listen, I'm convinced something supernatural is in play with Taylor." He exhaled. "Can you help me?"

After a long pause Garcia responded in a shaky voice. "What do you need me to do?"

"One way to verify my suspicions is to douse her in Holy Water. That'll get a reaction, right?"

"That's a complicated question."

"Come on, Javi. I think you believe she's possessed. Can't you help me?"

After another awkward delay, Garcia spoke. "I'll be there as soon as I can."

CHAPTER 37

Smokey parked in seclusion under a row of bushy trees with a clear view of Morgan's home. And, most importantly, Taylor's window. He ran his windshield wipers to brush the falling snow away. With his windows closed, the smell of his unlit cigar permeated the sedan's cabin. Dusk rapidly approached.

My instincts tell me to stand watch, and they rarely disappoint. Smokey shifted his attention to Taylor's bedroom window. He took his camera off the passenger seat. *If you go out tonight, I'll catch you in the act.*

The front door opened, and a tall man with spectacles walked away. Smokey snapped two pictures. *And who might you be?*

Morgan appeared at the doorway to shut it after the stranger left.

Smokey's cell phone vibrated. *The D.A.'s office? What do they want?* "Smokey."

"Detective, it's Campbell. I want you to bring Morgan and his daughter in."

"You found the witness?"

"No. I've decided it's best for everyone here to extradite them to Costa Rica. Let them deal with this mess."

Smokey sat up straight. "But I'm not done investigating the suspicious death of Michelle Morgan. Not to mention the bizarre happenings with kids linked to Taylor Morgan."

"Afraid you are."

"I don't understand. Why the rush to extradite?"

After a long delay, Campbell continued. "It's a win for everyone. My office receives calls all day about the Morgan's being a danger to the community."

"We have no evidence," Smokey interrupted.

"Listen. The crimes occurred in Costa Rica. If we can't prove he offed his ex, it's only a matter of time before we extradite them both to answer for killing their policemen. They have the bodies. There's no reason not to send them both now. It calms everyone down in Salem. And it takes this off your plate. Win, win, win."

Smokey's mind swirled. "I'm not in it for the win. I'm in it to find out what happened. What if he's telling the truth?"

"About not killing his ex? About not killing their officers?"

"All of it. Without that witness we've got nothing. And what if he and Taylor are in mortal danger in Costa Rica?"

"Not our problem."

Smokey slammed the dash. "I'm not comfortable with this."

"You think he's innocent?"

"I don't know. That's why I'm *investigating*. He believes they'll be at risk down there. They think he's a cop killer."

"He should have considered the consequences of his actions."

"So you're acting as judge and jury now?"

"You have your orders. Pack them up. Ship them out." The line disconnected.

Smokey pounded the steering wheel once more. His stomach knotted. *Morgan may be guilty of something, but this isn't right.*

Smokey rubbed his chin. *Orders, my ass. There's only one way to finish my investigation. I have to arrest the Doc. They can't make me extradite him if he's facing real charges here.* He chomped on his cigar. *But for what? Campbell won't settle for speculation. I need hard evidence to hold him.*

A movement near Taylor's window caught his attention. He

shoved his phone into his overcoat and raised the camera to get a better look. He expected to see Taylor climbing out. Instead, a silhouette lurked outside the window. *Who are you?* He focused his lens on the shadow. *Female. Hispanic. Don't recognize her.*

The figure wedged something into the base of Taylor's window. *What the hell? Someone's trying to get* in. *Now I have vigilantes?*

A blade flashed in the moonlight.

Shit. That's a knife. She's jimmying the window open. His breathing stopped. *That's not a knife. It's a machete.*

CHAPTER 38

Morgan recognized Smokey's voice yelling from out front. "Stop! Salem police."

He opened the entry door to find Smokey charging Taylor's window. *Oh, no. She's trying to get out again.* He rushed outside, hoping to keep Smokey from seeing Taylor's teeth.

But primal fear replaced his concern. Margarita stood at Taylor's window armed with a machete. She'd pried it open and had a knee on the sill.

Morgan reeled with a vertigo attack. *She found us.* Still in his slippers, the world spinning around him, he rushed outside towards Margarita, but lost his footing on the icy ground, and crashed into frozen dirt.

"Margarita's after Taylor," Morgan yelled to Smokey.

Margarita had her rump on Taylor's windowsill, and both legs were inside.

"Stop!" Smokey commanded. "I *will* shoot you!"

But Margarita didn't flinch. She dropped into Taylor's room.

With only seconds before Margarita would reach Taylor, Morgan overcame the merry-go-round in his head and scrambled back inside the front door and raced to Taylor's room.

Margarita stood over Taylor's sleeping body. Her machete poised to strike.

"No!" Morgan screamed.

Smokey shouted, "Freeze!" from outside the window.

But Margarita paid no attention. She swung the machete toward Taylor.

Morgan lunged across the room, landing on top of Taylor's body. A sharp pain sliced into his shoulder and a gunshot exploded.

Margarita shrieked.

Morgan rolled toward Margarita while still trying to protect Taylor. The machete lay on the floor, a red smear along the blade. *My blood.* She held her right shoulder, a bullet wound leaking crimson.

He checked Taylor, still sedated and unharmed, before he grabbed the machete and threw it aside.

"You bitch." He clenched his fist and slugged Margarita across the jaw.

She crumpled to the floor, and Morgan stood over her, like Ali over Liston.

"Stand down, Doc," Smokey said from the window. "I'll be right in."

Morgan kicked her in the side one more time before Smokey charged through the bedroom door, gun drawn.

"You okay?" Smokey said.

"I'm all right. Not too deep."

Taylor spoke. "Me smell blood."

Morgan turned and found Taylor sitting up, her eyes blazing red, with a longing expression, staring at his wound. He glanced at Smokey, afraid he'd see her teeth, but the detective was handcuffing Margarita.

"This the Costa Rican woman?" Smokey said.

"Yeah," Morgan said. "Margarita. I hit her pretty hard."

"Yeah. She's out cold." Smokey ran into the bathroom and came back with a wet towel. "Put this on your wound."

Morgan took the towel and Smokey dialed his cell phone. "This is Lieutenant Smokey. I have a gunshot victim at Dr. Morgan's home. And a knife laceration. Send paramedics, stat." He hung up. "Help's on the way."

"Thanks," Morgan said. "Glad you were here to stop her. We'd both be dead without you."

Taylor squirmed, but the sedative kept her stationary. "Want blood." She opened her mouth and flicked her tongue at Morgan's seeping shoulder.

"Holy shit," Smokey gasped. "Look at her teeth."

Morgan cut off Smokey's line of sight. "She's not well."

Smokey narrowed his eyes. "She bit those girls, didn't she?"

Morgan's vertigo kicked up a notch. "You read the DNA report. They cleared her."

"You can't expect me to ignore the evidence right in front of me."

"I think she's possessed," Morgan said, his voice fading. He passed out.

CHAPTER 39

Garcia pulled up in front of Morgan's home and gaped at the flashing ambulance and police lights. The snowfall had stopped, and the haze of the moon fought through the clouds on the horizon. *Oh, man. This is bad.*

He met the ER staff wheeling Morgan out the front. His heart sank when he saw his ashen friend, eyes closed and drool leaking down his chin. "What happened?"

The lead ER guy noticed Garcia's robe, collar, and stole. "Knife wound. Doesn't look too bad."

Thank God for that. The demon do this? "Where's his daughter?"

"Inside with the police. The other woman is on her way to the hospital."

"Other woman?"

"The one who attacked the daughter. Lieutenant Smokey says Morgan saved his daughter's life. The detective winged the perp."

Garcia charged into the bedroom. He screeched to a halt when he beheld Taylor. Her incisors poked out from under her lip. His heart pounded. "Jesus Christ."

"Padre!" Smokey said.

Garcia stepped closer to Taylor. She sat up staring at Lieutenant Smokey. "I saw the red eyes last time. But her teeth. What happened here?"

"That Margarita woman from Costa Rica tried to chop Taylor's head off with a machete. She took a chunk of Morgan's shoulder before I stopped her." He looked deep into Garcia's eyes. "Morgan was right about her. About the risk to them in Costa Rica. The D.A. wants to send them both back. I can't let that happen. No matter what Morgan did, there'll be no justice there."

Taylor sat back against her headboard. She grinned, exposing the full extent of her teeth. Garcia brandished his Bible in a protective stance between them.

"Hell of a thing, Padre. Ever seen something like this?"

Thank God I'm not alone with her.

"Padre?"

"Yeah, a hell of a thing." *Hell being the operative word.*

"Before he passed out, the Doc said he thinks she's possessed. What's your take on that?"

Garcia swallowed. "Demonic possession is very rare. Some medical or psychological disorder is more likely." *Except, it called me by the same name the other demon did. And that was no psychological condition.*

"Are incisors like hers a side-effect of possession?"

"No." A surge ran through Garcia's body. *Her teeth argue for this not being a demon. Maybe she doesn't need an exorcism.*

Taylor smiled wide at Garcia. Her eyes twinkled.

Is she reading my mind? He shivered. *Stop it! She's my goddaughter. I might be her only chance.*

Taylor cackled. "She's already lost."

Smokey cleared his throat. "I need to go down to the station to book Margarita, then check on the Doc. I'm leaving an officer to watch her. You going to be okay?"

Hell, no. "Do what you have to. I'll stay."

"Do you think she's dangerous?"

Hell, yes. "I'll be fine."

"The patrolman can wait in here with you."

Garcia remembered the holy water. "I need to be alone with her." *I must be crazy. But I must evaluate her in private. If she becomes hostile, I'll call for help.*

What if the patrolman's too late? What if the demon comes after me? Remember everything they taught you in Demon 101? Never be alone with it. "Tell him it's a religious rite that requires privacy. I'll let him know when he can come in."

"Humph. Whatever you say, Padre." Smokey let himself out.

Father Garcia crossed himself and approached the bed. *May Christ be with me.* "Hello, Taylor."

Taylor's irises converted from red to black, and her skin tone shifted toward green. "I remember you," Taylor growled.

Her eyes changed. What the heck?

Garcia steadied himself. "You see me all the time."

"That was the sow. *We* call you Father Chancho. Come to fail at another exorcism?"

The blood drained from Garcia's face. *The pig. What the demon called me at the exorcism.* He collected himself. "The sow?"

"Taylor. She doesn't live here anymore."

Garcia took a deep breath and sat on the edge of the bed. He clutched his Bible, keeping it between them. *Don't get too close. Even sedated, she's could be dangerous.* "That's too bad. I like Taylor."

"You like all the young girls, don't you, Father Chancho? Should I tell your friends your secret?"

Garcia stiffened. *Don't take the bait.* "I don't have any secrets. I came to talk with my friend, Taylor."

Taylor cackled. "We both know better, don't we? Your indiscretion in high school? Convicted of raping a fifteen-year-old. What would your parish say?"

Garcia made a fist. "I didn't rape her! I protected her from her abusive father!" He lowered his eyes. "I crossed the state line to take her to her uncle."

"Statutory rape is rape. So, how did your failure turn out? Oh, yes. The uncle returned the girl to her father. She was dead in a month. Nice job, Father Chancho. Another soul lost on your watch."

The room spun. "I was a minor. They sealed those records."

"You can't hide anything from me. I am omniscient."

Garcia tried to swallow, but his mouth was an arid wasteland.

"Your failure drove you to become a priest," Taylor continued. "To find absolution. How's that working out for you?"

Garcia fumbled the Bible onto the bed. *You're falling for its mind games. Stop it!* "Let's talk about you. Where do you come from?" When he didn't get a response he tried a different tack. "What's your name?"

"They call me *Bé.*"

"That's an odd name."

"Not my name. Who Bribri called me."

What does that mean? "Tell me *your* name."

"*Spero Latinam numquam perire!*"

You hope Latin never dies? What's that got to do with anything? "You speak Latin?"

A chuckle. "Doesn't everyone?"

Not everyone. He shuddered. *And definitely not Taylor.* "What were you saying?"

"Don't insult me. I *know* you understand Latin."

"Fair enough. Let's try this again. *Quis nornen tuus est?*"

Taylor's nostrils flared. "*Iratissimus sum et semper ero populi omnis esse!*"

"Why are you the angriest of all people to exist?"

"*Mihi iratum non face; tu me non amabis cum ego iratus sum.*"

Garcia flinched at the message: *Don't make me angry; you won't like me when I'm angry.* He inhaled deeply. "You still haven't told me your name."

"*Lilith sum.*"

"And how did you get here?"

"Columbus."

"Christopher Columbus?"

Taylor burrowed her chin into her chest.

Garcia pulled a small book out of his robe. His hands shook like he was jackhammering concrete. *The sedation seems to have her under control. Let's see how she reacts.* "Taylor, I'm going to perform an Exorcism Blessing."

Taylor hissed at him. "*Eam ab me potes capere.*"

You can never take her away from me? Is Taylor referring to herself in the third person? He wiped his forehead and began. "Our help is in the name of the Lord, who made Heaven and Earth. I exorcise this demon in the name of God, the Father Almighty, who made Heaven and Earth, the sea, and all that is in them. May God uproot and expel from you all power of the adversary, all attacks of the devil, and all deceptions of Satan. We make this prayer in the name of the Almighty Father, of Jesus Christ, his Son our Lord, and of the Holy Spirit. Amen."

Taylor belched.

Garcia pocketed the book. He studied her, looking for any sign of discomfort, and found none. "How do you feel, Taylor?"

Taylor suddenly lunged forward until her face was inches from Garcia's. The shock stunned him, and he couldn't move. Opening her mouth wide, she exposed her razor-sharp fangs, and hissed. A foul stench erupted from her throat, and Garcia gagged. He gathered himself and leaned back, then rose from the bed. In his panic, he lost the grip on his Bible, and it tumbled to the floor.

That smell. Nothing human about that.

Taylor lay back. "Priest afraid."

Garcia choked back his disgust and retrieved his Bible. He looked at it with renewed interest. "You know what this is?"

Taylor narrowed her eyes to tiny slits.

"It's the Holy Bible," Garcia said. "The Word of God. It also commands you to leave Taylor's body."

Taylor reached for his Bible and snatched it away. He stumbled after it out of instinct, and realized, too late, he was within her reach.

She scratched his neck with her fingernails, drawing blood. He withdrew, fear racing through his veins. "Give me that!"

Taylor's eyes glistened. "Priest is nothing without his book. You have no virility at all. Not like Adam."

Garcia grabbed his Bible. Adam? As in Adam and Eve? He pulled, but she resisted, surprising him with her strength, and they held the book in a draw.

Then Taylor released it, and Garcia fell backwards, landing on his ass. He crawled to his feet and secured the Bible in his robe. After a deep breath, he decided to try one last rite.

He pulled out a vial of the holy water. I don't know what to believe. The teeth argue against possession. But other behaviors argue for it. This should piss off the demon if it is one. He uncapped the water and threw streams onto Taylor. "I command you, with this holy water, to depart!"

Taylor screeched and churned, steam rising from her skin. "Stop!"

Garcia stumbled backwards. Holy Virgin Mary. She is possessed! He capped the vial, his face devoid of color. I have to stop. I can't go through this again.

The steam dissipated and Taylor calmed. "So, Father Chancho, now you understand. You must face me again. And you are more afraid than ever."

"You're not the same demon."

Taylor grinned, flashing her incisors. "Does it matter?" She curled up into a ball. "Lamia rest now. Change faster when sleeping." While he watched in amazement, her irises reverted to red, and her skin color shifted back to a light chocolate.

That didn't happen at the last exorcism. Something's different.

He recalled his failed exorcism, wondering how much faith he had left, and which demon he now faced.

I have to tell the Church. She's been through the medical and psychiatric hoops. She needs an exorcism. And I won't have to be involved. The Church won't let me take part because I'm her priest.

A sense of relief washed over him. But the feeling fell away. But what if they have no choice? It's not like there are a bunch of exorcists out there. What if I have no option?

Either way, I owe it to Taylor to tell Pennywise.

But he realized he wouldn't inform anyone.

CHAPTER 40

Saturday

Morgan woke up in the ER to fumes of alcohol and cleaning solvent. Tubes jutted from his arm, and bandages covered his shoulder, which hurt like hell. Momentary confusion about his whereabouts cleared. *Margarita found us.* He shuddered.

"Welcome back, Doc." Morgan's blurred vision focused on Smokey. "ER guys say you'll be fine."

"Where's Taylor?"

"The Padre is with her."

"By himself?" *Oh, shit.* He tried to sit up, but the pain kept him prone.

"There's a policeman on site. Margarita's in custody. She won't hurt Taylor."

It's not Taylor I'm worried about. "Is the sun up?"

"Yeah. Why?"

Morgan let out a breath. "There's plenty to discuss, but first, I need my phone." After Smokey handed it over, Morgan called Garcia. "Javi. You okay?"

"*Sí.* Concerned about you."

"Did Taylor do anything to you?"

"She's been asleep for hours."

"You're sure? You've been with her the whole time?"

"I'm sure. Listen, I gave her an Exorcism Blessing, and tried holy water on her."

"And?" Morgan held his breath. *Please tell me it worked.*

"No reaction." Garcia hesitated. "Pretty much eliminates a demonic possession. Are *you* all right?"

"I'm fine. Listen, I'll be home soon. We need to talk before the sun goes down. Taylor should sleep all day. If she wakes up, keep her in the house. There's a syringe loaded with a sedative in my sock drawer. Use it if you have to."

"I'm not going to sedate Taylor."

"Don't argue with me, okay?"

"Okay."

After Morgan hung up, he pried himself to a sitting position. His pain shot past the 10/10 level, and he grimaced. "I need to get out of here."

Smokey took the phone. "What's going on, Doc?"

"I'll tell you and Javi everything. Then I'll beg you both for a favor, and some mercy. First, take me home."

"Listen, Doc. I have tough news."

"Let me guess. You're arresting Taylor for attacking those girls."

"DA Campbell is granting the extradition request. I'm supposed to take you both in."

Morgan's stomach cramped and growled in angst. "You can't. They'll kill Taylor."

"I believe you. At least about the risk in Costa Rica."

"Can't you arrest me to keep us here?"

Smokey eyed him. "The DA won't go for it without a solid case. I tried to convince him about my fresh suspicions about the attacks on those girls, but he's using the DNA evidence to justify letting Taylor go."

"Can you interview Margarita and get confirmation they plan to kill us if we're sent back? Or use my injury to buy us some time?"

Smokey pulled out a fresh cigar and shoved it into his mouth. "Humph. That might work."

"Interrogating Margarita?"

"Convincing the ER doctor to say you're not fit to travel."

Morgan closed his eyes. The pain overtook his adrenaline spike, and wooziness struck. "Use any excuse. I'll tell you why when we get back to my place."

* * *

After a full day of waiting to be cleared, and constant check-ins with Garcia, who reported Taylor was still asleep, Smokey escorted Morgan home. Sunset approached, driving Morgan's fear to new heights. "Please hurry. We have to beat nightfall."

"Why?"

"I'll tell you at the house." Morgan watched the sun advance on the horizon, then switched his attention to the speedometer. His chest muscles clenched. *This'll be close.* "Can you use the siren?"

Smokey gave him a sideways glance. "Beating sunset is that important?"

"It's that important."

Smokey grunted, but placed his portable siren on the roof and activated it. The lights flashed, and the alarm blared, much louder than Morgan expected.

Morgan exhaled. "Thanks. And thanks for getting me the reprieve on the extradition. You must have been very persuasive."

"Don't thank me yet. It won't buy you more than a few days. So, tell me, did Taylor attack those kids?"

"When we get to the house."

* * *

Garcia met them at the front door, slightly ahead of sunset. Morgan grasped his arms. "You're okay?"

"*Bueno*."

Morgan patted him on the cheek, then went for his hardware drawer in the kitchen. He grabbed a hammer and nails and sealed Taylor's bedroom window. *There. No more walkabouts for you.* He lowered the shade. "The sun's setting. She'll wake up any second."

"Is this mental illness, Doc? Her skin looks almost green."

"That was my original diagnosis. Now, I think she's possessed by a demon. You can tell the demon's in charge when her complexion turns this color, and her irises turn black. Then, there's another beast who takes control, turns her irises red and her skin pale. Some kind of vampire. One that preys on young girls." Morgan turned to Garcia. "You *must* do an exorcism."

Garcia shifted, looking uncomfortable. "I told you. I tested her. There's no evidence of possession."

"Trust me. She's possessed. I need you to do this."

"Even if she is. I'm not allowed," Garcia said, his own complexion competing with Taylor on the pale scale. "The Church approves exorcisms at a level much higher than me. There are interviews, evaluations, prayers, many acts before deciding to take that course of action."

"Like what?" Morgan said, his impatience and desperation rising.

Garcia inhaled. "The Church will demand I've tried all medical and psychological options. Evidence of a demon, and a probability it can be removed. Only then will they put together an exorcism team."

"A team?" Morgan said.

"*Sí.*" Garcia swallowed. "It takes several priests, and a support staff. No one can be alone with the demon. Demons are liars, man. They attack where you are most vulnerable. Prey on your fears and guilt. It's takes months to decide, and they approve few. And they often fail."

"Doesn't the church believe the power of Christ can overcome any demon?" Morgan said.

Garcia held up his answer and lowered his voice. "At a theological level, sí. But not all decisions in the Church are made on doctrine. Sometimes the Bishops don't want to get involved. Finding capable exorcists isn't easy."

"What makes an exorcist qualified?"

"Because the fight gets so personal, the Church wants one with nothing to lose. People who feel they have a lot to forfeit have trouble going all in. And, they want someone with experience, who has gone into battle before, and survived."

"Some don't survive?"

"Sí. And some abandon their calling and quit. Few have the stomach for the fight."

"It's Taylor, Javi. What if you're her last chance?"

Garcia took a full two minutes to respond. "I did an Exorcism Blessing. I flashed my Bible at her. Sprinkled her with holy water. No reaction to any of them. I don't have any evidence to argue for the exorcism rite."

"She's your godchild," Morgan said.

Garcia squirmed. "And that eliminates me. Even if the Church agrees to go forward, they must find other priests. There aren't many priests with experience, and most aren't eager to go through it again."

Morgan's gut winced. *There's something else going on here. What aren't you telling me?*

Taylor stirred, then sat up. She grinned at Morgan. Her black irises mocked him. "Back for more?" Her tresses stuck to her face in streaks. She switched her attention to Garcia. "Should I tell them about the girl you raped?"

Garcia bolted forward. "Shut up!"

"Javi?" Morgan said.

"Father?" Smokey said.

"It's nothing," Garcia said. "You can't believe anything a demon says."

Morgan made a fist. "So you *do* believe it's a demon."

Garcia stared at the floor. "No. A slip of the tongue."

"Like hell," Morgan said. "You're convinced she's possessed."

"It doesn't matter. Without evidence, the Church won't act."

"You do not understand," Taylor said.

Morgan glared at Garcia before turning back to Taylor. "What don't we understand?"

"Taylor is gone. The sow's a lamia now." She pointed her head toward the sky and howled like a wolf.

Morgan retrieved another shot of sodium thiopental. He approached her, and she shrieked. "No! The lamia needs to hunt!"

Morgan jabbed her before she could stop him. She spit at him, but she showed the sedative's effects. He eased her back on the bed, and she fell asleep.

Smokey joined Morgan at her side. "Damn, Doc. What's happening here?"

"I need to keep her sedated at night," Morgan said. "Otherwise, she'll go after more girls. And turn them."

"Turn them into what?" Smokey said.

"Monsters like her." Morgan spun on Smokey and Garcia. "You see why she needs an exorcism? Why we can't throw her in jail?"

Smokey took a deep breath. "Why demonic possession, and not some vampire ritual?"

"The Catholic Church has vampire rituals?" Morgan said.

Garcia blanched. "Not officially. There were rumors centuries ago. The legend of vampires was strong in Europe in the dark ages. It wouldn't surprise me if the Church had a way to calm the people, even if they didn't believe in nosferatu."

Blood rushed to Morgan's face. "Javi, you've got to get her an exorcism. You're her only chance."

Garcia looked his friend in the eyes. "I can't."

"Why? You saw her. That's a demon in there. It talked to us."

"I'm sorry. Like I said, the Church won't approve it."

"You're afraid, aren't you?" Morgan said, his voice rising.

"You're damn right I'm terrified," Garcia yelled back. "You can't comprehend what it's like."

Morgan stewed. "Fine. Go!"

"Pennywise, don't."

"If you're too afraid to help your own goddaughter, you're no use to her. Get out."

Garcia's lips quivered. "I'm so sorry. I wish I could do more." He waited a moment, then lowered his head and shuffled out.

After an awkward silence, Smokey cleared his throat. "Doc, I have a problem."

"I know. You need to take Taylor in. But what good will it do? She can't assist in your investigation. Or answer your questions. All you can do is lock her up, with no hard evidence, because of her teeth. Which your own crime lab says aren't involved."

Smokey stepped up to the bed. "I'll admit I don't understand what's going on here. But demon possession? You believe that?"

"I do. She's a good girl. She deserves a chance."

Morgan and Smokey walked back to the living room and sat on the couch. Smokey pulled out his cigar and chomped on the tip. "What about her teeth? They match the folklore about the creatures of the night."

Morgan smirked at Smokey. "So, you draw the line at demons, but vampires are possible?"

"There are lots of unanswered questions, and this lamia thing is consistent with the attacks. I can't ignore it. And then there's Margarita. Coming here to kill Taylor. She must believe."

"Do what you need to do to me, detective, but let me save Taylor first. If an exorcism is out, I have another idea to heal her. Please give me that chance. I'll make you a deal. If you leave her with me, let me execute my plan, I'll confess to killing Michelle. Take that off your plate."

Smokey melted into the couch. "I'm not interested in false confessions."

If you knew about the drug log, you wouldn't dismiss a confession so quickly. "Maybe it's not false. I've admitted I don't remember, so perhaps I did it. Either way, I'll be grateful to you for giving Taylor a chance to survive. And you'll get a lot of glory out of the deal. They'll probably give you the keys to the city."

Smokey peered down the hallway toward her room. "All right, Doc. I'll keep guards outside so you can both stay here. At least until the ER doctor clears you. Then I'll have no choice but to extradite you to Costa Rica." He grunted. "The chief will have my ass in a sling if this goes sideways."

"Not to worry. I'll confess to Michelle's murder before extradition happens. That way Taylor will never get sent to Costa Rica. You'll lock me up and Taylor will go to her grandparents. The task force won't know where to find her, and she'll be safe."

"I'm not convinced, Doc. Even with motive, opportunity, and a clever cover-up my gut says you don't have it in you. And my gut has a damn good track record."

"I admit I'm having trouble with the motivation part. I've always cherished Michelle."

"Humph. Maybe that *was* the incentive. Couldn't stand her being with another man."

CHAPTER 41

Garcia drove to Saint Edward's, his vision clouded by tears and the road covered in dense fog. The wind rammed into the car, and he rocked and rolled like a fifties oldie-but-goodie.

I lied to my best friend. I'm abandoning my goddaughter in her time of crisis. Has there ever been a weaker priest?

After parking, he stayed in his car. *How can I do this to Taylor?* But another voice reminded him, *Her symptoms aren't classic for it. You can't be sure it's a demon.*

Exhausted by his internal debate, he cut through a heavy fog to the main entrance. The wind sliced through him like a blowtorch through ice. He clutched his Bible like never before.

Stop rationalizing. I know Taylor needs an exorcism.

He nearly bumped into a parishioner in the foyer. "Quite a morning we're having, eh, Father?"

You have no idea. "Sí. Everything okay with you? Anything I can do?"

"Oh, no. Lighting a candle for my husband. Been gone three years now. I'm surprised to see you down here. I heard you upstairs."

"No, I've been out. The storm, most likely."

She gave him a puzzled expression. "Wind doesn't make loud footsteps, Father. Did you run into the Peterson girl?"

"Jennifer?"

"Yeah. She went up to your room earlier." He looked down her glasses at Garcia. "Highly irregular, if you ask me."

Garcia shivered. He looked up the stairs toward his private bedroom. Darkness shrouded the hallway. "With her parents?"

"Alone." The suspicion hit him square in the head.

"Nothing to worry about. Her parents were bringing her by to talk about the youth group. You must have not seen them."

She frowned. "I see." She bundled herself for the frigid gust outside. "I better get back. My cats will worry." She exited through the front.

Garcia fought a surreal resistance to close the door. Once secured, he peered up the staircase.

Jennifer Peterson?

He walked carefully upstairs, his senses on high alert. The wind pummeled the side of the building, and the walls moaned.

He reached the summit and paused. His stomach lurched. *If I'm afraid to do my duty, it's time to get out.* He scowled at the heavens and screamed. "*Sí*! I admit it! I'm horrified!"

More loud moaning sounds replied.

A subdued light shone under the door. *Either somebody opened my blinds, or turned the light on while I was out.* He shook as he reached for the doorknob.

The light in his room snapped off. Garcia jumped back, holding his pounding chest. *Someone's still in there.* He swallowed. *Or something.*

He swung the door open. The blinds were sealed tight and pitch blackness met him, along with a putrid stench. *Oh, Jesus. It smells like someone died.*

"Hello?" No reply. "Anybody in there?" No answer. "Jennifer?" He steeled himself and flipped on the light switch. And stumbled into the wall.

The cross normally above his bed lay on the floor, broken into slivers. Shards of glass from his mirror peppered the cheap carpet.

And, on the opposite wall, fresh blood-red letters drizzled from the ceiling to the floor. The message warned him. "Stay away."

He collapsed to his knees. He looked at his Bible, held it close, and prayed for his own survival. *God, I know I'm not worthy, but please don't let the demon take possession of me.*

A sharp tug ripped the Bible from him. It flew across the room, slamming against the wall under the warning and landing on his pillow, open to the New Testament. The Bible vibrated, and pages tore, flying around the room as if in a tornado. Garcia instinctively threw his body on top of the Bible, pinning the pages.

The blast spoke to him. *Javier. Javier.*

Outrage at the desecration temporarily emboldened him. "You don't scare me," he yelled to the invisible voice.

Liar, liar, the squall responded.

And then the storm withdrew. He lay curled in a fetal position for five minutes before he felt strong enough to move. He picked up the torn pages and taped them back.

I've been warned. Interfere, and I'm next.

CHAPTER 42

The grandfather clock ticked into afternoon, the only sound after the morning's storm had cleared. Freshly brewed coffee gave off a comforting aroma. Smokey was gone, and Taylor slept in her room. In the dining room, Morgan searched for internet hits on Nathanial Quinn. *If Javi refuses to help, and Linda's solution sends us to our death in Costa Rica, what do I have to lose?*

He found only two posts. A woman in Australia claimed Quinn drove a demon out of her daughter, now five years clear of the life-threatening event. A second post asserted Quinn saved a young boy a year earlier.

Two? Not exactly a confidence builder.

Neither article mentioned an organized religion, or the term *exorcism*. Rather, they referred to a medical procedure, of Quinn's own design, which had done what the church could not.

A loud crash broke his concentration. *Shit. Taylor's room.* He raced to her door, dread overwhelming skepticism. He barged in and froze.

Taylor appeared to be asleep, but her bed sat several feet from the wall. *How did that happen? The wood frame and headboard weigh a ton.*

"Taylor? You awake?"

When she didn't respond he strained to push the bed against the wall. *No way my Taylor could have moved this.* He stepped back to the door and watched her. Her breathing came in starts and stops. Her lips were cracking. He applied vaseline with his finger, half expecting her to wake up and maul him. *Stop it. The sedative has her unconscious.*

Satisfied with her lips, he lowered his head, went back into the hallway, and closed the door behind him. He got only two steps when the loud noise repeated itself. He took a deep breath and swung the door open.

The bed had again moved away from the wall.

He pulled out Quinn's business card and made the call.

* * *

Quinn arrived within minutes. He wore a pitch-black suit with a red bow tie set against a white shirt, with scuffed dress shoes torn at the toes. "Dr. Morgan. I'm glad you called. I was about to move on."

Morgan motioned toward the couch. "Have a seat. I have questions."

"Of course." Quinn sat, and Morgan settled in the chair across from him. "Let's get down to business, shall we? You've seen your daughter's inevitable deterioration, and you're desperate for a solution. One only I can provide."

"You'll excuse me if I'm a little skeptical."

Quinn laughed, exposing yellow teeth. "You have questions. I'm happy to answer. As long as they aren't about my proprietary process."

"Let's start with the obvious. If you're so good at this, how come I can find only two articles? How many have you done? How many worked? And by 'worked,' I'm talking permanent. No ill effects from the disease, or your process."

"Excellent questions. I've done hundreds of these, and never a dissatisfied customer."

"Then why no mention of them?"

Quinn raised an eyebrow. "Do you want to advertise your child is afflicted with this? Will your daughter's life ever be the same if word gets out?"

"No."

"I never out my clients. The two you found on the internet are unique. The names of the families are all fabricated, by them, to protect their child. They were willing to go that far because they were so thrilled."

Morgan mulled that over. *He's right. I'd never advertise this.* "Okay. But why should I believe you've cured hundreds of people?"

"You don't. And, because I'm sworn to secrecy, you never will. If my unwillingness to out my clientele's a deal-breaker, I understand."

Is that a deal-breaker? What are my options?

"You said before you're not with a church, and this isn't a theological treatment."

"Correct."

"Yet you think Taylor is possessed by a demon."

Quinn angled forward. "Yes. It's a misconception demons are only susceptible to religious treatments. My process works. Every time."

Morgan raised his palms. "Look, you've got to give me something more. Some rational, medical reason to trust you."

Quinn stood. "It is an act of faith, Dr. Morgan. Much like religion."

"And how much does this act of faith cost?"

"I'm afraid it's expensive. The drugs themselves, well, there are no generic potions available."

Morgan narrowed his eyes. *He's not giving me anything to justify trusting him.*

"Perhaps this isn't a good fit," Quinn continued. "Is money an obstacle?"

"I didn't say that."

"I apologize. There's no price you can put on the health of your daughter."

He's right about that. If I'm convinced it will work.

"I'll tell you what," Quinn said. "I'll let you speak with a former client. Would that suffice?"

"One client isn't much to go on."

"Right you are. What if the client was so above reproach you'd find him unimpeachable?"

The bristles on Morgan's arm prickled. "Who?"

Quinn pulled out his cell phone and handed it over. "The Archbishop of New York. When the exorcism of one of his flock failed, he called on me. Go ahead. Call him. He'll tell you."

Morgan held the phone. *The Archbishop? Failed exorcism? He's worth talking to.* "How do I reach him?"

"He's in my contact list under 'A'. I'll let you dial it. His assistant will answer, and you'll know it's his office. Tell him Nathanial Quinn is calling. He'll take it."

Morgan found the listing and dialed.

"This is the office of the Archbishop of New York. How can I direct your call?"

Morgan drummed up his best British accent, which elicited a frightened stare from Quinn. "Um, this is Nathanial Quinn calling. May I speak with him?"

"Yes, Mr. Quinn. I'll connect you."

After a few clicks, a deep voice came on the line. "Nathanial! A blessing to hear from you. How's the demon business?"

Morgan swallowed. "Archbishop, my name is Richard Morgan. I'm with Nathanial now, and he asked me to call you."

"I see." *He's disappointed.* "What can I do for you, Mr. Morgan."

"It's Dr. Morgan. My daughter is possessed."

"And you want to know if Nathanial will cure her."

"Yes," Morgan said, barely above a whisper.

"He always has. Listen *Dr.* Morgan, Nathanial is a true gift from God. He saved my parishioner's life when no amount of religious doctrine or faith could. If you're calling me, you must have doubts. You can relax. He's the real deal."

Morgan's heart picked up speed. *The real deal!* "And his process didn't harm your daughter?"

"Not whatsoever. Completely safe."

Morgan thanked the Archbishop and disconnected the call.

"Satisfied?" Quinn said.

A fresh thought struck Morgan. "What about the other girls in Salem? The ones Taylor infected? Are you meeting with their parents?"

Quinn hesitated. "Not yet. I only have enough to treat one victim." His eyes drilled deep into Morgan's. "I'm giving you that chance. Imagine how you'll feel if you see another girl healed, and your daughter doesn't make it."

Morgan blanched. *I'd never forgive myself. Or recover.* Still, the psychiatrist in him gave him pause. "I need to think about it."

Quinn moved toward the door. "I'll stay in town through Monday. Then, I must move on. The demand for my type of work is growing, and I have an obligation to humanity to help as many people as I can. Call me if you decide to go forward."

Quinn vanished out the door.

The Archbishop vouches for him. What am I waiting for?

Morgan reached his personal banker with an hour to spare before they shut down on Saturday. "Tom, I need you to convert my 401k to cash. Can you transfer it to my checking account?"

"Richard, that's a horrible idea. It's your retirement fund. And you'll pay a stiff penalty for early withdrawal."

Morgan's stomach groaned. "I'm aware of the cost. And one more favor. I need a cashier's check delivered here today for the entire amount."

After an extended pause, the banker exhaled. "You sure about this?"

"It's an emergency, Tom. I'm positive."

"A courier will drop it off within the hour." Before disconnecting, he continued. "I hope you know what you're doing."

So do I.

Next he called Quinn. "I'll have your payment in sixty minutes. Let's do this."

"I'll be there."

* * *

Morgan checked on Taylor. She continued to sleep, the sedative doing its job. *What I wouldn't give to see her smile again.*

A rap on the front door interrupted him. *That was fast.*

But, instead of a chaser's check or a demon specialist, Linda Copeland stood on his porch in a pink ski jacket, jeans, and red tennies. "Dr. Morgan, I need to talk with you."

"What now?"

"I beg you to return with me to Costa Rica."

Costa Rica? Boy, does your salesmanship need work. "Yeah, that's not happening."

"If you don't go now, it'll be too late."

"Look, Costa Rica is the *last* place I'll be taking Taylor. There's a bounty on her head. Besides, how do I know you're not part of the task force trying to get her back in the country?"

Her posture reeked of defiance. "If I wanted to kill her, she'd be dead."

"I have another solution."

"No, you don't."

"Ever hear of Nathanial Quinn?"

Linda shook her head.

"I'm surprised. Seems like he's in your line of work. Demon specialist."

"Demon specialist? Preposterous. There's only one way to fix your daughter *and* capture the demon. The *Awá* at the Bribri village."

Morgan waved her off. "If going to Costa Rica is the only alternative, I'll take door number one. Now, if you'll excuse me, I'm expecting someone."

CHAPTER 43

The cashier's check and Quinn arrived simultaneously, as if he'd been waiting for it to appear.

Morgan thanked the courier, tipped him his last twenty, and motioned for Quinn to come in. "This better work."

Quinn reached out and tried to take the envelope with the check in it. "It will."

"It's my retirement savings. I need to know Taylor's cured before I hand it over."

Quinn tugged. "I won't begin without full payment. I've already invested in the medicine. It's quite expensive. So, you see, I've spent the full amount. If you aren't committed, I must find somebody else."

Morgan held tight. "Half now, final payment when she's healed."

"Dr. Morgan, if you don't want my help I'll be happy to wish you and Taylor the best and move along. Perhaps the Petersons will be more interested."

If this fails, Taylor's screwed. But if I don't do it, she's done for, anyway. Morgan released the envelope. "Okay. Do it."

Quinn pocketed it, then opened a satchel and pulled out a breathing apparatus with an attachment that could cover Taylor's nose and mouth. It had dials and lighted indicators along with a compartment to pour liquid into it. "Excellent. Bring her."

"You can't go to her?"

"No. That's the demon's lair now. I must do it on neutral ground."

Morgan shivered. *Demon's lair? Jesus.* "I'll get her."

Halfway down the hallway to Taylor's room Morgan stopped. *What's keeping him from leaving with my money?* He glanced back, but couldn't see the couch from that angle. "There's coffee on the counter. Help yourself."

No answer.

Morgan's heartbeat accelerated. "Quinn?"

Still no response.

Morgan's knees weakened. *Oh, shit. He stole my life savings.* He turned and hustled into the living room.

Quinn fiddled with his contraption. He looked up. "Where's your daughter?"

Morgan swallowed. *Thank God.* "Did you hear me about the coffee?"

Quinn gave him a puzzled expression. "I hardly think this is the time for social pleasantries. Please bring me the girl."

Morgan nodded and ran to Taylor's room. The window shade eclipsed the morning sun. She slept in a white nightgown. Morgan nudged her. No response. "Taylor. There's someone here to help you."

Taylor emitted a chuckle, but otherwise showed no signs of being awake.

"Taylor. We're going to end this." Morgan tapped her cheek. "For good."

She lay still. Morgan lifted her to a sitting position. She winced and groaned. "It's so bright." Her high-pitched voice carried a lisp. "And hot."

Jesus, she sounds like a snake. "It's okay, Sweetie. I'll carry you to the living room." He put his arms around her, watching her mouth with frightened interest. *That sedative better be working.*

He picked her up. Her eyes flamed right through him and she yawned, exposing incisors too long and sharp to ignore. *Keep moving. The cure is in the living room.* His stomach lurched. He took two more steps and Taylor grinned. *What if she goes for my throat?* He shuddered. *What if Quinn's gone?*

But Quinn was still on the couch, with his gizmo. Morgan sighed with relief and carried Taylor to the seat next to him. He positioned a dinette chair across from them and sat.

Quinn gripped her hand. "Hello, Taylor. My name is Nathanial Quinn. I specialize in helping people like you. And I *will* help you."

Taylor snarled, but Quinn showed no fear. He placed the contraption over her mouth.

"Hey," Morgan said. "What are you doing?"

Quinn didn't turn. "Dr. Morgan, I need you to be quiet."

"What's she inhaling?"

"You know I can't tell you."

Taylor took several strained breaths.

Morgan came to her side. "She can't breathe."

"She's fine." Quinn adjusted the dials while watching the monitor. A twitch to the left. A half-turn to the right. "Don't lose your nerve now. I'm saving her."

Taylor's pupils rose until only white showed.

Morgan gasped. "Look at her! She's dying."

"She's ridding herself of an evil force."

"You'll kill her."

"Almost done." Quinn pulled out a syringe and placed it near Taylor's arm. "Last step."

Morgan wanted to grab the hypodermic from Quinn, but stopped. *What if this the only way to save her? What if I stop it and she dies? I have to trust him.*

Quinn injected Taylor with a clear liquid. Morgan held his breath, waiting for a reaction.

Taylor reacted violently. She convulsed, then threw up. The ghoulish yellow-green almost cost Morgan his breakfast.

"It is done," Quinn said. "She'll sleep the rest of the day. But she'll be herself when she wakes up."

Almost on cue, Taylor drooped into Morgan's arms, ooze seeping down his shirt.

"You're sure?" Morgan said. He could recognize the hope in his voice.

Quinn stood and put his equipment in his satchel. "I guarantee it. If, for any reason, you aren't satisfied with Taylor's recovery, call me. You have your daughter back. Congratulations."

* * *

As the dark of night arrived, Taylor still slept. Morgan never left her side, each minute feeling like an hour. *Come on, Taylor. Wake up.*

He rechecked her pulse and temperature at five and again found them normal. A residual peppermint smell from the treatment lingered. *Come on, Sweetie. Come back.*

Bear stepped into her bedroom and licked Morgan. Morgan scratched him behind the ears. "Hey, buddy. Come to check on Taylor?" *Bear's not afraid of her any more.* Morgan's pulse picked up. Bear lay on the floor, panting. "You can tell, can't you Bear? Taylor's going to be fine."

The night dragged. Morgan took a break to feed Bear, who went outside to do his business, but otherwise, they stayed glued to Taylor's side. Finally, as the clock struck midnight, Taylor stirred. Bear stood and watched her.

Morgan took her hand. *Please, God. Let her be cured.*

She squinted, and Morgan's heart jumped. *No sign of black or red irises!* "Taylor?"

Her eyes twinkled and her cheeks blushed. "Dad?"

"I'm right here." *Oh my God! It's her!* Morgan seized his daughter and bawled. "I was so scared."

"Why? What happened?"

Morgan felt a chill. *She remembers none of it. What a break.* "You've been sick. But there's nothing to worry about now."

Bear sniffed in Taylor's direction. His tail dropped between his legs. He whined and stepped back. Milky drool fell from his mouth.

"What's wrong with Bear?" Taylor asked.

"I don't know," Morgan said. "What is it, buddy? Taylor's fine now." *Right?*

Taylor's arms turned rigid against Morgan. She pulled away. Her eyes reverted to black. She cackled. "You fool." The throaty voice again. "You think you can ever get rid of me?" She spit in his face.

Bear ran.

Taylor laughed.

Morgan sagged to the floor. *She was okay for a moment. Maybe if she gets one more treatment, it'll be permanent.*

He crawled away from the bed. Taylor's eyes burned. He pulled his cell phone out and dialed Quinn's number.

A twangy voice replied. "The number you're trying to reach has been disconnected."

He redialed and got the same response. Then he tried the Archbishop, but that link was also severed.

Taylor laughed at him. "I can sense your anger. You want to kill. Like your father. Like with Michelle."

"Shut up! I didn't kill Michelle."

"You can't fool me," Taylor said, her fangs sticking out from her grin. "I was there."

Morgan closed his eyes. His insides ached. *It's the demon talking. Don't listen to it.* He gulped down snot draining into his throat. "Go away."

"It is almost time for me to go. But the lamia will live forever."

Taylor's eyes shut, and she slept.

Morgan trudged to the couch, eyeing the phone. *I deserve a drink. I'm no good to her if I die from the stress. This will relieve the tension.*

No! One year sober.

He thought of easier times. Times with Michelle, and a normal Taylor. Times ruined with his drinking.

Look at me. Michelle dead. Taylor turning into a monster. And me, the alleged pillar of the community, hiding her symptoms, even though she's a threat. To girls. And now, my retirement, gone. What a loser.

He made a command decision and called his old liquor store. Yes, they remembered him, and yes, they still made deliveries.

CHAPTER 44

Morgan uncapped the Scotch bottle and set it on the floor. The sweet aroma excited him. *Peat. Cedar. The sweetness of florals and vanilla.* He took a swig from the bottle. A familiar warmth flowed through him. *Oh, yes. That is divine.*

But a panting in the hallway stopped him from taking a second sip. Bear, his ears lowered, stared him down.

"Don't look at me like that."

Bear whined.

Morgan guzzled a defiant gulp.

Bear barked, then sighed as if the weight of the world was on his shoulders.

Morgan gazed into the dog's eyes. *He's trying to save you. This is what unconditional love looks like.*

He capped the bottle. "You win, all right. Happy now?"

Bear rushed to Morgan, tail wagging. Morgan. Scratched him behind his ears. "Sometimes you can be a pain in the ass."

Bear licked Morgan's face.

A solid rap on the entry interrupted him. Morgan hid the Scotch bottle under a couch cushion and swung the door open.

Smokey and Garcia stood there. The night sky glistened with stars. Garcia looked scared to death. Smokey flashed a search warrant. "Doc, you lied to me. You get one more chance to come clean on the murder of your ex."

Morgan glanced at the authorization, then back at Smokey. "You found the witness?"

"Something more conclusive," Smokey said. "The hospital finished the drug inventory. You checked out Ketamine the day before you left for Costa Rica. That vial isn't in your office cabinet where it belongs. Care to explain?"

The alcoholic warmth inside Morgan turned to ice. *Shit.* Morgan sagged back to the couch and plopped down. The weight of his rear forced the Scotch bottle to the floor.

Garcia slumped. "You've been drinking?"

"One sip," Morgan said. He looked his friend in the eyes. "Yeah, I blew it. But no need to give me a guilt trip. Bear beat you to it."

"I'll call Dorothy," Garcia said.

"She quit. Taylor scared the shit out of her. But it doesn't matter. I'll take whatever punishment I deserve."

"That's the alcohol talking," Garcia protested. "We'll find you another lawyer."

Morgan swallowed. *Oh, Michelle. What did I do?* "It's time I paid for my sins, Javi. You, of all people, should respect that. And what are you doing here, anyway?"

"I called him," Smokey said. "Figured you'd prefer he watches Taylor, rather than child services."

Garcia gulped.

Javi, you look like you haven't slept. No. Something else. You're scared.

Smokey pulled out his notebook and sat across from Morgan. "Tell me what happened in Costa Rica, Doc."

"He's exhausted, man," Garcia protested. "You can't interview him now."

Morgan waved off his friend. "It's okay, Javi. It's time to come clean. I did find a receipt for Ketamine, stuffed down the side of my desk. Your guys missed it when they searched my office."

"Humph. My team never misses anything."

"Well, they missed this."

"Where's it now?"

"Top drawer at the office."

"I'll need that."

"Take it."

Smokey jotted something down. "So you stole the Ketamine, injected Michelle, then went on a dangerous hike. So she'd drown."

"I don't remember checking it out, and I don't recall giving it to Michelle."

"That's because you didn't do it," Garcia said.

Morgan looked up at Garcia. "Then who did? The autopsy found the drug. It's my signature on the invoice. My fingerprints on her neck. Everywhere the investigation turns, I'm implicated. Isn't that right, detective?"

Smokey inhaled. "Doc, I need to take you downtown to book you for Michelle's murder."

"We need to call her grandparents," Morgan said.

"I'll stay with her," Garcia said, his complexion moving from off-white to luminescence.

"You sure you're okay?" Morgan said. "You look like a sheet."

"Worried about you and Taylor."

It's more than that. You're spooked.

"Can I see her?" Smokey said.

"Sure," Morgan led them to her door. "The sun's up, so she should sleep until it sets."

"I don't understand," Smokey said. "She sleeps during the day? Is that caused by her illness?"

Illness? I wish it was that simple. "You could say that." Morgan pushed her door open, half expecting the furniture discombobulated, the window open, and Taylor nowhere to be found.

He was partially correct. The bed was centered in the room, but the window was closed, and she lay in a pool of green vomit.

"Jesus," Garcia said. "I'll get towels."

Morgan slumped against the wall. "I checked her every hour."

Garcia returned with wet cleaning rags. He lay his Bible on the bed, then inched closer to Taylor. When she didn't react, he cleansed.

Morgan knew he should help, but couldn't find the strength to move.

Smokey opened the window shades.

A beam of morning sunlight cut across Taylor's legs. Steam rose like through a teakettle's lid preparing to scream. Her upper body shot up to attention, her irises a bright red, and lisped. "Close those!"

Garcia backed away from the bed, a mask of horror etched on his face.

Morgan lunged to block the sun. "Smokey, the blinds."

Taylor writhed in pain. Steam turned to a darker smoke. Morgan gagged on the odor of burning flesh.

"Make it stop!" Taylor cried.

Smokey closed the shades.

Taylor calmed and lay down. The cloud and stench dissipated. She closed her eyes, arms crossed over her chest like a corpse laid to rest, and slept.

Smokey whistled like a man who'd seen something he couldn't believe. "You said you think she's possessed, Doc. I'd seen the teeth, but what's with the reaction to sunlight?"

"She's never reacted so harshly to the sun," Morgan said. He glared at Garcia. "Another sign she needs an exorcism."

Garcia ignored the shot across his bow, which he wiped with his sleeve. "The sedative keeps her under control?"

"For now," Morgan said. "I can see it losing its effectiveness. The demon is getting stronger. One of these nights, it won't work at all. I don't know what I'll do then." *But I'm seeing Linda's point of view. Killing her might be the most merciful thing I can do.*

"Maybe you need to restrain her," Garcia said.

"I thought of strapping her to the bed," Morgan said. "I detest the idea, but I might not have a choice."

"What's with her voice?" Smokey said. "She has a lisp."

"It's her lamia voice," Morgan said.

"A what?" Smokey asked.

Morgan put a sheet over Taylor's legs. "She's turning into some kind of vampire. And she's infecting the other girls."

Smokey frowned. "Is this your plan? Obscure the facts with witchcraft and voodoo, hoping we won't hold her accountable?"

"Just the truth, detective." Morgan looked at the floor. "I'm sorry I didn't confess sooner."

"How could you?" Garcia said. "The scientific tests ruled her out."

"Yeah, but deep inside I knew."

"Doc, you know how crazy this talk of vampires sounds, right? Demons is one thing. The Church has prepared me to accept those. But *vampires*?"

"I know how it sounds. And perhaps I *am* crazy. But I can't argue with the facts. Too many supernatural signatures. I'm convinced there's three personas in her. Taylor, the demon, and the lamia, all fighting for control. That's if Taylor's still in there."

* * *

Garcia winced. *I've got to do something. The demon is killing her. And a vampire? What evil are we dealing with?* He said a silent prayer over Taylor. *Please, Lord, give me the strength to face my fear.*

Taylor's red eyes popped open, and she grinned at him, showing off her fangs.

Garcia staggered back, slamming against the wall.

"Javi, what is it?" Morgan said. "She's weak when the sun's up. She can't hurt you."

Garcia recalled the chaos in his own room. *I wish that were true.* A sparkle lurked in her eyes. *I can't stay alone with her. The demon will attack me.*

Taylor cackled. "Yes, I will."

She's reading my mind! He closed his eyes, trying to block out the scene in front of him. Instead, a vision of Jesus on the cross floated past. Jesus's eyes, always loving, instead condemned him. *For my lack of faith. In Him. What's happened to me?*

In the distance, a radio started. Garcia recognized the song. *"This is Amazing Grace." Phil Wickham.* "Where's that music coming from?"

Morgan shook his head. "What music?"

Garcia focused on the song's message. "The music!" He looked at Smokey, who looked as confused as Morgan did. "You don't hear it?"

"Sorry, Javi," Morgan said.

The music stopped. But something inside Garcia gained strength and rebelled. He stood up taller and stared down Taylor. "You don't scare me, demon!"

Taylor's eyes faded. She curled up her lip and closed her eyes.

"I'll talk to the bishop regarding an exorcism investigation," Garcia said.

"You finally believe she's possessed?" Morgan asked him.

"*Sí.*"

"What changed your mind?" Morgan said.

"The evidence is overwhelming," Garcia said. "Something evil is in play here."

Smokey joined them at bedside. "Jesus, Doc. I'm speechless."

"I'll tell my superiors I believe she's possessed, based on my experience with demons," Garcia said. "Maybe we can find another priest willing and able to lead an investigation." He turned to Smokey. "But I need time. Please don't call Social Services. Put them both under house arrest. Guard the place. It's Taylor's only chance."

Smokey winced. "I can't ignore the risk she brings to the city."

"If I'm right," Garcia said, "locking her up won't save the community. Only exorcising the demon can do that."

"How long do you need, Padre?" Smokey said.

"I should know in a day or two if the Church will even consider it. But, even if they hear the case, their evaluation takes time. Months, even."

"I don't have months, Padre."

"There's another possibility," Garcia said. "There are former priests who aren't active but have performed an exorcism. It's possible to hire one, as an independent contractor."

Morgan perked up. "How long would that take to arrange?"

"Not sure," Garcia said. "My bishop might know someone."

"Humph. I can give you forty-eight hours, Padre. As for you, Doc, no leaving the premises. I'll have one officer in the house, and two in a car outside."

"Thanks, detective," Morgan said. "You won't regret it."

"You better hope I don't."

Garcia cleared his throat. "I need to inform my bishop. Tomorrow's Sunday, so we're both booked, but I'll try to get an answer by Monday." He took off.

"Thanks, Javi."

* * *

The remnants of the Scotch lingered in Morgan's mouth, a taste he both regretted and cherished.

"Funny thing about your in-laws," Smokey said.

"What's that?" Morgan asked.

"They're still here. Never left."

Morgan gave Smokey a quizzical look. "Really? I wonder why."

"Beats me. Also just got a text we retrieved the drug log from your desk. They're running an analysis on it now."

"For what?"

"Fingerprints, any sign of doctoring. Usual drill."

"You talk to Azra about Costa Rica lately?" Morgan said.

"Yeah. She's still defending you. Says she was with you the entire time, and you couldn't have injected Michelle."

"She *was* constantly with me." Morgan chuckled. "With Michelle there, she wouldn't let me out of her sight."

Smokey squirmed. "I have to take her word with a grain of salt. She clearly loves you. Plus, she could be in on it with you. Hell, she could have injected Michelle without you knowing."

"No. Keep her out of this. She didn't do anything wrong."

"Well, you're not the most reliable witness."

"You know what I can't figure out? Why would I leave it to the luck of Michelle getting washed out to sea? If I planned to kill her, why dose her, then hope for a storm to come along?"

Smokey looked up from the warrant. "Maybe you planned to dump her in the drink, but she drowned first."

"Maybe."

Smokey bit on his cigar. "You were hoping to bring her body back. No autopsy. Then the police showed up, and Taylor got bit. Messed up your plan."

"But why don't I remember?"

"Don't ask me. You're the shrink."

Smokey's phone rang. "Smokey. Yeah. You sure? Check it again." He hung up.

"Something wrong?"

"Crime lab. Something unusual on your drug log."

"What?"

Smokey shook his head. "I can't discuss it."

"And here I thought we were becoming such good friends."

"Humph. I may be rooting for you, but I will do my job."

Morgan ran his fingers through his mane. "Fair enough. You know, I never laid a hand on her. The claims of marks on her neck make no sense."

Smokey pointed his cigar at Morgan. "Laid a hand. Of course." He slapped his forehead. "I need to go to the office."

CHAPTER 45

Sunday

Morgan sat on Taylor's bedroom floor, watching her sleep at noon, exhaustion overwhelming him. *Go ahead. Doze off. The sun's out.*

He tensed. *Is her aversion to sunlight, or the time of day? If it's cloudy, is she not affected? Because if it's the latter, these sedatives will run out twice as fast. And they've barred me from writing any more prescriptions.*

He gave in and slept.

The nightmare of Costa Rica hit him hard. Michelle drowning. Taylor attacked. Shooting the guards on the beach. The empty eye sockets on the border.

And, in the background, a demon's voice. Taunting him.

He woke up drenched in a dark room. Body odor assaulted his nostrils. He panicked, certain Taylor had wandered off while he slept. But she sat upright on the bed. Staring at him with red irises. *The lamia.*

A frost ran down his vertebrae. "Taylor." He cleared his throat. "You okay?" *What kind of question is that?*

Taylor didn't react, other than to narrow her eyes.

Morgan checked the time on his phone. *Six o'clock. How long has she been awake?*

His stomach growled. *You haven't eaten all day. Neither has Taylor. And Bear hasn't since breakfast. Why isn't Bear knocking down the door for his dinner?*

"Taylor, what would you like to eat?" he said.

"Blood." The lisp.

I walked right into that one. "I'm asking Taylor. Let her answer!"

Taylor grinned, then sank her incisors into her lip. Plasma flowed into her mouth.

"No!" Morgan ran to retrieve a wet cloth and another syringe. He returned to find her licking the flow from her mouth, slurping the sticky liquid while her eyes blazed. He grabbed her arm, which caused her to convulse. Powerful in his grasp, she broke away easily.

"You cannot hold me," Taylor said in her lamia voice. "I am lamia. I am strong."

Morgan injected her in the leg. "Sorry, sweetie. I can't have you hurting yourself."

Taylor slapped the empty syringe across the room. "Your medicine won't work much longer. I adapt with each dose." She settled into the bed and closed her eyes.

Morgan wilted. *She's right. I can see it. I'm running out of time. And she's not eating. Azra can help with an IV.*

I don't want Azra's help. She'll freak.

Javi and Smokey have seen Taylor. There's no reason to hide her from Azra now. I'll call her after I hear from Smokey. Maybe he'll have good news.

The sound of a car in his driveway interrupted his thoughts. Hoping to find Garcia or Smokey, he rushed to the front door. The officer on duty sat at the dining room table. He looked up from his crossword and signaled his okay to open it.

Where he found Michelle's parents, Carter and Laila. Morgan sagged.

252

Carter looked even larger than normal in a massive overcoat. He stepped forward. "Where's my granddaughter?"

"She's asleep."

Carter stormed past Morgan toward the bedrooms. "In here?"

"Isaiah," Morgan called while following him, "we need to talk. I should tell you some things before you go in."

Carter turned. "No more stalling."

"I'm not stalling. She's sick."

Carter paused at Taylor's door. "What do you mean?"

He's a religious guy. Might even believe in possession. No. Better to ease them into it. "She has a second personality. And some physical ailments."

Carter glared at Morgan. "What did you do to her?" Before Morgan responded, Carter barged into Taylor's room. "Taylor. We're here to take you home."

Taylor, in her white nightgown, didn't respond, still under the influence of the sedative.

Carter treaded to the bed. "Taylor. Wake up." He patted her cheek. When she didn't respond, turned on Morgan. "What have you done to her?"

"I told you," Morgan said. "She's ill. I gave her a sedative to calm her down. She's stopped eating. I need to arrange for an IV so she'll get some nourishment."

Laila stood at the door. "Why isn't she eating?"

Morgan addressed her. "I'm not sure. The best thing for her is to let me treat her."

Carter grunted. "You killed her mother. I know it, and the police know it." He pointed to the closet. "Laila, get Taylor some clothes. We're taking her right now."

Laila walked timidly toward the closet. "Isaiah, she doesn't look too good. Maybe he's right."

Carter spun on his wife. "Laila, your husband asked you to do something."

Her shoulders sagged.

"You're not taking her anywhere," Morgan said.

Carter looked down on Morgan. "And who's going to stop me? You?"

Morgan glanced at Laila, who pulled clothes from the closet. Her eyes were tired and empty, and, something else.

Is she sedated? On drugs? Scared to death? "I have a plan to cure Taylor. I have full custody. So back off!"

"Is this your plan?" Carter said. "Drug her?"

Should I tell him she needs an exorcism?

No! Crazy bastard might kill her himself. He won't risk the news that a member of his family is possessed.

Carter reached over and grabbed Morgan by the collar. He pulled Morgan toward him, his face crimson with rage. "No more debating. She's coming with us."

Laila gasped.

Taylor was sitting up, mouth wide open, her irises a blazing red.

Carter turned, blanched, and released Morgan.

"Taylor?" Morgan said. "How long have you been awake?"

Taylor's eyes glimmered. "Going to kill each other, are you?"

Morgan took a step toward the bed. "No, sweetie. Just a discussion over how to care for you."

She pointed at Carter while continuing to stare at Morgan. "Go ahead. Slay him. I'll watch."

Laila stepped out of the walk-in closet, staring at the maniacal expression on Taylor's face. "Stop it, please. Both of you."

Taylor swiveled her head toward Laila. "Good. She can observe, too."

"What's wrong with her voice?" Laila said.

"It's an alter-ego talking," Morgan said. "She has several voices."

Laila turned to her husband. "Isaiah, I'm afraid. We should go."

"Hurt him," Taylor ordered, pointing at Carter. "You know you want to."

Morgan stepped to the edge of the bed. "Nobody's getting hurt."

Taylor sulked. "Too bad."

"You want us to get hurt?" Morgan said.

Taylor snarled. "All humans must die."

"You're human," Morgan said.

"No. Lamia now. Girl already dead." She flashed her teeth at Laila. "You like these? I can get you a pair."

Laila staggered against the wall. "Isaiah? What's happening?"

Carter gasped. "What the hell?"

Laila turned ghost-white and collapsed.

Morgan reached out to catch her when he picked up a blur of movement. Distracted, he missed Laila, and she crashed to the floor.

Taylor lunged through the window, shattering the glass.

CHAPTER 46

Taylor landed on her feet and, with wolf-like agility, vanished into the park. Despite the cloudy night, she noticed the minutest details.

Shards of glass poked out in multiple spots on her arms and legs. She brushed them aside, noting a lack of any pain, and watched in amusement as the wounds closed quickly.

Her enhanced hearing distinguished THE MAN calling her old name.

This is so awesome!

She considered returning. *To do what? Help him? Hurt him? Feed from him?*

No. She had no appetite for adults, or males.

Young girls. That's who she thirsted for.

CHAPTER 47

Morgan watched Taylor vanish into the woods from the window. He noted the crimson on the edges of the broken glass. Her blood pulsated on the shards. *She did that under sedation. How do I control her now?*

Carter's eyes bugged out. "Did you see that? She dove out the window like it was nothing."

Morgan checked on Laila, who breathed in stops and starts, her eyes closed. "Laila!" He slapped her gently. "Stay with me."

"What have you done to Taylor?" Carter yelled, gawking at the window.

Morgan checked Laila's pulse. *Too fast. Should I give her one of my sedative doses? No. Save them for Taylor. But what if Laila needs it?* "Isaiah! Over here! Laila needs you!"

Carter glanced at his wife for the first time since Taylor's escape. "Laila! Stand up!"

Morgan glared at Carter. *You asshole.*

Laila opened her eyes and coughed.

"Relax," Morgan said. "You're all right."

"Her teeth," Laila stammered.

"I know," Morgan said. "It's a lot to take in. Can you sit up?"

"I think so."

Morgan helped her to the bed. "Better?"

"I'm okay." She glanced at her husband. "Isaiah, whatever's going on here, I can't handle it. Can we go home now?"

"First, I need to locate Taylor," Morgan said. "You two stay here. If she comes back, well, have the officers deal with her. Their handcuffs will hold her."

"Handcuffs?" Carter said. "What's going on?"

Garcia's emerged at the bedroom door, his Bible held higher than normal. He acknowledged Carter, and then Laila, before noticing Taylor's absence.

Morgan put his finger to his own lips, signaling for Garcia to stay silent. "Javi, Taylor's escaped. We need to find her." *Before she attacks another innocent girl.*

The blood in Garcia's face rushed south. "Oh, man. How'd she get out?"

Morgan pointed at the shattered window. "Leaped out before we could even budge."

"But you're not allowed to leave," Garcia said.

"Yeah," Morgan said. "Isaiah, I need your coat."

"Why?" Carter said.

"I'll use it to leave with Laila," Morgan said. "You stay here. Javi, you keep that officer occupied. Don't want him realizing I'm not Carter. Once I'm clear, come out and drive me away. Laila, you'll come back in. Say you forgot to feed Bear. Then you and Isaiah wait in here, out of sight."

Laila looked terrified. "I don't know. Lying to the police is a sin."

"Would *you* rather go look for Taylor?" Morgan asked her.

"Oh, no," Laila said, shriveling up.

Morgan put on Carter's coat. "That's what I thought. Let's go. You'll be fine. Don't make eye contact with the officer. Javi, lead the way."

Garcia marched around the corner and spoke to the officer. "Want to see something hilarious?"

Morgan put Laila's arm in his and skirted into the living room. The policeman, his back turned, was huddled with Garcia. Morgan rushed to the front door, and outside.

"No!" The officer called out.

Oh, shit. Did he see me? Morgan kept walking.

Holding his breath, he reached Garcia's unlocked car.

"Stop!" the officer yelled.

Morgan froze. Blood rushed from his face. *Should I run for it? Would he really shoot me in the back? And Laila? I can't risk her getting hurt.*

"You're killing me!" the policeman screamed, his voice still within the house.

Puzzled, Morgan turned around. *Javi, what are you doing to him?*

Through the front window Morgan saw the officer laughing at something on Garcia's phone. *Javi. You devil, you.* The term's irony wasn't lost on him.

He ducked into the passenger seat. "Laila, you go back now. You remember what to tell the policeman?"

She nodded and shuffled back. Once she disappeared inside, Garcia jogged over and climbed into the driver's seat. He backed the car out of Morgan's driveway, and they drove away.

"Let's start at the Petersons'," Morgan said. "Then the Wilsons'."

Garcia grimaced. "They'll go crazy if Taylor shows up."

"Batshit crazy. Oops. Sorry."

Garcia shook his head while concentrating on the scene outside, searching for Taylor. "I couldn't have said it better myself, man."

"The last dose didn't stop her. When we find her, I'll need to sedate her again. Going forward, I'm doubling the amount in each shot."

"Is that safe?"

Morgan prepared a syringe for immediate use and then switched to upping the dosage. "It may cause an overdose. Her blood pressure would crater, and she'd have trouble breathing."

"That's not good."

Another in the long list of not goods. "No. But I have to control her at night."

"Man, sounds too dangerous."

"What choice do I have??" Morgan pointed to the corner. "Turn right up here." Morgan braced himself to ask the million dollar question. "What did you find out from your superiors? Does Taylor get an exorcism?"

Garcia didn't answer right away. "I tried to convince them to bring in a priest to do an evaluation. But they want more evidence."

Morgan sagged in his seat. "They won't even evaluate her?"

"Not yet."

Morgan bit his lip. "Any chance they'll reconsider? Can I talk to them?"

"I explained you're a psychiatrist and have exhausted all medical options. They told me to monitor her and return in a month if the symptoms don't subside."

"A *month?*"

"Yeah." Garcia's body shook. "I'd be expected to be there as an aide. I confess, the whole thing makes me question whether I should continue in the priesthood."

"What? Their refusal, or the possibility of being part of another exorcism?"

"Both, I suppose."

"It was that bad?" Morgan said.

"Worse."

"Jeez. And here I'm putting you through this."

"Not your fault. Let's focus on finding Taylor. And there's always the private sector we discussed. But even a private exorcist will still need to be persuaded she's possessed."

"You're convinced, right?"

Garcia kept his eyes on the road. "*Sí.*"

The Lamia

Morgan finished loading the syringes. *There. These better hold her.*
And if they don't?
Morgan's heart pounded. He shut his eyes and prayed.

CHAPTER 48

Smokey retrieved Morgan's drug log from evidence and visited his fingerprint expert. "Just one print in the bottom right-hand corner belonging to Dr. Morgan, right?"

"Yeah."

"What are the chances Morgan grabbed the page in the same spot for all those months and never touched another piece of it?"

The expert scratched his head. "Not possible. Even if he tried. there'd be smudges."

"Right. Can you tell if someone wiped this page?"

The specialist took the sheet. "I can try."

"How long?"

"Later today. I understand our original search didn't find this in his office."

Smokey pulled out a fresh cigar. "Makes me wonder if someone is trying to incriminate the Doc."

Smokey's phone rang. "Smokey here. What? Morgan and the Padre got out? The Carters helped them? Bring them in. And find Taylor and Dr. Morgan!"

* * *

The precinct doors flew open and two officers led Isaiah and Laila Carter into the room. Smokey shot out of his seat.

Smokey stepped up to Carter. "You helped Morgan escape?"

Carter waved his arms. "Taylor dove out the window. Took a dive through the glass! Morgan threatened us. What could I do?"

Heat spread through Smokey's face. "Oh, I don't know. Inform the officer posted in the living room?" Smokey looked at Laila. "And you?"

She lowered her eyes.

Smokey glared at Carter. "Stay here. Someone will take your statement."

Laila looked pale. "I'd appreciate some water. I don't feel well."

He led them to the break room and showed them two clean glasses. "Use these."

CHAPTER 49

Taylor sniffed the brisk evening air. She sensed blood nearby coursing through veins and arteries. The night briskness was a welcome change from the bedroom's stuffy confines.

She knew the loudest sounds belonged to adult humans. She tuned in to the softest heartbeats, those of children.

There. A child's pat-pat-pat.

She crouched in the brush, listening to the rush of blood, waiting for her prey to approach, fighting her ravenous hunger. She tensed, ready to launch onto her target, ripping open the jugular vein and drinking until contented.

A teenage boy came into view.

Damn.

But her craving overrode any chance at being selective. She pounced and knocked him to the ground. She pinned his arms and descended, her teeth closing in on his neck.

But she stopped. The boy smelled like rotten meat. Her desire to feed evaporated.

She ran. *I couldn't slice into him. Why am I only attracted to young girls?*

A deep voice in her head, the one counseling her for the past week, returned. "Do not worry, child. It takes time to mature into what you are becoming."

Her mind answered. *Who are you? What have you done to me?*

"Call me *Bé*. I have made you strong and powerful. Soon, an army will be at your disposal. And the humans will die."

Why do you want humans to die?

The demon laughed. "Humans destroy the earth. I must destroy them to save it. Besides, God loves them and pissing off God is satisfaction enough."

Why can I only feed from girls?

"Because you are lamia."

Are there more of my kind?

"You are already creating them."

She found herself at the police station.

The police will look for me. I should not be here.

"First, child, I will show you a new power. And now you have support."

Jennifer Peterson turned the corner, her face pale and her gait slow and gliding.

* * *

After no sign of Taylor at the Peterson and Wilson residences, Morgan and Garcia expanded their search.

Morgan's cell phone rang. He looked at the display. "Smokey."

"You going to answer it?"

"Maybe he found her." He tapped the connect icon. "Hello, detective."

"Don't 'hello, detective' me. We had a deal."

"Sorry," Morgan said. "I can't allow Taylor to be out unsupervised."

"You haven't found her?"

"She's not at the Petersons' or the Wilsons'. Not sure where else she might go." *Sure I do. Somewhere with young girls.* He shivered.

"Doc, there was another attack. A boy this time. Victim claims it was by a young girl in a white nightgown."

"Did she hurt him? Bite him?"

"No. Flashed her fangs, then made a disgusted face and ran. Listen, I need you to come to the station."

"Not yet. I need to find her."

"We'll find her. Turn yourself in before this gets any worse."

"And how does this get any worse?"

Morgan hung up and shut off his phone.

CHAPTER 50

Laila Carter stared at the interview room's blank wall, trying to make sense of the evening's events. The chamber smelled of Pine Sol and the water had left behind a mineral residue. *My husband wants Taylor to live with us, no matter how sick or dangerous.* The thought made her nauseous.

I'm trapped in a loveless marriage with a megalomaniac, my daughter is dead, and my granddaughter has vampire teeth. I can't bear it.

She considered asking for more water, but decided she needed fresh air instead. A young officer stood guard. "Excuse me. May I step outside?"

The policeman took one look and froze. "Jeez, lady, you're white as a ghost. You need a doctor?"

"Can I get some air?"

"Don't run off."

She fought back a tear. "Where? My husband's here, and I have nowhere else to go."

She stepped outside, hoping to see the stars. A night sky full of diamonds always calmed her. But the exterior of the police station was well lit, giving the aura of daylight. Dark clouds blocked the heavens.

You're not in Utah, anymore. How do locals survive in this constant gloom? The suicide rate must be astronomical.

Footsteps drew near. *I should go in.* But before she could do that she saw the figures of Taylor and a younger girl gliding toward her.

Laila froze, a panic attack rumbling toward her. "Taylor?"

Taylor and the girl approached in white nightgowns, blood stained, both with blazing red orbs.

Her eyes. What can do that? She trembled. "Please don't come any closer."

Taylor ran a black tongue across her lips. "I'm here to help. You want all this over,"

Laila stared into those eyes. Her body relaxed. *I see it now. She can help me.*

Taylor grinned and drove her canines into the other girl's neck. Blood spouted out like a Yellowstone geyser.

My God. She's drinking the child's blood. Laila stood her ground, feeling both fear and awe. *I don't know what she is, but she's magnificent.*

Taylor withdrew, her lips and chin covered in red gold, and lifted her eyebrows.

"You like watching?" Taylor said.

"Yes," Laila said. *So much.*

The other girl peered around Taylor. The wound on her neck closed.

"Can you to take me away from my horrific life?" Laila said. "Make me strong, like you?"

Taylor's voice beat into Laila's head. *You are too old to turn. But I can tell you how to free yourself.*

"Tell me."

* * *

Laila's long-time deception of hiding pouches of cocaine in her bra was about to pay off. She returned to the interrogation room. Following Taylor's directions, she dug out a week's worth. A page from the notepad on the table provided an impromptu straw. Soon, she'd float away to a safe place, one where her husband couldn't bully her. Taylor promised immortality and freedom from the memories haunting her.

She glanced at the door, pulse racing. If her husband came in, her secret would be exposed. *Isaiah will throw me out.*

Fuck it. She tore the pouch open. White powder spilled halfway across the table. She reached for the notepad and tore a sheet off, trying to be silent, certain the guard outside must have heard.

The door remained shut.

Scratching came from the window. She couldn't see through the opaque glass, but the scraping continued, and she approached.

A voice hypnotized her. A beautiful melody. With powerful lyrics. The voice of the coaxing devil.

When the chorus completed, she walked back to the table. She rolled up the sheet of paper, bent down, and inhaled the cocaine.

She tried to clean up the remnants of white powder, but a sharp pain struck her arms and chest. Her final thought was, *At least I finally contributed. Even if only the suicide rate.*

CHAPTER 51

Two blocks from the police station, Taylor and Jennifer stood in the center of the road, frozen in Garcia's headlights.

Morgan jumped in his seat. "That's her."

Garcia gasped. "Oh, man. Their faces are covered in blood. Is that Jennifer with Taylor?"

Morgan rubbed his forehead, trying to chase the pounding away. "Yeah. She's drawn to her."

"What did they do?" Garcia stopped the car.

Morgan got out first. "They fed."

* * *

THE MAN. He found us.

THE MAN took a few cautious steps toward her. He spoke, but the lamia didn't bother to listen. THE PRIEST followed him out of the vehicle.

"What do we do?" Jennifer asked her.

"They're irrelevant. We find a young girl and feed."

"On them?"

"Only young girls. Then turn them. Make them like us."

"What are we?" Jennifer said.

"Lamia."

The lamia returned her attention to THE MAN, who stood less than ten feet away now. She hissed at him, displaying her fangs, which caused THE PRIEST to take a step back and cross himself.

"I'm hungry," Jennifer whined.

"Be still," the lamia commanded.

* * *

Morgan's eyes met Taylor's. "Taylor. You need to come home with me. It's not too late to fix this."

Taylor cackled. "Fix? Me never better."

Morgan's knees buckled. *Me never better? That's the grammar Linda warned me about. Along with the high voice and lisp. Indications she's converted. Am I too late?* "You're sick, sweetie. You need help."

Garcia edged nearer to Taylor. "Taylor, it's me. Father Javier. From the church."

Taylor's tongue flicked across her mouth, making a clicking sound. "No closer."

Garcia inched forward and held his Bible higher. "Remember your youth group? How much you enjoy teaching them about God?"

Taylor laughed. "Me answer to different god."

Garcia took one last step before Taylor bolted forward, knocking him to the ground. She straddled him. "Your god help you now?"

Morgan injected the sedative into her back and pulled her off.

Taylor reacted by twisting and freeing herself. She landed on her feet, standing face-to-face with Morgan.

"I'm taking you home," Morgan said.

* * *

The lamia hissed, eyeing THE MAN's neck. She crouched and leaped, passing over THE MAN's head, landing behind him, next to Jennifer.

"Come, child," the lamia said. "We feed."

271

A warm sensation moved up the lamia's body. She peered at her leg. A syringe stuck out. "What you do?" she hissed.

"Gave you another sedative."

The lamia pulled the needle out. But the medicine advanced, overcoming her unnatural strength.

"Jennifer," THE PRIEST said, "come on over here. I'll take you home."

"Taylor?" Jennifer said.

Taylor turned to Jennifer. "Run! I come later."

"Don't listen to her!" THE PRIEST said. "Your parents are worried sick."

"Where me go?" Jennifer asked the lamia.

"Hide forest."

THE MAN reached out to stop Jennifer. "It'll be okay."

The lamia stepped between them and growled. "Leave daughter alone!"

* * *

Morgan braced himself to lunge after Jennifer. *What if I have to sedate Jennifer? I'm running out of sedatives.*

Taylor's knees buckled, and Morgan instinctively grabbed her, rather than Jennifer, who bolted away with eerie speed.

Garcia took several steps after her, but stopped. "She's gone, man." He turned to Morgan. "How can she run so fast?"

"I don't know. Call Smokey and tell him to search for her. We need to deal with Taylor." Morgan helped Taylor to the grass. "Her pulse and breathing seem okay. Her irises are changing back to black."

"How many times do I need to explain this to you?" Taylor said in her demon voice. "It's too late to stop it. Her change is complete."

Morgan swallowed. *I believe it. I can't believe I'm about to ask Javi this.* "Taylor's gone, Javi. She needs to be destroyed before she infects anyone else. Will you help me?"

Garcia cringed at his words. "Destroyed? Listen to yourself."

The medicine took control. Taylor's eyes drooped shut.

"Let's take her to the church," Garcia said. "Smokey won't look there right away. Maybe she'll give us some stronger evidence of demonic possession. Something I can use with the Church."

Morgan looked at her angelic face. "Sure." A flood of tears gushed. *But we're wasting our time. My daughter is dead.*

CHAPTER 52

Monday

The lamia's eyes shot open. Laying on cold marble, it recognized THE PRIEST'S church. The scent of candles burning. The statue of Jesus crucified hanging over the altar. And the sun through the stained glass, sneaking ever closer to its exposed legs. Panicked, it tried to rise, but found itself tied down. "Let me go!"

She recognized THE PRIEST'S voice. "Taylor, you're safe. You're with me at the sanctuary."

The lamia continued to fight its restraints. "Release me."

"Why?" THE PRIEST said. "Does being in the church bother you?"

The lamia bared its fangs and growled. THE MAN shuddered. *Ha. Still frightened.*

THE PRIEST set his Bible down and pulled a flask from his robe. "Do you know what this is?"

"Piss?"

"It's holy water. Blessed it myself. Remember the last time I sprinkled it on you? Would you like me to bless you with it?"

The lamia's eyes widened. *Holy water! Burns!* It tried to break free.

THE PRIEST watched it. "You seemed bothered. Why is that? You've been in here thousands of times."

The lamia spit in THE PRIEST'S face. "Me never here."

THE PRIEST stepped back. *He afraid. Use it.* "Release me, or creator take residence up in *you*."

THE MAN gave THE PRIEST a handkerchief which he used to wipe away the blood and spittle.

"Are you Taylor Morgan?" THE PRIEST said.

He shaking. Me scared him. Keep going. "You see note *Bé* left you? She here. You like her to switch, cross over to you?"

THE PRIESTS'S could barely open the vial. "What's your n-name?"

"One." *Almost got him.*

"One? Not *Bé*?"

The lamia stared at the liquid torture and strained against the rope. "*Bé* my creator. Named me. Now coming for *you*."

THE PRIEST moved the glass vessel above its face, his hands spasming. "And why does *Bé* call you One?"

"Me first."

"There are others?"

The lamia sneered. "Thousands. Legions."

"I see. Are you a demon?"

"Me lamia."

"Is a lamia a kind of demon?" THE PRIEST said.

"Me lamia."

THE PRIEST released a solitary drop of holy water onto its forehead.

A searing pain burned across her body. *Jesus. Fucking. Christ. Burns!*

"Calm yourself, child," came the deep voice from within. "You're a lamia now. The blisters will heal."

He hurting me! Take control of him!

"How dare you scold me? Me, who made you immortal. Don't worry. I'll take him."

* * *

Garcia blinked at the sizzling smoke rising into his eyes. They burned. Every candle in the sanctuary blew out. He stepped back to get clear while Taylor convulsed from side to side. *The holy water's working again. But I shouldn't be doing this without another priest.*

If Morgan's right Taylor doesn't have much time before integration happens. Then Taylor's soul will be lost forever.

"Javi, what's happening?" Morgan said.

"She's reacting to the holy water."

"Why this time?"

Garcia grabbed his gut. *Well, it also worked last time, but I never told you. How should I put this?* "Not sure. Let's try it again."

"Do you think Taylor's still alive in there?"

"Are you familiar with the term integration, as it relates to demonic possession?"

"No."

"It's where the demon takes over and the host's soul is lost. I don't know where Taylor is in that process. But once integration happens, an exorcism won't help."

Morgan slouched over the marble slab. "Can you tell if it's happened?"

"There are signs, but this is an unusual case because of the lamia aspect. I'm guessing the demon stays until the transmutation is complete. So I think there's still time."

Taylor's irises turned black.

"There. The holy water brought out the demon." Garcia turned to his friend. "Ridding her of the beast will be violent and painful to watch. Brace yourself."

Morgan stepped in closer. "I can handle it."

But can I? Garcia raised the holy water vial over her face with shaking hands. "Demon, you don't like the holy water."

Taylor sneered. "I *cherish* holy water."

It's lying. Trying to convince me it won't work. Garcia trickled a small stream on Taylor's face. "By the power of Christ, I command you to leave this girl at once!"

Her skin blistered, and she winced, but rather than shrieking, she let the water flow into her mouth. Her tongue boiled. Tears fell down her cheeks. But she didn't scream. Instead, she used the boiling liquid to spit in Garcia's face.

Excruciating pain staggered Garcia. He stepped back and wiped himself with the sleeves of his robe. "Holy Mother of God, that's hot." The smell of burning flesh assaulted his nostrils. "Help me, Pennywise. I can't see."

Morgan rushed Garcia to the holy water fount and shoved his face underwater. The cooling water stopped the burning. His vision cleared.

"You doused me in holy water?" Garcia asked Morgan when he came up for air.

"Yeah. I hope I'm not going straight to Hell for unauthorized use."

Garcia patted his face with a white cloth. "I'll make more. Am I burnt bad?"

"Some redness, but no blisters." Morgan stepped closer to Taylor. "The holy water still burned her. But this time the demon overcame the pain and used it against you. Do you know how?"

"I don't know." Garcia recomposed himself and returned to Taylor. He made the sign of the cross over her chest. "By the power of Christ, I command you to leave this sacred host!"

Taylor tilted her head. "Untie me, and I'll show you where the real power is."

Garcia continued. "By the power of Christ, I command you to leave!"

"Fuck you, Father Chancho!" Taylor shouted.

The force of her words knocked Garcia back. He turned to Morgan and shook his head. "I need the actual sacrament, and another priest. Sorry."

Morgan sat on the pew. "I can't allow her to live like this. I can't put others in danger. If we can't exorcise this demon, you know what I'll have to do."

A sharp pain pierced Garcia's chest. "I'll find a priest. Even if I have to defy the Church."

"You'll risk your career."

Garcia stared into the demon's eyes. *Trouble with the Church is the least of my concerns.*

"Her very soul is at stake." Morgan's eyes teared up. "Sometimes sacrifice is the only solution."

"What are you thinking?"

"Give Taylor last rites." Morgan looked his friend in the eyes. "I have no choice. For Taylor's soul. For humanity. I can't let it hurt any more children."

Garcia's face turned sheet white. "She's your daughter."

"She was. Not any more. By the way, I may have killed Michelle."

Garcia's gut wrenched. "That's absurd."

Morgan closed his eyes. "The evidence is pretty overwhelming. And I spent my retirement savings."

"You what?"

"I paid a guy to rid her of the demon. A con artist as it turns out. Lost everything."

"Oh, Pennywise." Garcia fell back into the pew. "This is my fault. If I'd taken your request for an exorcism more seriously."

Morgan looked up at the statue of Jesus. "God could end this if He wanted to. He could save my daughter." He raised his voice. "Right, God? What's that? You've got nothing?" He slumped.

Garcia cleared his throat. "I understand how you feel. I'm not sure I can be a priest any longer. My faith's not there."

"Faith in God?"

"No. Faith in myself. I'm too weak, too afraid. I've been contemplating leaving the church for a while. It's time."

Morgan eyed his friend, then moved in to give him a hug. "You're great at what you do. Don't make a decision you'll regret."

"That's the thing. I feel no remorse."

"This all started when I brought up the exorcism?"

Garcia teared. "I have a confession. I lied about the holy water. Taylor reacted the first time I tried it. I knew then she was possessed."

Morgan sat straighter. "Why didn't you tell me? Maybe the Church would have done something."

"You have every right to despise me. I should have fought harder for you. For Taylor."

"But, Javi, why?"

"Because I'm afraid to fight another demon, man."

Morgan stood and paced. "You should have said something."

"I'm sorry."

Morgan watched his friend. "Forget it, Javi. Based on all we've learned and seen, I doubt it would have made any difference."

Garcia looked up, his cheeks glistening in tears. "*Gracias.* You're kind to say that. If only I could forgive myself."

Morgan sat and pointed at Taylor. "I've always observed we face demons of our own making. I see it in my practice daily. And in myself."

"Scripture is full of testimony on demons. Christ exorcised hundreds. But we're influenced to alter our belief systems based on society, don't we? How many people, even parishioners who attend this church, acknowledge demonic possession, and that exorcisms still go on today? How many would believe what we've seen?"

"It's hard for me to accept, and I'm living it," Morgan said. "I've always believed in the battle between good and evil. Generic good, and generic evil. They make sense, two opposite forces we see in an ongoing, daily struggle. We can identify the good, and the evil. But this takes it to another level. A level I don't want to admit exists."

Garcia's cell rang. "It's Smokey."

"Take it. Just don't tell him I'm with you."

"Detective," Garcia said. "How can I help you?"

"Padre, listen up. I know you're with Morgan. Don't bother to deny it. Tell me you found Taylor."

Garcia shifted. "I can't do that."

"All right. But give the Doc an important message. The DA has booked the first flight to Costa Rica tomorrow morning for the two of them. I can't hold him off any longer. Tell the Doc he's out of time."

* * *

Morgan gazed upon his daughter. *Is there any way out of this?*

"The girl is gone," Taylor said, continuing in her demon voice. "Integration is complete. The transmutation is finished."

Morgan shivered at the idea. "You're a liar."

Taylor cackled. "Your arrogance causes all your problems. It's why you're always a loser."

Morgan peered into Taylor's eyes, looking for a sign of his daughter. "Is that so?"

"Let's review. Your fiancee. Dead, because of you. Your wife. Dead, because of you. And now Taylor. Destroyed, because of your arrogance to hike when warned to stay away. From now on you'll be The Arrogant Loser."

"Don't listen to it," Garcia said.

Morgan reached down and grabbed Taylor by the shoulders. He shook her, harder than he intended. "Stop it!"

"That's right. Strike me. Use your Army training. Slay me. Like your ex-wife. Better yet, hire someone to do it. Abdicate responsibility. Isn't that what Michelle used to say about you? Or go the way of your parents. Murder, suicide, wasn't it? Because their teenage boy was too much for them? You can follow in their footsteps. Kill your daughter, then off yourself. Like old times."

Garcia grabbed Morgan's arms. "Don't engage with it."

Morgan, rage in his eyes, gave her one last shake and let her go.

"Why are you doing this?" Morgan said, his voice dropping with each word. He fell limp against the table, easing to a seated position on the ground.

"You killed them," Taylor said. "You deserve to suffer."

Morgan gazed upon Jesus, tears rolling down both cheeks.

Taylor laughed. "And now, you will be responsible for killing *everyone*. The plague will spread. Lamias will be created. Efforts to stop the invasion will fail. Even humans can't kill that fast. Soon, there will be no girls left to bear children. The entire human population will die off. Thanks to you."

Morgan looked back at her. "Tell me something. How did Taylor pass the DNA tests?"

Taylor cackled. "By then her DNA had already been altered, as she changed to a lamia. Now, it is time for me to go."

"You're leaving her?"

"Yes. Integration is complete. I will enter a bat for a flight to Costa Rica. I have an old adversary to kill before I return to my original homeland."

The front door of the church flew open. Morgan turned, expecting the wind to be the culprit. Instead, a black blur descended on him.

What the hell?

The blur separated into a thousand pieces, and Morgan's knees buckled. *Bats. Hundreds.* He fell to the floor, covering his head. Garcia cowered next to him.

They swooshed around Taylor. She jerked, her back arching to the point Morgan thought it would snap in two. Then she plopped onto the table. As quickly as they'd arrived, the bats flew out in unison.

Morgan helped Garcia to his feet. "You okay?"

"Been better, man."

Taylor opened her eyes, now red, and hissed, showing her fangs. "*Bé* is gone. The girl's soul is dead. I am lamia."

"Then I have nothing to lose by killing you. And nothing you did will spread."

"Fool. Infection exponential. No one believe you."

"Some people believe," Morgan said. "Margarita believes."

Taylor's face contorted. "Margarita far away."

The lamia's afraid of Margarita. "She's here. In Salem."

The lamia hissed. It closed its eyes and fell asleep.

Maybe Margarita's the answer. She and her task force.

CHAPTER 53

Morgan stared at Taylor lying on the marble slab. Afternoon sun poked through the stained glass windows in the sanctuary. *I wonder if the sun will hurt it more in a church?* The smokey aftermath of the extinguished candles floated through the air.

He pondered his dreadful options. *Kill my daughter, or allow her to continue life as a monster?* He shook. *Life? That's no life. It's a horrific existence. And the contagion will spread. I can't permit that.* He wiped away tears. *But it's Taylor. How can I hurt her?*

He turned to Garcia. "If she's been changed into this lamia monster, what can I do besides kill it? It's the humane thing to do."

"You're not capable of harming Taylor. What about the *Awá* possibility?"

"Even *if* Taylor's still in there, she's dead the second we set foot in Costa Rica tomorrow."

Taylor's eyes popped open, her irises fiery red. She hissed at them, fighting to break free of the restraints. "Release me!"

What I'd give to have her yell at me again, in her own voice. "You're not going anywhere."

"Me tell *Bé* spare you." She leered at Garcia. "Otherwise, *you* his next host."

Morgan drew a deep breath. "Yeah? Bring it on."

"Richard!" Garcia said. "Don't invite it in!"

Loud clicking on the marble floor interrupted them. Morgan turned to find Azra approaching in high heels and a heavy coat. His head cleared at the sight of her.

"Azra?" Morgan said. "What are you doing here?"

"I'm worried about you. And I have horrible news." She took Morgan's arm. "Your ex's mother killed herself at the police station. I'm so sorry."

Morgan's heart jumped. *Laila? No!* "How? Why?"

"Cocaine overdose," Azra said.

Garcia crossed himself.

"My God," Morgan said. "You think losing Michelle pushed her over the edge?" He glanced at Taylor. "Or maybe seeing Taylor like this?"

She followed his attention to Taylor. "Why is Taylor tied down? There's blood on her. And her eyes and teeth. How can the other personality do that?"

"It can't," Morgan said. "Like I told you before, it's not psychological. I've been trying to build a case for an exorcism."

She faced Garcia. "You put him up to this nonsense?"

"No," Garcia said. "But he's right. And, trust me, I didn't want to go there."

"Have you treated her wounds?" Azra said.

"The blood's not hers," Morgan said.

Azra took his hand and pressed. "I want to help you, Richard. I do. But this talk of possession? You're a scientist."

"I know."

Azra tried to grasp Morgan. "We must run tests. Find a cure."

Damn, she still smells like orchids. Morgan held her at a distance and looked into her eyes, his anxiety boring a hole in his chest. "Taylor's gone. What's left is a monster. And if the church can't save her, no one can. I have to destroy her."

Azra glowered at each of them, her mouth agape. "Destroy? You mean kill?"

Taylor squirmed on the table, trying to free herself.

Azra withdrew from Morgan. "Richard, I'm trying to work with you here. How can you even bring up the possibility of hurting Taylor?"

"Taylor's soul is at stake," Morgan said.

Azra placed her hands on her hips. "I can call in specialists from all over the country. We can still solve this."

Taylor spiked her head toward Azra. "Bring me young girls? Me so hungry."

Azra made a disgusted face. "Let me start by taking X-rays of her mouth. Finding the cause of her enlarged incisors may help us with a diagnosis."

Morgan grabbed her arm. "What's wrong with you? Look at her!"

"Ow. You're hurting me." Azra pulled away. "You don't want my help. You want my blessing. Well, you don't have it. I have a responsibility to protect this girl. From all of you. It appears I'm her last chance."

Morgan realized the trouble Azra could cause him. *I can't let her leave or call for help.* He put up his palms. "Sorry. I shouldn't have grabbed you. I'm just so desperate to save her."

Azra glared at him. "Then stop saying crazy shit."

"I will. Can I ask for a favor?"

Azra folded her arms without replying.

"Can you do the X-rays here?" Morgan said. "And keep this between the three of us?"

Azra glanced at Garcia. "In a *church*? Why?"

Morgan reached for her and Azra let him hold her. "Because I don't trust anyone else. You have access to a portable X-ray machine. Please, don't get anyone else involved until we have more answers."

Azra pondered that. "If it's okay with Father Garcia, it's okay with me."

"It's alright," Garcia said. "Desperate times and all."

"Then I'll go pick it up and bring it back in the CME van. Promise me you won't do anything until I get back."

"I promise," Morgan said.

After Azra left, Morgan bolted for the door. "Watch her for a little while, will you? I'm off to the jail."

"The jail?"

"I need to break Margarita out."

"Break her out? Are you hearing yourself?"

"I have to try. She's the expert at dealing with this."

"She'll want to kill her," Garcia said.

Taylor flashed her incisors at Morgan again.

"I know." *And she knows how.*

"I can't condone killing Taylor."

Morgan walked away. "Then you'll have to stop me."

CHAPTER 54

Morgan called Officer Phillips' private line from the car. "Doctor Morgan. What's up?"

"I need a favor."

"Name it."

"Can you sneak me in the rear exit of the jail?"

Officer Phillips paused. "I guess. What's this about?"

"I need to see a prisoner. Alone."

Officer Phillips was waiting for Morgan at the rear exit. "Be careful." The sentinel pointed to bloodstains on the dirty floor. "She's a handful." With that warning, he left Morgan outside the locked barrier.

Without her machete, or a gun, Margarita looked benign. Smaller than Morgan remembered. She even grinned at him.

"Come to admit I was right, *señor*?"

"I came to ask for your help."

"Ah. You finally believe in the demon. And what your daughter is becoming."

"Yes. Can you kill it?"

"The demon? No. But I can kill the girl which will force the beast to leave."

"The demon's already gone," Morgan said.

Margarita knit an eyebrow. "Why do you say that?"

"She told me. Then a zillion bats showed up. Looked like your demon was hitching a ride home."

Margarita pondered for two minutes before responding. "The demon doesn't leave until the transmutation to lamia is complete."

"So, if the demon's gone my daughter can't be saved."

"She was doomed the moment the bat infected her." She sighed. "This help you mentioned. You want me to do your dirty work." It wasn't a question.

Morgan closed his eyes. "Yes. And then, one more thing."

"I know what you want, even if you cannot say it out loud. You want me also to kill *you*. Because you cannot live with yourself if you go through with destroying your daughter."

"Yes."

"It will not be pretty," Margarita said. "You may think you can see your daughter decapitated, but you will beg me to quit. And if you do try to stop me, I will be forced to kill you, and anyone else who gets in the way."

"There's a priest. I don't want him hurt."

"Not my problem."

Morgan winced. *What if Javi fights us?*

"By now, she has turned others." She reposed in her bunk. "Once their transmutation is complete I must destroy them."

"There's no other way?"

"Not if they've turned. I must behead them all."

Morgan's stomach erupted in pain. *Oh, Jesus. Beheaded? They're just children.* He fell to his knees. "How can we kill all these girls?"

"If I was allowed to remain in the shadows, I could have cleaned everything up. But, thanks to you, the plague has free reign over your city. And it spreads quickly."

Yeah, thanks to me, the entire world is turning to shit.

Margarita spit near Morgan's shoes. "I must kill her today. They are deporting me to Costa Rica in the morning."

Morgan reopened his eyes. "Me, too. And Taylor. I imagine your task force will be waiting."

"They will."

"I could let the extradition play out. We'll both be dead. Problem solved."

"But the turned girls will continue to multiply. Killing your daughter is no longer enough."

No longer enough. Meaning, if I'd let you kill Taylor in Costa Rica, all this could have been avoided. "Then we better hurry."

"How do you plan my escape?"

"Working on it." Vertigo struck Morgan. He held his head, hunched over. "What if I bring Taylor to you?"

Margarita laughed. "You want me to kill her in here? And you? They will arrest me for murder. You are *loco en la cabeza.*"

"No, of course. I'll get you out."

"To all the infected girls. Then, safe passage home."

"I'll find a way." *I need Smokey.*

Morgan sneaked out the way he'd come in and drove toward the church.

But the dizziness and nausea crippled him, and he pulled over. He turned off the engine and shut his eyes. *Never felt like this.*

He lay across the front seat in a fetal position, hoping for relief, until exhaustion overtook him, and he fell asleep.

* * *

Morgan woke up to a calm head and a setting sun. But his back and neck ached from the awkward repose in his front seat. *I slept all afternoon? Did the demon do this? I did invite it in.* He shivered. *Damn. Javi's alone with Taylor.*

He floored the car back to the church. He recognized Smokey's car, along with two police cruisers. *Good. Smokey's here.*

Morgan screeched to a halt in front of St. Edward's and ran into the sanctuary. Garcia stood behind the marble table where Taylor was still bound. *Thank God.* Smokey stood next to him, watching Taylor, who lay with her eyes closed. Four armed officers rose from the pews.

"Let him through," Smokey commanded.

Morgan rushed to the front. "Sorry. Something came over me. Fell asleep in the car."

Smokey twirled his unlit cigar. "Doc, you've got some explaining to do."

Morgan checked on Taylor. "I know. How is she?"

"The same," Garcia said. "Azra's come and gone. Took X-rays and vitals. Taylor slept through it. I begged her to keep all this to herself. I think she will, for now. Out of love for you."

"Thanks," Morgan said, then turned to Smokey. "What now?"

Smokey motioned to the officers. "You four. Wait outside." They hustled out amongst hushed whispers. Once the sanctuary door closed, Smokey let out a deep breath. "What were you thinking, bringing her here?"

Morgan shifted his weight. "We were hoping to get solid evidence to justify an exorcism."

Smokey turned to Garcia. "The Padre explained all that. Says the Catholic Church wants nothing to do with this."

"Yeah. Listen, I need another favor."

Smokey smirked. "Don't you think you've had your quota?"

Morgan grabbed Smokey's arm. "I need you to release Margarita. She knows how to destroy Taylor and save her soul."

"You're not serious."

Garcia stepped between them. "He's not. But we need Margarita's help. If the girls Taylor infected are also turning into lamias, sending Morgan and Taylor back to Costa Rica solves nothing in Salem."

"That's right," Morgan said. "The only way to stop it is to eliminate the afflicted girls."

"You're suggesting even more exorcisms?" Smokey said.

"No," Morgan said. "The original demon turned Taylor, and she infected the girls, turning them into lamias. The other girls aren't possessed. We must destroy them."

"That's not entirely accurate," came a female voice from the end of the sanctuary.

Morgan turned to find Linda Copeland walking down the aisle. Setting sun rays beamed around her.

CHAPTER 55

A sense of renewed hope coursed through Morgan's veins in the Sanctuary. "Professor Copeland. How'd you find us?"

"It's Linda, remember? I've been keeping an eye on you. Waiting for you to be ready to listen."

"Javi, Smokey, this is Linda Copeland. She's an expert on ancient cultures, like the Bribri. I'm sorry to say she lost a daughter to this demon."

Garcia took her hand. "I'm so sorry."

"What did you mean," Smokey said, "when you said the Doc's version isn't entirely accurate?"

Linda extricated her hand. "Exorcising the demon by a Bribri *Awá* before the transmutation is complete cures the offspring."

"I think the demon's already gone," Morgan said. "Taken away in a hoard of bats."

"That may have been an act designed to fool you," Linda said. "I thought my daughter's demon had fled, and her transformation complete. But, before the task force beheaded her, I heard the demon again. Saw the blackness in her eyes. It was still there. Lurking."

Garcia cleared his throat. "Why would it hide? Demons want you to know they're in control."

"This demon is different," Linda said. "Its mission is to convert the girl, not to mock us. So, it will only show itself to protect its interest. Gloating isn't enough for it."

Morgan's heart raced. *Maybe I can save Taylor!*

Hold on. All this is conjecture. Don't get carried away.

Screw that. This is my daughter we're talking about. Hope may be the only thing keeping me alive.

"So, the demon might still be in there," Morgan said.

"If the transmutation isn't complete, I'm certain it is," Linda said.

Morgan's heart raced. "And the girls Taylor's infected can be saved by exorcising the demon? Without killing Taylor?"

"Correct," Linda said. "But, if we can't exorcise the demon in time, we must destroy the infected girls."

Morgan sat. *This changes everything.* "I need to take her to Costa Rica. To the *Awá*."

Smokey turned to Garcia. "Padre, I'm way out of my league here. What do you think?"

Garcia looked at Morgan, then at Taylor and Linda. "I'm a believer, man. I think Taylor's best chance is to go see this *Awá*. Get the demon exorcised in Costa Rica, at the Bribri village. Apparently it's also the only choice to save the other girls in Salem."

"And what about these other girls?" Smokey asked him. "What do we do with them while we wait?"

"We need to quarantine them," Garcia said.

Morgan's head spun. *I'm taking Taylor to Costa Rica? They'll kill us both as soon as we step off the plane.*

But if there's even a chance it can save her, and the others, I have to try.

"No doctor will agree to that," Smokey said.

"One doctor might," Morgan said.

"Who?" Garcia said.

Morgan stood. "Azra."

Garcia almost choked. "Azra? She's not exactly on team Morgan right now."

"She'll do what's best for the community. I can't think of another option." Morgan turned to Smokey. "What do you say, Lieutenant? Are you willing to push for a quarantine?"

"I've seen enough to agree it's necessary. But how will you get to the Bribri village? The authorities will be waiting when you land."

A somber silence descended on the altar.

"I'll arrange my own transportation before the extradition flight," Morgan said. "Sneak past the police before the extradition flight lands. Fortunately, I know a pilot who will want to help."

Smokey bit on his cigar. "It won't stop the extradition, but I'm following a new lead on Michelle's death. If it pans out, you'll be exonerated."

"What?" Morgan said. "You didn't think to lead with that?"

"I said *if*. Don't get your hopes too high. Might be a pile of crap."

A charge ran through Morgan's body. *Maybe I didn't kill Michelle!* He lunged forward and gave Smokey a bearhug. "Thank you."

Smokey pushed him away. "Like I said, I'm investigating."

Morgan pulled out his cell phone and punched in Azra's name on the call list. "Hey. It's me. I'm at the church. Can you get back here? I have something important to talk to you about." He hung up. "She's close. We have to sell her on doing this for Taylor. Don't bring up anything she doesn't want to hear. Play to her ego about solving a big medical crisis. She won't be able to resist the opportunity."

He stood near Taylor, now panting like a wild animal, her eyes a red inferno. *Maybe this will work. Maybe I won't have to destroy her.*

"Untie me!" Taylor demanded. She strained against the ropes, which frayed. Then, her body lifted off the marble table. Inching higher. The ropes kept her tied, but she hovered several inches above it.

Morgan gasped. *Jesus. Is she levitating?*

Taylor slammed back onto the table and closed her eyes, suddenly sedate.

"Did you see that?" Morgan said. "Was she hovering?"

"Damnedest thing I've ever seen," Smokey said.

Garcia backed away. "I've seen it once before."

"Your exorcism?" Morgan said.

"Yeah," Garcia said. "Not something you forget."

The church doors squeaked open and Azra charged in, slamming the door behind her. "Where were you?"

"Sorry," Morgan said. "I had to check on something for Taylor. Thanks for coming back."

Azra glared at Morgan. "You've still got Taylor tied up." Then she noticed Linda. "You again?"

Smokey cleared his throat. "Azra, I'm asking you to declare a medical emergency. Whatever Taylor's got, it's spreading. You must set up a quarantine and isolate the girls that are showing symptoms."

Azra shifted her attention from Linda to Smokey. "What other girls?"

"Jennifer Peterson is missing," Smokey said. "So is the Wilson girl. And there was another attack an hour ago. An eye witness identified Jennifer as the attacker."

"That doesn't justify a quarantine," Azra said. "For all you know, it's teenagers acting out."

Taylor's nails dug into the marble top. The sound made Morgan's skin crawl.

Morgan approached her. "Taylor! Stop!"

Taylor grinned and flashed her teeth at him. Even longer now than that morning. "Come. Say close to my face."

Azra followed Morgan and gasped.

Garcia steadied Azra. "You see what we're up against. Imagine if Jennifer and Katy are infected like Taylor. Imagine if they're infecting others. I don't know what this is, but I know it's spreading. You can get it under control while you figure out what the medical cause is. You can identify an unknown pathogen."

Azra stared at Taylor. "Even if I believe you, I have no authority to quarantine anyone."

Morgan stepped forward. "Your mentor at the CDC has the authority."

"Joseph?" Azra said. "But what would I tell him? They have protocols in place." She pointed at Taylor. "I can't provide any evidence of a pathogen."

"I remember," Morgan said, "you telling me Joseph had a huge crush on you. It's time to call in a favor. The CDC has broad powers. Ask him to trust you while you gather evidence."

Azra continued to stare at Taylor. "If I agree to try, I assume Taylor will be part of the quarantine."

"That's the thing," Smokey said. "My orders are to extradite them both to Costa Rica in the morning to face charges of killing their officers. If Taylor's in quarantine I can justify keeping her here."

She turned to Smokey. "If I do this, we can also claim Richard's an infection risk due to his proximity to her. We can protect them both. I'll call the CDC." Azra studied him. "You're not bullshitting me, are you?"

Smokey swallowed. "I'll stake my career on it."

"Azra, what happens now?" Morgan said.

"I call Joseph. Ask him to mandate a quarantine and put me in charge until they get their people here. The police round up the affected girls and we put them inside the zone."

"Where will you set up this zone?" Smokey said.

"My lab has a medical containment area. It's big enough for eight or ten girls. It has all the safeguards we need."

"Let's do this," Morgan said. "Smokey, can you help me take Taylor to Azra's office?"

"Sure, Doc."

Azra's heels clicked down the aisle. "I need to go. Bring Taylor by 8 a.m."

"Will do," Morgan said.

Once Azra left the building Morgan wheeled on Smokey. "Taylor's not going into quarantine. She's coming with me."

Linda exhaled. "Thank God. I thought you'd lost your mind."

"I probably have, but that's a debate for another time. Smokey, once the CDC mandate comes down, you can pick up the affected girls."

"But without Taylor, will Azra play ball?" Smokey said.

Morgan pursed his lips. "Azra won't like it, but she won't risk looking like she yanked the CDC's chain. You'll have a few days to keep the girls isolated. Once Azra sees their condition, she and the CDC will realize they need to keep the quarantine going."

"Right," Smokey said. "What about avoiding the extradition?"

"Taylor, the professor, and I will fly under the radar, and travel to the Bribri village. Once we've taken off, you tell the DA we escaped and ran. Tell them we drove toward Canada. That will keep them off our trail for a while. I hope you won't get in too much trouble."

"Don't worry about me," Smokey said. "I've got a ton of goodwill banked."

"You're forgetting something," Garcia said. "Azra will know you lied, and she'll out you to the DA. The Costa Rican authorities will be waiting for your private plane."

The room went quiet, which, in the marble-filled sanctuary, struck Morgan as eerie.

"You're right," Morgan said. "You'll have to convince her Taylor is still here, and will be brought in soon. Buy us time to land in Costa Rica."

"*I* have to persuade her?" Garcia said.

"You're the only one who can," Morgan said. "She'll trust you. Costa Rica doesn't have much law enforcement near the Bribri's village. We should be able to avoid capture if we can get out of the airport."

Taylor clapped. "Me home? Good. Me infect girls there, too."

Morgan drooped. *I must be mad. This will never work.*

Don't give up! It's her only chance. "Smokey, what time are you supposed to have Taylor and me at the airport?"

"Nine in the morning."

"Is that Margarita's flight?" Morgan said.

"Yep."

Morgan looked over at Taylor, who was chewing on the ropes binding her. "I need to make a call."

Linda stepped next to Morgan. "Taylor's not likely to be cooperative, and her appearance will be conspicuous."

"We only need her to look like my patient when we land in Costa Rica," Morgan said.

Linda touched Morgan's arm gently. "I'm with you, all the way."

Morgan smiled at her. "Thanks. The flight should be fine. It'll be daylight the whole trip. She'll be calm."

CHAPTER 56

Tuesday

At eight sharp Garcia stepped into Azra's office. Medical personnel in matching white lab coats were sealing the quarantine area.

Azra glared at him. "Where's Taylor?"

Garcia's face warmed. "They're right behind me." He swallowed. The smell of rubbing alcohol and bleach burned his eyes.

Azra narrowed her eyes. "You're a horrible liar, Father."

Garcia looked down.

"I'm ashamed of you," Azra said, vile dripping in her tone. "Is Smokey complicit in this?" Garcia kept focusing on the linoleum floor, afraid to look Azra in the eyes. "Fine. No more fooling around with you and Morgan's posse. I'm calling the chief."

Sorry, Azra. I've got no more shame to take on.

* * *

Morgan held Taylor, freshly sedated, in the back of Smokey's car on the one lane road toward Lusardi Field. Based on his destination, he'd chosen lightweight clothing, and he shivered in the early morning Salem weather. Linda sat in the front with Smokey.

Hurry, hurry, hurry. Azra won't be patient.

Bob Allister met them at his Gulfstream G450. "Morning, Dr. Morgan. Beautiful day for a flight."

Morgan slipped out of the car with Taylor in his arms. "Bob. I don't know how to thank you."

Allister waved him off. "After saving my marriage? Don't be silly. Let's get her loaded up. The cops could show any moment." He led them aboard his eight passenger jet. "We'll be in Costa Rica by mid-afternoon."

Morgan got Taylor situated. After he and Linda seated themselves, Morgan checked the medical paperwork again. *She should pass for a patient.*

His stomach growled. *If we haven't been flagged.*

"Be safe," Smokey said, standing on the runway.

"Thanks for this," Morgan said. "I know you're way out on a limb here. They'll suspect you helped us."

"Don't worry. I'll accept the consequences for doing the right thing."

"I can tell them I forced you."

Smokey gave Morgan a look that said, "as if you could."

Morgan laughed. "At least I can explain why."

"As Rick said in Casablanca—after the plane leaves, Louie."

"Is this the start of a beautiful friendship?" Morgan said.

Smokey shook his head. "Unlike Louie, I'm not able to cover your expenses. Godspeed."

Allister secured the door. "Time to rock 'n roll."

Moments later, the engines fired up, and the Gulfstream glided down the runway. It lifted over the top of the nearby tree-line. Morgan glanced down at the pavement.

A police car approached Smokey, lights blazing.

Morgan's skin crawled. *Oh, shit. So much for getting to Costa Rica before they're tipped off.*

"The cops are here," Allister yelled back.

"Yeah, I see them," Morgan responded. "Maybe this is a bad idea. Too much risk for you."

"Will Smokey tell them you're aboard?" Allister said.

"No chance."

"Then they can't prove it. Even if they call me to turn around, I'll ignore it. What are they going to do? Shoot us down?"

Morgan paled and glanced at Linda. Her washed-out face showed the etchings of stress. *I don't know. Will they?*

The jet merged with the thick cloud cover. Morgan watched wisps of white cotton candy float by. "The DA will have law enforcement meet us in Costa Rica."

"When we land, it'll be in the private aviation terminal," Allister said. "Your paperwork should get you through customs. Even if our country tries to convince them to stop you, word doesn't travel fast down there. You might slide by."

A gap in the clouds gave Morgan a view of the airstrip. He watched Smokey being handcuffed. "That's a lot to hope for."

"Do we have a choice?" Linda said.

"No."

* * *

Smokey stepped into the Chief's office. DA Campbell stood off to the side in yet another navy blue suit. *Doesn't he own a different color?* Tension was two cents a ton.

"What the hell were you thinking?" the Chief yelled at Smokey.

"Not sure what you mean, Chief."

"You let two suspects escape," the Chief said. "Dr. Khan told us everything."

Of course she did. Bitch. "Like I told you on the phone, Morgan slipped away when I was arranging for Dr. Khan to set up a quarantine."

"And you just happened to be at the airport?" Campbell said.

Smokey pulled out a cigar. "Once I heard they were on the run, I went looking for them. I checked the airport, but they weren't there."

"Bullshit," Campbell said. "I can have you charged with aiding and abetting."

Smokey popped the cigar into his mouth. "Go ahead. In the meantime, Chief, am I free to go back to work? I have a fugitive to track down. And some girls to quarantine."

Campbell gave Smokey a sinister scowl. "I've already reported that plane to the Costa Rican authorities. If it touches down there, Morgan and Taylor will be captured and tried in Costa Rica, and you'll be fired."

"Knock yourself out," Smokey said. "But you're wasting your time, and the taxpayer's money. They weren't on that plane. Now, if you'll excuse me." He turned to go.

"Lieutenant," the Chief said. "For your sake, I hope you're right. For now, you're restricted to desk duty."

A young officer barged in. "Sorry to interrupt, but four more girls are showing the same symptoms as the Peterson and Wilson girls."

"Get them to the quarantine zone," Smokey said. He turned back to his boss. "You sure you want to restrict me? The shit's about to hit the fan. You'll need all hands on deck if we're to get out in front of this contagion."

Campbell scoffed. "Dr. Khan assures me it's under control."

"Have it your way," Smokey said. "Call me when you come to your senses."

Smokey retreated to his desk and nearly jumped with excitement at the sight of the file he was expecting. *There it is!* He opened the folder and scanned the contents. *Yes! I was right.* He opened an intercom line. "Carter still here?"

"He's down the hall waiting for us to release his wife's body."

Restricted, my ass. Smokey barged in on Carter. "Guess what I found?"

"Lieutenant, I'm in no mood for games. I lost my wife and daughter. My grandchild is sick and my deranged son-in-law abducted her."

Smokey tossed Morgan's drug log, protected inside a plastic evidence bag, onto the table. "Your fingerprints are on this log from Morgan's office. The log that showed Morgan checking out the drug Ketamine."

Carter squirmed. His face added a shade of red. "What are you talking about?"

"You tried to frame Morgan for Michelle's death."

"That's absurd."

Smokey reached into his pocket and withdrew a cigar. For the first time in his career, he ignored the no smoking policy and lit it. "Let me explain it to you. You doctored Dr. Morgan's drug log. You thought you wiped it clean, but after you wedged it between Morgan's desk and cabinet, you took your gloves off. Then the log shifted down, and you reached under the desk to move it back up, thinking you only touched the bottom edge. But the paper bent enough to leave a partial on the back."

Carter showed no reaction. "I want a lawyer."

"Humph. I bet you do."

* * *

Azra watched the officers bring in another girl. "In there. With the others. Do their parents know?"

"We found her wandering the streets alone. No sign of an adult. No ID."

"All right. Do your best to find their families."

That makes six. All with violent thrashing behavior, similar to Taylor's convulsions. I think Smokey was right. This is *a medical emergency.*

She prepared more doses of sedatives. *Might even be a paper in this.*

She put on her surgical mask and stepped into the quarantine zone. After administering the opiate to the latest drop-off, she studied the other girls while they slept.

Bite marks. On each neck. I'm definitely getting an article out of this.

* * *

Garcia stood on the front steps, waving goodbye to the last of the afternoon's youth group, when Smokey pulled into the church parking lot.

"Padre! Glad you're here."

"I'm always here." *At least until the Bishop finds a replacement.* "Any word from our mutual friend?"

"No. But I can't sit on the sidelines on this one."

"What's that mean?" Garcia said.

"It means I'm going to Costa Rica."

You're what? "Don't you have work to do here? Containing the plague, and all?"

"Azra has the girls in CDC lockdown. Besides, I'm stuck at my desk for helping Morgan and Taylor escape. Once Morgan lands, the department will know I helped them and they'll fire me."

Garcia rubbed his fingers through his hair. "I'm not sure what to say, man."

"I do. Come with me."

"What?"

"Come with me. I've arrested Isaiah Carter for trying to frame Morgan. The Doc deserves to know he didn't kill Michelle. And, maybe, we can help him get Taylor cured."

Garcia shivered. "I can't."

"Sure you can. I can see it in your eyes, Padre. You need to see this through to get your faith back."

Get it back? Or lose it forever?

"Come on," Smokey said. "We're only half a day behind Morgan. We should be able to catch up at the Bribri village."

Garcia peered at the church. *Maybe the answers I seek are in Costa Rica. They're sure not here.* "I'm in."

CHAPTER 57

Liberia, Costa Rica

The Gulfstream glided to a soft landing at Daniel Oduber Quirós International Airport in Liberia at three in the afternoon, local time, and rolled to a stop on the asphalt runway. The plane pulled up to their appointed checkpoint. Security officers in black and red uniforms and automatic weapons stood guard.

"Are those guards here for us?" Morgan asked Allister.

"Not necessarily. You'll see policemen with guns along the roads, too. The main highway links Columbia and Mexico, so there's a lot of drug traffic the military is determined to stop."

Morgan checked Taylor, still asleep in her seat. A big, floppy hat and long pants and sleeves covered every inch of her skin to keep the sun's rays from scorching her. "We need to get Taylor somewhere isolated before the sun goes down. Let's hope customs believes she's sedated due to illness."

"I've been through this part of the world many times," Linda said. "As long as they don't suspect drugs, they'll be cooperative."

When Allister opened the door, heat and humidity assaulted Morgan. The feeling brought back painful memories of Nosara.

Allister climbed down the stairs first, carrying a wheelchair. Then Morgan carried Taylor and placed her in the chair on the tarmac. Linda followed. The guards stood their ground, like Buckingham sentinels on duty.

Morgan studied the row of guardians, looking for eye contact, but got none.

A uniformed man emerged from the customs office on the far side of the sentries. He held a clipboard, and a frown. He stepped with purpose toward Allister.

"Show time," Allister whispered. "Stay calm. Routine check."

The customs officer walked past Morgan to Allister. Morgan held his breath until his face changed color. He forced himself to breathe, but the short staccatos of air gave off a wheezing sound, which caught the officer's attention.

He slowed to stare at Morgan, his eyes narrowing. "Are you okay, *señor?*"

"I'm fine."

"You look nervous."

Morgan shook his head. "Don't like flying. Glad to be on the ground."

The officer broke off his gaze to ogle Linda. He gave her a more thorough perusal than appropriate, then returned his attention to Allister. "I am Officer Ruiz of the Costa Rica Customs Department. Papers, please."

Allister handed him the flight and landing authorization, along with customs forms.

Ruiz gave them a cursory glance, then looked back at Morgan. "How is it an American, with a sick daughter, comes to Costa Rica for treatment? Our medical facilities pale to yours."

"It's a specialized therapy," Morgan answered. "Involves research using pharmaceuticals extracted from insects in your rain forests. Once she's inoculated, I'll take her back to finish her treatment."

Ruiz checked the paperwork and signed the form. "Insects. You sound like the medicine men in the jungle."

"I'm returning to the US. I'd like to take off as soon as possible," Allister said.

"You are free to leave." Ruiz waved toward the building. "Of course, there is a fee for leaving the country."

"Understood. In those doors?"

"Yes," Ruiz said. He turned to Morgan. "You will follow me to get processed. It's a different section, so say *goodbye* to your friend."

Morgan didn't care for the emphasis on the word "goodbye."

Allister took Morgan by the arm and drew him away while Linda stayed with Taylor and Ruiz. "I'll wipe down everything in the plane. Even if they suspect I brought you down, they'll never hear it from me, and they won't find any evidence. Good luck, my friend."

"Thanks," Morgan said. "You're a lifesaver."

Allister glanced at the guards one last time, saluted to Morgan, and walked to the customs office.

Morgan returned to Linda and Taylor, intending to wheel Taylor. He didn't get far.

"Stay here," Ruiz ordered.

Morgan turned to him. "What's up?" It was only then he realized the guard's automatic weapons now pointed at him. Morgan's stomach lurched.

Ruiz pulled a match from his shirt pocket and lit a cigarette. "I know who you are, Dr. Morgan."

Morgan glanced at Allister going through the customs door. *If I cooperate, maybe they'll let Allister and Linda go.* "What happens now?"

Ruiz pulled out a sheet of paper. "I have a fax. Says you and your daughter fled the US to avoid extradition. To us." He gave Morgan a puzzled expression. "And yet, here you are, right where we wanted you. Strange choice, *señor.*"

Morgan sagged. *I've got to get past this guy.*

Ruiz studied Taylor. "What is wrong with her?"

"She's very sick," Morgan said. "If I don't get her to that doctor soon, she *will* die."

"That is unfortunate." Ruiz turned to Linda. "There is no mention of you. What is your connection to these two?"

"I'm escorting them."

Ruiz grunted. "Then you have come a long way for nothing. These two will be transported to Nosara, to be tried for murdering a policeman." He eyed her. "But I have no orders on you. You can return with the pilot."

"I'm not leaving," Linda said.

"Then you can enter the country through customs." Ruiz pointed to the entrance. "It makes no difference to me."

"I'm staying with them," Linda said.

"No, Linda," Morgan said. "It's over for us. You need to go live your life."

"My life is killing that demon."

"Demon?" Ruiz said, shaken.

"Yes," Linda said. "The Bribri plague has infected this girl. Only they can save her."

Ruiz took a step back.

"You know it?" Morgan said.

"I have three daughters, *señor*. And cousins who live in those mountains. They tell me about the plague. Most around here don't want to believe it, but I do."

"Then you know what's at stake," Morgan said. "I must get my daughter to the *Awá* up there. He's her only chance."

Ruiz shook his head. "They will not even try to cure her, *señor*."

"Maybe," Morgan said. "But what choice do I have? You said you have daughters. What would you do in my place?"

Ruiz looked Morgan in the eye. "Even if I want to I have a dilemma, *señor*. Once we register your passport, your government will know you are here. As will mine." He tipped his head to the left. "I will lose my job."

A bank of dark clouds passed overhead, moving ominous shapes across the tarmac. Taylor squirmed.

"There must be something I can do to convince you to let us pass," Morgan said.

"My boss handed me the fax," Ruiz said. "I can not pretend I did not see it."

"But you can deny seeing us," Morgan said "I bet a man of your stature can escort us through customs, and avoid having our passports registered. Claim we're a special witness for the police, and the drug cartels are after us. It won't be the first time you took charge of an explosive situation and handled it personally."

Ruiz narrowed his eyes, remaining silent.

"What about the guards?" Morgan said. "Do they know about the fax?"

"No. They will accept any story or command I give them."

"Then you're golden," Morgan said. "You just have to escort us through. Use the drug cartel explanation. I'm sure that's plausible."

Ruiz looked at Taylor. "It is too risky."

"I know how hard it is to raise a big family like yours," Morgan said.

"We grow our own food, slaughter our own chickens and pigs. Yes, it is a challenge."

"Maybe I can help." Morgan pulled out a wad of hundreds. "I like you, Ruiz. A family man, who cares for his children. You're a lot like me. I'd like you to have this to take care of your daughters. No strings attached. One father to another, honoring the commitment we made to keep our daughters safe."

Ruiz slid over to stand next to Morgan, slipping the wad into his pants pocket. He turned to the guards. "This man is a witness against the drug cartels and needs special treatment. No one will talk of this meeting. Understood?"

The sentries lowered their weapons and stood at attention.

Ruiz looked at Morgan. "We shall escort you around the normal process. You will need a car. As luck would have it, my brother runs a rental car shop down the road. You have more cash?"

Morgan pulled out the last of his currency. "A little."

Linda stepped forward. "Don't worry. I'll help cover our expenses." She handed Morgan half of her money.

"You sure?" Morgan said.

"Positive."

"Thanks."

Linda charged ahead. "Let's go. It'll be dark soon, and I'm guessing that will bring a whole new set of challenges."

* * *

Her US Marshal escort removed Margarita's handcuffs and handed her over to a customs official in the main terminal. "She's all yours. Didn't say a word on the flight down other than complain in Spanish about some Morgan bastard who stood her up. In case she doesn't understand English, tell her not to come back to the US."

Margarita glared at the marshal. "I understand you fine, *chancho*."

The customs official pulled her away. "That's enough. Your husband is here to take you home."

"Juan is here?"

"*Sí*. Move."

Margarita glanced out the window at the tarmac. She froze at the sight of familiar faces.

It's a miracle. Taylor Morgan is here! Now I can complete my mission. I will kill the lamia.

CHAPTER 58

Morgan drove as fast as the brutal highway conditions allowed. Potholes and narrow lanes surrounded by dense jungle created hazards around every bend. The sun disappeared over the mountains to the west. Taylor moved in and out of semi-consciousness.

"We'll make the Atlantic coast by sunset," Linda said, seated in the back of the run-down Sports Utility with Taylor. "Then up the highway until we reach the dirt roads that take us up the mountain to the Bribri village."

She'll be awake soon. Will the drugs keep her calm? They turned right along the coast. *No streetlights. I hope Linda knows the way.* "She still secure back there?"

"She's not escaping these ropes."

"Not too tight, right?"

"Don't worry. I won't let her get hurt."

She's not the one I'm worried about. "Watch yourself. She's powerful."

As if on cue, Taylor awoke. "Home!"

"We're going to the Bribri village." *I wonder if it's afraid of the Bribri village?* "To fix you."

"Me fixed. You broken."

Doesn't seem to bother it. Morgan regarded Taylor in the rear-view mirror. "Can I speak to *Bé?*"

She showed off her incisors. Then her voice changed to the deep version. "Nice of you to bring me home. Saved me from finding a ride."

Morgan's heart raced. *The demon! There's still time!* "So the bats at the church were for show."

"What can I say. I'm a drama queen."

Morgan recognized the voice. *My mother. She used to say that. How does it know?* He shook it off. "Can I talk with Taylor now?"

"I already told you," Taylor said. "She's dead."

"I don't believe you," Morgan said.

Taylor sniffed at Linda. "I know you. We took your daughter."

The color drained from Linda's face.

"Easy back there," Morgan said. "Don't let it get in your head."

Linda leaned forward until her face almost touched Taylor's. "I will kill you, demon."

Taylor laughed, and Linda slapped her, hard. Taylor stopped laughing, and strained to break free. "You don't want to mess with me. Especially now. I'm even stronger here."

Morgan held his breath. *Don't lose it, professor. I need you.* "You okay back there, Linda?"

"I'm fine."

You don't sound fine.

Taylor cackled, then reverted to the lamia voice. "Much to do. Me do it here now. Offspring infect others in Salem."

"Jennifer and Katy are in quarantine," Morgan said. "There won't be any spreading of anything."

Taylor opened her eyes wide. Her tongue clicked across her teeth. "Think can stop us? Fool."

The last shimmer of sunlight vanished, and they were in the dark, the road lit by two dim headlights. Shadows reached across the road from all directions, like tree limbs expanding and contracting.

Like the "Wizard of Oz." The branches are reaching for me. His throat, having lost all its moisture, gagged on dry air and dust.

The SUV hit a deep divot, knocking Morgan skyward until his head slammed against the roof.

"Me drive," Taylor said, matter-of-factly. "See perfect in dark. You get you killed." She shrieked with laughter. "Me mention lamia side benefit? Immortality. No need worry about new Taylor."

Shut up!

Another wild bump landed Morgan halfway across the front seat, his worn seat belt snapping. He pulled himself back in front of the wheel.

Great. What else can happen?

He glanced in the mirror and almost fainted.

Taylor's eyes flared so brightly he lost control, and the car swerved, crashing into a roadside boulder. Morgan's chest rammed into the steering wheel, sucking all the air out of him.

Taylor wailed in wretched laughter. He gasped for oxygen. Then he passed out.

* * *

Morgan awoke to heavy metal music in his head. A deep bruise in his chest limited his breathing. *Oh, shit. They're both gone. Taylor's restraints are chewed through.*

He inhaled several deep breaths. He ran his arm across his face and came away with a smear of blood. A quick check in the mirror showed a cut along his forehead. He pulled his handkerchief out and tied it over the wound. *Awesome. Now I look like Rambo. The locals will probably shoot me on sight.*

He called out. "Taylor? Linda?"

No answer.

"Taylor, come back. I'm trying to help you." *Yeah, like calling her will work.*

He strained to hear a sound, any utterance, but fell back into his seat in defeat.

Now what?

He tried the ignition, which didn't flicker. The driver-side door was pinned, so he slid out the passenger side. The surf crashed to his left, the jungle loomed on his right. A moon sliver provided a hint of light, but he couldn't see anything beyond twenty feet.

"Linda? Can you hear me?"

What if Taylor attacked her? He shook his head. *Don't go there. Taylor's only after young girls. More likely Linda's in pursuit of Taylor. Have to find them.*

He plodded forward, his head pounding and the cut stinging in his sweat.

Up the road, a dirt path bisected the jungle. He looked down. *Yes! Two sets of footprints.* He followed them. "Linda! Taylor! Can you hear me?"

Still no response.

He entered a clearing and Taylor stepped out from the jungle, her eyes burning red. Startled, Morgan stumbled over some rocks, falling to his knees. A crimson trail from her lips ran down her chin on both sides of her face.

Morgan drooped. *Please don't be Linda's blood.* "What did you do?"

"Feasted."

Morgan sagged. "You killed a girl?"

"Oh, no. Offspring not die. Quench thirst and infect."

"Oh, Taylor. How can you do this?"

"Taylor dead."

His eyes rose to hers. "You're hurting innocent children. Dooming them."

Taylor's demeanor shifting from laissez-faire to darkness. "Immortal now."

"There's no such thing."

"*Bé* tell me."

Morgan shifted to one knee. His eyes bored in on Taylor, who returned his glare. He reached into his jacket pocket. "*Bé* lied. You're still my daughter, and they *will* kill you if you continue this. Let me help you."

She hissed. "*Bé* never lie."

"Really? Ask yourself this. If you're immortal, how come there aren't more of you? If *Bé* has been transforming girls for centuries where are all those immortals? Why hasn't humanity been overrun?"

Taylor's brow creased, her eyes drifting off, and Morgan used the distraction to lunge at her leg, injecting her with another sedative. She screamed and slapped him, hard, knocking him to the ground. But he'd given her a double dose, and her eyes lost some of their luminosity.

"Fool," she said. "You no win."

"Sorry, sweetie, but this fight's not over. Now, where's Linda?"

Taylor cackled. "In jungle. With friends."

"Friends?"

"Bats. Wolves. *Bé* allies."

Taylor took a threatening step toward Morgan, but her knees buckled, and she fell forward. Morgan caught her. He lifted her over his shoulder. "You sleep, Taylor. Help is on the way."

He stepped deeper into the jungle. "Linda! Where are you?"

He waited for a reply, but the jungle was eerily silent. *Dammit. Answer me. I don't want to leave you out here.*

And I don't relish going alone.

"Linda! You out here?"

Nothing.

Now what? Search the jungle for her? Wait at the car?

No. I need to get Taylor to the Bribri village.

He returned to the main road and began the trek toward the Talamanca Indigenous Reserve.

If Linda dies out here, that'll make three women on my watch.

Shut up! Taylor didn't hurt her.

And the bats? The wolves?

He pressed ahead, carrying Taylor. *Linda knows where we're going, and how to get there. She knows the jungle. Hell, she's probably safer than I am.*

Satisfied with that rationalization, he considered his own situation. *I'm down to three sedative doses. Can't afford more sedatives tonight.*

And what if she grows stronger, and these double portions stop working?

He shook the thought away.

After an hour hike, he tired—*how can it be so damn hot in the middle of the night?*—and needed rest. He lay Taylor on her back in the dust and took out his water bottle.

A blur swished by. He froze, then braced himself. *Bats.*

Something scratched his face. "Shit," he screamed, panic rising deep inside him.

Another attack struck him in the back of the head. He gyrated his arms to shoo them away.

But the raid continued, taking synchronized shots at his upper torso, scratching and clawing their way deep into his skin. The blood pouring from his face soaked into the collar, and he knew he was losing the battle, and maybe, the war.

A break in the assault gave him a chance to catch his breath and think. *They don't want me to take Taylor to the Awá.*

Morgan's pulse picked up. *Which means we're not too late. Otherwise, why would they care?*

He considered the absurdity of his thinking. *I'm talking about bats having that kind of awareness. If Azra could see me now.*

The bats flew in for another assault, this time ripping the water bottle to the ground.

Then the bats, working as one coordinated entity, carried the bottle away.

What the hell?

Taylor stirred, eyes closed, and whispered in her demon voice. "Turn back. Or I'll continue to send my army to attack you. Leave the sow and go home. If you do, I'll spare you."

Morgan grabbed Taylor by the arms. "I'm not afraid of you, demon. But you obviously fear me. I'm coming for you. Right after Taylor's healed."

He picked Taylor back up, threw her over his shoulder, and continued his march.

CHAPTER 59

Father Garcia stepped off the commercial plane in Liberia under a blanket of stars, followed by Lieutenant Smokey. The rental car counters were all closed, but a chap with a dangling smoke and torn t-shirt was all-too-happy to drive them across the country to their destination at the base of the mountains, for a price so exorbitant Garcia laughed. But Smokey produced American C-notes, and their passage was secured.

Smokey fell asleep quickly on the drive, but Garcia found slumber impossible. Jungle shrieks kept him on edge. The car's headlights were caked in mud, and he saw demonic shapes in the blurred darkness that terrified him.

Hang in there. You're only a few hours behind Pennywise.

They careened into another pothole the size of Rhode Island and Garcia's head slammed into the roof between torn cloth. He closed his eyes and prayed.

And hoped God could hear him in the jungle.

* * *

Linda woke up in a pitch-black rain forest, her body covered by vegetation and dirt. She tried to establish her bearings. *Deep wilderness, no lights visible, no sign of Richard or Taylor. Great.*

She stood and couldn't recall how she'd gotten there. *Last I remember, the car crashed, and Taylor broke free. I chased after her. But she was too quick. Next I know, I'm out here by myself.*

But a cry in the distance told her she wasn't alone. She tensed. *Where did that come from?* She rotated her body, in search of the sound. But she was met with an eerie silence. Even the crickets stopped chirping.

Richard will be looking for us both. She gulped. *If he's alive.* She shook that thought away. *No. He survived the crash. He had to.*

Having no idea which direction the road was, she picked the path of least resistance. Fifteen feet along she stepped into a clearing.

A young girl lay on a blanket of leaves, her throat gauged. Linda rushed to her and found a faint pulse. *Taylor's been here.*

The girl opened her eyes. "Help me."

Linda caressed her. "What's your name?"

"Hanna. Please don't leave me."

Linda brushed away a tear. "I know you won't understand this, but the only way to save you is to catch the girl that did this to you. I must go help my partner cure her. That will heal you."

"I'll die out here."

Linda released the girl and rose. *And you'll die if we can't get Taylor to the* Awá. She clenched her hands and followed the same trail, leaving the girl screaming alone in the dark.

* * *

Margarita smiled as Juan rushed into her arms.

"Thank God you are home safely," he said. "I was so worried."

"No time for that. Take me to our Bribri Village. I have a lamia to slay."

CHAPTER 60

Wednesday

Morgan reached a small town at daybreak. Exhausted, aching, and parched, he set Taylor down on the sun-damaged wood bench outside the bus station. He checked the departure schedule. A converted school bus was leaving for Bribri town within minutes.

Finally, a break.

He bought a quart of water and gulped all but a couple of sips. He tried to give Taylor some, but she coughed it up.

It's only been three weeks since you were bitten by that bat. Seems like an eternity.

He loaded Taylor on the rusted carriage, put his arm around her, and fell asleep.

He woke up when they pulled into the marketplace in Bribri, at the base of the indigenous reserve. The structures featured rotting wood walls and thatched roofs. The air reeked of burnt animal flesh. Fruits and vegetables sat in rain-damaged cardboard boxes.

Morgan set Taylor in the shade, protected from the sun's rays, on a bench at the bus terminal. She continued to sleep, her complexion ghoulishly pale.

He asked a middle-aged man if he knew how to arrange a trip to Yorkin, the last populated town and the staging area for trips to the Bribri Village. The man looked at Taylor and gasped. He gave Morgan a frightened look, then crossed himself, backing away from the bench.

"It's okay," Morgan said. "She's asleep."

The man turned and ran. Morgan inspected Taylor. Her two incisors were sticking out. He shoved them back in beneath her lips and scanned the area.

Linda warned me about this. That guy's liable to tell others, and I may have a mob on my hands. Have to hurry.

A sign on another bus caught his eye.

Adventuras Naturales Yorkin.

Six young adults with full backpacks stood next to it, and an enormous man in tan shorts and a tee shirt reading "I Beat Anorexia" took tickets.

Morgan approached the driver. "Excuse me. I'm looking to join your tour group."

The driver looked up. "Do you have a reservation?"

"No. But I can pay, and I see you have room."

The coachman considered Morgan, then focused on the cash.

"How many?"

"Two. Me and my daughter. She's asleep over there."

The driver reached for the money. "Welcome to Adventuras Naturales Yorkin, home of the finest volunteer programs in Talamanca."

A new thought pierced Morgan's soul. *What if the Awá won't help? What if he wants to kill Taylor?*

* * *

Talamanca Indigenous Reserve, Costa Rica

The Yorkin farming community wasn't the end of the world. But Morgan could see it from there.

After a two-hour bus ride on a gravel road winding parallel to the Sixaola River, they arrived in the Bambu Community, where they transferred to a boat that took them upriver by motor and pole on the Río Yorkin. Since the bus and river trips were both in full sunlight, Taylor slept and Morgan avoided using any more of the sedative.

They arrived in Yorkin beside the Río Tsqui at 5p.m., beating sundown by thirty minutes. The sky was cloudless and the air was warm and sticky. Morgan stared at the setting sun and the reality of his dilemma and likely fate hit him brutally. He suddenly resented the clear sky. *Better the cold and drizzle of Salem on this day.* He shook the thought away and found refuge in a simple empty shack on stilts. He pulled out a syringe and injected Taylor.

This should hold her. I need to go find the Awá.

* * *

The powerful sedative pierced the lamia's skin, making it sleepy. But the drug couldn't control its hunger. *You must feed, and you must kill THE MAN.*

* * *

Darkness surrounded the hut.

Taylor's sedate. Time to find the Awá. Morgan rose from his perch at the side of her cot and peered outside. Torches around the family of huts provided enough illumination to notice a cable bridge crossing the river, wide enough for one person. On the other side, deeper in the jungle, a subdued light and a low hum suggested a gathering.

Follow the light. Maybe the Awá will be there.

He took one last glimpse at Taylor, decided she wasn't going anywhere, and headed for the brightness.

* * *

The door closed, and the lamia opened its eyes.

* * *

Morgan crossed the bridge, entering a clearing set up for a barbecue. Volunteers milled around, along with camp guides, who doubled as cooks. Morgan saw no one dressed uniquely. Like an *Awá*. *Whatever they look like.*

*Forget the Awá. I need nourishment. About to faint, h*e grabbed a plate and walked up to a line being served grilled chicken and pork, corn on the cob, and baked beans. The combination of smells reached up his nostrils, creating a divine sensation. His body tingled.

He took his first bite. *Oh, that's good.*

Then screams started across the river. *That's not good.* His skin wept, and a river of perspiration drizzled down his arm.

Morgan dropped his plate and turned back toward the bridge. *That's not Taylor's voice. But what if she got out?*

Two women ran toward him from the overpass, their arms waving, yelling in a foreign language. A guide listened to them, his face drawn firm, then reached up and rang a bell. The alarm clanged as if being rung from the gods. The ground shook.

The guide signaled for everyone to stand in a circle. "You're safe on this side of the river. The threat will be captured and killed."

Morgan tensed. *Killed.* He broke ranks and ran toward the bridge.

"Señor. It is not safe. The beast can not cross water."

That's my daughter you're talking about.

* * *

The lamia swooped around the torches, blowing them out, and found itself in total darkness. But it saw everything in perfect clarity.

Hunt.

* * *

Morgan reached the grassy area in the center of the huts. He'd seen the lights go out, and he found himself unable to recognize more than eerie shapes in the starlight. "Taylor, stop! These people will hurt you."

Her unmistakable cackle shook the night from straight above him. He froze, trying to figure out which direction to go.

A woman's scream to his left jarred him. *Too old to be Taylor.* He rushed after the voice.

He made it ten feet before his forehead clipped a tree branch, and he fell, hitting his head. Everything went black.

* * *

The lamia crouched at the edge of the jungle. Hunger ravaged it. *Been through entire village. Where are girls?*

And when will damn sedative wear off? So tired.

Footsteps approached, treading lightly, from four sides.

It wanted to stay and fight. Devour whoever came near. But it recognized its weakness from the drugs and decided to run. Even in its weakened state, it was confident it could blow past them, a blur in their eyes.

It tensed to make its move when a bevy of ropes cinched its arms.

Four men with machetes descended on it. It howled.

* * *

"Wake up, *señor*."

Morgan grunted and pried one eye open. "What am I doing here?"

"That is our question, *señor*."

The cell was a nest of shadows. A wood structure, with narrow wooden bars reinforced with a metal strip across the middle. A thatch roof. He lay on bare ground. Insects scurried around him, and a quick check of his left ear confirmed he was bleeding. A single torch lit up enough to see the reflection of a man standing guard outside with a rifle.

"I came from the United States to see the *Awá*. To heal my little girl."

The guard creased his forehead in the dim light. "The *Awá* is finishing important business. He will arrive to decide your fate presently."

"And my daughter?"

"We have her. He will also decide her future."

"I'm told he knows how to heal her."

The guard grunted. "We have been fighting the *Bé* a long time, *señor*. We evacuated the few surviving girls, trying to save our tribe from extinction. And now you show up from America. We did not think the plague could reach beyond our borders."

"I was in Costa Rica in October. She was attacked and infected then."

"Sad for you, then."

"Where is she?"

"Chained in another jail. One made for lamias."

"Is she awake?"

"We have an herbal mixture that makes the lamia sleep. Without it, I don't know if our village would have survived."

"So she's okay?"

"She is a lamia, *señor*. She is anything but okay."

Morgan sat up, fighting to keep from vomiting. "She didn't hurt anyone, did she?"

"There are no girls left to infect."

Morgan tried to stand, but his knees failed him, and he plopped back onto his ass. "Can I see her?"

"No, *señor*. Not until the *Awá* comes."

"Then he can help us."

The guard shook his head. "Do not get your hopes up, señor. Most likely, the Awá will put you both to death."

CHAPTER 61

"Wake up. My name is Ramon Valverde. You have been asking for me."

Morgan rocketed up to a seated position, opening his eyes. His eyesight adapted to the bright sunlight outside. He focused in on a short, thin man outside the hut, dressed in dark jeans, black tennis shoes, a black Fleetwood Mac tee-shirt, and a Dodgers cap. The wrinkled skin of too much sun. The man slouched, hands in his jeans pockets. *This is the Awá? I expected more.*

"My daughter is possessed by your demon." Morgan swallowed. "Will you help us?"

"*My* demon?"

"Yeah. *Bé.*"

Valverde glared at Morgan. "Do you even understand what *Bé* is?"

"The demon possessing my daughter. Turning her into a lamia."

Valverde grunted. "As I thought. I am afraid someone misinformed you."

"Like hell. The symptoms are irrefutable."

"Oh, I believe your daughter is possessed. And transforming into a lamia. But *Bé* is not the demon responsible."

What's he trying to pull? "Then who's invading my daughter?"

"Allow me to explain. The story of *Bé* goes back to ancient times here in the Bribri tribe. It is a race of demons that have plagued us since time began."

"So not just one."

"Correct. This race of demons attacks humans when they are a danger to the forest. As man's infringement has spread near our land, those onslaughts have escalated."

"So when it attacked Taylor, my daughter, that was a random attack? Taylor's done nothing to hurt the ecology."

The discussion was causing Valverde's face to redden. He took a cleansing breath. "*Bé* never assaulted Taylor. That was a different demon."

Morgan's head swam. "I'm confused. Why do you say it's not *Bé*?"

"Because *Bé* cannot turn anyone into a lamia. The demon plaguing Taylor came here from Europe with Columbus."

"Christopher Columbus?"

"The same. It arrived from Europe when he landed and it settled here. That is when we first experienced lamias."

Morgan licked his parched lips. "So you admit there's a demon that creates lamias. Can you exorcise it?"

"I can. Honestly, I know why I can exorcise the *Bé* demons. It is a power that comes with the Awá responsibility. I am blessed by *Sibú*, creator of the Bribri world. It is not clear why I am also effective with this other demon."

"Does this other demon have a name?"

"It must, but I do not recognize it. It took on the *Bé* moniker centuries ago and uses it to this day."

"This demon inside Taylor fears you."

"Yes. I have exorcised it before. Perhaps my power extends to all demons."

"Look, I don't care the reason. I just need you to exorcise it from my daughter."

"Tell me," Valverde said, "how did she get infected?"

Morgan stood and approached the bars holding him captive. "My daughter got bit in Nosara last October."

"I see." Valverde looked years older at this revelation. "That demon has always been constrained to our village. To have your daughter infected in Nosara, it is a shock. And terrible news."

"Then my daughter carried it to Oregon. I brought her back yesterday. Praying you can help."

"If the demon is already gone, then it is too late." His expression hardened. "If I am unable to exorcise the demon, for any reason, we must destroy the lamia. It's plague would be a major pandemic. It could doom humanity."

"How do you tell if the demon's inside?"

"I have incantations. But I must warn you. This demon is clever. Because I am the only one it fears, it might stay hidden, even if it is inside her. If it does not show itself, I must assume it is too late for your daughter."

"The demon's still in her," Morgan said. "It has a unique voice, different from the lamia's. I heard it last night."

"Then, perhaps, we are not too late. But, I remind you, that is no guarantee of success."

"When can we start?"

"Once the sun goes down," Valverde said.

"And, if she fails your test, you'll kill her."

"For what it is worth, she will die the innocent young girl you love, and it will save her soul."

"That sounds like my department."

Morgan turned toward the interruption. Garcia stepped into view, still wearing his black pastoral robe, purple stole, and carrying his Bible, along with a second book.

Two guards surrounded Valverde in a protective stance.

"Javi! What the hell are you doing here?"

"You didn't think I'd let you have all the fun, did you?"

"But, how?"

"Caught the first commercial flight to Costa Rica and drove to Limon. We ran into your bus driver, and he confirmed you and Taylor were up here. But what happened to Linda?"

Morgan's side cramped. *I wish I knew.* "We got separated in the jungle. I'm scared to death for her."

"My money's on her. She's a tough lady."

Smokey appeared behind Garcia, perspiring profusely in tan shorts and a beige button-down shirt. "Howdy, Doc."

"Smokey!" Morgan exclaimed at the sight of him.

"You know these men?" Valverde asked Morgan.

"Yeah. Friends from home."

Smokey smiled at the inclusion.

Valverde signaled to the guards to stand down.

Smokey stepped up to the bars. "I have good news, Doc. You didn't kill Michelle. It was an accident, and then your in-laws tried to use it to their advantage to get custody of Taylor."

Morgan slumped against the slats to keep his balance. "You're sure?"

"You didn't do it," Smokey said. "Your father-in-law is under arrest for trying to pin it on you. He paid that witness, he called Costa Rica. Hell, he's the one who told Margarita where to find you." He smiled. "I told you I was good at my job."

Morgan laughed. "You did. I can't believe you two came."

Smokey grinned. "And don't worry about Bear. He's the new mascot for the station. Until you get back."

Morgan motioned to his surroundings. "If I get back. The Costa Rican authorities are still after me."

"Oh, you're coming back all right," Smokey said. "This is my last rodeo, and I'm not going to have you muck it up."

"Last rodeo?" Morgan said.

"I'm retiring."

Morgan squirmed. "I got you in some hot water back home."

Smokey grinned. "Humph. You sure as hell did. And you can buy me a beer to make up for it. After we help Taylor."

"Where *is* Taylor?" Garcia said.

"They're holding her down the road," Morgan said. "She's worse. They'll test her tonight. If they believe she's turned into this lamia, they intend to kill her."

Valverde stepped up to Garcia. "I am Ramon Valverde. I am the *Awá* in this community."

Garcia pointed to his Catholic collar. "Nice to meet you, man. I'm sort of the *Awá* in my community. And this is the sheriff back home."

Valverde bowed. "Welcome. I wish the circumstances were better."

"You intend to hurt the girl?" Garcia said. "Isn't that a violation of everything you stand for, as the *Awá?*"

Valverde narrowed his eyes. "Keeping the community healthy requires I rid the region of the lamias."

Garcia lowered his voice and pointed to his other worn-out leather book. "This is the Rite of Exorcism for the Catholic Church. On the way down I read about the Bribri history, and your beliefs. We both believe in demons, and we both know we can exorcise them."

Valverde's eyes narrowed. "The test will tell us. If she's possessed, we can try."

Morgan's knees turned to jello, and he slid to the ground. *It's all about the test. She must pass.*

Garcia kneeled and took Morgan's hand through the slats. "Hang in there, man. We'll see Taylor through this."

"Thanks for fighting for her. I know your faith has been tested."

"I've got my second wind."

"Glad to hear it," Morgan said. "Taylor will need you."

Garcia stood. "Is keeping him in a cage necessary? He's not a threat."

Valverde motioned to the guards, who unlocked the door.

Morgan stepped out into the late afternoon sunshine and stretched. "Thanks. What now?"

"Now," Valverde said, "we wait for the sun to set. To see if there is anything left of your daughter."

CHAPTER 62

The sun finally set though it had no effect on the stifling temperature or humidity. The smell of grilling pork would have been welcome at home. Here, Morgan had lost his appetite.

Valverde led the group to Taylor's hut, surrounded by three guards with machetes.

Morgan approached the chained door of the shanty and found Taylor sleeping on a slab of rock, five feet off the ground, encircled by plants. "The plants really keep her calm?"

"They do," Valverde said.

Morgan eyed the machetes. "She's just a girl. Please remember that."

Valverde signaled to a guard to unlock the chain, then entered the hut by himself. The guards relocked the links. He stepped up to Taylor and chanted.

"What's he saying?" Morgan asked Garcia.

"Beats me. Not in the Catholic playbook."

Valverde continued chanting. The guards around the hut readied themselves.

Jeez. They'll protect Valverde at any cost. Taylor's cost.

"How long?" Morgan called to Valverde, who ignored him.

Taylor's eyes opened, and the guards shifted back.

Morgan choked a swallow. *They're afraid of her.*

Valverde didn't retreat. Rather, he put his palm on Taylor's chest and chanted to the heavens.

Taylor leered at Valverde.

Morgan's body shook. *Oh, shit, She's going to strike.*

Maybe that's good. It might convince Valverde the demon's still in there.

Valverde shifted his hand to Taylor's forehead. Taylor's mouth opened, exposing her fangs.

"No, Taylor!" Morgan yelled. "Don't!"

A guard grabbed Morgan's shoulder and pinched, as if to say, keep quiet.

Easy for you to say. That's my daughter.

Taylor widened her mouth. Her tongue flicked over her gums, like a lizard.

Valverde stopped chanting and stepped back. He took a plant and set it on Taylor's chest.

Taylor cringed, then faded to sleep.

"What's that mean?" Morgan said.

Valverde stood over her for several minutes. Taylor remained sedate until Valverde removed the plant.

Taylor reacted with a contorted face. "You *Awá*!"

Morgan winced. *No, not the lamia voice. He needs to hear the demon voice.*

"I am," Valverde said. "And I command you to depart."

"Demon gone," Taylor said. "You no power over me."

Valverde shook his head. "You are wrong. I have authority over all evil." He tossed the plant back onto Taylor's legs.

Taylor swept it aside. "You too late, *Awá*." She swung her torso around. "I command *you*. Bring me girl!"

Valverde gasped and stumbled back into the gate. The guards unlocked it, and Valverde scrambled outside. The guards closed the exit and locked it before Taylor slammed into it, shaking the hut.

Taylor's red eyes bored into Morgan's. "Let me out!"

Morgan fell to his knees, his heart beating too fast for comfort. *Jesus. The plants don't work?* Garcia and Smokey helped him up.

Valverde stepped in front of Morgan. "She is lamia, now. Nothing I can do. I am sorry." He grasped Morgan's shoulder. "We will take care of the body."

"There must be something else you can try," Morgan pleaded.

"This is best for her," Valverde said, despair in his eyes. "For everyone."

Garcia crossed himself. Smokey chewed through his cigar.

Tears leaked down Morgan's face. "I should take her body home for a proper burial."

Valverde bit his lip. "I am afraid our solution does not allow that."

"What do you mean?" Morgan said.

"I mean," Valverde said, "I must bury her ashes in the river, to assure the destruction of the lamia."

Morgan listed and vomited. "She's my little girl."

"I wish that were true," Valverde said.

Morgan stepped to the cell bars, standing face to face with Taylor. "Taylor, if you're in there, you need to show us. Now."

Taylor growled. "Hungry."

Garcia took Morgan by the arm. "Come with me. Let's find a quiet spot to pray."

Morgan yanked his arm away. "That's my daughter in there!"

"You know she is gone," Valverde said. Then, to the guards, "Take her."

"Stop!" came a cry from behind them.

Morgan recognized the voice. *Can it be?*

Linda emerged from the jungle. Her face, scratched and bleeding, beamed with relief, and she walked with a pronounced limp.

"Linda!" Morgan broke free and ran to her. They embraced. "I was so worried."

"You weren't the only one. But I'm fine."

"I'm so sorry I left you behind. I looked everywhere."

"Don't apologize," Linda said. "I'd have done the same thing."

"Really?" Morgan said.

"Absolutely," Linda said. "Getting Taylor here before it was too late was all that mattered. Tell me, where are we?"

Morgan wiped his face with an enormous green leaf. "The *Awá* says the demon's gone. Taylor's gone. There's nothing he can do."

"Bullshit," Linda said. She surged past Morgan and stopped inches from Valverde. "You're not giving up."

"I am sorry," Valverde said. "But who are you?"

"Professor Linda Copeland. I lost my daughter to this demon, and I'm here to help you capture it. After we're through, you'll never have to worry about it again."

The guards looked at each other.

"How do you know this?" Valverde said.

"I studied this demon in the Vatican archives," Linda said. "The Bible, the Dead Sea Scrolls, other ancient texts. Her name is Lilith."

"Lilith?" Garcia gasped. "The demon? The stuff of legends?"

"The one and only," Linda said.

"I heard Taylor use that name once. But I didn't pay much attention to it. How did you get access to the Vatican archives?" Garcia asked.

"A Catholic priest in Peru knew about my daughter and got a Vatican Cardinal mentor of his to ordain a visit."

"That's phenomenal," Garcia said.

"It was crazy. This Cardinal showed me documents that go back centuries. These scrolls showed the long history of Lilith attacking girls. Converting them to monsters. Then, the Catholic Church captured the beast and tasked Columbus to take it somewhere where no one would ever find it, somewhere it would find no hosts."

Morgan rubbed his eyes. "And it landed here?"

"Yeah," Linda said. "Columbus first made landfall in Costa Rica, and buried the box containing the beast, thinking it would die a lonely death in the deserted jungle. But he didn't plan on the Bribris digging it up. My guess is they saw the disturbed earth while farming, and natural curiosity compelled them to open it."

"That is an interesting story," Valverde said, "but it changes nothing."

"Actually," Garcia said, "it changes everything."

"How?" Morgan said, reaching for any reason for optimism.

"It means the Church exorcised the demon and captured it," Garcia said. "There must be a way."

"And I learned how they did it," Linda said. "If you can exorcise it, I can trap it."

"If a Catholic exorcism will work," Morgan asked, "why the insistence to expose Taylor to the dangers of Costa Rica? Why didn't we stay home and let the Catholic Church do it?"

Linda shook her head. "It's true the Catholic Church had success, but the Bribri *Awá* is the only one with a recent successful track record. Also, the Catholic Church moves slowly on such matters. Taylor's out of time." She turned to Garcia. "Am I right?"

"*Sí.*"

"So this path is the best chance to save her."

"But I'm here now, armed with the full power of the Rite of Exorcism," Garcia said. "It can't hurt to attack it with both of us."

"You won't get in trouble with the Church?" Morgan asked.

"Screw them." Garcia stood tall. "Let's exorcise this vile demon."

Valverde shut down the conversation. "Look, I appreciate the offer of help. I have exorcised this demon from many girls. *But not after a completed lamia transmutation. It is too late.*"

"Taylor's still possessed by the demon," Linda said.

Valverde glared at her. "If *I* cannot tell, *you* cannot tell."

"I mean no disrespect, *Awá*," Linda said. "Let me ask you this. Those plants are meant to slow down the lamia, right? And they always work."

"They always have," Valverde replied.

"But they didn't, right?" Linda said, "They're scattered all over the ground. By your own admission the lamia can't do that. But the demon can. I say it's still in there."

Valverde looked back at Taylor, who stood at the gate, her eyes flaring red. "I am not sure."

Morgan came up to him. "And if you're not sure, we can't kill her. We have to try to save her."

Valverde turned to Morgan. "You would say anything to convince me."

"That's true," Morgan said. "But you saw what happened. Linda's explanation is plausible."

Valverde stared at Taylor for a full minute which seemed like an hour to Morgan. "Okay. We can try one more time."

"No!" came a booming voice from behind. Margarita stepped into the clearing from the jungle, followed by Juan.

Oh, my God. Can this nightmare get any worse?

Margarita raised a machete. "*Awá*, step aside. This is task force business."

Morgan blocked her path. "No!"

"You have no jurisdiction on the reserve," Valverde said to Margarita. "Put your weapon down. My guards will defend our territory."

The guardians pulled their machetes, poised to strike.

Morgan steeled himself. *Jesus. I'll die in Costa Rica after all.*

Juan came up to Margarita. "He is right. This was our community. Our people. We fought to keep our independence, to save our culture."

Margarita flinched. "We can not let the girl live."

Morgan stepped forward. "I have a compromise. Let Father Garcia and the *Awá* do their best to exorcise the demon. If it works, there will be no need to kill my daughter."

"And if it does not?" Margarita said.

Morgan turned to Taylor. "Then you'll destroy her."

338

Taylor flashed her tongue at him, then withdrew from the steel bars and lay back on the table.

Morgan approached Margarita. "I know what you lost." He glanced at Linda. "What you both lost. I won't let Taylor infect another girl. But give her this chance. Linda believes it will work. Our holy men are ready to try." Morgan turned back to Margarita. "Please. If it was your daughter, wouldn't you do anything to get her back?"

Tears streaked down her cheeks. Juan lowered Margarita's machete. "You have a deal, *señor*."

Thank you, Lord. I need you more then ever. Stay with us on this.

Valverde cleared his throat. "There is more to consider. Exorcisms are hard, dangerous, and can last for days. We do them when we know there is a demon in there. But in this case, how will we know when to admit defeat?"

Garcia cleared his throat. "The demon will show itself, because it seeks the conflict. It revels in beating a man representing good."

Valverde turned to the guards. "Prepare the altar. Bring the girl."

Morgan faced Linda. "So, when were you going to tell me you can capture it?"

Linda blushed. "I needed you with the *Awá*, or it didn't matter. It's all predicated on the exorcism."

"Fair enough. What's the plan?"

CHAPTER 63

Valverde invited Garcia into his personal hut to prepare for the exorcism. The abode had a single bed surrounded by open cabinets full of bottles filled with amber liquid and green vegetation.

"You have quite an assortment of stuff," Garcia said.

"Holistic medicines, mostly," Valverde said. "Some you'd be familiar with. Some unique to the rain forest."

Garcia's exorcism experience from long ago barged into his mind. When a teenage girl, Patti, had counted on him for salvation. *I failed miserably. The demon beat me and killed the girl. And going against Lilith? This time, she won't just settle for the girl. She'll probably kill me. Or worse.*

"Are you okay?" Valverde asked him.

Garcia put on his stole and kissed the leather cover of the Rite of Exorcism. "Honestly, I'm a little freaked out. I was prepared for an exorcism. But not for Lilith."

"Tell me about Lilith."

"She's like the queen of demons. Some believe she was Adam's first wife. Our task couldn't be harder."

"We will win."

More likely I'll die, and the demon will live.

Shut up! God is with me! Have faith!

"Tell me," Valverde continued, "if this demon is from your world, and not mine, how do you think I have been able to exorcise it?"

Garcia smiled. "God has empowered you. Same as me."

"But my God is not your God. My Diety is *Sibú*."

"We may have different names and traditions, but there's only one God."

Valverde crumpled his brow. "I am still confused about why this demon left our village after centuries here."

"You said you removed all the girls. My guess is you took away its food source."

Valverde groaned. "That is troubling. If it can travel anywhere, the entire world's in danger."

"All the more reason to capture it. You ready?"

"I am. You?"

Not even a little. Sweat dripped from Garcia's chin onto his Rite of Exorcism, leaving an imprint. The perspiration formed a message.

Die.

CHAPTER 64

Morgan stared at the altar, an arm's length away. The gigantic stone tablet balanced on four large rocks in the center of the hut reeking of animal feces. Taylor lay on the slab, her arms and legs tied with thick rope, quiet and sedated, her eyes closed. Garcia stood on the far side. Valverde, Linda, and Smokey stood next to Morgan. Margarita, Juan, and three guards stood behind them.

"Is she asleep?" Morgan said.

"No," responded Valverde. "*It* is awake. But under the influence of the herb potion." Valverde lifted the corner of her mouth. Her incisors extended as her watched. "Her teeth are morphing as the Dìwö sets. Time to begin."

"So," Morgan said, "how does your exorcism ritual differ from Javi's?"

"Father Garcia has his rite, I have mine. The principles are similar. I suspect mine might be more violent."

Morgan squirmed. "Excuse me?"

"Do not worry," Valverde said. "I only do what is necessary to chase the demon away."

"Do you both talk at the same time?"

Garcia cleared his throat. "I'll be silent while the *Awá* works. He tells me he may chant in Bribri while I'm working. We'll start by trading off, then see what's effective."

Morgan stepped to Taylor and took her bound hand in his. "It's me, sweetie. Father Javier is here. And the *Awá*. Relax and let them do their thing."

Taylor's red eyes flew open at the mention of the *Awá*. She snarled at Morgan. "Release me."

Morgan, desperate to hear the demon's voice, rather than the lamia's, grit his teeth.

Valverde, wearing a black robe and still in his Dodger cap, checked the ropes. "There are no *alàköls* within miles. Nobody for you to turn."

Taylor spit at Valverde.

Valverde slapped her, hard. Morgan tensed at the welt on Taylor's cheek.

"I am your worst nightmare, lamia," Valverde said. "Either the demon leaves the *alàköl*, or I cut off your head."

Valverde raised his arms. Before he could strike, Morgan grabbed his wrist. "Keep your hands off her!"

Valverde spun on Morgan. "If you can not handle this, you should leave. Exorcisms are not for the faint of heart."

"That's my daughter in there."

Valverde pulled his arm away and poked Morgan in the chest. "She is *not* your daughter. It is a monster. Remember that. If you want to save her, let us work."

Morgan looked to Garcia.

"He's right," Garcia said. "I know it's painful to watch. Maybe it's best if you sit this one out."

"I'm not going anywhere."

Valverde motioned toward the edge of the hut. "Then go stand over there. No matter what, do not interrupt. It will do anything to distract us. It will use your feelings against us. You can not listen to anything it says. It is a devil, and a liar. Treat it as such."

Smokey took Morgan by the arm and led him to the side of the hut. "C'mon, Doc. We'll watch from over here." Linda, Margarita, and Juan joined them.

Valverde signaled to the three guards standing outside the altar. "Bring them all chairs. Fresh *di'* and food every few hours. We may be here for days, and we will need all our strength."

Garcia, in his vestigial robes, purple stole, and collar, pulled out his sacramental instructions, a miniature statue of the Crucified Christ, a picture of the Holy Virgin Mary surrounded by angels, and placed them on the slab. Taylor fought to reach them, but her ropes held.

"I'm ready," Garcia said.

"You sure, Javi?" Morgan said. "You don't look so good."

Garcia kissed the cross hung around his neck. "As sure as I'll get, man. You guys know the responses. Be strong and have faith."

Valverde took a deep breath and pounded his fist on Taylor's chest. "By the power anointed me by *Sibú*, creator of all, I command you, *Kudo*, to expel your demons from this girl. Send them back to the *dakúrs* from which they came."

Morgan gasped at seeing his daughter hit, but stayed back.

Taylor didn't cry out in pain, but rather, lunged at Valverde's neck with her fangs.

Valverde grabbed her by the chin, forcing her back onto the slab. "No, lamia, you have no power over me. Even as night falls, you are helpless."

"Me rip throat out," Taylor hissed.

"You will do nothing," Valverde said. "*I* am the *Awá*, and you are an insignificant affront to *Sibú*. I can squash you any time I want."

Morgan started toward Valverde, but Smokey held him back. "Hold still, Doc. Let's see how this plays out."

Valverde signaled to Garcia to begin. Garcia traced the sign of the cross over her, himself, Valverde, Morgan and the others. He then took out a vial of holy water and splashed it on each of them.

"We begin with the Litany of the Saints," Garcia said, nodding toward his responders.

Taylor shifted her attention to Garcia. "You wasting time."

He ignored her. "Lord, have mercy."

Morgan, Linda, and Smokey responded, "Lord, have mercy."

"Christ, have mercy."

"Christ, have mercy," they repeated.

Garcia continued the Litany until he'd repeated all sixty entries. After each name, the group replied, "Pray for us."

Garcia then recited the Lord's Prayer, Psalm 53, and began praying. "God, whose nature is ever merciful and forgiving, accept our prayer that this servant of Yours, bound by the fetters of sin, may be pardoned by your loving kindness."

Linda embraced Morgan's arm. He looked down on her and forced a smile.

"Holy Lord, almighty Father, everlasting God and Father of our Lord Jesus Christ, hasten to our call for help and snatch from ruination and from the clutches of the devil this human being made in Your image and likeness."

Taylor's tongue extended five inches from her lips and flicked toward Garcia. Morgan gasped.

"Strike terror, Lord, into the beast now laying waste your vineyard. Fill Your servants with courage to fight against this dragon. Let Your mighty hand cast him out of your servant, Taylor Morgan."

Morgan, Linda, and Smokey replied, "Amen."

Taylor's black tongue flung near Garcia's face. He took a deep breath. "I command you, unclean spirit, whoever you are, along with all your minions now attacking this servant of God, that you tell me by some sign your name, and the day and hour of your departure. I command you to obey me to the letter, I who am a minister of God despite my unworthiness."

Taylor withdrew her tongue and stared at Garcia with pure hatred.

Garcia turned to Valverde. "Hold her head down."

Valverde moved behind her, grabbing both sides of her head and locked her into position. She strained against the ropes binding her arms and legs.

Garcia laid a palm on her forehead. "They shall lay their hands upon the sick and all will be well with them. May Jesus, Son of Mary, Lord and Savior of the world, through the merits and intercession of His holy apostles Peter and Paul and all His saints, show you favor and mercy."

Morgan, Linda, and Smokey replied, "Amen."

"The Lord be with you," Garcia said.

"And with your spirit," they said.

Garcia opened his book. "A lesson from the holy Gospel according to Saint John. John One, verses one through fourteen."

Garcia signed himself, and then Taylor, on the brow, lips, and heart. She hissed.

When he finished his reading from the Book of John, Garcia signaled to Morgan, Linda, and Smokey, who replied, "Thanks be to God."

Garcia took a deep breath and put his shaking hand over Taylor. "May the blessing of the almighty God, Father, Son, and Holy Spirit, come upon you and remain with you forever." He sprinkled Taylor with holy water. Each drop sizzled on her skin as they landed. Taylor strained more desperately against the ropes, her face tortured, but her eyes still glowed red.

Morgan's body shook. He spoke in a hushed voice to Linda. "Damn. Still no sign of the demon."

"Still too early," Linda whispered. But her face showed anxiety.

"Patience, Doc. The Padre has a lot more ammunition."

Does he? And are we too late?

Garcia removed the stole from around his neck and placed it around Taylor's. Taylor fought, but couldn't get it off. He crossed himself and Taylor, then put his right palm on her head. "See the cross of the Lord! Begone, hostile powers! Let us pray. God and Father of our Lord Jesus Christ, I appeal to Your holy name, humbly begging Your kindness, that You graciously grant me help against this and every unclean spirit now tormenting this creature of Yours. Through Christ our Lord."

Linda and Smokey answered, "Amen."

Morgan stared into the darkness.

"In the name of our Lord Jesus Christ I cast you out. It is He who commands you. Begone, then, in the name of the Father." Garcia gave the sign of the cross on Taylor's forehead. "And of the Son." He repeated the sign. "And of the Holy Spirit." He completed the signage. "Give place to the Holy Spirit by this sign of the Holy Cross of our Lord Jesus Christ, who lives and reigns with the Father and the Holy Spirit, God, forever and ever."

Linda poked Morgan in the ribs. "Hey. Stay in the game."

Morgan joined Linda and Smokey in replying, "Amen."

Garcia again gave the sign of the cross on Taylor's brow. This time, her face turned beet red, and her skin smoldered. Valverde grimaced, but held on.

"Let Your servant be protected in mind and body. Keep watch over the inmost recesses of her heart." Garcia switched to signing over her breast. "Rule over her emotions. Strengthen her will. Let vanish from her soul the temptings of the mighty adversary. Through Christ our Lord."

The responders replied, "Amen."

Garcia looked up at Valverde, who released Taylor's head and stepped to her side. Garcia stepped back and wiped his face.

"Javi's tiring," Morgan whispered to Linda.

Valverde pounded his fist on Taylor's chest again. "By the power anointed me by *Sibú*, creator of all, I command you, *Kudo*, to expel your demons from this girl, and send them back to the *dakúrs* from which they came."

The two exorcists stepped back and waited. Taylor looked from one to the other with red eyes. "Your idea good cop, bad cop?"

Morgan's heart sank. *Still, the lamia.*

"It's a long race, Doc. Stay strong."

"And united," Linda said.

Valverde signaled for the guards to enter. "Give her another dose of the herbs. We need to keep her subdued while we rest."

Morgan shook his head. "You're stopping?"

Garcia approached Morgan, breathing heavily. "For now. We refresh our strength and come back at it hard."

"Did anything happen there?" Morgan said.

"No sign of the demon," Garcia replied.

Taylor's head turned toward Morgan. "You think keep me down? They weaker. Me stronger. Herbs soon do nothing. You all die."

Morgan's knees buckled, and only with Smokey and Linda's support did he stay upright.

CHAPTER 65

The lamia awoke, its vision acutely sharp, even with the plant's medicinal restraint.

THE PRIEST stood over it, with the Goddamn book, reciting more gibberish. *Blah, blah, blah.* It wanted to reach up and rip his throat out, but couldn't find the strength to break through the ropes. *But this weakness won't last. I'm adjusting to the herbs.* And while the cross and holy water bothered it, the words did not.

Watch. You see real power.

It realized the *Awá* and the others were also in the hut. Even THE MAN, who now bored it. But THE *AWÁ* made it nervous. *Me do something. Shake faith. Make quit.*

More crossing and blah, blah, blah. The lamia laughed to itself. *What supposed to do?*

THE PRIEST, again. "Depart, then, transgressor. To what purpose do you insolently resist? To what purpose do you brazenly refuse?"

The lamia's strength was returning. It also picked up a whispered conversation between THE MAN and the bitch next to him. "Her eyes are brighter," THE MAN said. "We need to sedate her."

THE PRIEST slowed, and the lamia recognized what would happen next.

THE AWÁ. Going to pound chest again. Bad. But once close enough I will kill.

THE PRIEST finished, and the responders recited, "Amen." THE *AWÁ* thrust his arms above his head and launched them toward its thorax.

But the lamia reached up in a blurred movement, tearing the ropes, and grabbed both of his hands. *Now who got power?*

It sneered at the *AWÁ*, snapped the bones in both of his wrists, and stretched for his throat.

CHAPTER 66

Morgan cringed at the sound of Valverde's bones cracking. Taylor shredded the ropes and grabbed Valverde's throat. Valverde's eyes bulged. Blood oozed down his chest.

Morgan's extremities went numb. *Oh, shit.* He rushed the slab. "Taylor, stop!"

She cackled and her irises blazed a brighter red.

Morgan injected the lamia with a double dose of sodium thiopental.

Taylor hissed, then released Valverde, who crumpled to the ground. She turned toward Morgan, bared her teeth. "You dare defy me?"

Her glare drilled deep into Morgan's soul. "Get the fuck out of my daughter."

Taylor's eyes lost their shimmer. "You fool. Daughter dead."

For the first time, Morgan believed. *We're too late. Taylor really is gone.*

Taylor lunged for his throat.

Her claws came within inches before Morgan pulled away. He grabbed her wrists. Her pulse was stronger than normal. Morgan shivered at the realization.

With her arms pinned, she switched tactics. She thrust her teeth at Morgan's neck.

Morgan gripped her chin to stop her, but now one wrist was freed. He inclined back, but not far enough. A sharp pain sliced across his cheek.

Garcia came to his rescue. He grabbed her arms and held them in place behind her back. "I've got her."

Morgan released her and wiped the blood from his face. "She's strong."

"I have her. How long until the sedative kicks in."

"Should have happened by now." Morgan looked at his crimson sleeve. "She's getting more immune to it every time."

"Move away from her!" Margarita commanded. She raised her machete.

"No!" Morgan shifted to keep his body between Margarita and Taylor. "The drug will put her to sleep any moment."

"I was willing to kill you in Nosara," Margarita said. "I am amenable to decapitating you now. Do not test my resolve."

Taylor broke free of Garcia's grasp and darted for Morgan. He steeled himself for the inevitable. But before she could reach him the sedative took effect. Taylor collapsed into Morgan's arms, her red eyes fading. *Maybe there's still time.*

Margarita lowered her knife.

The guards rushed in and retied Taylor with fresh rope.

Valverde rose to his knees. "It broke my wrists. Another second and it would have torn my throat out."

Morgan checked Valverde's pulse. "She mangled your wrists. I need bandages, antibiotics, splints."

Valverde motioned to a guard, who ran off to retrieve medical supplies.

Linda leaned next to Morgan. "Is he going to be okay?"

Morgan put pressure on Valverde's throat wound. Blood leaked through his fingers. His stomach tied itself in knots. "He's losing a lot of blood."

Garcia addressed Margarita. "Her infection can't spread like this, right?"

"No plague," Margarita said. "Only via the teeth, and only with young girls."

Morgan cleared his throat. "You under control now? You see Taylor's sedated?"

"*Sí.*" Margarita said. "But for how long?"

"I don't know," Morgan said. "Stay alert. We may need you and your machete before this is over. But only when I say so. Agreed?"

Margarita hesitated. "Agreed. Just do not let your emotions get in the way of what you see."

The guards returned with medical supplies, and Morgan bandaged Valverde's throat. "That should stop the bleeding. How are you feeling?"

"Weak. A lamia has never beaten the herb cocktail before. It is getting too strong for us. And I do not see any sign of the demon. We need to kill the lamia while we still can."

Morgan applied splints to Valverde's wrists. "No. We're not finished."

"I will not risk the community," Valverde said.

Morgan begged Valverde. "I have one more dose. It still works. I'll be ready next time. And daylight will come soon."

Valverde took a sip of water from Garcia. "You have one more dose?"

"Yes."

"Okay," Valverde said. "But the next time we are forced to dose it, we have no choice but to kill it while it is weak. I cannot risk it waking up when we are out of medication."

"Fair enough." Morgan turned to Garcia. "Let's get back to it."

Morgan situated himself next to Linda, Smokey, Margarita, and Juan. He wiped the sweat from his forehead. *Come on, demon. Show yourself.*

Garcia began again, holding a palm over Taylor, who continued to sleep. "Begone, now! Begone, seducer! Your place is in solitude. Your abode is in the nest of serpents. Get down and crawl with them. You might delude man, but God you cannot mock. It is He who casts you out. It is He who repels you."

Taylor flinched and her eyes sprung open.

Morgan stepped up to the slab. "Taylor?"

She turned her head toward him. "Taylor dead."

Morgan wilted. *Still the lamia. How'd it wake up so fast? They'll kill her now.* He stared at her, his own rage boiling. With a sudden burst, he jumped on the slab, straddling Taylor. "She's not dead," he screamed, clutching her throat. "Leave her, you bastard. Leave her!"

Garcia and Smokey grabbed Morgan's arms, pulling him off.

"Richard, that's not the way," Garcia said.

Morgan fought to free himself. "We're running out of time, Javi. We need something to work! Now!"

Taylor laughed. "Me told you. She gone."

Valverde signaled for the guards.

Morgan turned on Valverde. "No! We haven't used the sedative yet."

"But she is awake," Valverde said. "You need to use it now."

Morgan shook his head. "She hasn't freed herself from the ropes. Until she can, we don't have to drug her."

"We agreed when she woke up, we would inject her and put her to death," Valverde said. "I feel for you, but I can't risk any more."

The guards reached the slab, machetes out.

Morgan fell into an abyss of pitch-blackness. *Valverde is right. Taylor might surprise us, and might escape. Still, I can't give up on her.* "What time is it?"

Smokey checked his watch. "It's three."

"It's 3AM?" Garcia said. He shared a concerned look with Valverde.

"Yeah," Smokey said. "Why?"

Garcia's head drooped. "It's the hour when evil is at its strongest. The inverse of the time Christ died on the Cross. The witching hour."

"Please," Morgan begged. "Let me dose her one last time. The cumulative effect should keep her calm. She's my little girl."

Valverde stared at Morgan. "I will agree to the injection, plus fifteen minutes. After that, if the demon has not been removed, the lamia dies."

Yes! Still a chance. Morgan injected his final batch of sodium thiopental. "Javi, you heard the man. Let's go."

"Valverde's up next," Garcia said. "But he's in no shape to pound her with his fists."

Valverde lifted his mangled wrists. "It is our culture to fight the demons with violent confrontation. Someone will have to strike her for me."

Morgan approached the slab. "If anyone's going to hit her, it's me. Besides, the demon knows me. Better chance I can lure it out." He climbed up over Taylor, straddling her and clenching his fists. "Okay, what do I do?"

"Whenever I pause, you pound on her chest. Show authentic rage to get the demon's attention."

Morgan grimaced, looking down on Taylor. *I'm sorry, Sweetie.* "Not a problem. Let's do this."

Valverde raised his voice and yelled with authority. "By the power anointed me by *Sibú*, creator of all, I command you, *Kudo*, to expel your demons from this girl, and send them back to the *dakúrs* from which they came."

Morgan pounded Taylor in the chest.

"Demon," continued Valverde, "I command you, in the name of *Sibú* himself, to vanquish you allegiance to *Kudo*, and show yourself, so *Sibú* may show you mercy when you leave this girl."

Morgan hit her again, a tear forming in both eyes.

"Demon, are you a coward?" Valverde continued. "Do you hide inside this young woman, instead of facing me? Come out now, or else be branded a coward forever amongst your peers."

Morgan struck again.

Taylor moaned.

"Demon, I strike at you, and you do not defend yourself?" Valverde caught his breath. "Is that all you are? A coward who will not defend itself?"

Morgan jolted her again.

Taylor opened her eyes and grinned at Morgan with black irises. "So, if it isn't the Arrogant Loser, back for more defeat."

Morgan's heart tried to clear his ribcage. *The demon! We're not too late!* He turned to Valverde. "That's the demon! Taylor hasn't been turned!"

Valverde looked unconvinced. "Demon, call out your name, so I know my adversary."

Taylor rolled her head toward Valverde. "I am Lilith, and you are nobody." Taylor strained against the ropes, which stretched and began to fray.

Garcia approached the slab. "My God. It really is her."

Taylor spit at Father Garcia. "Back away, Father Chancho. You have no business here. This is hell's work."

Valverde turned to Margarita. "Behead her!"

"No!" Morgan yelled. "You have the proof you need. The demon can still be exorcised."

Valverde shook his head. "But the sedative is not working. That was our deal."

Vertigo struck Morgan, and the world turned upside down.

CHAPTER 67

Lilith raged. The Arrogant Loser on top of the host. The *Awá* chanting. Father Chancho reciting something irritating. *And, dangerous.* Lilith commanded the sow to attack, to use her lamia powers.

The priest splashed more holy water. Steam rose from the host's burning flesh. Even in the possessive state, Lilith felt a tortuous pain. For the first time, it wanted to depart the girl's body.

No. If I leave for another host, the transmutation fails. I just need a few more minutes. I'll show them my true power.

A flash of lightning struck the thatched roof, which caught fire. Instantaneous thunder rocked the hut.

Yes! More! Unleash the bats! Release the wolves!

* * *

Morgan held his breath while the scene spun around him, waiting to see if Margarita would honor Valverde's command.

Margarita's brow puckered into deep lines. She turned on Valverde. "If Taylor is in there, I cannot kill her. He has ten minutes left."

Valverde glared at her, then at Morgan, finally settling on Taylor. He exhaled. "Agreed." He stared down Morgan. "Not a second longer."

Morgan's vertigo calmed. "Thanks." He glanced up at the growing flames on the roof. "Somebody got the fire?"

"*Di!*" Valverde commanded.

Guards raced away, then returned with buckets of water. Smokey and Juan helped them douse the flames, but not before the roof turned to ash and crumbled onto Morgan's unprotected arms.

Morgan ignored the searing pain and held Taylor tight. But one ember landed on his sleeve and sparked, starting a fire. He tried to blow it out, but instead caused it to spread and grow. "Help!"

Smokey splashed his arm. "You okay, doc?"

Morgan blew the last of the ash away and hung on to the writhing Taylor. "Good, thanks." He returned his attention to Taylor. *Come on, Taylor. Keep fighting.* "Javi, time's running out."

"On it." Garcia continued reading. "The Word made flesh commands you. The Virgin's Son commands you. Jesus of Nazareth commands you. It is God Himself who commands you. The majestic Christ who commands you."

Morgan kept the thrashing Taylor secured to the slab, his heart racing, time running short. "Give up, demon. We know you're in there. It's over."

Garcia raised his voice. "God the Father commands you. God the Son commands you. God the Holy Spirit commands you. The mystery of the cross commands you. The saving mysteries of our Christian faith command you."

Taylor grinned like she knew something they didn't. Something terrifying. "You think it's over? I'll show you *over.*"

Morgan shook off chills from seeing the confidence in her grin. *Don't listen to the demon. Focus on the positive. That's Lilith's voice. It's still in there! We're not too late!*

An approaching sound caught Morgan's attention. He looked to the sky, puzzled. *I've heard that before.* He stiffened. *Oh, shit.* "Incoming!"

Valverde reacted to the noise. "*Dakúr!*"

Bats flew into the hut. Too many to count. They circled the slab in a blur, then launched.

Morgan covered up with one arm to protect his eyes, and held on to Taylor with the other. The bats sliced into his face with sharp talons.

The bats also covered Garcia. "Get them off!"

Get them off Javi. He's the important one. But before he moved to his friend, a horrific stench permeated the hut. He gagged, and his eyes watered. The bats stopped biting and fled.

"It is safe, *señors*," Valverde said.

The stink almost knocked him off the slab. A guard held an open container, the source of the miserable odor. "What the hell is that?"

"Something we use to repel *Kudo's dakúrs*," Valverde said. "It disrupts their sonar. They become disoriented and seek refuge in the jungle."

"How long does it last?" Morgan said.

Valverde laughed. "The smell? You will take that home with you. Welcome to Bribri life."

You can keep it.

"*Kudo* has other animals at his disposal," Valverde said. "And without the roof, we are exposed to more lightning. You need to hurry."

* * *

Lilith forced Taylor to arch her back and flail her tongue wildly. *Hit them again!*

"And now as I adjure you in His name," said Father Chancho, "begone from this woman who is His creature. It is futile to resist His will."

Lilith opened Taylor's eyes, focusing in on the priest's throat. Another lightning bolt hit the hut. It struck only the side, and the guards put the fire out. The priest and the Arrogant Loser wouldn't budge.

Father Chancho is trouble. Making me weak. Shut off his words. Regain control. Lamia can break the ropes. Once she regains strength, she can kill them. And I can move on to safety.

The priest continued. "Depart, then, accursed one, depart with all your deceits, for God has willed that man should be His temple. Why do you linger here?"

Lilith thrashed, summoning the lamia to free them both.

"Give honor to God the Father almighty, before whom every knee must bow. Give place to the Lord Jesus Christ, who shed His most precious blood for man." The priest sprinkled another dose of holy water. "Depart, then, transgressor. Depart, seducer, full of lies and cunning, foe of virtue, persecutor of the innocent."

This time, the holy water burned too much. Lilith shrieked in torment. *Forget the lamia. Save myself.*

With one final push, Lilith fought for control. Lilith bared Taylor's fangs. She strained against the ropes, the restraints fraying, her skin smoldering. With a gigantic grunt, she popped the last strand and aimed her teeth at The Arrogant Loser.

But The Arrogant Loser pushed back. Lilith looked into his eyes. *He's no longer afraid.*

* * *

Morgan fought Taylor's surge toward him, even as her fangs moved ever closer. But his arms were tiring. "I can see fear. It's working. Hurry!"

"Five minutes," Valverde said. "My guards will not hesitate at the deadline."

"You might delude man, but God you cannot mock," Garcia said. "It is He who casts you out, from whose sight nothing is hidden. It is He who repels you, to whose might all things are subject. It is He who expels you."

Taylor's teeth neared Morgan's throat. A guard raised his machete.

Morgan held his position. *I'm not afraid of you, demon. The power of God is with us.* "Finish it off, Javi!"

Garcia continued. "I adjure you, ancient serpent, by Him who has the power to consign you to hell, to depart forthwith in fear, along with your savage minions, from this servant of God, Taylor, who seeks refuge in the fold of the Church."

Morgan held her off, watching Taylor's eyes, hoping for a return to her natural brown. "C'mon, sweetie. I know you're in there."

A growl interrupted him. *That's not the demon.* Then, another snarl, and another.

"Wolves!" Valverde yelled. "Brace yourself!"

"Will the smell keep them out?" Morgan said.

"Nothing will keep them out," Valverde said.

The growls surrounded the hut. Then the wolves rammed into the walls. Several wood slats cracked.

Margarita raced to the hut's exit and threw the door open.

"No!" yelled Juan.

But she paid no attention. She left the safety of the hut and secured the barrier.

"What's she doing?" Morgan kept Taylor pinned to the slab. "They'll shred her."

Violence erupted outside. Growls, baying, and scrambling feet. Tearing clothe. Then, the sound of a machete whacking into flesh and bone.

Juan ran to the door and tried to follow Margarita, but a guard stopped him.

"Should your guards help her?" Morgan said.

"They will defend me, and the hut," Valverde said. "She is on her own."

The growls and baying stopped. "Open the door!" Margarita yelled.

The guard unlatched the barrier and Margarita entered, carrying the head of a wolf. Covered in blood, her clothes in tatters, she tossed the head away. "*Kudo's* wolves are dead."

Juan held her and turned to Valverde. "She needs medical attention."

"No!" Margarita said. "Finish the job!"

Garcia gave Morgan a hysterical glance, then pressed on. "I adjure you again, not by my weakness but by the might of the Holy Spirit, to depart from Taylor, this servant of God. Yield, therefore, not to my own person but to the minister of Christ. For it is the power of Christ that compels you."

Dread passed through Morgan. He glanced toward Smokey and Linda, wanting to make sure they were unharmed. Instead, his parents stood inside the hut.

Morgan's father aimed a shotgun at Morgan's mother.

"No!" Morgan screamed. He started to release his grip on Taylor.

"Pennywise, stay focused!" Garcia yelled.

Morgan's father pulled the trigger, and his mother's head splattered against the wall.

Morgan released Taylor.

His father put the gun in his own mouth and fired. The back of his skull blew open.

"Richard!" Garcia called out. "Whatever you see isn't real. It's the demon. Don't let go of her!"

Streams poured into Morgan's eyes, blinding him. He grabbed Taylor before she sank her teeth into his neck and shoved her back onto the slab. *Nice try. But the only way out is to leave my daughter.* Another quick glance confirmed Smokey and Linda stood in their spot.

* * *

Garcia gathered himself for a final push. He gripped his temples and twisted his head side to side, relieving the tension. He looked at Taylor.

But Taylor was gone. In her place, Reggie, the teenage girl he'd escorted across state lines.

"Javier," Reggie said.

"Reggie?" *No. You're not here.*

"Javier, please save me. There's only one way. Stay with me. If you don't, you know I'll die. You know you want to."

Garcia closed his eyes.

"You lust for me. Want me. So many times you've felt the heat of the flesh. The desires of a mere mortal. I'm here to save you. Take me, Father. Fuck me like a real man. The pain will leave you forever."

"Stop!" Garcia screamed. "You're a vile demon, and I reject you."

Reggie faded away, replaced by Patti, the victim of his failed exorcism. Her face was torn apart with lesions, blood leaking down her neck. Yellow eyes that almost shimmered. "Father. Why couldn't you save me? You damned me to hell."

Garcia's knees wobbled. The room spun. Only Patti stayed in focus.

"It's okay to stop, Father." Patti's teeth were chipped and rotting. "No one should have to fail at this twice."

She's right. He shuddered. *But if I stop, I forsake Taylor.*

"Walk away, Father. Before it's too late. Can you live with another spiritual and physical death on your hands? Depart, before the demon comes after *you.*"

Garcia's willpower drained from his body. As much as he wanted to fight the feeling, he knew he was being overrun by hopelessness.

"Last chance," Lilith said.

Yes, I should walk away. While I still can.

* * *

Morgan turned to Garcia. "Javi. You okay?" *Jeez, he's looking right through me. Like in a spell.* "Javi! Taylor needs you!"

When Garcia didn't react, Morgan slapped him. Garcia's nape snapped back, creating a cracking sound.

Christ. Don't break his neck. "Javi? You okay?"

Garcia quivered. His eyes focused in on Morgan "I'm okay." He took a deep breath and wiped the sweat from his forehead. He dipped closer to Taylor. "Nice try, demon. I'm not going anywhere. You are."

Taylor hissed, her black tongue darting around her nose. Her visage contorted itself until she appeared to wear a hideous mask, barley recognizable as human.

Morgan gasped. His entire body shivered. *Her chin is moving left. Her whole face is angled, and her mouth looks like one of those "Scream" masks. How is that possible?*

Garcia raised his voice. "Unholy demon, it is God Himself who commands you. The majestic Christ who commands you. God the Father commands you. God the Son commands you. God the Holy Spirit commands you. The mystery of the cross commands you. The saving mysteries of our Christian faith command you."

With each command Taylor's face morphed further into something inhuman. Her eyes flickered. The black faded to brown, then back to black.

"Keep going!" Morgan yelled.

Valverde stepped in. "The beast shows itself. That is good. I know how to finish it." He put his bandaged hand on Taylor's shifting forehead. "Demon, who must succumb to the power of *Sibú*, leave this girl at once. The power of *Sibú* compels you. The power of the *Awá*, handed down for generations by *Sibú* himself, compels you. Retreat, before *Sibú* reaches down and yanks you away to the underworld, where you will perish in infinite and hopeless damnation."

Morgan forced his eyes to move from Margarita to Linda, who held the silver box. *You better be right.* He grabbed Taylor around the throat and squeezed. He bent over her crimson face. "Demon, you accuse us of being cowards. But it is you who took on a defenseless little girl. You avoid anyone who can challenge you. You are the ultimate coward."

Taylor's eyes bulged.

"Careful, Richard," Garcia said.

"Linda," Morgan said. "Now!"

Her feet shuffled behind him. "I'm ready."

Morgan applied relentless pressure to her throat. "You don't have the nerve or the strength to attack someone like me. You use my little girl. Well, here I am. If it's me you want to torture, come on. Come on! Take me on instead. Or are you only able to control little girls?"

Morgan released Taylor's throat, and she gasped for air. Her eyes raged an inferno of black hatred. Morgan pounded on her chest again, and she spit up blood.

"You feel that, don't you?" Morgan said. "You're nothing but a coward. A sniveling wimp. You'll die in there. The only way to save yourself is to leave her."

Taylor shrieked, a nerve-jarring scream that rocked the hut. She narrowed her eyes at Morgan. "You want me? Be careful what you ask for." Taylor's body shook and the black in her irises faded to gray.

Morgan grabbed the hidden cross hanging around his neck under his shirt and flashed it at the demon. *Linda better be right.*

Taylor spasmed, then fell limp.

* * *

Lilith departed Taylor and moved toward Morgan, intending to take up residence there. But the cross stopped it in midair. Danger! Find another host.

But everyone in the hut brandished a similar crucifix.

Find an animal.

It altered course for a nearby vampire bat.

* * *

Linda held the box of pure silver. Inside, surrounded by the *Awá's* herb mixture, a tethered vampire bat fought to escape.

She wanted to watch Taylor, but knew not to. Her eyes stayed riveted on the bat.

The bat jerked, its eyes flashing a glossy black. *Now!*

She slammed the lid shut, trapping the bat and the demon. If the Vatican documents were accurate, the demon couldn't escape the silver lining.

"Got it!" she cried out. "Taylor should be free of the demon!"

CHAPTER 68

Outside the hut, howler monkeys wailed. A stiff wind razed the shack, bringing with it a stench reminiscent of an overflowing septic tank. Thunder rumbled in a sky devoid of stars.

Morgan felt Taylor's cheek. Tears fell from his chin onto her. *We did it!*

But Taylor's eyes remained closed.

Morgan checked her pulse. He blanched. *No!* His body shook. He began chest compressions. "C'mon, Taylor. Wake up!"

Linda stepped up next to Morgan, holding the box, which vibrated violently. "She's not breathing?"

C'mon, Taylor. The demon's gone. Come back to me! "No."

The bruises on Taylor's neck turned darker. *Did I press too hard?*

"C'mon, sweetie," Garcia said. "The demon's dead. Come home now."

Morgan kept pumping. "She's not responding."

Garcia bowed over her and began administering Last Rites.

Morgan continued the compressions. "Shut up, Javi. She's not going to die."

Garcia continued. "She deserves to have her soul prepared."

"I said she won't die!"

"You can't know that. And I can't afford to take the chance."

A guard ran in with another medical bag and opened it.

"The blue one," Valverde said to his lead guard. The guard withdrew a satchel and opened it. "Put it under her nose. If there is life in her, this will bring it out."

"What's that?" Morgan continued the chest compressions, and Garcia continued to pray.

"Herbs from the jungle," Valverde said. "They have unique healing powers. *Awás* have been using them for centuries. Dr. Morgan, you need to step aside."

"Like hell."

Valverde signaled to a guard standing off to the side. He moved in and pulled Morgan from the slab.

Morgan fought to free himself, to no avail. "Let go of me! I have to save her!"

The guard with the herbs picked up a pinch and set it in front of Taylor's nose.

"Force it in," Valverde instructed.

"You could suffocate her," Morgan said, struggling to get to Taylor.

"She is not breathing, *señor*."

The guard stuffed the herb mixture into Taylor's nose.

"It is done," Valverde said.

With a final push, Morgan threw the guard off of him and rushed back to the slab. Morgan climbed up and lay next to Taylor. He searched for Garcia, barely making out his features through his tears. "I killed my girl, didn't I?"

Garcia hung his head.

Full-on vertigo attacked Morgan. *To come this far. Why, God?* Morgan pounded his fist into his forehead. *Please take me instead. I'll do anything. Let my little girl live.*

"What now?" Smokey said, his voice unsteady.

"We wait," Valverde said.

"How long?" Tears streamed down Morgan's face.

"If it is to work, it will happen soon."

Morgan pressed his ear against Taylor's chest. "Please, Taylor. Come back."

A subtle murmur.

Morgan's eyes shot open. His vertigo dissipated.

Stronger now.

He lifted himself up, looking at her face. "Her heart's beating." He checked her pulse. "She's breathing."

Garcia and Smokey edged in while Valverde motioned to the guards to be ready.

Taylor inhaled, a long, tortured breath that rattled her chest and throat, followed by a cough.

"She's alive!" Morgan said.

"Praise be to God," Garcia said, crossing himself.

Valverde approached to see, his guards at his side. Margarita and Juan followed. Margarita pulled her machete.

"Stay back," Morgan ordered. "She's not a threat."

"We do not know that," Valverde said. "We have no experience with an exorcism this late in the process. She might still be the lamia." He motioned to a guard. "If you see any sign she is infected, take her head off." Then, to Margarita, "If we need to kill her, my guards will do it. Understand?"

Margarita eyed Taylor with suspicion. "I am the most qualified. I will do it."

"Nobody's doing anything." Morgan slid up the slab, putting himself between her neck and the guards. "She's not infected."

Taylor's eyes opened. Their bright redness bored into Morgan's skull.

He wilted. *Oh, shit. It didn't work.*

"The eyes!" Valverde said. "Guards! If she moves, kill her!"

But Margarita didn't wait. She raised her machete and charged the slab.

Morgan grabbed Margarita's arm and held the machete at bay. "No, you don't!"

Smokey and Garcia grabbed her by the waist and pulled her back. Juan joined in holding her. A guard wrangled the machete away from her.

"I must destroy the lamia!" Margarita pleaded. "Can't you see?"

"My guards will handle it," Valverde said.

"Dad?"

Morgan turned back to Taylor. *Her voice. It's normal.* His heart raced.

But her eyes are still red.

"Taylor, is it really you?" Morgan said. He lifted the corner of her mouth. Her incisors were long and sharp. His breathing came in fits and starts. *No. I know she's in there.*

A guard with a raised machete gasped at the sight of her teeth.

"Stay away!" Morgan demanded. "The demon's gone. We need to give her time."

"Kill her!" Margarita yelled, trying to pull away. "While we still can."

"Guard," Valverde said. "You have your orders."

"Wait!" Linda said. "Look. Her eyes are changing back."

The red glint faded, her natural brown taking over. Morgan kissed her on the cheek. *Praise the Lord. It worked.* He embraced his daughter.

Garcia and Smokey leaned in close.

"Of course it's me." Taylor said in her normal voice. "Who else would it be?" She noticed Garcia. "Father Javier? What are we doing here?" She examined her surroundings. "Where am I?"

Morgan checked her teeth. *They're shrinking. The process is reversing.* "Costa Rica."

"Again? Why?"

Tears gushed from Morgan.

"Dad, why are you crying?"

"It's a long story, sweetie. I love you so much."

She swung up and held him. "I love you too, Dad."

Morgan held her tight. "You've been sick. Do you remember?"

"It's a blur since Mom died. Are we here to bring her home?"

Morgan looked at Margarita, who nodded. He touched his daughter's chin. "Yes. We're bringing her home."

The box in Linda's possession rattled. She shifted. "The demon's pretty pissed in here."

"It's really in there?" Garcia said.

"It really is," she said. "I don't suppose anyone wants to take this thing. It gives me creeps."

Morgan stepped over to Linda. "I'll take it. If it knows I'm holding it, it'll piss it off even more." He smiled.

"It appears we are witness to a miracle." Valverde turned to Margarita. "I trust this ends your interest in this girl."

Margarita gazed at Taylor. "It does." Juan took her arm, and she sobbed. "I miss our daughter so much."

Juan led her away. "Let's go home. It's not too late for us to try again."

"A child?" Margarita said.

"Sí. Maybe another daughter. This time, we will be safe."

"Juan," Morgan called before they got out of earshot. They turned back. "Thank you both."

"*Gracias*. If you are ever in Nosara, *señor*, you know where to find us."

Morgan waved them goodbye. *No offense, but I hope I never see either of you again.* An uncomfortable gnawing turned his stomach. *A premonition?* He shook the thought away. *It's just stress.*

CHAPTER 69

Morgan rested in the morning sunshine. The howler monkeys were silent. The wind had calmed, and the air gave off the scent of orchids. Taylor slept next to him. The silver box lay sealed and in view of Morgan, Garcia, Smokey, Linda, and Valverde. They drank from the *Awá*'s private stash—a 120 proof community-made rum.

"I make this for medicinal purposes," Valverde said, laughing. "That is my story, and I am sticking to it."

Garcia lifted his glass. "If this isn't a case for remedial treatment, what is?"

After a short pause, Morgan spoke to Valverde. "I'm sorry about your man."

"*Gracias.* He gave his life protecting our community. We will honor him forever."

After a moment of silence, Smokey piped in. "Padre, what are you going to tell your Bishop?"

"I don't know. Telling him about the demon is one thing. But, vampires? Even if they believe me, they won't want that getting out. I might get tossed out on my ass."

"They'll be too afraid of you telling your story to do anything to you," Morgan said. "They'll keep you in the fold."

Smokey changed the subject. "How long before Taylor's transmutation was irreversible?"

"We'll never know, man." Garcia drained the rest of his drink. "But my gut tells me not long."

Morgan examined the imprisoned demon's silver box. "Are we sure the box is sealed? The demon can't escape?"

"My Vatican Cardinal assures me once a demon is captured, silver is the only element that can overpower it and keep it constrained." Linda shivered. "He should know, right?"

"And I thought the power of silver was a legend from horror novels," Garcia said.

"What about the box?" Linda asked. "Sink it in the ocean?"

"Humph." Smokey took another swig. "Someone might find it and think it's treasure."

Garcia moaned. "There's nowhere on earth we can assure it stays hidden."

"There is." Morgan put his arm around his friend. "But Javi, you're not going to like my idea."

They all stared at Morgan, waiting.

"It needs the most protected place on earth. The Vatican. They're best equipped to securely lock it away."

Garcia shifted. "That makes sense. But why won't I like it?"

Smokey smirked. "Because you're the only Padre here. You have to escort it to them."

Morgan laughed. "And tell them Lilith is in there and convince them to store it for eternity."

"I've never seen the Vatican archives before." Garcia perked up. "And their support will add to my creditability at home."

"The advantage of my job is I answer to no one. It is me and *Sibú*. But without our combined beliefs, we lose. Taylor would be dead." Valverde raised his glass. "To God. Each version of Him."

Morgan thrust his glass toward Linda. "To Doctor Linda Copeland. She made all this possible. I only wish we could have done for her daughter, what she did for mine."

Linda blushed. Morgan gazed at her, feeling like he could see her soul.

Linda raised her glass. "To you, Dr. Morgan. You made it possible to catch the beast. I'd give anything to have my daughter back, but this is sweet revenge, and as close to justice as I can get." She broke down.

Morgan shifted to her and embraced her. She melted into him, and he stroked her locks. "It's okay. Let it out."

After a moment, Linda eased back, wiping tears from her cheeks. "Sorry."

"You have nothing to be sorry about." Morgan looked around at each of them. "I can't thank you all enough. You saved my little girl."

"You as much as anyone. It was you who rid Taylor of *Lilith*. You took quite a risk, *señor*." Valverde elevated his mug. "A final toast. To accepting things we can not comprehend."

"Hear, hear!"

Garcia cleared his throat. "Speaking of things we don't understand, what was the stuff we put down her nose? Did it really bring her back?"

Valverde lowered his voice. "A recipe handed down for centuries. It can restore life if administered promptly."

Garcia pressed on. "Do you have any idea what that's worth? Pharmaceutical companies would kill for it."

Valverde's face darkened. "You must tell no one. If they knew, they would ravage the rain forest for the secret. That would only make *Kudo* angrier, and the demons would descend unlike anything we have ever seen. I barely survived this last confrontation. I need a break."

"But it could be a medical miracle," Garcia said.

"Leave it be," Morgan said. "It's not ours to discuss, and not ours to take."

Valverde relaxed. "Thank you. This medicine belongs here. I doubt it would even work anywhere else. *Sibú* himself provides the power to make it work. Not me. And not some corporation intent on making money."

Morgan took his last sip and turned to Smokey. "So, retired detective, is Taylor in the clear?"

"I follow the evidence, Doc." He took another swig of rum. "And all indications are Taylor is no threat to anybody. Case closed."

Morgan slapped him on the back. "You're a good man, detective. And I still owe you a beer."

"It'll have to be special to beat this rum," Smokey said.

"I wish we had reception up here," Garcia said. "Be nice to know what's happening back home."

Linda smiled. "Those girls'll be fine."

Morgan turned to Linda. "You're sure, aren't you?"

"I am."

I believe you. Her radiant skin scintillated in the midday sun. "So, what's next for you?"

She blinked, and when her eyes opened, they sparkled. "Back to teaching. I need to find a new college. What do you think of the ones near Salem?"

CHAPTER 70

Salem, Oregon, two weeks later

Morgan sat at Taylor's side with a cup of hot chocolate, the sunshine bursting in through her bedroom window. The iciness in the air was a comforting change from the stifling Costa Rican heat. Taylor opened her eyes and Bear jumped on the bed.

"Morning, sweetie," Morgan said.

"Hi, Dad. What are you doing in here?"

"Watching you sleep. I made you some cocoa."

She took the cup. "Thanks." Bear cuddled next to her, and she pet his white head.

"I'm going back to the office today," Morgan announced. "I'm giving up my marriage counseling practice. From now on I'll work only with the patients at the hospital."

"Why's that?"

"Most are criminally insane. But some are victims of unexplainable circumstances and need a therapist who can relate."

"You'll be a good listener."

Morgan blushed. "Thanks. Then, I'm going by the church to see Javi. He's returning from Vatican City today. I've been a poor Catholic for a while, and it's time I fixed that."

"Can I go back to leading a youth group someday?"

Morgan kissed her forehead. "Once you're at full strength. And you'll be going back to school soon."

He left Taylor and Bear to their morning ritual and returned to the kitchen. A sharp knock on the door stopped him halfway through brewing a pot of coffee. "It's open."

Smokey stepped in, wearing his usual trench coat, brandishing his trademark cigar. "Hey, Doc. How is she?"

"She's great. Remembers nothing."

"That's a blessing. Just like all the other girls. The wounds on their necks healed, their incisors and nails reverted to regular size, their eyes are normal. I think Azra's kind of pissed. They all recovered before she could figure out what was wrong with them. The parents are so relieved they're either accepting the CDC's explanation it was a fluke, and there's nothing to worry about, or they can't process the alternative and aren't willing to go there."

"I can relate. As for Azra, she'll never accept the truth. Coffee?"

"Nah. I need to get back to the station. They're throwing me a retirement shindig. But they want me to consult for them. Just as well. I'd go bonkers without some kind of detective work, and I'm not inclined to help suspicious wives track their husbands, or whatever it is PIs do."

Morgan laughed. "That sounds like a nice gig. Good for you."

"Thanks, Doc. So, I ran into Professor Copeland yesterday."

"Yeah. She'll be teaching at the college."

Smokey smiled. "Convenient. You two have a lot in common. Went through stuff nobody else will ever be able to relate to."

Morgan grinned back. "Subtlety isn't your strong suit, Detective. But, yeah, I'm glad she's here."

"Two more things. No charges are being brought against Allister. They're satisfied with my retirement as sufficient punishment. But our national alert on your Mr. Quinn struck gold. They've arrested him in Colorado."

Morgan's heart rate surged. "And my money?"

"We froze his accounts. It'll take awhile to sort out all the folks he scammed, and figure out a fair way to distribute what money's left, but you should get some back. Who knows. Maybe most."

"Do me a favor and put him away, will you? I could use the money if it's returned. Mostly, I don't want him taking advantage of anyone else. Parasites like that deserve the worst."

"Will do." Smokey came up and shook his hand. "I'm happy for you, Doc. You're a good man." He gave Morgan a sheepish expression, then ambled off to his car.

As soon as Smokey left, Morgan's phone rang. "Yeah?"

"It's Javi."

"Javi! Did the Vatican take the box?"

"*Sí*. What a powerful experience. And once I got back to my parish, they even gave me a new Bible. Said my old one was ready to be retired."

Morgan laughed. "We've all been thinking that for years. It served you well. And nothing like a successful exorcism to get your faith back, eh?"

"Pennywise, do me a favor. Can we never bring up exorcisms again? Two in a lifetime is at least two too many."

"But you won this time!"

"I'm glad Taylor is free of the demon, but there are no winners in an exorcism, man. Only survivors."

Morgan exhaled. "Yeah. I know what you mean."

"I'm not sure you do. Once you see the darkness like that, there's no way to escape it. It will follow you everywhere."

* * *

The message light flashed on Morgan's answering machine, from Azra two days before. He'd chosen not to take her call, but knew he couldn't avoid her forever.

She'll never believe me.

He picked up the land line. *Hell, I was there, and I hardly accept it. And maybe I'm already nuts. She deserves to hear it from me.* He dialed.

She answered as if she'd been hovering over the phone. "Richard! I heard you're back, and Taylor's fine now."

Morgan tensed. *No thanks to you.*

When he didn't respond, she pressed forward. "Smokey told me Taylor's better. What a relief!"

"Yeah. It's a miracle."

"The girls we quarantined are also fine. Whatever it was, it's passed."

"What do you think it was?" Morgan said.

"I haven't figured that out. I'm still running blood tests. We need to be ready in case someone relapses."

"It's not coming back."

"How can you be certain? It's still unexplained."

"I know exactly what it was."

After a long silence, Azra continued. "You know there's a medical explanation for all this."

"Goodbye, Azra." Morgan disconnected the line.

Linda used the house key Morgan had given her and entered in a flowery pink dress. She beamed like a teenager going to the prom. Morgan kissed her.

* * *

That night Morgan sat with his arm around his daughter Taylor watching TV in his living room, with Linda Copeland sprawled next to him, each wearing casual sweats. His yellow lab Bear slept at his feet. On the evening news, a CDC rep explained the Salem quarantine was over, and the Hantavirus, carried by local rodents, had been contained and eradicated.

So that's how they explain the unexplainable.

"I didn't expect them to tell the truth," Linda said, "but Hantavirus?"

Morgan lowered his voice and did his best Jack Nicholson impression. "They can't handle the truth."

Taylor squirmed. "Why would they lie? Is that what I had?"

Morgan's insides clenched. *Can Taylor handle the truth?* He clutched her tighter. "You picked up a different virus in Costa Rica. Nothing to worry about." He thought about the demon, Lilith, eternally trapped inside the silver box. "You're okay now, and that's all that matters."

He felt the warmth of Linda nestled into him. A blaze fired his face. *I'm finally turning the corner on my relationships. This one feels so right.* Gray streaked the long locks at her temples, much like what he'd seen in his own reflection, although his brown hair helped camouflage it more than her black. *Too much stress. Losing her daughter and facing the demon.* He kissed her cheek, grateful she was interested in him after all they'd been through. *Probably* because *of all we've been through.*

A text message buzzed. "Sorry," Linda said. "Forgot to turn my phone off."

"That's another dollar in the fine jar," Morgan kidded.

She smiled and reached for the phone, then stopped. Morgan felt her muscles tense.

She sat up with a wild look. "It's Cardinal Vitelli at the Vatican. The one who gave me access to the scrolls with the instructions to capture Lilith. What do you think he wants?"

A chill ran the gamut of Morgan's bones. And his stomach grumbled like it had when Margarita threatened Taylor in the Bribri Village. *Taylor's still in danger.* He held his breath, unable to peel his eyes away from Linda's phone.

Linda opened the message, and Morgan gasped.

Lilith loose. Help!

MY GIFT TO YOU

Visit my Fan Club website page to download the
first three chapters of the sequel to *The Lamia*

Available for purchase in Spring 2021

Get your free gift at:

www.StevenGJackson.com/Fan-Club

ALSO FROM STEVEN G. JACKSON

Novels:

The Zeus Payload

Short Stories:

"Full Service" - *It's All in the Story*

"Life Dies, and Then You Suck" - *It's All in the Story*

"Noma" - *Culinary Delights*

"The Asylum for Rejected Characters" - *Masquerade*

Produced Stage Plays:

"The Johnson Case" - Lincoln Elementary
School Graduation Ceremony

"The Loan Officer" - Camino Real Playhouse - ShowOff!

"The Loan Officer 2" - Camino Real Playhouse - ShowOff!

"The Asylum for Rejected Characters" -
Camino Real Playhouse - ShowOff!

"Fade to Crazy" - Camino Real Playhouse - 24 Hour Creative

"The Master Playwright" - Camino Real
Playhouse - 24 Hour Creative

"Life Dies, and Then You Suck" - Camino
Real Playhouse - 24 Hour Creative

"All I Want for Christmas is You" - Pure Fiction League

"The Optimism of Youth" - Camino Real
Playhouse - 24 Hour Creative

"Psycho Therapist" - Camino Real Playhouse - 24 Hour Creative

"The No-Goodnick, The Bad, and The Ugly" -
Camino Real Playhouse - ShowOff!

"Pharmaceuticals for Dummies" - Camino
Real Playhouse - 24 Hour Creative

ACKNOWLEDGMENTS

I am grateful to my publishing team, including critique groups Pure Fiction League (whose members were dedicated to my success from the beginning); WriteOn! (whose members helped me in the critical end-game); beta reader (and gifted writer) Annette Lahr; content and copy editor Sandy Homicz (also a gifted writer), who sees every detail and knows precisely how to fix anything that is less than perfect; and Jeniffer Thompson and her phenomenal team at Monkey C Media. Thank you.

And, as always, I am grateful for my wife, Yann, who makes my dreams come true every day.

CPSIA information can be obtained
at www.ICGtesting.com
Printed in the USA
LVHW010911151220
674215LV00002B/43